# TRIAGE

He froze, his hand still clawing the doorknob. Across from him the man's hands dangled from the armrests, shaking like a Parkinson's victim. His swollen face was blanched except where subdermal hematoma had painted mottled blotches beneath the chin, which dropped like a trap to grab at air. Eyes white plates, pupils dilated but unresponsive, not tracking Farnes' arrival. Nostrils fluttering, breathing shallow, rapid. Pulse, judging from the swollen jugular vein, the same. A portrait of terror. A mask screaming shock. This shouldn't be happening to me.

And there was nothing Farnes, or anyone, could do.

Not now.

# THE LAST PRISONER

## DAVID LORNE

AVON BOOKS NEW YORK

To
My Father

THE LAST PRISONER is an original publication of Avon Books. This work has never before appeared in book form. This is a work of fiction, and while some portions of this novel deal with actual events and real people, it should in no way be construed as being factual.

AVON BOOKS
A division of
The Hearst Corporation
1350 Avenue of the Americas
New York, New York 10019

First Avon Books Printing: December 1991

AVON TRADEMARK REG. U.S. PAT. OFF. AND IN OTHER COUNTRIES, MARCA REGISTRADA, HECHO EN U.S.A.

Printed in the U.S.A.

RA 10 9 8 7 6 5 4 3 2 1

With apologies to those many who contributed to this book in small but important ways, major thanks are due to my wife, Marsha, who both supported and endured the process of its creation; to my agent, Philip Spitzer in New York, who found the right editor and house to back this book; to Bob Mecoy at that publishing house, Avon Books in New York, for his unflagging support and superb suggestions to improve the story; to Christine Myles of Chicago, in belated recognition of editorial contributions; to Captain R. Al Frost, USN, Ret. of MacLean, Virginia, for his superbly detailed and highly informative review of the submarine scenes; to Lt. Col. Joe Curry, USA of Potomac, Maryland, for his critical appraisal of the current battlefield arsenal, tactics, and strategy of both the United States and the Soviet Armies; to Dr. Lester Marion of Potomac, Maryland, for examining the material on the pathology and epidemiology of viruses; to Dr. Peggy Arps of the University of Alaska, Fairbanks, for her helpful comments on genetic engineering of microorganisms; and to Alexe M. Block, formerly of the Atlanta Convention and Visitor's Bureau, for a detailed photographic, cartographic, and informational profile of the city of Atlanta. Each of these folks contributed marvelously and willingly, and thanks are not enough. Nevertheless, as every work of fiction alters the truth to suit its own objectives, so has this one. The author alone is responsible for inaccuracies, often introduced deliberately for literary and dramatic effects.

*"US–Soviet relations remain fragile."*

—*Mikhail Gorbachev*
*February 25, 1991*

*"It is a national scandal
that we are not better prepared
for this threat."*

—*Frank Gaffney*
*Center for Security Policy*

# Atlanta Constitution Headlines 1996

January 1
**Revised German Constitution Allows Standing Army**

January 22
**Unrest Spreads in Ukraine, Soviet Crackdown Shapes Up**

February 3
**Soviet Tanks Conduct Exercises Along Ukrainian Border**

February 15
**Ukraine Closes Border with Soviet Union,
Invites Germany for Joint Military Maneuvers**

February 16
**Soviets Warn Germany to Stay Out of Ukraine**

March 15
**German Army Conducts "Rapid Response" Movements
Along Polish Border**

March 22
**Invoking Warsaw Block Status, Poland Invites
Soviet Maneuvers Outside Warsaw**

April 9
**Economic Woes Seen as Reason for
President's Defeat in New Hampshire Primary**

April 12
**German Army Masses on Polish Border,
Warns Soviets Against "Menacing Presence"**

April 17
**More Soviet Tanks to Poland,
First MiGs Land in Warsaw**

May 1
**German Credit to Soviet Union Frozen,
Ruble Tumbles on World Markets**

May 6
**German Technical Experts Withdrawn from Russia**

June 1
**Soviets Close Natural Gas Flow to Western Europe**

June 2
**Dow Jones Loses 70 Points in Panic Selling**

June 10
**Secretary of State in Moscow Reports "No Progress"**

June 22
**Talks Collapse; US Introduces Resolution to United Nations—Get Out of Poland, Ukraine**

July 4
**US Embargos Grain to Soviet Union, Bars Purchase of Soviet Oil**

July 7
**More Red Tanks to Poland Bolster Soviet Air Power**

July 16
**Germany Advances UN Deadline for Soviet Withdrawal with Its Own: Out by August 15—Or Else**

July 22
**US Offer of Troops, Battlefield Nukes, Assures Germans; Bases Reopen for Influxing Soldiers**

July 24
**Soviets Embargo Atlanta Olympics, Oil, Raise Ante; Brinkmanship Returns**

July 31
**Eleventh Hour US Delegation Leaves for Moscow, Berlin**

August 12
**Republican Convention Opens in Miami; President Short Votes for First Ballot Victory**

August 15
**Olympic Games Open Without Soviet Athletes**

August 16
**German Deadline for Soviet Withdrawal Passes**

# DAY ONE

The disembodied synthetic voice spilled down from the concealed speaker behind Larry Farnes, telling him, "**When the automatic door slides open, you will have four seconds to move to the holding area beyond. Once inside, do not turn or move until the door has shut automatically behind you. If you do not understand these directions, step back from your position, turn and face the camera, and raise your hand.**"

Farnes said nothing, stood empty and still, feeling nothing at all beyond the thudding in his chest, the stale air pulsing in his lungs, only once the blinking of his eyes.

Again the voice droned from the speaker, "**Wait for the green light over the holding area door to go on. The green light will signal that the door will slide open in exactly two seconds. When it does, move as directed.**"

Above and in front of him the green light ignited.

Exactly two seconds later, the gleaming frame of chrome bars whooshed aside. As instructed, he stepped inside, keeping his eyes on the wall ahead until the door hissed shut behind him.

Pneumatic float, he guessed. It would be simpler to rig, easier to maintain, and less expensive to operate, in the long run, than a magnetic suspension. In magnetic systems, hysteresis could be a problem. Do-able, sure, but basically an R&D exercise. Aside from the other problems, it could lead to jamming, even kill an inmate. And they wouldn't want that, not here at Prison Perfect.

"You may turn," said the synthavoice, sounding as patient as a new mother on Valium.

"Thank you," Farnes said back.

The responder program cut in automatically and began cycling through its sequences. "**The prisoner has spoken. Is there a problem?**"

Farnes muttered to himself, "Is there a problem?", bit off a short laugh and said, "Yes."

"**Is the prisoner distressed?**"

"Yes."

"**Please respond to the choices for describing your distress in order that the system may provide attention.**"

The man in the cage beside Farnes gurgled laughter and said, "You believe that asshole thing?"

Farnes speared him with a contemptuous glance. Fat, tall, bald. Bushy eyebrows. Blowtorch breath he could smell at fifteen feet. Same starched prison grays that Farnes had, but no shoes. Why?

"**Are you experiencing acute medical problems?**" asked synthavoice.

"Say yes, start rollin' around and screamin'," whispered Fatty. "It always works."

Farnes wanted to tell Fatty to shut up, to mind his own business, but just kept watching the camera.

Synthavoice rolled on, "**Are you being assaulted by another inmate?**"

"What does it look like to you?" Farnes asked back.

"**Is your environment degrading?**"

Farnes imagined the intent of the question was to establish whether something was wrong with the air conditioning or plumbing, or whether rats were attacking him. Instead, choosing to hear it another way, he smiled and said, "Yes."

"**How is your environment degrading?**"

"Because no string quartets are playing Pachelbel?"

A brief silence as the computer stormed its keywords and came up dry, then automatically rolled into citing a checklist. "**Answer yes or no immediately after the following questions. You will have two seconds to respond. If you do not respond, it will be assumed that you have no problem in this area.**"

Farnes stood back and waited.

"What are you in for?" said Fatty.

"**Is your plumbing working?**" asked synthavoice.

Farnes ignored both questions, folded his arms, closed his eyes.

"Hey, asshole!" Fatty hammered the chrome bars.

"**Is your air clean?**"

Farnes couldn't be bothered.

"Who the hell you think you are?" Fatty snarled.

**"Is there electrical danger near you?"**

Farnes began wondering about sleep cycles and lights, temperature control, optimizing. He wondered what the library was like and if he could borrow from the outside, what computer systems were available to inmates and how soon he could access them. He even wondered how similar the area commands in the synthavoice controller were to programs he had written or modified.

"I get you in the yard down there, assbreath, and I'm gonna knock your fucking teeth out and stick my big one down your pussy mouth."

**"You have not responded to the basic problem menu. This conversation is now terminated. Proceed immediately to your cell at the green light."**

In two seconds, as promised, the green plastic bubble over his cell glowed. Again, as promised, his cell door slid open. And, as directed, he moved inside. After three seconds the cage sealed itself.

Farnes moved to the rear wall, sat down, folded his arms across his chest, rolled his head back, and closed his eyes. The intense overhead fluorescents pinked through the lids.

The voice could be dismissed. Fatty was more troublesome. Farnes would give good odds that Fatty had hyperpituitarism, perhaps an undiscovered benign tumor straddling the corpus collosum and invading the deep nexi of the R complex. He was surprised the defense lawyer hadn't sought mitigation for that.

"I raped my grandmother," Fatty confided.

Farnes popped one lid open, rolled his head Fatty's way, watched the spittle roll down the big man's chin, and turned away.

". . . and my mother . . ."

Farnes sighed and leaned back, raising his ennui to understate his response. "So did I. In fact, I raped her, impregnated her, then kept her arms bound to the bedposts so I could force-feed her during the pregnancy. And I delivered the child, which had two heads, but lived. I delivered it Caesarean but forgot to close. Mommy bled to death. That made me very angry, so I cooked her and ate her. By then the baby was crying too hard, so I cooked her alive and ate her for dessert."

"No shit?" whispered Fatty.

Farnes refused to respond, closed his eyes, leaned his head back again.

Fatty then said, "I killed 'em both, too. Granny and Mom, otherwise they would tell, you know, be witnesses in my trial."

"Smart move," Farnes said, his eyes still closed. "Otherwise they could have put you away for life."

"That's what I was thinkin' . . ."

Fatty seemed to descend into a long, deep silence, as if he were trying to figure out, in the dim margins of his mind, whether Farnes were making fun of him or not. Before Fatty could decide, the blockhouse corridor belched with a powerful hiss, admitting visitors. A confident voice, bubbling with enthusiasm and pride, led them in.

Farnes kept his lids shut. There was nobody he wanted to see. Instead he listened, because it was too much trouble, exhausted as he was, to cover his ears.

The escort's voice, full and resonant, rang off the naked walls as his charges shuffled behind, their steps measured, tentative. "Here we have a Versatile Exclusion Area, or VEA, which can serve both for isolation of problem cases and for preliminary staging of recently admitted prisoners, as well as for Federal Witness Security."

The shuffling stopped. Farnes could almost hear the heads nodding, the notepads coming up, as the tour continued. "Unlike the overcrowding in many contemporary prisons, the MPMS prototype has accommodated every lesson of twentieth century confinement and provides a tutorial in excellence with its profusion of multifunctional areas."

"Sorry, Dr. Gray," interrupted one visitor, "but what, again, does MPMS stand for?"

Warm chuckle from Dr. Gray. "MPMS is not, as some feminist critics have charged, for *More* Premenstrual Syndrome . . ."

Responsive laughter, muffled.

". . . but rather," Gray's rising voice, "Model Prison, Maximum Security. You see, for both men and women inmates in a community environment it provides answers to both major criticisms of modern penology: first, that prisons dehumanize inmates without rehabilitating them, and second, that prisons are vulnerable to innovative escapes."

Fatty's thunderous fart was absorbed without notice by Dr.

Gray's continuing exposition. "In response to the first concern, we have advanced some of the enlightened penological methods proven by Alexander Maconochie in the nineteenth century on Norfolk Island by establishing at MPMS a work-incentive and trade-skills program that leads graduates into secure halfway houses, controlling the problem of over-crowding."

"What about recidivism?" Old woman's voice, quavering.

Dr. Gray bellowed, "None. At least not yet. And while there may yet be problems, we are incomparably better than any other rehab system ever tried.

"And as far as escape goes," Dr. Gray said, "we decided, based on the success of Alcatraz, to have the Army Corps of Engineers build MPMS here on Morisset's Island, which is little more than a barrier sandbar. Each launch crossing the three miles of open water from St. Andrew's Sound is controlled by computers and requires coordinated permission from our system here and at Jekyll Island."

"Couldn't they swim it?" one man asked.

"You mean if they defeated the seven-barrier containment system?" Dr. Gray wanted to clarify the question with its apparent absurdity.

"Well, yes."

"In that case they'd have to make it ashore against the Gulf Stream sweeping up the Georgia coast. On a lazy day the Gulf Stream makes about five knots. A world-class swimmer can only manage about three, and not very long at that. Alcatraz had rip tides, but no current like this. Nor did it have the size or frequency of sharks we have."

"Sharks?"

"Yes, Mr. Owens, sharks."

In the silence that followed, a woman cleared her throat.

"More questions?"

"What about these two?" Another man's voice, maybe thirty. Hard, brittle. Farnes was not curious enough to open his eyes. What good would it do? Dr. Gray had made up his mind.

"With a caution to stay out of spitting range," Dr. Gray said, "we have on your right Stanley Ernest Dross, a convicted murderer. Raped and killed his own mother and grandmother. Sentenced to life imprisonment, eligible, by law, to consideration of parole application in eight years. So far no rehabilitation. In fact, Mr. Dross is something of a unique disappointment, to himself and the system.''

Dross exploded a belch that reverberated off the hard concrete walls.

"What if he doesn't reform?" The old woman again.

Dr. Gray missed just half a beat before saying, "He stays."

"Forever?" The thirty-year-old man.

"Until the day he dies."

"So some don't make it?" New voice. Young woman, throaty, with a little lisp.

"Some never will," Dr. Gray admitted.

"What about him?" The same young woman again, punctuating this question with a paroxysm of coughing so deep and raspy that it opened Farnes' eyes. What he saw hit him like a battering ram. But all he could do at first was blink, let his arms drop to his sides, brace them on the hard bench for stability.

She coughed again and buckled over, getting Dr. Gray to say, "Goodness, would you like some water, perhaps?"

Water will do her no good, Farnes knew. Jesus, nothing would. So they finally did it. Jesus Christ, they finally did it. And how to get out. How?

He got up and moved forward.

The crowd of visitors, almost as one, moved back.

Dr. Gray laughed. "Oh, he is not a murderer. This, unhappily, is only, or perhaps, just simply, a traitor. This man is Lawrence David Farnes, the man who . . .''

The young woman coughed again, her eyes wet, her face flushed, and rasped, ". . . the one who exposed the biological warfare lab at the Edgewood Arsenal?"

"That's the one. He arrived today. He's only in VEA for preliminary holding until . . ."

Farnes raised his finger, leveled it at Gray. "I'm a medical doctor and I demand that you get this woman to a hospital!"

The visitors surged back, muttering in fear and confusion.

Dr. Gray stepped forward to snarl, "Do you want to end up in the restraints? We have order around here! Order! Do you understand?"

Farnes spoke up. "Look Dr. Gray, if you knew as much about disease as you pretend to know about penology, you would see the characteristic external markings of advanced *Pneumocerebritis stravanski* infection, tertiary stage and runaway. You see the purple blotches beneath the makeup on her neck? Want to take her temperature? I'd say about a hundred and three, maybe four, on the way to a hundred and eight before she goes into convulsions and dies. Two hours. No more. My recommendation? You medevac her to CDC, *RIGHT NOW!*"

"You goddamn prima donna! You think some stunt like this is going to win sympathy for what you did to your country?" Shaking and flushed with anger, Dr. Gray stood back, as if he were more afraid that he would catch something from Farnes.

The woman descended to one knee with coughing, got up wobbling, began to fall when the others caught her. Then she seemed to call on some inner strength that forced her chin up, made her smile, swallow hard, protest, "It's just the flu. Honestly. I just need some rest."

Still muttering, casting doubtful glances over their shoulders at Farnes, the visitors began to drain out, shaking their heads.

Dr. Gray came back and struck the heels of his hands on the bars of Farnes' cell. "Goddamn you, Farnes, I won't tolerate this kind of thing. You little bastard! We made this hell for slime like you and you'll never get out, not as long as . . ."

A cough hit Gray and brought him to his knees. Slowly, leaning on the bars for support, he dragged himself up. Quickly, before he could react, Farnes seized his wrist.

Above them the monitoring cameras whirred and panned, a soft gong went off again and again, the anodyne synthavoice oozed from the speaker, **"The prisoner will now release his hostage. This instruction is final and nonnegotiable. Repeat. Release your hostage now or we will anesthetize the entire unit. You will have three seconds, after the green light goes on, to obey this instruction. One, two . . ."**

He released Dr. Gray, who pulled himself back and started to lurch away.

Farnes shouted after him, "Two hours and she's dead, Gray. Longer for you and the rest. But she's contagious as hell right now. It's just a matter of time." Before his last word died in echos on the hard concrete walls, the outer cellblock door whooshed shut.

Closing his eyes and squeezing the chrome bars hard, Farnes screamed, "GODDAMNIT, MAN! LISTEN TO ME! I'VE SEEN THIS BEFORE!"

# BEFORE

Larry Farnes kicked off his loafers, shuffled back to the Chesterfield sofa, settled in, and perched his steamy cup of Mocha Java on the armrest as Assistant Lab Director Bill Wentworth finished his diatribe with, "The Renaissance man is obsolete. In the twentieth century he's impossible."

They sat on opposite sides of a sprawling oak table in Conference Room Three of what resident scientists called The Bunker. Thirty feet beneath the roots of the blossoming forsythia coating the overlying Maryland landscape, The Bunker sprawled the length and width of a football field, a hundred yards square packed with offices, conference rooms, computer rooms, machine shops, and laboratories, each segment methodically divided and separable from others and from the central library. Half a mile from the lapping waves of the Chesapeake Bay, buried and invisible to Soviet reconnaissance satellites, a staff of seventy Q-cleared scientists, technicians, and support personnel entombed themselves daily and carried on their work. Officially they didn't exist. At the Pentagon and National Security Council they were known to only a handful as Project Trump.

Farnes was the chief immunotherapist, a graduate of Cornell and the Johns Hopkins MD-PhD program. After rushing through his medical degree in two years he added PhDs in molecular biology and computerized immunologic epidemiology simultaneously at Cal Tech and Harvard. If anyone began to disprove Wentworth's pessimistic opinion, it was Larry Farnes.

Still, he only sipped on his coffee, raised an eyebrow, and asked, "Oh?"

Which drove Wentworth crazy. "Of course, 'Oh!' " he

said. "First of all, much of what was called knowledge in the early sixteenth century was resurrected classics, like Ptolemy in geography and Galen in medicine. And since guys like Mercator and Vesalius not only learned something but overturned absolute error, they came to look like genius-heroes. Today there's no way we can look that good because we're not that stupid to begin with."

"Tell me more, Master," Farnes said, smiling.

"All right, wise ass. Think of it. You know how many scientific papers are published each week? There's a hundred times as much science in print each *week* now as everything that was printed in the *century* Gutenberg's press was introduced. And have you calculated how long it would take even Evelyn Wood to read that much?"

Farnes shrugged. "Maybe you don't need to."

"Even if you didn't . . ."

Farnes had waited long enough and now seized his turn, refusing interruption. Circling the air with an expository coffee cup, he began scoring counterpoints. "First of all, there *is* a lot published. Too much. Some of it is dead wrong and shouldn't have passed peer review. The bright reader knows that after the abstract. A lot more, maybe most of it, is inconsequential, publication for publication's sake, the glorification of the obvious in quest of tenure. So who cares? That leaves you with the important papers, and there are few enough of those. So it's still possible."

"Will you grow up?"

"What? I look underdeveloped?"

"Larry," Wentworth sighed. "For Christsake you're only twenty-nine. You simply can't expect to dance with the giants without getting stepped on. Now you're a very bright guy, but with what we're really doing here it's not wise to be so visible."

"What are we really doing here, Bill? And who is 'we'? Me, I'm coming up with vaccines for the little nasties you folks cook up, and antitoxins or antidotes for those that resist vaccination. According to Hippocrates there's nothing sinister about curing diseases, Bill. Making them, maybe."

Farnes stopped long enough to raise his coffee cup and sip, and long enough for Wentworth to counter. "Don't get holy so quick, Larry. You also—if I'm not mistaken—plot the epidemiology of morbidity and mortality for released vectors."

Farnes didn't even start his rejoinder before the overhead

alarm light pulsed red, the warning horn bleated, and the calm, almost perfunctory synthavoice recited, "Attention. Attention. Breech in Laboratory Seven. The area has been sealed. Unaffected personnel are directed to report to the lobby for ascent to the surface. Essential response personnel report to Central Command. Thank you. This is not a drill. Repeat. This is not a drill."

Farnes shot a glance at Wentworth, feeling the adrenaline lance through him. Reflexively he jumped up and numbly raced after Wentworth to Central Command. Like scrambling SAC pilots they shot along the corridors, dodging evacuating personnel coming the other way. Left, sprint, then right, two corridors down in a hermetically protected inner sanctum ruled by complex floor plans and indicator lights, they burst through the hinged door.

The instant they entered, Wentworth took charge, gasping his demand for "Status!" at Cindy Chin.

Chin's troubled eyes flickered back, her Adam's apple bobbed as she answered, but her words were steady. "We have contamination indicated and confirmed in Lab Seven, Dr. Wentworth."

"Cause?"

"Broken glove box. Number three . . . that's the middle unit."

"I thought we abandoned glass containment."

"Roger that. We *had* impact resistant silicone polymer laminate sheeting, but the explosion blew it out."

"What explosion?"

Farnes jumped in, guessing, "Exothermic propagation, right?"

Chin nodded. "Incredible kinetics."

"I was afraid of this," Farnes whispered.

"You want to shut up, Larry?" said Wentworth. "Moralizing gives us zip."

"What's the overall containment status?" Farnes asked.

Chin turned to technician Ted Slovkowski, who reported, "The whole unit is hot. Beyond the secondary barrier window seals and outside is clean."

"What about the traps and filters from the fume hoods?" Wentworth yelled.

Slovkowski checked his instruments, turned back, and said, "Holding. Evidently the transient overpressure was localized, didn't develop a detonation front. That would explain why the remote primaries survived. Instruments show the particulates still retaining, the bubblers and cryotraps intact and functional. Beyond the lab itself we get no indications of breech, nothing aboveground. At least we show nothing.''

''Who's in there?'' said Farnes.

''Dr. Karlsen—''

''Jesus, Karen?'' Farnes felt the shock seep through him, fought it with disbelief, denial.

''Yes,'' said Chin, ''and Drs. Von Heiden and Brandon, along with Dennis Ulrich and Sandy Iatrogena.''

''We have visual and voice?'' asked Wentworth.

''I can patch you in,'' said Chin.

''Do it.''

Chin placed Wentworth beneath the camera, so the isolated scientists could see him. Holding back his reaction, he tried for hope. ''Karen, how are things in there? What's the status?''

Karen Karlsen's terrified face leapt on the screen. Gulping short slurps of air, she struggled to regain her professional detachment, to remain calm. ''My ears are still ringing. I'm having trouble hearing. But it's bad, Bill. Ulrich got the first burst, including shards of the glove box window, before the hood fans could dilute the stuff. Between the bleeding and the bug there was nothing we could do. He's dead.''

''Dead?''

Karen tossed a curl off her forehead, stuffed her hands in her lab coat and went on. ''Hans Von Heiden was close by. He's down. Pupils full open, breathing shallow, temperature maybe one-oh-five Fahrenheit and rising.''

''Brandon?''

''Shock, I think. Not responding.''

''Sandy Iatrogena. How's she?''

''She was away from it, tried to give mouth to mouth to Dennis Ulrich when he stopped breathing. Since that contact it's only been three minutes and she's already comatose.''

''And you, Karen?''

''I'm scared, Bill.'' She began to sob. ''I've never been so scared in my life. God, I'm terrified!''

''We'll keep this channel open, Karen, while we try to figure something out,'' said Wentworth.

Farnes burst in, ''Karen, do you have any specific derivative monoclonal antibodies in the lab?''

She shook her head no, fought back a sob.

"What about interferon?"

Again a shake, no.

"Gamma globulin?"

Another no.

"Macrophagic factor promoter?"

Still another shake of the head, no.

"For God's sake, why not?" Farnes yelled.

"We didn't want to damage the growth medium for developing species," she said, hardly able to get the words out.

"What's out?" demanded Farnes.

"*Pneumocerebritis stravanski* for sure, from the primary damage to Glove Box Three. The good thing is that it's slow. But it looks like the blast breeched adjacent glove boxes. It looks like Five lost it for sure. That would mean we have modified botulin toxins, too. And if Four is gone, you might as well sit back until we're all gone and decontaminate after. If we've lost Four, don't do anything stupid. Please!"

"Just hold on in there," he said, taking Wentworth to a far corner of the Command Center, whispering, "Why don't we try to multiply isolate? Raise the level of contamination by one after we let someone in, someone with something that may turn it around?"

"Who?"

"Me."

"Too dangerous."

"I'm immune to everything here, Bill."

"What?"

"You heard me. I'm immune. You don't think I'd come down here if I weren't."

"Are you crazy? You . . ."

"Self-inoculated. Boosters and all that. Now do I go in?"

"We don't know we can bring any of them back, Larry."

"We sure as hell can try."

Wentworth shook his head, no. "Too risky. We've got to limit this thing."

"Limit?" Farnes couldn't hide his shock. "Those are people in there, Bill! You used to call them your friends!"

"They knew the risks."

"Jesus, you sound like you're discussing a pro halfback's knees! At least let's try to get something in by interconnecting air lock; we could work it from the adjacent lab and—"

"We don't break the seals, Larry. That's my final decision."

"So you're just going to let them die?"

Wentworth shrugged. "Maybe they won't."

"Maybe they won't?" Farnes coughed up a laugh. "There's enough *Pneumocerebritis stravanski* in there to kill the Cuban army and you can say, 'Maybe they'll make it?'"

"It's not that simple," Wentworth said, clenching his teeth.

"I'm going back there," Farnes told him.

"No you're not!"

"It's my risk. The rest of the complex will be secure."

"It's not an option."

Farnes made for the Command Center door, hit the button. It would not open. "Open the door, Bill."

"Not yet."

"Open the door or I'll break your goddamn neck."

Wentworth knew that Farnes, if he never became a new Renaissance man, had already won an eighth degree black belt in karate, so he could only say, "All right."

The door slid open. Flanking either side were Marine guards in combat fatigues, service .45s two-handed, cocked, leveled. From behind Farnes came Wentworth's voice, "Place this man under arrest."

Three hours later Bill Wentworth slipped quietly into Larry Farnes' holding cell. "We're contained. And decontaminated. We limited. We kept a lid on the thing. The system worked."

"Where's Karen?"

"With the others, topside."

"How is she doing?"

Wentworth missed a beat before saying, "She's dead, Larry. They're all dead."

"Surprise, surprise."

"Accidents happen."

"No doubt."

"Take the day off, Larry. In fact, take a couple of days off. I can see this hit you hard."

Farnes shook his head. "No. No, Bill," he sighed. "The one lesson today has taught me is that we all have to make sacrifices."

"Agreed."

"So back to work."

"You sure?"

"Absolutely. There's lots of work to be done. New protocol for accident abatement, including emergency antibiotic responses available inside all the labs, required."

"I can see that, sure."

"And the Unusual Incident Report."

"I think not," said Wentworth.

"Bill, it's in the Op's Manual. Each accident or off-normal event at this lab must result in an Unusual Incident Report, followed by a Board of Inquiry, followed by Recommendations, Responses, Modified Guidelines, and Final Approved Guidelines. That's this glorious system you've been saluting."

"Sometimes the rules have to be ignored."

"Sorry, I didn't quite get that."

"Grow up, Larry. What we're doing here has been illegal since 1972, for Christsake! The last thing we're going to do is raise a great paper trail for some cub reporter to unearth with an FOI request after declassification. Get real."

"So that's it?"

"Forget it."

Larry Farnes got up, sighed, rubbed the back of his neck, felt Bill Wentworth clap him on the back and heard him say, "Atta boy, I knew you'd come to your senses."

That night at his apartment, Larry Farnes packed a cartridge of bond paper into the laser printer of his computer, booted up his Word Perfect 5.1, and created a new document. On page one he entered the name and address of the editor of the *New York Times*.

Under that he wrote quickly and without error, "My name is Larry Farnes and for two years I worked as a civilian scientist for the Department of Defense in secret laboratories at Edgewood Arsenal, attempting to create invincible biological weapons. Despite the fact that the Soviets are similarly engaged, this does not justify our illegal efforts.

"Known as Project Trump . . ."

# CABAL

Rolling west from Siberia like a Mongol horde, the massive cell of Arctic air stalled here, two hundred kilometers northwest of Moscow, casting the domed sky a hard, Wedgewood blue. Through thick stands of pine and fir enclosing the Czarist dacha, brilliant shafts of April sunlight lanced onto the snow, etching jagged shadows into talons that clawed at the shifting white powder. Crunching ahead, four men leaned into the howling wind, mounted the porch, and pushed inside.

Closing out the gale, they stomped the snow off their boots and stepped across the thick carpet to the fieldstone hearth, where they circled and ignited a kindled stack of wood that had waited weeks for their arrival. Against the chill that still frosted their breaths, they kept bundled in greatcoats and peaked astrakhan wool caps while the nascent flames crackled and spread. Reflexively they rubbed their hands together, sometimes blowing into cupped fingers, none wanting the burden of speaking first. Yet as the fire grew, scenting the room with aromatic sap, their reluctance seemed to thaw.

Officially each of them was elsewhere.

They might later need to prove that.

Or be ready to die.

And they knew that instinctively, as they waited for the first word. Drawing a deep breath and holding it like a prayer, Boris Ochoiski, Soviet Minister for Planning and Production, checked the others, one pair of eyes at a time. Then he crossed his powerful forty-three-year-old arms and said, "So we are here, all but one."

Surprise snapped the other faces his way, deepening the silence that followed. Finally the shortest and most feared of them, KGB Director Igor Saranov, stammered, "I expected just four, us only."

Ochoiski smiled and said, "One more. One only. But a crucial one."

"Who?" asked Koertsin, pacing like a caged tiger. When his bald head bobbed, the glint of sunlight flashed off his wire-framed glasses. As the ranking Politburo member and key figure in the plan, he had the right to ask.

Hearing the engine of an approaching auto, Ochoiski slid to the window and said, "Soon enough, comrades." Turning slowly, he drew the lace curtain back and scraped the rime from the edge of a pane of glass. Seconds later a sleek black Red Army staff car pulled up outside. Instantly the driver leapt out. Puffing condensation, he raced to the porch, pounded up the steps, and hammered on the door.

Ochoiski opened.

The driver stiffened and threw off a sharp salute, starting to say, "Sir, General—"

Ochoiski cut him off. "Tell the General we will see him in a few minutes."

"Yes, sir." The soldier wheeled and fled back to the Zil limo.

Ochoiski closed the door, turned to the others.

The last man to keep his silence was the biggest and ugliest, Yuri Rostenkov, Chief of the Soviet General Staff, who had been fighting in uniform since he was a Leningrad teenager. Almost hissing the words, he said, "Say what you must, but say it quickly, Boris."

Ochoiski nodded. "I say nothing new. The agricultural ministry projects a crisis in the coming wheat harvest. In Kazakhstan an Islamic jihad is building, threatening our underbelly. Striking Ukrainian coal miners may soon spread to the resource miners in Siberia. Western and Japanese capital is loosening our socialist ties. Workers expect more and do less. But these are all problems, and time solves problems. Now there is more. The Ukraine successionists. First declaring independence, then closing the borders. When we massed tanks, the Hitler-lovers invite the new German army for maneuvers. Then Poland sees Germans on one border, maybe a German army in Ukraine on its eastern flank. And they remember Germany. As we do. And that, comrades, is why today the first MiGs land in Warsaw, to support out tanks. But where from here?"

A silence swallowed his question, so he arched his eyebrows and answered it himself. "From here it escalates. From here no one backs down. We have already seen the Americans in Iraq. And in Iraq we have seen the outcome of Western technology against Soviet tanks—"

"If unsupported by air power," Rostenkov growled.

Ochoiski nodded, held up a hand. "Perhaps. But our problems are larger than air power. They go to the core of the society. Everywhere discipline is breaking down, threatening national unity, forcing us into a situation where we can, perhaps, win the war, but lose the economy, meaning . . ." he drew a long breath, "revolution."

Koertsin cast a glance at the others. "But what are we to do about it?"

The question.

Ochoiski could feel the tension grip them as he sighed, raised his eyebrows, and said, "You know how I feel."

Koertsin prompted him now. "We all feel the same, Ochoiski, but talk is talk. Either we break open vodka and drink ourselves into a stupor, or we go beyond talk."

"Yes," he said, feeling them out.

He did not know exactly where the KGB Director stood, how reliable the man was, whether he could be trusted. So in the very Russian way, Ochoiski turned to dwell in the thick black pools that were Saranov's eyes, asking, "Don't you agree, Igor?"

"Agree?" Very Russian again, and expected. Answer a question with a question, never be the first one out of line. Not good enough. Not if Ochoiski was going to be that man.

"Do you think Russia can survive without change?"

"No," said Saranov.

"And what needs change?"

"Policy," said Saranov. Equivocal. A hedge? Draw him out.

"And how do you change policy, Igor?"

"To change the direction and conduct of government is to . . ."

"Yes?"

Saranov stopped, swallowed hard. Looking around, he asked, "Is this what we are discussing?"

Ochoiski nodded, but did not commit. Instead he said, "And how is it you build a strong, modern nation from stubborn, stupid Slavic moujiks? You treat them as you would hot iron. You put them to the hammer, hit them again and again until they assume the shape you want, then quench them quickly of any heat that remains, so that you can seize and use them like the tools they ought to be. And then you push them hard, knowing that they are forged by your will, that they will not bend or break. You do not lead Russians, you forge them. To put Russia to work again needs a man like Stalin.''

Each of the other men recoiled as if hit. Eyes darted around the room, seeking denial. The fire grew and crackled, roared and glowed intense heat. Inside their greatcoats, the men began to sweat.

''When?'' asked Koertsin.

Ochoiski felt a wave of relief. Now he had the Politburo. ''When circumstances warrant, when times demand it.''

Saranov said, ''You have a plan?''

Ochoiski looked up, asked the Chief of the General Staff, ''Can we rely on the Army?''

''The Army supports no man,'' said General Rostenkov, pitching two logs on the fire, ''but rather the Soviet people. In a crisis the Army looks to the Politburo.''

''Koertsin?'' Ochoiski pressed.

The fire hissed, popped, erupted in sparks. Koertsin's eyes flashed. ''We cannot go much longer down our present road. But we can build no other without a plan.''

''I have a plan,'' said Ochoiski.

''It must deal with the whole problem,'' said Koertsin.

Ochoiski nodded. ''It does.''

''That means the source of hope for all defecting nations. That means the United States.''

''Yes.''

Rostenkov said, ''But how? Certainly not . . .''

''Certainly not,'' affirmed Ochoiski.

''Then how?'' Rostenkov demanded.

''Quickly, silently, irreversibly, using our General outside to finish what Soviet science will start.''

''An invasion?'' Koertsin said.

''That is a necessary part of it, yes,'' said Ochoiski.

''But,'' Rostenkov objected, ''we are many thousands of kilometers from America.''

''But Cuba is not,'' Ochoiski shot back.

Rostenkov scoffed up a laugh, bit back his astonishment

with a shake of the head. "Invade from Cuba? You forget the last Soviet build-up in Cuba. President Kennedy—"

Ochoiski cut Rostenkov off like a gangrened limb. "President Kennedy also gave America the Bay of Pigs. That is what America remembers best. And after Kennedy was dead and gone his legacy included Vietnam. Since Vietnam, America has sent troops only to Beirut. And what happened there?"

"You forget Iraq," snapped Rostenkov.

Ochoiski ambled back to a cushioned wicker chair, sat down. Taking a deep breath, he tented his hands, shook his head, and said, "No, Comrade General. I *remember* Iraq. America sweeps to victory over a horde of starved, groveling cowards. But I also remember Grenada, where America answers a distress call from an island nation. So how can they object if we do the same?"

"From Cuba?" Rostenkov looked lost.

Ochoiski turned to KGB Director Saranov, said, "Can you get to Castro?"

Saranov nodded. "At any time."

Rostenkov kneeled before the raging fire, thrusting the poker angrily between hissing pine logs, wrenching bursts of sparks with sudden twists. The flickering flames cast deep tenebrist shadows in the furrows of his face, transmogrifying it to a mask from hell. Turning his eyes to Ochoiski, glaring up in an even, unyielding stare, he measured his words carefully as he spoke. "I have so far agreed to listen, Comrade Ochoiski, to this hypothetical discussion. But suddenly a man I know for shrewdness and sobriety babbles like a lunatic. What madness has convinced you to slaughter a dozen battalions of Soviet troops on the beaches of America? And how is this insanity measured against the risk of nuclear annihilation?"

Ochoiski took on a beatific smile. This was the moment he had waited for. Drawing a deep breath, spreading his hands and raising his eyebrows, he said, "Because, Comrade General, our so-called invasion will come disguised as a mission of mercy . . ."

"What are you talking about?" Koertsin demanded.

"And," Ochoiski continued, "before the first amphibious wave turns north to land, the American President and most of the defenders will already be dead."

"What?" The question leapt from the others like a startled bird.

Ochoiski continued to smile as Rostenkov rose, letting the

poker clang on the hearth behind him. Taking his time for the astonishment of the other conspirators to thaw, Ochoiski explained, "Our biological warfare research group at Sverdlovsk has used the space program to develop methods of genetic engineering to produce a virus of unprecedented lethality. An accidental release three months ago killed all seventy people exposed. One hundred percent fatalities, despite the best efforts of our immunologists to save them. Nothing they tried worked, so they isolated the epidemic until it ran its course."

"And you propose to infect a whole continent?"

Ochoiski nodded. "I am assured it can be done. A seeding of several dozens of strategically placed initial infections, quickly followed by transmission from person to person. Mild symptoms at first, then increasing severity, disability, madness, paralysis, finally death in thirty-six to forty-eight hours."

"And when is this possible?" Koertsin asked.

"At the right time. Now, as Comrade Saranov knows, we can arrange that time, perhaps create confusion by sabotaging a hidden American biowar facility. In the panic that follows, the public, being told of the resulting contamination, will blame the government. And what does the government do? Perhaps nothing."

"Nothing? You propose to kill a nation and the government does nothing?"

"But who would respond, take responsibility?" Ochoiski returned the doubt.

"The President," said Koertsin.

"But taking action involves admitting responsibility. If we choose a time when the President can't afford to admit responsibility, we should not expect reprisal, but paralysis."

Saranov shook his head, sighed, "And when is it, Ochoiski, that the President must deny responsibility?"

"When," Ochoiski said, meeting the hard stare unblinking, "the President is weakest. When admission may cost him everything. Then and only then."

"This is still hypothetical," Rostenkov objected, "and we cannot keep a military invasion prepared and secret indefinitely. To succeed, you must know the timetable of events."

"I do," said Ochoiski.

Another gasp exploded, the others turning, muttering. Ochoiski raised his voice over the din, said, "In fact, the Republican Party has been kind enough to announce exactly when the President will be weakest, most distracted, least effective.''

"And that is?" Koertsin asked, confusion on his old face.

"At his party convention in Miami. Mid-August.''

"And when to invade?" Rostenkov asked.

"Perhaps three days later, as I understand it," Ochoiski said. "By then, America will have its hands full fighting for its own life. And the Soviet Union will have offered assistance through the American ambassador here in Moscow to provide medical relief by redeploying its martial police force to provide pure food, pure water, and to assist in repressing a disease which, we will selfishly admit, threatens all the world's people. By the time they discover the real nature of our unopposed landings, the American military chain of command will be severed at the top. Tactical nuclear strikes are already forbidden to American field commanders. The American policy refuses the option, at any level, of nuclear *first* strike. And no one below the President can authorize an intercontinental nuclear strike of any kind. But the real trick will be to keep our mission disguised as long as possible.''

"Trojan horse," guessed Saranov.

Ochoiski nodded.

"But even a Trojan horse must first be pulled through the defender's gates," Rostenkov said. "When, exactly, does your imagined schedule say that will happen?"

Ochoiski raised an eyebrow and smiled, not so hard his yellowed teeth would show, but just enough to tighten his lips. Then he said, "Our exact timing will be revealed to us.''

"Revealed?" Saranov scowled. His expression alone demanded an explanation.

Ochoiski gave it. "We watch from the sky. Reconnaissance satellites will show the soil littered with dead. By the time the dogs are chewing on corpses, our General will bring our troops ashore.''

"And who have you chosen for this mission?" asked Rostenkov.

Like the chess grandmaster he was, Ochoiski had correctly anticipated who would ask this, and when. "That man is just outside. His name is Yustechenko.''

"The Lion of Afghanistan," whispered Koertsin.

Ochoiski had only to nod.

For the first time, Rostenkov smiled.

Saranov continued to frown.

Ochoiski knew he needed a chain that bound them all. Saranov was the weak link. Quickly he said, "Comrade Director, you are troubled by Yustechenko?"

Saranov shook his head. "I am troubled, Comrade Minister, by tourism. If we infect America, what is to keep a tourist from carrying the infection right home to Rodina?"

Again Ochoiski was ready. Whispering as if they could be overheard, he said, "Several days before we infect, one of our UN delegates will defect. We demand his return. The US grants asylum. We react by closing the borders."

Saranov smiled, the first time for him. "Good," he whispered back.

"And Yustechenko mops up," General Rostenkov guessed, "then establishes the first occupational government."

Ochoiski shook his head slowly. Turning to each man as he spoke, he explained, "Yustechenko has two jobs, each important. His first mission is to buy time, to preoccupy the American defenders with repulsing their first invasion since the War of 1812. Think of how many Soviets died in that very effort in the Great Patriotic War, Comrade General Rostenkov."

Rostenkov nodded, let Ochoiski continue, "And while Yustechenko fights north, the epidemic runs on."

"Can we be so sure?" Koertsin asked.

Ochoiski raised a finger and asked, "Can we? Koertsin, you are the historian. What has happened throughout history when an army invades?"

Koertsin's old face wrinkled as he recited, "In addition to the inevitable death comes upheaval, destruction, dislocation . . . social services, utilities down, communities uprooted and . . ."

Ochoiski finished, ". . . fleeing in the face of the invaders. Anyone who can move will re-concentrate, bunch, and surge ahead of Yustechenko's forces, therefore multiplying the number of human contacts wildly beyond the static pockets of quarantined individuals who would survive a purely biological attack. So Yustechenko's invasion is not just a military preoccupation; it's an epidemiological tactic to mix the contact between the defending forces moving toward him and the civilians moving the other way. The beauty is that Yustechenko will kill more Americans by public panic and military reaction that he does by rockets and bullets."

Koertsin raised a hand, signaling the conversation to stop.

Agitated, he said, "I am still confused about what you said before. To invade and not conquer, what is this?"

Ochoiski told him, "Yustechenko's orders will be to win, to beat back the resistance, to secure victory, prepare for the occupation force to follow. But he will not succeed."

Saranov flattered himself to guess, "But his presence will occupy the American defense system with a problem at home until . . ."

Ochoiski finished, ". . . they all die."

"Americans and Soviets alike," Saranov guessed.

Ochoiski nodded. "Unfortunate, but necessary."

Rostenkov cleared his throat, said, "Why not protect our men, inoculate them?"

"Consistent with our biological war policy, we will give all of our soldiers shots. They will go into battle believing they are immune . . ."

"But in fact . . ." Rostenkov, the soldier, was suddenly bothered.

Ochoiski shrugged. "But we have no vaccine."

"No?" The gasp leapt from all three other men as one word.

Ochoiski said, "And that is why we cannot lose."

Saranov became the second man to sit. Rubbing his chin, losing himself in a troubled grimace, he shook his head. "The lesson of world wars is never to underestimate Americans. Even now. What is to prevent the Americans from discovering a cure? Is it not true that they have men like Larry Farnes who also have created these viruses? And what is to say they have not made this same one, that they have vaccines ready?"

Although Saranov's questions came rapid-fire, as the elfin man punctuated each with a stab of his finger, Ochoiski could only laugh. When he stopped, he said, "Comrade Saranov—dear Igor—it is exactly because of Larry Farnes that we are sure they will not be ready. Whatever evidence those labs have of illegal efforts are being destroyed as we speak, before Congressional investigators discover them. And as for Larry Farnes, by the time we strike, he won't even be able to help himself."

# THE LAST SUPPER

Above his stiff bunk was a window. Not a barred opening, but a vista sealed off by a shatterproof polymer similar to the one blown out by explosion in Glove Box Three in The Bunker. At first it surprised him to see a large area so completely exposed. Then he realized there was nothing to smash it with. Nothing was loose in MPMS. Everything was built in, welded on, or attached with recessed, headless bolts, down to the contoured ceramicized titanium toilet seat.

How could he break it?

He could have struck it with an edged hand, but that would only have broken bones. Ditto a roundhouse kick, even if he had the spring and rotational velocity to get into it. Sure, he had broken timbers and cinderblocks that way, but this was different. The window did not resist force, it permitted it. The plastic nature absorbed shock with deformation. The window yielded slightly when hit, then recovered to its original position, like a spring. You could beat the hell out of it, without effect.

Pulling himself up with his fingertips, he looked down.

The external wall was made of a smooth, reinforced high-density concrete. Vertical. Perhaps even canted a degree of arc inward, so objects falling got farther away as they fell, with no possibility of decelerating. From a hundred feet up, the first point of contact would be the bezeled revetment that slid into the slapping gray waves of the Gulf Stream.

No way out.

Looking farther, he re-examined the interlocking revetments, how they were joined into a forbidding series of notched walls, the kind he had seen in medieval fortresses. Except for the canopied tunnel receiving the launch, there were no landing or mooring spots on MPMS.

Farther out, beneath the gliding terns and gulls riding the gilded crests of afternoon waves, a pair of quixotic longhairs zipped along in a Zodiac. On the inflated gunnel was AMNESTY INTERNATIONAL. Fluttering from a flexing pole, a flag in handwritten letters said, "FREE LARRY FARNES, POLITICAL PRISONER."

He smiled.

The world is full of fools. And full of foxes, too.

He let his mind wander to the report by Connie Chung on the day of his arraignment. Dressed in an austere blue-on-white summer pin-striped suit, she squeezed the microphone before her as he was hauled, in irons, up the Federal Courthouse steps in Baltimore. Letting her dark eyes drop to muster all her poise, she said, "Facing an almost certain congressional investigation into a major treaty violation, the President continues to insist that all activities carried out at the Edgewood Arsenal, Fort Dietrich, and elsewhere, were, in his words, 'Strictly defensive and in compliance with the provisions of the treaty.' Other high sources in the Pentagon admit privately that there may have been more, but justify this activity as, in their words, 'Prudent anticipatory countermeasures to the very real Soviet biowar threat.' What the real situation is will remain a matter of blind speculation. For reasons of national security, much testimony in the Farnes trial was presented in camera, leaving many of us to wonder what considerations, exactly, are being balanced in Justice's hands." Then drawing a quick breath, she flashed her eyes directly into the camera and asked, "But should the provisions of Federal law that exist for the protection of national security also allow the government to violate treaties, defy restrictions of Congress and the will of the people? And if not, how can those same laws punish any individual who has the courage to stand up and blow the whistle? That, and only that, is what the case against Larry Farnes is about."

Nice words, but empty.

Ten years.

In the next call, Fatty woke himself from a snoring nightmare with a whimpering and flailing of arms, finally screaming the words, "No, NO, NONONONONO!"

Farnes was drilling Fatty with a stare when the murderer finally looked up and said, "What the fuck's your gripe, asshole?"

Without acknowledging the question, Farnes looked away,

watching the Zodiac skip waves while a Coast Guard patrol boat and an Atlanta news crew followed.

Looking down again, he heard Fatty cough. "I don't feel so good," he said, shaking his head.

"You're dying," Farnes told him.

Fatty lurched to his feet and stormed the bars, grabbing and rattling them as the sweat rolled from his forehead. "What are you fucking talking about? You little shitsucker. Wait till I . . ." A spasm of coughing dropped him to one knee, forced him to prop himself up with a quivering arm.

Detecting an increase in acoustical energy, the maternal synthavoice cut in. **"The prisoners are directed to remain in their own areas, away from the interfaces. You have five seconds to respond before action is taken. Five, four, three, two . . ."**

Fatty looked up, quiet now, nothing but fear in his eyes. Swallowing with difficulty, he asked Farnes, "What you said, about them people . . ."

Farnes said nothing, only listened.

"They really sick, huh?"

Farnes nodded.

"You know that for sure?"

"Better than anyone."

"They gonna die?"

"Depends."

"On what?" Fatty was just able to get the question out before he exploded in a paroxysm of coughing.

**"Is the prisoner distressed?"** asked synthavoice.

"Help me!" Fatty screamed at the speaker.

**"Please respond to the choices for describing your distress in order that the system may provide attention."**

"Help me!" blubbered Fatty.

"Play with it," Farnes told him. "If you want help, you've got to play with it."

"Fuck you!" he screamed at Farnes, turning to the speaker and saying, "Help me! Oh, God, I don't want to die!"

**"Are you experiencing medical problems?"**

"Yes," Farnes answered for him, seeing a chance.

"Fuck you!" Fatty screamed, hammering the bars. "It's not him. Can't you see? It's not him! It's me!"

Synthavoice syncopated, returned. **"The prisoner is instructed to be quiet. This instruction is final and nonnegotiable. Repeat. Be quiet or the entire unit will be**

**anaesthetized. You will have three seconds, after the light goes on, to obey this instruction.''**

"Quiet!" Farnes whispered. He understood what Fatty might never, that changes in decibel level apparently triggered certain subprograms without regard to preceding programs in progress. Fatty's rage had bumped the medical intervention interrogation and put them on the brink of an automatic, unarguable reprisal.

"AHHHHHHHHH!" Fatty wailed, the tantrum on him.

**"One,"** said synthavoice.

Think, Farnes. What does the fat boy want? He wants to be better. Sees the computer as his only chance. But can't control it. So what?

**"Two . . ."**

Give him another option. Give the fat one hope. Give him . . . what? Of course! Farnes just got the word "Antibiotics" whispered before synthavoice said,

**". . . Three."**

But Fatty went silent and the program sequence cycled.

Fatty's feverish eyes lifted to find Farnes, who had pulled a simple plastic bottle of aspirin from his pocket.

Don't let him off, Farnes told himself. "How do you think I stay well?"

"Give me some," said Fatty.

"Quiet or they'll gas us."

Fatty nodded, held out a quivering hand. Farnes instantly saw the nicotine stains, got a flash.

"Matches," said Farnes.

"What?"

"I'll give you a pill for your matches."

"Not allowed," said Fatty, flicking a glance at the camera.

"Bullshit," said Farnes. "Give me the fucking matches." He snapped his fingers.

Fatty's trembling hand buried itself in his denim pants, pulled out a red and yellow booklet. "What you want these for, huh?"

"Never mind. You want the pill?"

"It makes me better, right?"

"Right," Farnes told him, knowing it was not entirely a lie. Psychoneuroimmunology had shown that patients who believe they will get better actually do improve, at least temporarily. Even terminal patients who believe they will get better actually feel better and last longer than those who resign. Fatty would feel cured. His symptoms would remit, even while the disease ran him down.

Farnes gave him the aspirin.

He gobbled it down.

Farnes held the matches and thought.

Fatty turned his head and smiled, coughed up a laugh. "Don't burn, you know?"

Farnes eyes worked along the ceiling, searching. Only distantly did he hear himself respond, "What?"

"Don't burn, you know."

"Matches?"

"Not the matches, dogshit, the sheets, bedding. It don't burn. That's what you was thinkin', right. Torch the bed, get out?"

"Maybe." There it was, outside the cells, near the middle of the corridor. On the way in he had walked right under it without noticing.

"Your food will now be served," said synthavoice.

A whirring noise spilled into the cellblock, not from inside it. Elsewhere. As he waited, he analyzed the computer system, which seemed to run multiple independent programs serving all the functions. A medical program offering help overridden by a control program threatening punishment followed by an automatic, clock-activated program for feeding. No cross talk. Or was there?

Hatches in the floor, just outside his cell and Fatty's, popped open as food trays emerged and were drawn by conveyors inside the cell, where they stopped.

"You have twenty minutes to finish your meal. After twenty minutes, a red light will inform you to stop. When the red light appears, replace your tray on the conveyor and step back while your tray is recovered. You may now eat."

Farnes was amazed. The food at MPMS was evidently not part of the punishment. Supper was snow peas, mashed potatoes, chicken breasts, a bun, some Jell-O, a carton of whole milk. He chewed and thought.

Beside him Fatty inhaled his dinner with long, slurping sounds. In seconds the big man finished. Another second spawned a burp. A minute passed before the first fart. Fatty had no apologies, no regrets, only one concern. "How many more them pills you got?"

Farnes told him, "Twenty."

"Enough to get us better?"

Farnes nodded. "The problem is, everyone else is going to be dead."

"You're shitting me."

Farnes shook his head.

"What are you sayin'?"

"Unless we find a way out, we're going to starve."

"Bullshit." Crossing his arms on his lardy chest and leaning back, Fatty yawned. "Somebody'll come from the world."

But Farnes knew, as no one else did, that the world itself was dying. And ironically, they'd not only locked up the only person who could help, they'd thrown away the key.

To the right, Fatty slipped into a postprandial stupor, letting himself drift off into what Farnes knew would be death. He would never again awaken. He had eaten his Last Supper and was off for Judgment Day. Farnes, with his comprehensive immunity, would remain uninfected. But unless he could get out, he would end up just as dead.

# INVASION

Idiots!

General Igor Yustechenko clung to the starboard bow rail of the huge Ivan Rogov class landing ship as the helmsman on the bridge heeled her sharply to lee, heading east by northeast at flank speed. In the same moment, responding to the same satellite signal, the whole armada of ships turned together, with the precision of Kirov dancers. Twenty kilometers ahead, due east, lay the white sand beaches of Florida's west coast. One hundred kilometers to the southwest, its high swirling clouds staining the horizon, was what the crippled American weather service had named Tropical Storm Clyde, its fury lashing out in running swells that ebbed and fell at the vessel's flattened bow.

Gritting his teeth, squinting his eyelids at the driving seaspray, he remembered in vivid detail his spring meeting at the dacha north of Moscow. Saranov had been so glib. "By the time you will come ashore, the American President and Vice President will be dead. When that announcement is made, we will broadcast that the President's last wish to us by the hot line was to enlist any nation with expertise that could abate this epidemic. In response, we will then divert vast supplies and manpower from Cuba. They will land in Florida at the earliest moment to assist."

Yustechenko turned to Rostenkov, the only other soldier among them, and asked, "And if the President isn't dead?"

"We wait until he is."

"And if the weather isn't . . ."

"Comrade General," Rostenkov sighed, "no campaign is perfect. That's why we need a good general."

"You realize, Comrade General," Yustechenko snapped back, "that you are giving me fewer men than Henry V had against the French at Agincourt."

Saranov said, "And fewer opponents as well."

"And," Rostenkov said, draping his huge arm over Yustech- enko's broad shoulders, "we equip you better than Henry V ever dreamt of. What the Japanese showed at Pearl Harbor is that it is not the number of men, but the validity of the attack plan."

"But the Japanese had no plan to occupy. And in the end, what good was one decisive thrust? If you mean for me to secure territory, there are things I must know. Who covers my flanks as I advance with this few men?"

"The Supreme Soviet Air Command, of course." Rosten- kov smiled.

Yustechenko raised his eyes to the swirling gray clouds, smiled at the remembrance, then whispered, "Of course," into the howling wind.

Directly below his feet, under the thick steel-plated deck that held him up, within the hold of the five-hundred-foot- long supership were forty workhorse FST-2 armored tanks, thirty specially modified BTR-60 armored personnel carriers, and a battalion of elite Soviet marines with field experience in CBW. Stretched out in a wedge along a thirty-kilometer line led by the landing ship *Aikhal* were twenty high-speed Aist class air cushion vehicles, each kept skimming over the waves by three eight-hundred-horsepower gas turbines. Be- hind that were two more waves identical to the first.

Eight thousand men committed and no way out.

Idiots!

What could they be thinking?

And Rostenkov himself approved!

Yustechenko, the Lion of Afghanistan, Field General of the Soviet North American Invasionary Army, hammered on the rail with one hand, unable to contain his rage.

Now they could not turn back.

The storm called Clyde was cutting west, would hit them in hours. If they fell back now, it might be a week until the weather broke. Too late to help the second Soviet Army due to put ashore overnight on the southern Massachusetts shore. So now they face a few, unanticipated enemy. And they have raised suspicions, risking the precious element of surprise. Why, the American commanders might ask, would the Soviet Union risk such weather for a mission of mercy? If there was no good explanation, neither was there an alternative. Even if they could turn back now, Clyde would overtake them and sink all the ACVs in the stormy sea.

Ahead, just now in sight below the dull gray scud, a ribbon of sand appeared. He lifted his field glasses, focused, and scanned. Magnified ten times the tops of the palms ruffled in the wind. But along the shore, a shore normally crowded with vacationers, he saw no one, nothing, in fact, but rows of still, tidy houses. Once he saw something, perhaps a body, carried in and out, over and over, on the lapping waves.

Unconsciously a shiver seized and shook him. Shaking off the feeling, cocking his wrist, he checked the time, estimated ten minutes until they were safely ashore. As if to mock him a burst of wind exploded over the pitching bow, soaking him with salt water.

Suddenly a sailor appeared before him, snapped off a salute, shouted, ''You must come below now.''

Yustechenko nodded, tottered his way aft on the heaving deck, steadying himself on the rail. For him this was the worst part: belowdecks, in the hold, fighting off the welling sickness. Even pills seemed not to help. He was a soldier and hated the sea, its relentless pitching madness. And he hated the wait, the taut minutes stretching to infinity when a missile could rip through the hull, killing them all, igniting the ship in a consuming firestorm. He hated . . . Stop! He tried not to think of these things.

Instead, he thought of the men.

As he clicked down the steep steel ladder, his footsteps clattering back off the tight compartment walls, he thought of them, those depending on him. The first went ashore last night on inflated boats launched from submarines. Sappers of the Iron Hammer brigade, they were ordered to secure a United States system highway number 41, preparing for a rapid passage when the main landing came ashore.

They should meet little resistance. Florida had no active army units, only the three National Guard reserve posts: the 227th Artillery Brigade in Miami, the 53rd Infantry Brigade in Tampa, and the 164th Artillery Brigade in Orlando. If American press reports confirmed Soviet intelligence estimates, all three units had been redeployed to face the current civil emergency. Two were assigned local police duties to preserve order, and the Tampa unit had been flown out to provide logistical support for the Centers for Disease Control in Atlanta.

The plan was to shoot north fast under the cover of air support, fanning out in three spearheads once they reached the city called Tampa. From Tampa . . . Yustechenko found himself smiling. Listen to me! Have I learned nothing from war?

Plans are points of departure.

First let's get ashore.

Steadying himself on the railing, Yustechenko dropped through a second deck, following the sailor ahead, arriving at a terraced catwalk with a view of a lower deck, a deck that stretched the entire length of the cavernous landing ship. Lined up in perfect order were ten rows of four showcase FST-2 tanks, ready to spill through the gated bow as soon as they hit the beach. Mustered in the center was a tangled mass of troops, knotted on a single figure, a young officer in the pale blue uniform of the KGB.

Yustechenko marched forward, his hands knotted behind him, his ears keen. The KGB officer, Myeloskeo, shouted hysterically, "You will not be in danger of infection unless you contact the enemy. If so, you must shoot. Shoot to kill. Take no prisoners. Allow no stranger within fifty meters."

Yustechenko's echoing steps stopped as Myeloskeo turned suddenly, then smiled. "Comrade General, I was . . ."

"Go on, please."

Myeloskeo turned and faced the full-geared assault force, their faces streaked in camouflaging greasepaint, shouting, "You will not consort with the enemy. You will not consort with their women. You will drink only State-approved water, eat only our food. Disobedience will be punished by death. Am I understood?"

Not a man blinked. When no one disagrees, the government assumes that everyone agrees.

Myeloskeo turned his cruel blue eyes to Yustechenko and said, "Is there anything you want to say, Comrade General?"

Yustechenko hoisted the straps of his combat pack over his shoulders and picked up his AK-47 assault rifle. Leaning forward to redistribute the weight, he cinched up the harnesses with his free hand and said, "Follow the assault plan we have studied. Protect yourselves and your comrades. Keep your heads down and your spirits up. And when in doubt, follow orders. Are you with me?"

A huge shout exploded through the hull.

Then Yustechenko pulled himself close to the KGB colonel's ear and whispered, "My good colonel, in seven minutes we will be in a war, not a political indoctrination seminar. Some of these men are going to die. Some of those who die may save you. Make it easier for them by changing into combat gear. Running around out there in *that*," Yustechenko poked a stubby finger hard into the center of Myeloskeo's blue uniform jacket, "is going to make some American think you are more important than you are. And that will get you the first bullet."

Myeloskeo narrowed his eyes, opened his mouth just enough to say, "May I remind you, Comrade General . . ." before Yustechenko wheeled and walked forward to join his men.

Standing before them as they ran through a final check of their gear, Yustechenko held his AK-47 assault rifle high above his head and said, "You see this?"

"Yes, sir!" the shout came back.

"This," Yustechenko walked it around, "is your Soviet identification. Otherwise, as you know, we look like American infantrymen. So hold your weapons, raise and use them. Let your comrades see them. And listen to your commanders."

One pale soldier, almost too young to shave, raised his hand.

"Speak," said Yustechenko.

"What is our opposition?"

"Mostly dead, I am told, Comrade Private. Those American soldiers who remain are being deployed for emergency epidemic relief. The rest are committed to quarantined bases."

"Do we shoot civilians, sir?"

"Shoot anyone who gets in your way, but don't follow if they run. We have a mission."

Or do we, wondered Yustechenko. They had told him to secure major population centers, beat off scattered and disorganized defenders, prepare for Soviet occupation. An ambitious plan for eight thousand men invading America. And reinforcements? Three thousand paratroopers to drop in tomorrow. Although Rostenkov had promised as many more as the job took, there were not many more organized units in Cuba. And the storm would determine when any of those would arrive.

Idiots!

Myeloskeo stepped between Yustechenko and the men, said, "Any more questions?"

But by this time Yustechenko had ordered, "Stations!" and the men were running. For a week the *Aikal* had been pulling them out of open boats departing Cuba, then provisioning and equipping them on board. And the American press, suddenly taken with this shocking sickness, had lost interest in what the President had called, "a dangerous communist presence."

With the distraction of the hyperinfection plus Saranov's Trojan horse, they had gained surprise.

In time they would need it.

How far did Moscow expect him to get in these conditions? The ship was pitching and yawing as it approached the sandy white beach, reminding him of his immediate enemy, the weather. Sometimes, as Napoleon learned, that alone is enough. But here?

He simply could not afford to think about it.

Not that he didn't know. The FST-2 tanks, Soviet's finest, would be naked without the air support of the Hind-D helicopter gunships. But not even American all-weather interceptors could fly in a hurricane. And when the great technological toys and trinkets disappear, it comes down to the will, resourcefulness, and health of the common solider. It always has.

"Two minutes," the loudspeaker blared in Russian, echoing through the cavernous hold. Like the low growl of a pack of rabid dogs, forty mighty FST-2 tank engines fired up and revved.

When the bow's landing gates yawned open and splashed its huge gray metal tongue into the shallow water, the palms lining Venice were already quivering like reeds, their fronds plaintive and frantic in the shifting winds. As his APC sped down and hissed through the boiling surf, Yustechenko was hammered by knuckle-sized drops of rain.

They churned ashore unresisted, one tank after another, followed by the BTR-60 APCs. Although not as much as a single rifle had fired at them, their first enemy was already bearing down on them with unexpected ferocity.

To meet the invasion schedule, they would have to beat it.

Yustechenko felt the wind rake his fatigues, watched the power lines overhead flutter with the strain. Under his breath, so the troops could not hear, he cursed. The plan, the glorious Soviet plan on which so much more than the lives of his men relied, depended on continuous American electricity for the gasoline station's fuel pumps.

Idiots!

What had they told him at Voroshilov Academy? "A soldier's duty is to die in service to the country."

And so he may finally do his duty.

As soon as the Americans discovered Saranov's dysinformation, the instant they knew the real intentions of the Soviet presence, they would strike back with every measure of strength available.

How far can we get,· how long can we hold out without relief?

Without air support and against the weather, Yustechenko knew that his forces would be slowed, maybe stopped. If crucial bridges were washed out, highways flooded . . .

Stop it!

He tried to think ahead of the present, put his mind on the inevitables. Assuming they penetrated, sooner or later they would encounter resistance. It was only a matter of where.

How many American troops?

And how soon?

Never mind. He had to move. By whatever means, they must secure southern Florida. If not, the next wave of paratroopers would be slaughtered before they could drop their harnesses. But the supporting reinforcements who would drop like confetti from long-range Ilyushin IL-38 transports would have to wait the mercy of the storm.

Yustechenko's BTR-60 APC burst from the waves and spun up the deserted beach, smashing through a row of abandoned cars and onto the town's asphalt roads. What was it they had told him at Kiev? "American roads are so perfectly marked that all you need is surprise, a Rand McNally map, and you can read your way to Washington."

Unless all the signs are blown down by a hurricane.

Idiots!

As Yustechenko lifted his Gableidov Mark-7 field glasses to survey the distance, the other tanks began cresting behind him, sweeping their 125mm smoothbore guns in search of targets, advancing a secure perimeter around their commander.

Behind him, charging up the beach alone, on foot, waving a Polish Laskoy 7mm automatic pistol, the KGB Colonel Myeloskeo shouted, "See her! Over there!"

Yustechenko turned and saw an old woman, perhaps eighty, wrapped in a loose red housecoat, her thin white hair matted in rain—or was it sweat?—crawling along the wall of her beachhouse, trying only to hide.

Myeloskeo screamed, "Kill her! Kill her or I will have you . . ."

Yustechenko's own Graz-Burya automatic took Myeloskeo's throat in its sight, seven meters away. When he pulled the trigger, Myeloskeo's eyes had just shifted up, seeming to implore the General to support his leadership.

The round fired alone, the first shot ever fired by an army

invading America from Russia. Exploding blood and connective tissue from the exit wound in the back of his neck, Myeloskeo jerked back and hurled his pistol high in the air. Then he quivered, gagged, and stiffened, reeling once before falling straight back and crunching into the sand. His eyes rolled back and stared up as the red blood drained onto the beach.

Yustechenko turned to his adjutant, Lieutenant Drosnenski, and said, "You will report that Colonel Myeloskeo was the first Soviet casualty, killed on landing."

"Yes, sir."

"But in his honor, I will support his last wish. Obey orders."

"Yes, sir." The lieutenant paused only a second to gauge his commander's mood before speaking. "General Yustechenko? The quartermaster asks if we should now don protective gear."

Yustechenko knew there would be a time they might need it. When the Americans gathered that they had been attacked by a vicious little germ, they would strike back with their own. That, Rostenkov had argued, would be the greatest concern. But it did not explain why his men had not been inoculated against the attack virus.

Turning to his adjutant, he said, "Not now, I think. In those suits and this weather, we sweat. And we have not so much safe water we can afford to waste it."

"I will pass your response, sir."

"And Lieutenant Drosnenski?"

"Yes, sir?"

"Check Colonel Myeloskeo carefully."

"Sir?"

"See if his body shows any sign of recent inoculation."

"Yes, sir."

"And report your findings to me. Only me. That is a direct order. Do you understand?"

Lieutenant Drosnenski's narrow face turned and stared at Colonel Myeloskeo, understanding what it meant to disobey an order. Snapping his eyes back to his commander, he said, "Yes, sir."

# PRIMARY CONTAINMENT

One way out. Whatever options he had afterward, he had to beat what security specialists called primary containment, what institutional penologists called the single cell barrier. Control access made it easier to break in than to break out. Breaking in gave a better opportunity to study, to gather information from public documents, libraries, and allegedly secure computer data banks. A planned entry had infinite control of timing, a broad variety of manpower and technology, and a certain measure of influence over the terms of assault. Breaking out was tougher. A lot tougher.

Breaking out from the inside, without help from the inside or outside, was regarded as so nearly impossible that its probability for MPMS had been estimated by expert witnesses at congressional testimony to be "near zero."

As Farnes examined the bars, he understood why.

Contrast cases.

Inside, the inmate loses freedom and control. Lost freedom means lost resources, whether money, men, or information. Lost control means lost access. Lost resource plus lost access means limited opportunity with minimum leverage. In practical terms—the kind that Larry Farnes faced right now—it meant taking down barriers one by one using whatever means circumstances provided. For most prisoners it meant no information, no understanding, no mechanical or technological advantage. Taken together, for most prisoners it meant no chance. But Larry Farnes was not a typical prisoner.

He stood upright but relaxed, cupped his hands in front of his mouth, and breathed deeply, easily, into them. It wasn't cold, not offshore Georgia in mid-August. But Farnes had developed the habit as a kid in Vermont, when he trekked off

into the snow for a weekend to be alone with thoughts that
wouldn't go away.

He never brought books. Sure he read, storing everything
away in that amazing brain of his, cramming it to seeming
overflowing using Luria's mnemonic tricks, ones that went
back to Cicero, even Aristotle, to a time where books were
rare and the need for information, in dialectical philosophy,
immediate. Everything went in, stayed exactly in place in his
mental rooms, ready for recall, ready to cross-link, like a
wonderful computer.

Farnes looked at the bars and wrote a program for that
amazing natural computer, a search program to bring all the
facts to bear. The bars, hard, gleaming, and dense, seemed
unimpressed. Seamlessly welded into a cage with one sliding
door, a door beyond his immediate control, they seemed to
stare back implacably, slave to only one master.

All commands were issued by that master, a central
computer.

Fact.

Security control and access systems, by common functional requirements, had underlying program control sequences.

Fact.

Larry had designed, programmed, debugged, and deployed
such a system for the underground complex at Edgewood, for
the place where Karen died . . .

Discard.

He pushed the wave of emotion aside and pressed on.

Facts.

More facts.

What was the best system available, the one any programmer intent on devising a fail-safe, life-and-death area control
program, whether for bacterial isolation, safeguarding plutonium, or containing Federal felons, would use as a model?

One and only one answer.

Gerhardt Siemens' classified report, LANL/SS-1009, the
same one he used for designing the Edgewood Lab system,
which had directly comparable isolation and security areas.
In fact, Siemens' algorithm was regarded among experts as
fundamental to integrating artificial intelligence into security
systems of any kind. Many features were generic, including
system designers' need to bypass and access a threatened
area.

Fact.

But did the designers of MPMS have access to the classified Los Alamos report?

Unknown.

Possibilities?

High. It is a Federal prison. The report is a Federal report. Such systems, as at Edgewood, are frequently designed with Siemens' advice and consultation. Even if no one in the Justice Department knew how the program worked, the primary automator and guardian here was, in high probability, the product of Gerhardt Siemens.

Meaning what?

The bars seemed to stare back, cold, hard, but most importantly unmoving.

Think.

Think? The bars would not be thought away.

Or would they?

Come on!

Farnes considered the alternative, that the human custodians of the facility would be swept into oblivion by their next sleep, leaving him alone. In the cell to his left, Fatty was already speeding down the freeway of death, the deadly virus busily, dispassionately, relentlessly invading the synapses of his respiratory and cardiac systems, slowly pushing his vital functions into an irreversible slide. Three billion years of evolution fought futilely for life, convulsing in stertorous gasps, rhythmic wheezing, slobbering coughs. Collapsed and entirely involuntary, the huge body flinched, its arms reduced to quivering flippers as the life drooled out into a pool of pink saliva.

I did this, Farnes thought.

No.

I tried to stop it.

Karen.

Stop.

Think.

Karen.

The pain recycled, stabbed deeper this time.

Stop.

Primary containment. The bars. Focus.

Gerhardt Siemens.

Think.

Interdict. What was in the deep logic? What had Siemens

said, almost an aside, almost now forgotten, in that phone call? A mischievous thing, the kind of thing hackers love to do, just to show who's in charge. The back door.

Of course!

The question was, did they delete Siemens' back door or not? And if not, was it identical to the Los Alamos version?

But were those the questions?

Would it be more effective to raise Fatty into a perithanatic rage, have him lower his senseless head and batter the automatic lock with it? Seriously? With so few options, Farnes had to take it seriously. Especially since Fatty's time was running out.

He went to the sliding door and touched the bars. Before coming to MPMS he had read everything available on the system. He had called in favors from sympathetic colleagues who weren't even supposed to talk to him, who could have been hurt if someone found out. From them he learned a lot. Of what he learned, he knew that the primary cell lock was a multiple independently sequenced Rabson Cyberus-II, a miniaturized variation of the time-lock used on bank vaults, this one computer controlled.

A charging elephant couldn't break it.

A Roman battering ram would tear the lattice of bars from the reinforced concrete before the lock yielded.

Using Fatty would only succeed in opening his cranium. Farnes gave up the possibility, returned to the computer angle. Back door.

Gerhardt Siemens. Said what? Think. Farnes went deep into his marvelous memory and replayed the conversation, his eyes shut, ears plugged to shut out distractions, listening carefully to exactly what that bearded pixie had told him.

He heard the discussion as if he were listening. "The program, of course, either has to be used as is, the logic intact, all forty thousand lines compiled and debugged, or the architecture has to be duplicated, the program rewritten, the language translated and recompiled, debugged, installed, and verified in demonstration, which would take, say, three years. What's easier? What's cheaper? Who wants the headache of doing this? So what happens? Unless you're a masochist, you lift it intact and accommodate new needs. Basically, though, most of the program is unchanged. How many times have I done this? Don't ask."

There it was.

Any help?

Siemens' voice leapt into his mind again. "The point is that all this automated help is just so wonderful as long as the system is unperturbed. It's a future world where all the vacuuming is done by robots. The problem is that real systems behave unpredictably, Larry. You know that and so do I. So if a sensor goes dead or gives a nutty reading, or if your keyboard locks up and doesn't respond, or if you get a power surge that shuts things down, you're going to want a quick override until you can get to the problem. Now if everyone knows the override,. you've got a security problem. But, ah, if only the programmer knows, you've got a solution."

A solution.

Siemens' voice again, perfectly recalled, as if they were talking this instant. "And you've got to put access where you can get to it right away. Since the speed of events is often, as with nuclear reactors, occurring too fast already, you don't want to create a situation that puts you in worse shape than human control if your system crashes. It's best to have your 'in' right up front, staring you in the face, but so nobody else recognizes it. And you know how I did that?"

Farnes did.

He turned to face the synthavoice speaker, jumped up and down, waved his arms. Right and left, in the cellblock corners, cameras whirred.

Program perfect, synthavoice cooed, "Is the prisoner distressed?"

The initiator sequence, just a variation on Siemens' main program. Run the program.

"Yes," Farnes said. Command word in.

"Please respond to the choices for describing your distress in order that the system may provide attention."

Response sequence one, correct and complete. Let it run.

"Are you experiencing medical problems?"

Option menu, introductory item. If Siemens left the back door in, it was here. It not . . . well, if not . . .

Farnes' heart rattled, his lungs pumped his throat dry as he voiced the word that made no sense, "JABBERWOCK."

Synthavoice went mute, but only for a second. When it resumed, it said simply, "Open system command. Please enter command."

"System control abort," Farnes said. Siemens' phrase, not his. But then, Siemens' program, not his.

Synthavoice died, leaving Farnes in terrifying silence.

Power loss?

What?

Eternal seconds passed.

Farnes screamed, "Shit!" spun, and raced to the window. As he dug his fingertips into the narrow sill and pulled himself up, a whooshing sound erupted behind him. Snapping around, he saw the cell door open. Dropping down, he spun back and shot through it, stopping fast and panting hard in the cellblock corridor outside.

To his right was a large, hinged door, heavy and metal, hardcased steel. But without a conventional tumbler lock. Pushing hard, he found it fixed. Not jammed, still locked.

Why?

Should have been open. Didn't he. . . ?

That was it!

In Siemens' compartmentalized control system, no global commands could be entered by a system broken by inside input. That unique feature prevented unauthorized movements to restricted areas. If he were sitting at central control in the complex, he could open and close areas at will. But he was inside. That limited him to one move. When he had told the system to abort control, it had obeyed, but locally and forever.

Overhead, within the affected area only, the microphones in the synthavoice unit had switched off automatically. They no longer heard him, could no longer help.

Another way.

"It's never easy," he muttered to himself. "But what fun would that be?"

He whipped around, searching for the next move. As he completed a full circle, he saw Fatty sprawled in death, his eyelids popped open in astonishment at his own passing. His door had slid open with Farnes', but the other inmate would never walk through it. Seeing him made Farnes remember the matches. That was it.

Fires.

He rechecked the ceiling and found it.

Bingo.

He smiled. Prison Perfect may have done everything possible to prevent fires. They may have made the mattresses and clothes incombustible. They forbade smoking in cell-block areas, or tried to. But they could not prevent accidental fire any more than a nuclear reactor could prevent an unanticipated malfunction. So the system had to protect prisoners against fire. The last thing authorities wanted was a suit from a surviving family because their boy had sizzled up in a jailhouse barbecue.

And the system would have to be decoupled from central computer control, hardwired in, redundant, the same as at Edgewood.

The best systems were just like the one he was looking at, exposed bimetal eutectics in parallel with redundant americium capacitance detectors, normally run off modified line current, backed with lithium batteries in case of power failures.

"Let's see what we've got," he said to himself, opening the matchbook. In front of a picture of a naked girl straddling a Harley Davidson were three matches. One by one he examined them. Leftmost looked frayed, crumbly, as if it had been wet. The two others looked okay.

The detector array projected half an inch down from the ceiling above him.

Farnes was just over six feet tall. The length of arm above his head gave him twenty inches more. Together that gave him seven-eight. On tiptoe he fell short of holding a brief flame against the detectors.

Turning around again he looked for something to raise him up. The cellblock was sparse. Aside from the permanent beds and toilets, nothing but gleaming bars. Nothing movable, nothing he could stand on. Nothing at all except for . . . "Fatty!"

Peeling off and stretching out his shirt, he tied the automatic door on Fatty's cell open to prevent accidental closure. After checking the improvised cinch, Farnes stepped inside and slid the three-hundred-pound corpse through its own fluids in short bursts. Spraddling the body directly below the detector, Farnes checked a last time. He looked up, down, up, then down. He stepped on Fatty's chest and said, "Make your mom proud and don't move."

As Farnes put his full weight down, a jet of bile nozzled through the dead man's mouth. The eyes, still open, saw nothing. Farnes steadied himself, testing his reach.

"Perfect," he whispered. Removing the crumbling match, he set to strike it. "May get lucky," he told himself.

Fast and hard, he drew it across the scratched black strike strip. Without luck. Not even a spark.

Like a surgeon he stripped the damp head and replaced the unburned shaft in the open matchbook.

Far away a gurgling mechanical sound rumbled through the walls. Farnes ignored it, focusing on the second match. Striking this one, a spark shot back. But no ignition. Again. This time the tip hissed white and consumed the head before settling into a neat conical yellow flame.

"Easy, easy," he said, talking to the flame as he raised it to meet the detector. As the flame's mantle kissed the button, a burst of air erupted from the louvered duct to his right as the fans began to turn over the air in the cellblock, snuffing the flame.

Cupping his other hand, he pushed the smoldering match closer, hoping that the smoke itself would trigger the americium detector.

No luck.

Damn. The design probably accommodated the prisoners' unauthorized smoking by increasing response time and decreasing sensitivity.

Farnes stared at the matchbook. One to go. Then what? Rub sticks together? "Don't look beyond," he told himself. "Focus."

He waited for the air handler to cut off. Then he grabbed a deep breath, planted his feet steadily on Fatty's chest, and struck the last match.

A hissing scratch crackled into a white spark.

Again.

The head crumbled, arcing a white burning shard that died in smoke as it fell to his left.

One more.

The sparking woof fragmented the tip but left a flickering flame that Farnes nursed in his cupped hand. Rolling the matchstick as it grew, he urged that flame to ignite the matchbook itself. Sputtering at first, the flame began to grow, consuming the naked woman's right thigh as it ate into the front tire of the Harley Davidson. Farnes' eyes flickered away. After first checking the louvered vent over his shoulder, he raised the burning matchbook to bathe the detector in the growing flame.

Still nothing. What had they done? Time delay? Temperature threshold? Simply forgotten to install batteries? Or had they neglected to hook up the system at all?

Farnes felt the bottom drop out of his stomach, draining all his hope away. But he kept the dying flame right on the detector until it burned down to his fingers, began charring flesh. The instant he dropped it, grabbed his hands, and muttered, "Shit!" he heard the bell.

"Unbelievable!"

Behind him the cellblock doorbolt released with a heavy clunk, as pneumatic jets blew the door into a mechanical locking bracket behind it. His head throbbing with the beautiful wail of a fire claxon, the bare-chested Farnes lept off Fatty and rushed through the open cellblock door. After a short interlock area, the connecting passageway beyond was boxed in with administrative offices, each fronted by a Plexiglas window. No more synthavoice. Whoever was left out here would have to help him raise the alarm. Precious time was draining away. Not hours now. Minutes. He remembered—how he remembered! Karen's image. Her eyes. Her voice. Now he had to convince them what was going on. Hard as that might be, he *would* do it. No one knew better than he what they were up against. He needed just *one* reasonable human being to see Fatty's corpse.

Certainly he could find one reasonable human being. Passing the first cubicle, he turned, saw a man in a striped red tie and white shirt propped up behind a desk. Throwing open the door, he got as far as the words, "You've got to see what's going on here . . ." before he saw it himself. And what he saw made him numb.

# TRIAGE

Farnes rushed through the cubicle doorway, then froze, his hand still clawing the doorknob. Nine feet ahead the man's hands dangled from the armrests, shaking like a Parkinson's victim. His swollen face was blanched except where sub-dermal hematoma displayed mottled blotches beneath the chin, which dropped like a trap to grab at air. Eyes white plates, pupils dilated but unresponsive, not tracking Farnes' arrival. Nostrils fluttering, breathing shallow, rapid. Pulse, judging from the swollen jugular vein, the same. Portrait of terror. It's always the same with sudden death. Unantici-pated, unexpected, unarguable. A mask screaming shock. This shouldn't be happening to me.

And there was nothing Farnes, or anyone, could do.

Not now.

In med school, future doctors see a lot. As interns, more and worse of the same. Emergency rooms teach as much humility as the value of sound judgment. Some Humpty Dumpty is gurneyed in, a paramedic hammering on his chest, blood sluicing off in slick red rivers from a body so cracked and broken that no merciful God would want to put it back together again. Part of the training makes you accept all that, because you can't help the patient if you're buckled over barf-ing your guts out or collapsed in tears. In most cases the patient needs prompt, correct response a hell of a lot more than sympathy. There's always plenty of time for sympathy, no need to rush. Sorry you're hurt, sorry you're not healing, sorry you're dying, sorry you're dead. But never sorry I didn't respond quick enough.

It's when you get a blessed break, a few precious hours to escape behind a heaping plate of tender veal and vintage white burgundy that makes the madness tolerable. It's then when you have no appetite for sickness, crises, or dying, feel it should leave you alone.

But this was unimaginable, worse than that. The doctor, society's God on earth, was suddenly impotent. Only in *grand mal* nightmares were you alone against death, the victims frozen in endless lines at the admitting desk, one hand outstretched, the world "help" silent on their lips, buckling and tripping over each other, as you fling open the dream-cabinets and find them empty. But now the nightmare was real. Now there was only one thing to do.

In disasters and wars, when time and help is limited, doctors practice triage. Triage separates victims who would most benefit from immediate care from those who will probably die no matter how much care they get. Triage gives life to the living and lets the dead bury the dead. Triage lets doctors play God based on their mortal limits. And at Prison Perfect even the triage was automated, not by Siemens' computer control but by microorganism.

But which one? At first he was sure it was *Pneumocerebritis stravanski,* the irreversible microbic assassin that took Karen. But after his first close look at a victim, he wasn't sure anymore. Whatever it was worked faster. And the symptomology, while similar, was distinct. And if it wasn't, what was it? And where did it come from?

Pushing aside the question, Farnes approached the man, a heavy, jowled gutbucket of about fifty years, gray hair receding from the temples. He touched the victim's left wrist, just below the Timex watch. Pulse one fifty, fluttering. Irregular. Tachycardia, runaway. Temperature soaring. Maybe a hundred and six. Burning up.

Farnes waved a hand before the man's eyes. The pupils did not respond.

Nothing.

"Can you hear me?" Farnes shouted.

Nothing.

"I'll put my hand in yours. Press when I get to the right answer to my question."

Eyes dead ahead, lids fluttering. Not long. Hurry.

"How long have you been like this?"

Nothing.

"One hour?"

Nothing.

"Two hours?"

Nothing.

"Three hours?"

Small squeeze. Or was it his imagination?

"Three hours?" Farnes repeated.

Another squeeze?

"If you want help, you'll have to help me get out of here. Do you understand? If everyone is sick, I can't phone for inside help. Do you understand?"

Squeeze? Or choreaic tremor. Hard to tell.

"Do you have a key?"

Nothing.

"Hang in there. Is there a prison doctor?"

Squeeze. Certainly. Hope brings strength. He wants to live. Strongest force of all.

"Keys. Do you have any keys?"

Squeeze?

An explosion of coughing convulsed the man, shot bloody, tangled sputum eight feet across the office, Rorschached it on the enclosing Plexiglas. His lungs sucked horribly for air, groaning like ruptured bellows. Heaving toward Farnes, his eyes rolled back in their sockets and stared up, as if reaching for God. A final shudder, then nothing. With unnecessary care Farnes leaned the casualty back, closed the lids, pushed him away from his desk on the castored chair.

Farnes shivered. The prison air felt cool, even cold. Without hesitation he reached down, loosened the dead man's tie, slipped it off. Then he carefully unbuttoned the yellow poly-ester shirt and put it on. Too big, but better and less con-spicuous than remaining bare-chested.

Next he leaned down and opened the top desk drawer. Inside lay a snakepit of clutter. Security badge on necklace chain. Take it. Spill of paper clips, interlocking. Scissors, sturdy, six-inch blade. He placed it on the ink blotter. Tickets to Thursday night's Braves game.

"Won't be needing these."

It erupted without thinking, the endemic professional black humor that saved doctors' sanity and wrecked their mar-riages. Callousness was the cost of wrestling nature against the odds, because you may win rounds but you always lose the fight. But without that humor you lose the detachment needed to go on to the next patient, next case, next bed. And now, at this instant more than ever in human history, going on was vital. And going on meant somehow getting through the next prison barrier.

How? His attention returned to the messy drawer, looking for an answer. Three-by-five lined index cards, loose, unmarked. Professional poker cards, plastic-coated. He took them out, placed them down on the ink blotter next to the scissors. He shuffled the index cards aside, looked underneath. Taped down was an air-brushed composite photo of George Bush *in flagrante delicto* with Marla Maples, flashing his read-my-lips grin. State of Georgia government pens, ballpoint, refill model. He took one, laid it aside. Zippo lighter, transparent, a jazzy fishing fly in the fluid chamber. He took it. Toothbrush. Colgate toothpaste. Black vinyl comb, some of the fine teeth missing. Norelco electric razor. He placed it atop the desk, kept fishing. Eyeglass cleaner. RayBans and case. Sold to the man with the life. He pocketed them. Loose change in dimes, nickels, and pennies, less than a dollar in all. But Farnes had nothing, and phones needed coins, so he took them.

Money.

And credit. This guy wasn't going to be calling in stolen cards very soon. Farnes stepped over the dead man's knees and sidled to the coatrack, three brass hooks on a polished oak wallboard. On the top hook hung a polyester leisure suit top, powder blue matching his slacks. He riffled the pockets. Keys. GM ignition and door. House key, Kwickset. Others, one industrial format. Luck? Too much to hope for. He took them anyway. And the wallet. Thirty-seven dollars in tens, fives, and ones. Studio pictures of a plump wife, scowling in a perm, embracing a young boy and girl trying to smile. MasterCard, VISA, Discover, embossed in the name of the now late Alfred Walton Spatz. What did they used to call him, Farnes wondered. Alf? Fred? Spatz? Or just "hey you"? He took the plastic, along with the driver's license.

"Prisons make criminals," he said to himself.

Back to the desk, avoiding the corpse, he circled to the front of the desk and grouped the things he had selected. Opening the pack of playing cards, he removed the top two cards and turned them over.

Aces, hearts and diamonds.

"If I were superstitious," he said, letting the thought drift.

Using the scissors he cut the cards into narrow, matched strips, pocketed the strips in his new yellow shirt, then looked down at the man. Pants, too? But why? No one inside was going to stop him, so there's no need of disguise. And before worrying too much about fashion on the outside, he'd better get there.

Next he seized the electric razor and snapped on the cord, a sharp black belt motion that exposed the cord coupling from the housing. Taking up the scissors he cut the wires away and tucked them in his pocket, dropping the Norelco housing in the trash.

Reaching across the desk, he gathered everything he wanted together and looked around. In the corner beneath the coat-rack stood a filing cabinet. Stepping over, he opened the top drawer, withdrew an accordion folder, emptied its contents on the floor, filled it with his needs, and stepped into the corridor.

Without delay he strode toward the heavy door sealing off the corridor directly outside from the less secure area beyond. After seeing Alfred Walton Spatz, he knew that the chance of anyone inside challenging his exit were almost zero. In this kind of crisis, people's first impulse is not to shoot one another. That stage comes later. Their first impulse is to panic, run if they can. If sickness hits before they can flee, they beg for help. And Farnes was the only game in town.

But there was nothing he could do, not now.

It was too late. Each cubicle he passed was a little mausoleum for its occupant, displaying them through the Plexiglas in their last moment. A thin man, balding, holding his throat, one hand stretched across his desk. Reaching for what? Maybe air. Dying creates strange, incongruent actions.

To the right beyond, a young man, twenty-two or so, in a khaki suit too big and crumpled, as was he, in the corner, coiled up fetal style, motionless, dying, comatose, or dead. Whatever this was, whoever had cooked it up, it was sneaky fast. If this was the dominant pattern, it didn't seem to knock you down in two steps or leave people strewn on streets where somebody could see that something was terribly wrong in time to react. Unless he missed his guess, this bug was seductively deceptive. It first said, you're not feeling quite right, so why don't you find yourself someplace where you can just sit down or lie down until it passes? Maybe a touch of something, maybe something you ate, maybe the start of a cold, maybe a little flu, but just a little, something that if you're careful and patient, will back off and let you through the day if you can just find a place to be alone.

Then when the victim is alone, Farnes bet, because he *knew* how these people thought, the symptomology would abate while the infection roared ahead, asymptomatically. The next time symptoms exhibited, they would be quick and disabling, striking the victims in the refuge of that privacy they had sought to bide their time. After this point, the disease would quickly, savagely run them down like a Mack truck crashing through their bedroom wall.

Maybe a moment to wonder, a fear they might have to choke down some bile, that they would embarrass themselves, but by the time they knew they needed help, they would be paralyzed. By that time, they wouldn't even have the strength or control to knock a telephone handset off its rack. By then they were just waiting to die, each one, all alone, isolated, unable to give the slightest warning that anything was wrong. Outside closed doors of offices just like these, the world would go on, waiting for its turn.

Farnes walked to the end of the corridor. To his right was an office in oak veneer. No Plexiglas window. Upper level management. A polished brass door placard announced "Violet Hamilton, Assistant Wing Warden, Security."

"Okay, Violet," Farnes muttered, "let's see what you've got."

The door opened effortlessly. The hinges opened without noise as the solid oak door swung back. At Prison Perfect the only essential locks were run by Siemens' computer program. In theory, they eliminated all other worries. In theory, nothing here ever went wrong. The door banged to a stop.

Inside, backed into the far right corner, was what Farnes assumed used to be Violet Hamilton. Like the rest, she had sought her sanctuary, a brief respite. But what else?

Why was she arched into the corner in her slip, one hand shoved in her panties, a smile sliding into a grimace on her face?

No answer.

Guess.

Like Spatz, Violet Hamilton had burned up with fever, began pulling off her clothes before she died. There she lay, taking her last delight. All decorum gone, her fingers coiled and *rigor morted* on her clitoris, and free at last. Farnes shook his head, began to riffle her desk, looking for anything that

might help get him out, when the console desk phone
screamed a ring.

Farnes snapped away, sucked in air.

"What?"

Again, another ring.

"But everyone's dead," he whispered into the silence.

Right away he knew it was wrong, felt embarrassed that
his mind was not focusing, that the orgy of death was breaking him down with fear. The unerring rule of epidemiology
is that someone always survives, that someone's immune system can take anything. During internship, Farnes himself had
examined a number of them. A field entemologist returned
from jungle studies in Venezuela with antibodies for *Pasteu-
rella pestis*, bubonic plague, who remembered only a slight
fever and dysentery. Another homosexual actor who did macho movies, who had tested positive for HIV antibodies nine
years ago and lived completely asymptomatically. A thirty-
year-old homemaker, the only one of forty people who didn't
die of botulism in an Oregon restaurant tragedy. Somebody
always lived. Species don't vanish overnight to other species.

He picked up the phone and mumbled, "Hello."

A woman's voice, high and southern, gasped back,
"Where's Violet?"

"Who is this?" Farnes asked.

"I asked first." Her voice came in bursts, syncopated by
panicked breathing. Don't hyperventilate on me, he thought.
Calm her.

"Who is this?" he asked again.

"Who the hell are you?"

"Larry Farnes."

"I don't know you. You must be new."

"Yes."

"What the hell is going on around here?"

"Runaway infection," Farnes told her.

"Infection, bullshit! Everybody's fuckin' dead!"

"Not you. Not me."

"What's goin' on?" Crying now, lost it. Come back to
me, he prayed.

"Someone's really screwed up this time," he told her,
keeping his voice calm.

"No shit, Sherlock. Listen, I think it's the water."

"What's your name?"

"Lorraine."

"Where are you?"

"I'm near my desk. Central Admin. You know it?"

"No."

Silence.

"What?"

"I don't know it, you'll have to help me to find you."

"How can you not know it? We all pass through it on the way in and out from shifts, you know, after the launches let us off . . ." Hesitation. "It's your first day, okay? So let me walk you back. Unless . . ." Another hesitation. "You're not staff, are you?"

"No, Lorraine, I'm not. But I'm a doctor. I can help."

"Sure. Right. Well, why don't you stay right where you are, Larry Farnes, because I may be scared and I may be desperate and everybody around here that I can see is as sure as hell dead if I've ever seen dead, which I never have, but, shit! I can't be dumb enough to ask some psychopathic rapist serial murderer con me into helpin' him out."

"So what are you going to do?" Farnes asked calmly.

"I'll tell you what I'm goin' to do. I'm goin' to get off this goddamn island and get myself some help. I mean, I might have this thing, you know. And if I *don't,* I sure as hell don't want to hook up with some con who *might,* you understand?"

"So why don't you just do it, exactly as you described?"

"Get off the island, right?"

"Exactly."

"As soon as I can raise the launch dock on shore, I will."

"You've tried?"

"They don't answer."

"Why?"

"Coffee break, maybe?"

"You've tried just once, Lorraine?"

"No," she sobbed. "I keep callin' and callin' and callin' and it keeps ringin' and ringin' and ringin', and nobody answers and I don't know what the hell is going on, goddamnit!"

"Why do you think they don't answer? Why would the primary control point for a maximum security prison, the one point needed to interdict and respond to an emergency, a riot, a fire, wouldn't answer?"

An eternal silence, a longer sigh, then, "Nobody home. They're all . . ."

"Dead or fled," Farnes said.

"What should I do?"

"Get me the rest of the way out."

"Why?"

"So I can get us both out, because if we don't, we're going to die."

"Like the rest?"

"No, not like the rest. We'll starve."

"We're not sick like them?"

"If we were sick like them, we'd be pretty far along to being dead like them, don't you think?"

"How do I know you're not tryin' to trick me?"

"Why should I do that?"

"You need me to get out, then you'll kill me after."

"Lorraine," Farnes sighed. "If I needed you to get out, how did I get to Violet Hamilton's office on my own?"

"How?"

"I understand enough of the security system to take it one step at a time. But I don't know the whole setup. Can you help me?"

"I'm not a locksmith, Farnes. And what I know about computers you could put on the head of a pin."

"What do you know?"

"For Christsakes, Farnes! I'm just a public information officer and I'm scared!"

"Okay, Ms. Public Information Officer. What is the security concept in this place. Is it all by computer?"

"No. Part is by computer, the rest is mechanical locks with decentralized alarms and actuators. That's what the blurb said. I memorized it, is all. I don't understand this shit. You understand?"

"You're doing fine."

"No, I'm not, Farnes. I'm really not, I'm scared and tired and upset. I can't get ahold of anyone on the coast and I'm runnin' out of my distilled water."

"It's not in the water," Farnes said. "Don't dehydrate. Drink."

"How do you know?"

"Because I used to make the kind of bugs that killed everybody."

"Great."

"Help me."

"Why?"

"You've got a better choice?"

"Look, I don't *like* this."

"Can't say I like it much myself. So what do we do?"

"What can *I* do?"

"Tell me how people like Violet Hamilton get out of the door at the end of this corridor at the end of their shift. That's the next step."

"Is Violet. . . ?"

"Gone. Everybody I've seen so far."

"Same here. Listen. It's ten of eight. Her shift, mine, too, goes off at eight. So at eight you'll see a red light go on over a little box on the wall. You see it?"

He did, told her, "The Rabson chamber?"

"That's it. Now it don't open automatically. Everybody has to put in their own PIN, like for personal identification number. Y'all see the digital windows with the buttons underneath?"

"Yes."

"Y'all punch in Violet's number when the red light goes on and the little gate slides open. You have five minutes to turn the key, take it out, and that lets you out. The guard on the other side will take it and replace it—"

"I don't think so," Farnes said.

"Oh, yeah. I forgot."

"It would be nice to know Violet's PIN."

"666."

"How do you know?"

"Friends share."

"I'm sorry. I didn't know."

"We weren't really, I mean, close. There just aren't many, you know, women staff, and she liked to talk, you know, about her Satanism, so she chose triple six as her PIN."

Two minutes left. Farnes held onto the handset and stretched out the phone cord to reach the wall. Keep her talking. "What about beyond?"

"Computer-secure."

"Dandy."

"Whaddaya mean, 'dandy'? You think I haven't figured out that you had to beat the computer to get out of isolation?"

"This is different."

A minute remained.

"What do you mean different?"

"Before I was just trying to move one step at a time. The only way I could beat the first barrier was to override the

central program using a back door command. The problem
is that I aborted the voice control when I overrode, so I lost
access. So now I've got to find another way.''

The red light popped on. Farnes would have to enter triple
six, turn the key, remove it, and slip through.

"This should be no sweat. You've got five minutes to
clear."

"What about successive barriers?" he asked. "Don't they
go down to let the shifts off, too?"

"Not automatically. The guard gets a new number code
every day."

Worry about that later. "What's your extension, your number? I may need to reach you if there's a snag."

"From any phone enter five numbers. Six-one-five-zero-
zero. Got it?"

"Got it."

"You want for me to wait right here, by my desk?"

Then it hit him. "Absolutely not. You've got to clear your
time-locked area, too. Right?"

"Yeah, sure, but—"

"No buts, just get out. Get past the barrier to the next
area."

"Without the guard I'll be stuck. He—"

"And if you don't move I have to beat one more barrier
to break you out. And I don't know where you are. I'm not
even sure you could *tell* me where you are."

"I'll shut out all the lights behind me as I leave. There's
plenty of windows on the low security walkways. Just look
for the blackness and I'll be in the area beyond."

"I'll find you," he said, "in the light beyond the darkness.
That's all we have to hold us together, any of us."

# THE LIGHT BEYOND THE DARKNESS

The late Violet Hamilton's key came in two parts, chained together. One element was a concentric barrel key, an elaboration of a night watchman's station key. The second element was a card key, like some parking gates use.

The door facing Farnes housed a socket for the barrel key. That hole punctured the frame where a handle should have been, but wasn't. Even on close examination he found nowhere, even around the raised doorjam or frame, where the card key might fit.

What had Lorraine left out?

Maybe nothing for now. Maybe she wasn't holding back. Maybe she just forgot in panic. The digital clock over the hallway door read three minutes past eight.

Farnes examined the configuration of the barrel key and apposed it carefully into the corresponding posts and glides in the Rabson lock. It still was unclear how the door was grasped. Not by the key, which would simply disengage. Nor were there any hidden grip slots or raised edges to hold. The door was perfectly flush with the wall, forbidding purchase.

Drawing a deep breath, then letting it out, he tried a counterclockwise turn. If the key worked as a bolt, it must be to the right, since the simplest mechanical response would be a counterclockwise turn.

He tried it.

Nothing.

The key moved, but nothing happened.

What next?

Clockwise didn't make sense but . . . One second later, the tumbler clicked, tripping a loud buzzer as the door threw itself open.

He stepped ahead to exit just as a huge uniformed man

charged in. Stunned, Farnes fell back before he could spin, disengage, and regain his balance. All shock and fear, he turned to face the guard. But the man, now a body bibbed in puke and gore, crashed forward, hit the floor, and bounced hard before sprawling across the administrative hallway.

Farnes shook off his shock, pulled himself together.

Think.

Always think.

Daily number code. Didn't Lorraine say the guards had it? But had it how? On a card? In a coded message? Or in their heads?

He frisked the motionless body. Shirt pockets, trousers, holster, inside uniform cap, inside belt buckle. Bottom of shoe? Inside shoe? Where?

The digital clock showed four minutes past eight before he realized that he was still *inside*. Think! Hurry, but think! Stabbing back one hand, he grabbed the accordion file he had packed with scissors, electrical cord, playing cards, credit cards, and cash. With the other, he grappled the collar of the fallen guard, hoping that he might, somewhere, have written down today's pass number. As the digital clock began rolling to five past eight, he tucked the file under one arm and dragged the six-four corpse through the opening just as the door snapped shut behind him.

Releasing the man's collar, he let the body drop and looked up. Before him, latticed across a ten-foot gap, welded into a surrounding flange, was a nest of double bars, similar to the ones in his cell. Unlike the preceding door, this gate lacked a keyhole.

Be sure, he told himself. Don't assume. He looked down. The fallen guard had no keys. None.

In a perverse way, the system made sense. In Prison Perfect, no inmate could defeat primary containment, then simply breeze through a series of conventional locks, each increasingly simple. Here containment was redundant, and escape almost impossible. Certainly no one could force their way out. To escape you had to be smart, smart and clever, clever and knowledgeable. Not exactly the resume of your average homicidal maniac.

Farnes leaned against the wall and wiped the dripping sweat from his forehead, looking at the bars ahead. All right, it was one thing to be clever, smart, analytical. He could do that well enough. But clairvoyant?

The gate ahead responded to a number. But Farnes had no number, and no idea what it was.

Clutching the packet of objects under his left arm, he approached the console on the gate and checked the keypunch. Linear three. About a thousand possibilities. Is it time limited? Would he have to beat it by, say, ten past eight? Even if not, how long to run through all the possibilities? Probably can't attack it consecutively or it will shut down after about three errors. That's the way. Access denial was a standard countermeasure against random tampering.

So what now?

Might as well, he thought. It's worth a try.

The light port on the synthavoice transceiver above the gate was out, had been since he aborted control in isolation. And the computer controlled the gate. But the computer was deaf. Being deaf it had become dumb.

But Farnes recalled something Siemens, the Los Alamos security whiz, had joked about while he consulted with him on the Edgewood system. "Okay, so I build in the back door and nobody knows about it. And it's only for me, right? So there I am in a terrorist situation or a plutonium release and what, I want to get caught up in that? I look crazy to you?"

Farnes remembered Siemens' roaring belly laugh, the old man wiping the tears from his eyes, the strong hand on his shoulder, his confession. "So I tell some friends about this back door. I don't want them caught either. Now they suspect I've done it because everyone does it, so why not tell them? Just don't tell the guys in crypto, okay? Because crypto has these very diabolical theoretical mathematicians who always try to beat you on a convergence program, just number crunching, bypassing, comparators, loops, that sort of thing, all with their multi-megabyte Crays. So I say, okay. Maybe. Who's going to break out with a supercomputer? What inmate is sitting around in his cell with a Cray?"

Farnes remembered the old man sipping on java, picking up, telling him the back door, and then, something more. "Then I think, you know, there may be, what, a handful of jokers who know this back door? And I do mean jokers, like the noveau hackers who would like to see the masterful inventor stymied. And I can just see myself leading a tour of DOD brass around when they lock up the system using my back door. And there I am with my head up my ass having to call out for release. Now how does that look for next year's grants?

"So I gave myself another option," Siemens said, tapping his pocket. "I created another override using an ultrasonic signal. A dog whistle. Simple, commonly available high frequency generator. Wash the spectrum and it pops. The beauty is that it activates the canine response, too, so no holes."

Farnes didn't know if they left the ultrasonic gate in. But debugging a rewritten program could be such a bitch he was sure they wouldn't do any more tampering than absolutely necessary to adapt. If so, all the buried garbage stayed in.

Although Farnes had no dog whistle, he had, in his folder, what might work as well. Piece by piece he took it out, laying the components on the concrete deck. Ballpoint pen, sans refill. Front barrel only. Plastic playing card strips, matched, variable. That's it. Simple but workable.

He picked up the barrel of the ballpoint pen and put the collar in his mouth. Then he picked up a pair of plastic strips, the thinnest, and stretched them out, using the thumb and index fingers of each hand. Raising the nozzle of the pen, using the orifice where the ballpoint usually fit, he blew over the cards, producing a shrill whistle.

Nothing.

Again.

Nothing.

He put the strips down, was overwhelmed with the thumping of his heart, the pulsing of blood in his temples. They'd shut off the high frequency egress gate. It was gone, he feared.

Think.

Knowing that different thickness and width produced different ranges of frequencies, Farnes picked up the next set of plastic strips, stretched them out as a kid does grass blades, and forced air through the pen tip. The resulting flutter tickled his fingers but was silent, all the sound energy channeled above the range of human hearing. He raised the flute and aimed it, pushing as much of the energy as he could into the transceiver.

He blew variably, scanning up and down the scale of notes, until he ran out of breath. The gate remained unmoved. When the last trace of air was expelled, he dropped the pen tip from his mouth and gasped, buckled over and refilled his lungs.

Doubled over, braced up by both hands on his knees, still grabbing breaths, he suddenly heard forced air whoosh into the pneumatic glides beneath the metal frames. Almost instantly a solenoid clicked, releasing the bolts. The gate glided open.

"All RIGHT!" Farnes yelled, grabbing his packet and charging through, knowing from Siemens that at this level of containment, gates were going open all over the complex. Somewhere on the other side of blackness, Lorraine would be watching a similar barrier sliding open. Would she be stunned and frozen, or would she rush through before it re-closed?

In either case, he improved his chances of escape and survival by getting to her. She knew the prison plan and procedure, including the arrival schedule for launches and maybe the emergency communication system. And she knew the mainland, its banks, roads, police stations, everything.

As Farnes waltzed through the displaced grid of bars, he momentarily relaxed, took a deep breath, then gagged. Until now it hadn't hit him. Until this moment he had been so consumed by fear that he had nearly stopped sensing. In that fight-or-flight paralysis he had only one thought, a thought that literally shut down normal sensation: get out. And as a doctor he had learned to shut out the wave of stench that overtook him now, the smell of decaying flesh, the smell of human rot, the smell of wholesale slaughter, of death.

It had been eking from lifeless bodies for how long? Three hours? Four?

Before long it would get choking bad. In the end no discipline could keep him from puking. And in Prison Perfect there were no screens, no open windows. The ubiquitous air handlers added little fresh air, concentrating the decay.

From what he knew, neither he nor Lorraine would die from infection. And if they kept making progress, they wouldn't starve. But unless they made tracks fast, they might suffocate or become disabled with convulsive vomiturition. So now, more urgently than before, he pressed on, looking for the next gate out of the charnel house and wondering, at the same time, where and who Lorraine was.

Farnes stepped around fallen bodies, heard the buzz of stray flies, pushed past the open gate, through a pair of fire doors and onto a walkway.

Enclosed, as Lorraine told him, by Plexiglas windows overlooking a court, Farnes was able to see the organization of the prison. The walkway was one of at least three spoking out from what appeared to be a central administrative building into separate cellblocks, each isolated and separate from the others, but each admitting prisoners to a common exercise yard. The exercise yard sprawled continuously beneath several crosswalks, a crescent-shaped grassy field etched with a baseball diamond here, a short football field there. In the mid-August twilight and intense floodlights, Farnes counted three bodies. All uniforms, guards. If the terminal phases of infection had struck during exercise, the yard would be littered with dead.

The prison architecture suited Siemens' computer control, which used a master program fed by local area control networks. Before a certain point, barriers opened up independently in each cellblock, leaving the others secure. That way a fire in one would not breach security in another. But the closer he got to the central facility, the more doors would open with each command. The planners' logic held that there's no sense in everyone, even convicts, being killed in a major fire, pipe-fed flood, or other disaster. When disaster exceeded a certain point of control everyone was released, captives and captors alike.

He looked up and out, over the yard, and traced the pattern of lights igniting the outline of the cylindrical administrative building. To a level of about fourteen feet up, the building was dark. Looking more closely, Farnes saw there were no windows. Because the admin building touched the yard, its lower levels were blank walls, denying access. Above them burned circular tiers of light, stacks of circumferential dots, regular, repetitive, except for one break.

On the fourth level a slice had been blacked out.

Lorraine.

Meaning what? Assume she passed the analogous barrier, was out. Where did that put her?

Farnes had no detailed picture of the floor plans beyond what his outside reading had given him, only a good notion of what compartmentalization would require. And in the admin building, it would require damn little. In fact, in the admin building, the gates he had just beaten would be the last barrier between the employees and the outside. Wouldn't they?

He pressed forward, his hard shoes tapping and echoing

across the catwalk, and pushed against the fire doors separating him from the admin block itself. The doors seemed to push back.

He stepped away, examined the paired doors.

The last barrier had been computer-controlled, meaning, according to the design scheme, that this one should be a mechanical lock. Or was it?

He took his time studying the doors, found no keyhole, no cardslot, nothing. Unavailable for examination, the hinges must be hung on the opposite side. No other possibilities for entry suggested themselves.

Think.

He ran his hand along the doorframe, seeking something tricky. A mercury microswitch, a magnetic read switch, a simple, hidden toggle. Even a reset-access button. Something.

A minute's search gave nothing. Farnes sucked in a deep breath and went into his head. Think.

What?

There must be *something*.

He went over the door itself, wondered about the possibility of a latent panel to the side, behind the wallboard. To explore that possibility he took out Violet Hamilton's card and began moving it around the wall, trying to trip a hidden magnetic scanner that would pop a bolt.

Still nothing.

"Hell with it." Stepping back, he raised his foot and smashed it into the door. The panels fluttered as the hinges squeaked. A slit snapped open, then shut, between the two panels. As it did he saw a simple, bezeled bolt, something you can beat with a credit card.

Nothing more.

Then why didn't it open?

He hit the door again with his foot. Again it budged, this time staying open. Looking through the slot revealed the problem. On the other side, a huge guard's body had fallen across the door, jamming it. Three hundred pounds of dead lard made a formidable wedge.

"So much for elegant solutions," Farnes said, putting his right shoulder down and driving the door back. After forcing an eighteen-inch crack, he slid through, stepped over the corpse and into the admin block.

Farnes still had one computer-controlled barrier to beat,

the one he hoped that Lorraine could make on her own. Only one. At this point he had no higher motives, no ambitions for heroism, no needs other than to eat. If he didn't eat, he would starve and die. And around the new Prison Perfect it was self-service or none.

Whatever happened later he would worry about later.

He walked ten yards, intersecting a corridor that moved in an arc, right and left, probably tracing the shape of the cylindrical structure. On each side were lighted offices. In each office, the images of marked and broken bodies reminded him of fourteenth century woodcuts illustrating the descent of the Black Death on Europe. That or the faces of the condemned, rendered by Hieronymus Bosch or Pieter Brueghel the Elder, slipping into hell. And the one aspect of that horror that only lived in death—the stench of vomit, feces, decay—was poisoning the air. So maybe eating wasn't the only problem. Maybe keeping the will to eat. Or maybe, more immediately and more urgently, breathing.

"Out," he said aloud to himself, moving away from the cellblock. That way led to lower security areas. That way was out. That way, maybe, was Lorraine. And if not?

When the time comes, he said, he would answer each question. Right now he had a gate to beat. With his packet of riffraff he strode down the corridor, wading through the growing stench.

"Out," he reminded himself aloud, focusing his attention away from the rank odor, turning the corner and coming to the gate. For a second, only a second, he couldn't believe what he saw, almost thought it must be a mirage, that somehow his mind had snapped. But if it hadn't . . .

His feet took off, sprinting toward the barrier, the lattice gate that stood, incredibly, open. Crashing through, he rolled left and posted himself against the wall, grabbing at air. He closed his eyes, unable to believe his luck, when a voice suddenly demanded, "Where the hell you think you're goin', shithead?" The question was punctuated by the sharp action of a riot gun.

He opened his eyes and saw the guard, his feet spread, his eyes riveted, his breathing steady.

Jesus, Farnes thought. Another survivor. Just what I need.

"Get 'em up, shithead!"

Farnes raised his hands, assessing the disturbed look in the man's eyes. Hysteria? Situational insanity? Religious fervor?

"Put down the pouch, shithead."

The guard motioned with the muzzle of the scattergun where, exactly, he wanted it put. Farnes dropped it. The scissors clattered out.

"You figure on pokin' me with that?" The guard clicked his head toward the scissors. "Hey, shithead?"

Farnes shook his head, no. "Just trying to find a way out."

The guard riveted him with reddened eyes, smirking, snorting laughter. "You just what? Say what, shithead?"

"Everybody's dead," Farnes started to explain.

"I'm not dead. You're not dead, shithead. So why don't we just turn around and start back to the cell, until we get orders from the outside." Again the guard motioned with the muzzle of his gun.

Farnes forced a calm deep inside. All his advanced karate prepared him for his level of confrontation, this psychological assault. In reaching that state his mind actually sped up, ten and more times its normal speed, so that actions external to him were delayed. Reality slowed. As it did, his eyes reached inside the guard's mind for a deeper level of vulnerability.

The guard just blinked. Then his gun barrel dipped, his lips went slack, the sound "Uh" gurgled from his mouth as his eyes flooded with confusion, but not enough to crush his will. Even deep in this mental state, each second Farnes was more aware that he might have to improvise.

But how?

Lazy images floated on his field of vision as he heard, slow, cadenced, sharp footfalls to the right. Reflexively the guard's head pivoted, followed by his riot gun. Entering his ears came the low question, "Farnes?"

The guard dropped to one knee, the stock of his gun planted on his hip.

Lorraine! Farnes rocketed ahead as the guard's doubled muzzle drifted back his way. A volley of double-ought buck thundered a slow explosion. He could actually see individual pellets exit the barrels. But the aim was way off, spraying shot far left.

Farnes spun into a deadly reverse roundhouse kick. Striking below the guard's left eye, it caved in his face, threw him senseless across the deck, where he fought to prop himself up, failed, collapsed in a groan.

Suddenly, the crisis past, Farnes' mind stopped racing.

Sounds, images, sensations accelerated to normal speed. Suddenly he was back in the world of common experience.

His eyes left the fallen guard and tracked the sound.

"Farnes?" Still in the hallway to the left, hesitant. "Farnes, who's shooting?"

"A guard. He tried to kill me."

"Why?" The voice rattled out of the corridor, its originator still hidden.

"Because I'm a convict, that's why."

"I'm not showing myself till I'm sure it's safe out there."

"Lorraine, you do what you like. I'm getting the hell out of here."

He was marching for the front lobby when she popped into view, raised a service .38. It shook in her hands as she said, "Take me along . . ."

". . . if I love you?" Farnes snapped. But what he saw made him smile, the first thing since Karen that had. Latched on to the Smith and Wesson was a beautiful woman. Full green eyes, slender nose, sensual lips, all framed in crashing ringlets of blond hair. For today, which must have seemed at dawn like just another day at the office, she had grabbed a short, revealing dress off the rack. The fabric dipped and tucked and gathered around a body where the swirling curves tucked and intersected in Praxitelean perfection. Good breeding stock for the Brave New World, promise of things to come, hope for the . . .

She waved the pistol barrel, said, "Let's go."

"My very idea."

They walked, silent. Finally she said, "This doesn't scare the shit out of you?"

"Fear is no advantage."

"Advantage? For what?"

"Survival," he said. "Nothing more, nothing less."

"You mean this isn't just bad water? This isn't just here?"

" 'Fraid not."

"Jesus, Farnes, if it isn't just here, how bad is it? I mean, how many people . . . what the hell's going on?"

# GIFT OF GLASNOST

"You sure you want to know?" Farnes asked, marching in front of her, one arm raised in deference to the gun, the other clutching the packet of paraphernalia from Alfred Spatz's office.

"Of course. I want to understand *why*. Just . . . *why*?"

"Why is easy. I thought you would be more interested in who."

"Turn left here, then straight through. The main lobby's at the next set of fire doors. It leads on to the wharf. That's where the launches arrive."

"If they arrive."

She directed him with the gun, protecting her distance, waving him ahead.

He moved, trying to loosen her up. He didn't sense she wanted to shoot, but guns in nervous hands have a nasty habit of going off. And now that kind of mistake wasn't affordable. "Lorraine, do you think there are more?"

She shook her head, no. "I called everyplace. Every admin unit, every ward, every wing. Except for you, nobody picked up."

"The Soviets really did their homework on this one."

"What do you mean, Farnes? I don't see any Russians."

"They'll be along soon enough."

"How could Russians do all this?"

"Because they were desperate and it was the only chance we left them. They're smart and they're thorough. They're smart enough to make themselves a bug that mimics flu symptoms, but that puts people away fast. And they're smart enough to chose the right time, when the leaders are preoccupied with renomination at the convention and the public is hysterical about possible releases from the four U.S. biological warfare centers, to create confusion about *where* this came from. And they're smart enough to fix the release right after summit talks added another ban. They're also thorough enough to be sure that all of their agents were in place, none of them detected or followed, no indication of their presence, before they activated the infection."

"You mean," Lorraine said, her face showing vexation, "put it in the water?"

Farnes shook his head no. "Water's too frequently monitored at the source. Even if officials didn't know what it was, they'd isolate the systems and post a quick warning. I bet they used a large institutional food service, something that makes deliveries to schools, businesses, hotels, airports. That way it would hit all at once. Anyone left to coordinate a response wouldn't know where to look until it was too late."

"Jesus, Farnes," she said, still training the gun. "Why would they do it?"

"Why? What do you do when you're drowning and somebody pushes your head underwater?"

"The Russians?"

Farnes nodded once. "We'd held out our hand and they'd taken it. Credit, grain, technology, personnel. Suddenly they accept Poland's invitation to maneuver across the border from the Fourth Reich and overnight the helping hand is gone. Credit withheld. Grain delayed. Technology stopped. Personnel withdrawn. Finally, their oil embargoed. The one chance to pull themselves up in the world market, gone. But do we stop there? Oh, no! Then comes the ultimatum to withdraw from Poland or face eviction, like the Iraqis from Kuwait. And look what happened to Soviet hardware in Iraq. Their bluff was called. Suddenly, their back was to the wall and what did we do? We gave them no way out. The only question was how they would come at us. And that answer was easy: surprise attack by germ warfare."

"But if everybody just, like, drops dead—" Lorraine said.

"Then the Soviets just pick up the title and carry on."

"What pricks!"

"They can be. So can we."

"What a flock of assholes!"

"That's what I decided about biowar generally."

"What can we do, Farnes?"

Together they moved into the lobby, Farnes leading. "First we get out."

"The lobby door to the wharf is locked, too," she told him. "Mostly to make a good impression, but one of the guys in maintenance told me it was a good lock. I don't have a key. I mean there isn't a key."

Farnes looked up, saw the oversized doors, paired, sans lock compartment or raised mechanism housing.

"How does it work?"

"Time lock on an override radio signal from the shore for emergencies. I don't understand much more'n that."

"So," he turned back, "not controlled by the central computer, like other gates."

"Nope," she said. "Not as I know, anyway."

"Then it's got to be local control, somewhere in this room."

"You're the expert," she said, shrugging.

"When is the time lock due to release?"

"Twelve minutes ago for just ten minutes. We missed it until tomorrow at six."

"Let's see what we can do." Moving to the reception desk, he passed through a swinging half-door and moved the body of an elderly woman from its chair, laying it down almost gently, then sitting down where she had been. Using his scissors as a wedge and screwdriver, he broke into the housing of one of the desktop personal computers and removed the disk drive. Again using the scissors as a lever, he disassembled it and pulled off one of the electromagnetic poles.

"What are you doing?" she asked, the revolver now lower, across her waist.

"Snooping. Hoping to luck out."

"Hey, Farnes. Talk to me, huh? I'm here."

"What?"

"Your head's somewhere else, like getting out of here is some game, like I'm just, you know, here for the ride."

Farnes looked up at her. Scared. Gun hand trembling. Adam's apple bobbing. Eyelids fluttering. "You want to put down that gun?"

"No. I still don't know more'n you're tellin' me. And if you belong in here, like the rest, odds're good you're a liar."

"Fair enough. Just don't shoot."

"Then just don't try anything."

"Look." He stopped, sighed, put the magnet down on the desk. "You shoot me and no one is going to save me. Bullets make big exit holes, bleeders. Believe me, I've seen some beauts in emergency rooms and it makes the movie stuff look pretty.''

"You're really a doctor?"

"If you think I'm a liar and I *am* a doctor, should I say no if I want you to believe me?''

"Farnes, goddamnit!''

"Do you mind if I try to get us out?''

"Maybe we should wait, you know, until they come in the morning.''

"Lorraine, I don't think anyone is coming in the morning.''

"That's what you'd say, wouldn't you, if you thought you had a better chance of escaping now than waiting, because of this—whatever it was—they put in the water.''

"It isn't in the water.''

"Bullshit, Farnes! Look, I'm the only one who drinks just spring water. I bring a couple of bottles every day. People think I'm weird, okay? But now they all drank the *other* water and they're dead, and I didn't and I'm alive, so . . .''

"The guard back there was pretty much alive, no? And me, I'm alive, huh?''

"It could still be the water if . . .''

Farnes stormed away from her, up to an upright water fountain, leaned over, pressed the button, and drank deeply.

"Farnes!''

"*Not* the water.''

"If you're wrong . . .''

"If I'm wrong, I still have a hell of a lot better chance of catching one of your bullets than from anything in the water. So you might as well put the gun down, because if you're right, I'm going to be dead soon anyway. And if I do start to have trouble, I'm going to need your help getting me to a hospital. So if you're right, Lorraine, I need you desperately, or soon will. Now why should I think about killing you?''

Lorraine put a hand to her head, trying to sort all that out, and said, "Okay. Maybe. Oh, look, I don't know—''

"Make a call.''

Lorraine blinked back, apparently unable to tell what he was up to.

"You've got the gun, Lorraine. Just pick up the handset on one of these phones and make a call.''

The gun in her hand was shaking, her control going. Tears welled up in her green eyes.

"If the problem is with the water here at MPMS, just buzz someone on the mainland." Farnes hurdled the counter and snagged a handset, put it to his ear. "Dial tone. Open line. Just make a call."

"I don't know who to call," she sobbed.

"Call any major TV station in Atlanta."

"Why, Farnes?"

"Because, Lorraine, this," he swept his hand across the carnage, the bodies sprawled and stinking with death, "is going on all over, right now."

"No," she gurgled, shaking her head.

"Call."

"You're lying, Farnes! You've got to be!"

"And what about the launch for the eight o'clock departures, Lorraine? Where do you suppose it is?"

"Waiting," she screamed back, "on the other side of that door, the same as it does every night."

Farnes snapped a look at the digital clock behind the counter. "At eight-thirty?"

"It doesn't *leave* till eight-thirty."

"But surely the crew would think something was wrong, if *nobody at all* came through for thirty minutes after quitting time. That would be a little odd, don't you think? They might even suspect a little problem with the inmates. And that would bring some kind of response, no?"

"I don't know, Farnes. Jesus!" Still crying, still angry. Gun still in her hand.

"Shall we go outside and find out?"

She nodded.

Farnes picked up the magnet, began tracing it along the exterior wall about shoulder high.

"What're you doin'?"

"Looking for the control box for the front door."

"I told you it came from the mainland."

"That's the signal," he said. "The actual mechanism and primary electronic actuator is here."

"You sure, Farnes?"

He nodded, kept moving the light magnet, waiting for it to pull against the steel housing that controlled the door. He figured it had to be at about this level for convenient maintenance or repair. At about shoulder level a serviceman would work for hours in safety and comfort, could develop easy purchase and apply controlled force, if necessary. Any higher or lower and the box would be either dangerous or difficult to work on, not to mention inconvenient. His best guess was that he would find it soon.

Getting nothing, he started on the other side of the door and moved away, all the way to the far wall.

Still nothing.

"What's the matter, Farnes?"

He held up a hand.

Think.

He moved the magnet back toward the door frame and stopped. Walked across to the other side and reversed what he had done. Then, to satisfy himself, he repeated what he had done. When he was done, he smiled and said, "I'll be damned."

"Farnes!" Lorraine screamed. "You're talking to yourself! Nothing pisses me off more about a man!"

Farnes laughed until he collapsed against the wall. When he stopped, he managed to say, "Karen used to say that, from time to time."

"Who's Karen?"

"Used to be a . . . friend, a very good friend."

"Old girlfriend, you mean. What happened?"

"She died."

"I'm sorry."

"So am I."

"Accident?"

"Sort of," Farnes said. "She died like the rest of these people here. And they wouldn't let me try to save her."

"Jesus. More assholes."

Farnes tried a weak smile. "Well, if it's any comfort, there'll be fewer assholes now."

Lorraine put down the gun, knelt down, shook him by the shoulder. "Farnes? You gonna be all right, honey?"

He drew a giant sigh, held it, let it go slowly, "Yeah, sure."

"We gonna get out of here tonight?"

"Let's see. Hand me my scissors."

"You gonna cut our way out?"

"In a way. You see this?" He knocked on the wall.

"It's a wall, Farnes. You can't think I'm that dumb a blonde."

"It's a sheetrock wall, Lorraine. Nothing fancy, but that's the point."

"Why, lots of wall is made of sheetrock. My daddy's a contractor."

"Sure, lots of walls are made of sheetrock, Lorraine, except in prisons. In the security areas, everything is reinforced concrete or chrome-molybdenum steel. It looks like whoever squeezed this contract out of the statehouse decided to cut a few corners in the lowest security area. I'll bet he figured that no one would ever know."

"So what? We're gonna bust through the walls?"

"No, we're gonna cut through." He took the scissors from her outstretched hand. "Right here, right next to the metal door jam, where the magnet pulled a little more than expected. At first I thought it was just the door, but the force was too much."

Farnes heaved back and rammed the double-bladed scissors through the wallboard, punching a small hole that he enlarged by rotating the double blades. Recovering the scissors, he heaved back and drove another hole, this one higher, then widened it the same way. Then another, lower.

Next, using the edges of Alfred Spatz's scissors, he began furrowing the wallboard, etching a groove that he deepened with each stroke as the gray powder flew around him, clouding the air. When all the grooves were cleanly and deeply etched, circumscribing the area, he inserted the scissors and began working slowly back and forth. As the adhesive facing came away, a huge piece of wallboard flapped open.

"Bingo," Farnes said. Behind it was a steel box fed by thick, sheathed cables. The control panel inside was protected by six countersunk Allen bolts.

"We're gonna be here a while," he told her.

"What's the matter?"

"Nothing I can't handle."

"Let me have a look," she said.

Nearing anger, Farnes turned. "Maybe, if you just sit down, I can get started here."

Lorraine posted her hands on her hips, cocked her head, narrowed her eyes. "Farnes, the second thing that pisses me off, next to a man who talks to himself, is a man who sits there all limp and good for shit and tells me nothin's wrong. And the third thing that pisses me off is the man who's so damn sure, just because I'm a woman, that I can't get his little business straightened out for him. You following all this?"

"Lorraine—"

"Just let me look at the pissy little thing, Farnes! Jesus!"

Farnes threw up his hands. "You going to think it open, Lorraine?"

"Maybe." Her face screwed up as she looked, touched a few things, then stopped. "Oh, I get it. We've got to get past this plate here to get to some switches or stuff inside, right?"

Farnes wanted to say "Brilliant" but didn't. Biting his tongue gave him, "Yeah. Okay, that's right. So?"

"Meaning we have to get off these little bolts, right?"

"Right again."

"The ones with the little holes in them, right?"

"Right."

"But there's no edges on 'em, so you can't, like, grab 'em with pliers."

"You're beginning to figure it out."

"Let me guess, Farnes. There's somethin' you've got to put down those little holes, something shaped just like them, you know, with six sides on it, that lets you turn the bolts, right?"

"Right."

"So how you gonna do that, genius?" she asked. Her head was cocked, a smile on her face, her tongue sticking provocatively between her teeth.

"I'm not. I'm going to wedge the plate off using the scissors and snap the bolts at the stress line between the head and shaft."

"Why?"

"Because you work with what you have. And what I have is scissors. What I don't have, incidentally, is a set of Allen wrenches. You're the public information officer. You must understand that they're not standard prison issue."

"Why don't you use what you have?" she asked. Farnes couldn't understand the devilish smile on her face. How could she be enjoying this? What the hell was wrong with her?

He sighed. "Five minutes ago I had a gun at my back. Right now I'm considering myself lucky to be rid of that."

"Now there's a thought. What about the gun?"

"You mean *shoot* the box open?"

"Hell, you're gonna rip it open anyway. Why not shoot the bolts off?"

Farnes sighed, brought his eyes around to her, blinked as the stinging sweat dripped off his forehead. "Because," he whispered, "the control panels on most security systems are wired to fail in the lock position. If the controls suffer any trauma, such as violent shock, they lock us in, forever, or at least until someone responds."

"So I guess you'd rather use those Allen wrench things?"

Farnes had already turned back to his task and was already inserting the thin leading edge of the scissors beneath the bezel of the plate when Lorraine asked her question. Impatient and a little angry, he said, "That would be just great if you could get some for us."

Behind him came the sound of jingling keys. Lorraine's voice said, "Now lookie what I got here."

Farnes closed his eyes, dropped his shoulders. He was too tired for games, and they still had a long way to go. He turned around and was raising a finger to lecture her when he saw it.

Dangling from the key chain was a small case, twice as long as wide, a few inches on the longest side. Inside the snapped case was a set of Allen wrenches.

"Why didn't you say so?" he asked.

"Why didn't you ask?"

"I didn't know."

"How can you know if you don't ask? You think you know that much, Dr. Farnes?"

"It just . . ."

Lorraine filled in, ". . . never occurred to Mr. Macho that a sweet little thing like Lorraine would have a handy set of Allen wrenches. Well, let me tell you something. You know what you get for Christmas when your daddy's in construction? Tools. Cute little ladylike tools, so you don't have to ever hitch a ride or depend on the kind of asshole construction lechers that good old daddy works with every day. So how about that? You wanta see my handbag, Farnes? I got more ratchets and levers and blades and spring-loaded extractors and wrenches than you'd ever believe."

"Why didn't you say?"

"Two choices, professor. One, I like watchin' dumb men fret. Two, I know it's damn near impossible to get a stubborn man to ask for help when he's goin' down in quicksand. Now whadda you think, Farnes?"

Farnes stepped back. Once again he was afraid Lorraine was going to hyperventilate, not from fear but anger. "You want to do this?"

"Watch me," she snapped.

As he moved aside, she brushed past and whirled off the bolts in clean, continuous spins, grabbing the wrench shafts just before the bolts popped and fell, moving on, bottom to top, keeping the plate in place with the pressure from her free hand. When the last bolt released, she pocketed the wrench and used both hands to lower the cover plate away.

Inside, a bewildering array of microchips was bread-boarded through four input wires, all snaked through conduits toward the door.

Lorraine shook her head. "I expected, you know, keys or switches or somethin'."

Farnes stepped in. "It is keys and switches, in a way."

"You understand this stuff?"

"Enough to get by."

"How's it work?"

"Two ways," Farnes said. "By a coded signal from shore directly through the antenna into an actuator that sends current to the solenoid and opens the door. Or by internal commands, like a timed signal or this computer, that open the external door in case of emergencies."

"You think this is an emergency, Farnes?"

"We've got to convince the system that it is. You want to hand me those two wires from the packet?" Lorraine stepped back and retrieved the wires Farnes had stripped from Spatz's Norelco razor.

"I don't suppose you have a penknife and flatblade screwdriver?"

"You're gettin' smarter, Farnes." She handed him a Swiss Army knife. Farnes quickly stripped the end of the wires.

"What are you doin'?"

"Basically, a sloppy job of short-circuiting the system. Get ready for an alarm. You can get through most of these systems real quickly if you don't lose your hearing."

"All alarms signal the mainland," Lorraine said.

"If they don't know already, they should."

Farnes hooked up the two terminals on the bypass, taking the control switch out of the circuit, passing the mainline electricity directly through the step-down transformer and DC converter to the actuator. When the current surged into the solenoid within the door itself, the bolts would fire back, freeing them. At least that was the way it was supposed to work.

Before he tightened the last terminal screw in the bypass, he turned to Lorraine and said, "This ought to work, unless the system responds to a through-space signal generator external to the door. In which case, it locks up on us." He closed his eyes and thought. "But if they built it that way, why pin your control and power units next to your door? It doesn't makes sense."

"Farnes," Lorraine said, "you're making me crazy again, talking to yourself. Just tell me what's the bottom line if this doesn't work. And don't tell me we're stuck!"

Farnes found her eyes and held them, savoring, for the briefest flicker, something wonderful. Then he told her, "No. We're not stuck. If it doesn't open it just means we're back to cave man solutions."

"Meaning what?"

"Meaning I find a way to reach those clerestory windows." Farnes pointed to the narrow line of windows twenty feet above the lobby floor. "We shoot one out, bash one out, or pry one out, and then I pull you up and through."

"Through *there*?" she squeaked.

"That's it."

"Goddamnit, Farnes. This better work. 'Cause if it don't, you're gonna owe me a brand new pair of pantyhose."

Farnes smiled. "That's okay. I think there'll be a surplus." With a quick snap, Farnes tightened the last terminal screw. Instantly the lobby exploded with the throbbing wail of the alarm claxon. Lorraine pressed her hands over her ears, clenched her teeth. But the door remained shut.

Farnes went to it, put one hand against the seam, keeping the other over an ear.

The claxon howled.

Lorraine's lips shaped out "You asshole" at Farnes. He shrugged, pressed his fingers lightly. An instant later what he felt relieved him. The bolts were rolling back. The system, evidently, had built in a capacitance time delay to allow guards to respond before the door itself actually opened. If the microbe hadn't killed everyone, by now the lobby would be swarming with armed guards.

Instead, as the doors parted, there was only the painful *woop, woop, woop* of the claxon pushing them onto the covered wharf. Without delay they moved out, their hands welded to their ears.

They walked to the end of the wharf, forty feet down,

leaned out, and stared into the Atlantic. The late summer sun still cast twilight off high clouds to the west. Already the dark shore twinkled with house lights. Lorraine was the first to say, "The launch left."

"Or never came."

"So what do we do?"

"Swim?" he said. The only option? He didn't know. Until now he had been taking one barrier at a time. Until now he didn't consider any grand strategy because he had no confidence he would actually beat the next challenge. Now that he had beaten them all, he stared out, remembering what Dr. Gray had said about the current. But it was Lorraine who told him, "Farnes, there really are sharks out there. That's no bullshit."

"Worst time, too," he said, almost inaudibly.

"What's that?"

"Worst time for sharks is dusk. They're dusk feeders. Daylight, too. Usually not at night. Not very active at night, unless they're frenzied. If we wait . . ."

"Are you crazy?"

"What?"

"Jump in here and you turn up all puffy and blue in Newfoundland, if that. More likely you end up way out in the ocean. Maybe you're going to try, Farnes," she yelled over the wailing siren, "but I'm going to sit right here and wait for help."

"Could be a long wait."

"Could be a long swim, Mark Spitz."

"Give me another option!" he yelled.

She kept her hands pressed to her ears as she shook her head, mouthed the words, "I don't know."

Farnes didn't hear the outboard at first, saw only Lorraine's face turn as the dull running lights came into view at the end of the tunnel. Once inside the concrete canopy, the motors throbbed and putted as the vessel approached.

Lorraine yelled, "Hey, y'all!" and thrashed one hand back and forth over her head.

The vessel came nearer, its inflated gunnels now ignited by the garish yellow sodium vapor lamps lining the tunnel. As it glided toward the dock, its engines throttled down to idle, the bearded skipper came into view, his face drawn with tension. "What the *hell's* going on around here?" he yelled.

"You don't know?" Farnes said, gathering in a mooring line the man threw.

"All I know is that I'm going to be out here as long as the weather holds. Around five the press boat takes off like a bat out of hell. I mean, not just packing it in for the day, but full throttle. Then the Coast Guard cigarette boat takes off, too. Then about an hour ago a Coast Guard chopper bears down on me, all spotlights and speakers, you know, saying, 'All vessels clear the area.' So I bug out about ten miles seaward and work my way back, figuring to wait for the launch and find out from the departing shift what's up. But the launch never shows. Now you two—"

"Listen carefully. I'm Larry Farnes."

The man's eyes came up quickly. "By God! You *are* Larry Farnes! So the commutation came through!"

"What commutation?"

"Amnesty International filed a suit in Federal District Court for commutation of your sentence based on an obscure codicil in the Geneva Accords, and so they've let you go!"

Farnes cut him off. "Everyone's dead."

"What?"

"Except for us, everyone inside is dead."

"Jesus, what happened?"

"Biological warfare."

"Accidental release?"

"Soviet attack."

"What?" The man's face blanched, his jaw dropped.

Farnes nodded. "Can we get a ride to shore?"

The skipper of the Zodiac, still bearing the banner demanding Larry Farnes' release, stammered, "We . . . we . . . we . . . well, yeah, yeah. Jesus. But we're just a couple minutes ahead of a wicked squall line to the south. We'd better move if we want to beat the storm."

Beyond the arcing mouth of the canopy, the sky lit up with the first varicose jag of lightning as Farnes helped Lorraine into the Zodiac.

# ESCAPE

When the skipper reached up to ease Lorraine into the Zodiac, Farnes yanked her back and yelled, "Don't touch her! Don't touch either one of us! We might have dust bearing the germs. Just move to the bow and I'll drive. Let's keep your face in the wind and the spray will clean us up."

The man swallowed hard, blinked, and edged to the bow. When the skipper was seated, Farnes lowered Lorraine in and followed, sitting on the metered fuel can, taking up the helm. The Johnson outboard was still idling, spitting puffs of gray exhaust, straining the mooring lines. Quickly Farnes uncleated the line and eased the boat away from the dock, through the yawning portal, into the dusky pinkcaps of the Gulf Stream. Squinting at the glimmering waves, he took his bearings and nosed the rubber boat toward St. Andrew's Sound five miles west.

As soon as they cleared the tunnel, Farnes wasted no time in throttling up the engine and heading for the Georgia shore. He didn't know if the Coast Guard was still patrolling the area, but he was sure they would take a dim view of escaping prisoners. So he pushed hard, flicking his glance around for signs of trouble. Due south, the twilight sky curdled with towering clouds, sparking white lightning from black bellies. Ahead of the squall line, a stiff breeze was running northwest, slapping the blue-gray water into frothy combers. As the wind rose, the waves began to hiss with the first faint traces of rain. Tear-sized droplets hit Farnes' face.

In the bow, the skipper turned around and yelled, "Ten minutes, no more. Then it's going to piss all over us. Could get gusts of fifty, maybe sixty. You read me?"

Farnes nodded, kept a steady bearing. Astern, towering clouds growled.

Think.

A wave lifts a pneumatic pontoon, a strong gust catches the hull, and over it goes. Then they might as well be swimming. Or waiting for the sharks. He throttled the engine up, pushing harder.

The flexible bow lifted and slapped, lifted and crashed, struggling against the sea and wind. Below the hull, combers were building and breaking, transforming from marching lines of neatly ordered ripples to riotous crests and troughs, three feet and growing.

"Where to?" Farnes yelled.

The skipper held up a cupped hand to his ear as the lightning flashed.

"WHERE TO?" Farnes yelled.

"MAKE FOR THE BREAK TO THE RIGHT. INTO ST. ANDREW'S SOUND! LET'S GET OUT OF THE GULF STREAM!"

Farnes nodded.

Her knuckles bloodless, Lorraine hunched down between the gunnels, clutching at the line that traced one, holding on. Even ducked down, the wind raked and whipped her hair. The waves exploding over the low pontoon plastered the thin dress to her body.

Not a hundred feet starboard a bolt of lightning pierced the water with a ferocious hiss. Farnes' lips were shaping the words, "Get down" when the shock front of expanding air blasted the Zodiac, skipping it ten feet across the churning sea.

Farnes shot a look down. Lorraine was huddled safely, a heartbeat away from a "JESUS!" Near the bow, Farnes saw nothing.

Where was the skipper?

He looked again and saw the hand grappled to the rope that circumscribed the rubber boat. A second later a gasping mouth broke and then an arm threw itself up.

"I'm coming," shouted Lorraine.

"Don't touch him!" Farnes told her.

"He'll drown!"

The skipper tried to heave himself up, appeared to be moving safely into the boat when another wave crested over the Zodiac and washed him overboard again. All around them, rain flattened with fierce wind into horizontal sheets.

"He's not going to make it, Farnes!"

"Then get him!"

Lorraine threw herself forward, her lanky legs thrown up as

the boat pitched. Forcing herself low, wedging herself on the yielding pods, she lashed her left hand forward and caught the skipper's wrist. Tangling her feet in the anchor line beneath her, she brought her free hand up to join the first and hung on.

Farnes maneuvered the boat into the wind, not just to stabilize the Zodiac against capsizing, but hoping a strong gust would push the man in.

A second later another hand joined Lorraine's grip on the man's wrist as he pulled with her, once, twice. He was balanced on the bow when a wave slid across from port, striking broadside. The skipper held on. When the wave cleared and drained, he had made it back aboard. Prostrate, still gasping, his eyes cried out to Farnes louder than his voice. "Let's go! Go, go, GO, man!"

Farnes could not hear. Only part of the sounds reached him. But it was clear what the skipper was indicating with his jerking hand. Beyond the straights to port lay the calmer waters of St. Andrew's Sound. This side was the Atlantic, with no landfall till the Azores.

"HOLD ON!" Farnes screamed.

Lorraine and the skipper nodded, tucked down flat, mooring themselves in the anchor line. As Farnes brought the boat about, he saw the skipper valiantly bailing with his free hand, clearing bucket after bucket of wash into the gale.

Beneath them the Zodiac buckled and straightened, the force of the storm twisting it like rubber band. But the outboard kept pushing as the pontoons channeled through the troughs, lifted and crashed as they passed over the crests and dropped like stones, smacking and lurching.

Above them the deep pink sky grayed and curdled into towering black monsters that growled and shook the air. Just behind them came the giant silent sparks and, seconds later, on the wind, the sweet smell of ozone. And beneath them the sea was running, pushing them along at twelve knots, dragging them irresistibly away from the mouth of St. Andrew's Sound.

We're going to miss it, he thought.

Damn!

No neat solutions here. No storybook endings. Forget wishful thinking. Just make land. Head due east. Settle for where the current drops you, but make land. Make land before the darkness blinds you, before the rain washes away any traces of shore lights, before the engine floods or stalls, or the fuel runs out. Before the storm, and the sea, swallow you alive.

Farnes could figure a thousand disaster clocks all ticking off the last minutes of his life, all running full tilt. He couldn't slow them down. All he could do was to aim the bow east, power the boat into the waves, hang on, and ride out the slapping that was beginning to deflate the Zodiac, softening its form, hammering it into useless flotsam. Whether or not it would work, he could do the most sensible thing.

Below him, her hands clutched together, Lorraine was almost inaudibly praying, "Our Father, who art in heaven . . . deliver us from evil . . . forgive those . . ."

The rain fell thickly in the failing light, casting a lined gray curtain ahead. Minutes ago Farnes was dead sure of his heading. On the shore ahead, perhaps only a quarter of a mile off, he saw lights. Now, suddenly, nothing, even a hundred feet beyond his bow. Now he was unsure that the wind had not buffeted them a hundred and eighty degrees off course. Now he could not say, with any confidence, that if he gunned the outboard motor he would not be heading straight into the Atlantic.

Inside he felt hollow, lost, almost defeated.

Almost, but not quite.

Think.

Beside him Lorraine whispered, ". . . and forgive us our trespasses, as we forgive . . ."

The skipper, one hand still heroically bailing.

Then, as if time had frozen, just stopped for his sake, Farnes realized something. Subtle but powerful. The sea, he saw and felt, was not just running but undulating behind them. Behind. When does the sea run behind? In a current, sure. That. But if that, then they were well out, far offshore. But they weren't. Just a minute ago they were a quarter of a mile from lights. Just a few heartbeats ago, they were that close to the beach.

Above him the thunder cracked.

Around them blinding sheets of rain lashed.

The skipper's bailing hand had slowed, moved up and down slowly, more a gesture of surrender than hope.

Soon.

One way or another, soon.

Farnes kept his hand on the tiller, seeking a sense of direction.

Think.

That's what his mind told him. But beyond his mind, or above it, out of somewhere he couldn't have guessed or known, a voice inside him said, with an almost paternal deliberation and calm, "Feel." It was just there, out of nowhere, subliminally subcognitive. He listened, repeated it aloud, whispered, "Feel?"

Beneath him the motion of the waves was still rhythmic, undulating. What did it mean? Periodic troughs. Rising and falling and running.

Below him, soaked and terrified, Lorraine raised her head and sought Farnes' eyes. She blinked once, spat out a mouthful of salt water, and said, quite calmly, "We gonna die out here, ain't we?"

Farnes didn't think his way to the answer. He simply felt it and believed. "No," he told her. "We're not."

But beside him the fuel gauge showed fumes. Almost no gasoline left in the tank. He seemed not to care. With insane confidence he throttled up and gunned the limping Zodiac ahead.

A long minute drained away before he actually figured out why, to know the reason for the impulse. The sea only runs and undulates one place, when waves are cresting regularly. Which they only do when they feel bottom. And they only feel bottom near shore.

The Zodiac was running, shuddering, bulling water aside when the engine sputtered, coughed, and died. Out of fuel.

Finis.

All around them, in every direction, Farnes could still see nothing but unremitting sheets of rain, now closer than before. Fifty feet of visibility, maybe less. But beyond that, nothing but endless gray. Still, if what he felt—and thought—was right, the beach was close.

It had to be!

With the engine dead, the Zodiac became another piece of shapeless flotsam swept along by the storm. Without power, it was going out to sea. Nothing could stop it except . . .

"DROP THE ANCHOR!" Farnes screamed.

The skipper stopped bailing, raised a soggy head, his glasses speckled with rain, and shouted, "WHAT?"

"DROP ANCHOR!" Farnes shouted back.

They both went for it, a thirty-pound aluminum model with retractable cleats. A heave and a grunt later, over it went. The wind and thunder and driven rain devoured the splash. From a loose coil on the watery deck, the line played out and suddenly stopped.

"Nine or ten feet deep here," the skipper yelled. "That's it."

"Let's wait out the storm and wade ashore," Farnes shouted back.

The skipper shook his head, no.

"Why not?" Farnes screamed.

"It's slipping on the bottom. It's not catching in the sand. Here, you can feel it on the line."

Farnes grabbed the line and felt the movement of the anchor transmitted along it like a plucked guitar string. "You're right. What are the options?"

"Options?" Lorraine screamed. "Goddamnit, Farnes! You promised me we weren't gonna die out here!"

Maybe I was wrong he thought, turning his eyes, and mind, back to the skipper.

A stray wave broke over the Zodiac, drenching them all again and quenching Lorraine's anger. Shaking off the sea, the skipper looked like a wet rat as he gasped, "Drift with the storm and hope somebody picks us up . . ."

"Or we can *swim* to shore," Farnes countered.

The skipper nodded, then qualified, "Unless we're on a sand bar,"

"No way," Farnes told him.

"How can you know?" the skipper asked.

"I saw the lights. There!" He pointed. "This is no sand bar."

Lorraine looked in disbelief and blinked. "This is a *hell* of a time for a dip."

"Can you swim?" the skipper asked her.

"Can Casanova screw? Of course I can swim! You point the way and look after yourselves."

Farnes brought their heads together and told them, "Swim with the waves, toward the beach. It can't be more than a hundred yards. Let's stick together." He looked around. "You ready?"

Lorraine and the skipper nodded.

"Let's go," Farnes said, shucking his shoes and socks.

"Hey, Farnes," she said. "Aren't you forgetting the sharks?"

"For sure," he said, dropping over the side. "I don't think they're stupid enough to buck this kind of a storm."

"What if you're wrong?" she shouted.

The skipper discarded his footwear, dropped over the sagging pontoon, and joined Farnes in the water.

"If we're wrong," Farnes nodded at the skipper, "since sharks are solitaries, only one of us dies. That's a fifty percent chance of dying. If you stay behind in this boat, you've got damn near a hundred percent chance of dying. If you join us, even *with* sharks, you improve everybody's chances."

Lorraine sighed, peeled off her thin dress, leaving her in brief panties and a low-cupped pink lace bra. "I'm not sure I like your math," she told Farnes as she slipped over the sagging pontoon side and joined them. "But what the hell."

Together they pushed off from the drifting Zodiac and stroked for shore.

Farnes led, his shoulders raised, stroking and breathing alternately, swimming in the direction he imagined shore to be. After what seemed a hundred yards, where he should be able to hear the storm waves crashing on the beach, he stopped, treaded water, and raised himself up, squinting ahead. Beyond the wall of rain was nothing. And, except for the loud hiss of falling rain, nothing that sounded like waves cresting and falling on a beach.

Lorraine came up behind, panting, grabbed his shoulder, gasped, "Where is it, Farnes?"

He shook his head, turned to her, said, "Where's the skipper?"

The both looked back, saw him struggle up, winded. He couldn't go much farther.

Lorraine was the first to see it. No beach. A light, maybe more than one. But the image off to the right, blurred by driving rain.

"What is it?"

Again Farnes shook his head, then put it down and began stroking that way. After five strokes he decided to sound. It was a simple test. If the anchor line told them they were in ten feet of water when they left the Zodiac, and if they swam in the right direction, toward shore, then the water had to be shallower here.

He grabbed a breath and let his feet drop straight down, releasing the breath as he sank to decrease his buoyancy. He kept his hand raised, hoping that it would remain above the surface when he touched.

Just barely, when his feet hit the bottom, the fingers were still being hammered by rain.

Less than eight feet.

Good enough. But there was something different. His feet struck something hard, a little sticky. And there were small rocks. Not sand. No sand. So what?

He surfaced and took a breath.

Lorraine screamed, "Farnes, don't do that, you shit! You promised me we weren't going to die."

Farnes turned to the skipper. "You okay?"

He nodded, gasped, "How much more?"

They were all shouting to be heard. "Not much," Farnes said. They treaded water in a close group. The current now seemed to push, push, push against them. Something vital had changed. Where he had figured the waves should actually drive them to the beach, now they were losing distance to a current.

Farnes squinted. Around them the waves had flattened, almost to ripples. And they were moving against the march of the waves, as if . . . as if what?

Snapping his eyes quickly right, he noticed the light slipping away, getting smaller. Instinctively he put his mouth in the water, sipped. "It's fresh!" he shouted. "Fresh water! No salt. We're in a *river.*"

"What do we do?" Lorraine said.

"We *don't* swim upstream," he said. "Swim to the side, for shore. Follow me."

"Farnes!" she screamed. "If we get out of this alive, I'm gonna kill you."

"Just swim," gasped the skipper.

Forming up, they followed Farnes. They swam what seemed another hundred feet, Farnes raising his head every tenth stroke to check the retreating lights. Then he decided to stop and check on the skipper.

When he looked back, he found Lorraine had kept pace but the skipper was ten yards back, his hands feebly pawing at water, his body going vertical, appearing more to float and drift than swim. Farnes would have to save him.

As he drew his knees up to make the turn and go back, they hit bottom.

"We made it," he told Lorraine.

She nodded, began to stumble, slip, crawl ashore.

Farnes dived back and stroked, grappling the skipper by his shirt collar, pulling him in. When he joined Lorraine on shore, they all collapsed, lay back, and grabbed at air.

Five minutes passed before Farnes could say, "Let's get to the light, find out where we are."

Lorraine and the skipper nodded, got up to follow. But it was Lorraine who said, "You better listen up, Farnes."

Farnes was already three steps ahead, mushing toward the light on the other side of the blackness when Lorraine caught up.

"You just want to *wait*?"

Farnes turned around, saw her anger.

"Okay," he said. "What?"

The rain was still coursing down in bullwhip torrents, the wind hammering in hard strokes that bent them over, the lightning hitting so close its spokes ignited the riverbank like a point-blank strobe.

Lorraine strained to make herself heard as the skipper struggled to catch up. "You go marching off straight to that light you're so eager to find and you're going to end up dick-deep in some marsh with a cottonmouth fanged to your nose. Now my daddy hunts these places and he taught me, if I was lost, to keep to the riverbank. It won't get us right there, but it won't get us killed neither. You get that?"

Farnes nodded.

In that moment the skipper caught up and said, "Something wrong?"

"No," Farnes said. "We're going to follow the river so we don't end up dick-deep in quicksand, as I understand it."

"She's right." He nodded.

"You okay?" Lorraine asked him.

"Fine, now. Let's go."

They pushed along, tracking the edge of the swollen river, still knowing only that they were headed inland. Turning to her, Farnes asked, "You recognize anything yet?"

"You crazy, Farnes? This is good ole Georgia wetlands, hundreds and hundreds of miles of little inlets just like this, and it all looks the same. Not to mention, in case you didn't notice, that it's only pitch dark out and the river's a little swole just now. So if you don't mind real much I'd just like to get my cute little ass on a little higher ground before I take my Rand McNally quiz."

Farnes found himself smiling. Maybe she was right. Quicksand and cottonmouths. And he thought the worst of it was over when they made land. Dreamer. The worst of it, the very worst of it—the real nightmare—had just begun.

# QUARANTINE

They held to the water's edge, mucking through the sticky clay, black except when lightning cast it orange. The pelting rain ran off hard, pouring sheets of cold water off the riverbank, making each step uncertain. The skipper fell first, going down hard.

"You all right?" Lorraine turned and asked.

He grunted and got up. "Okay. Just my pride, I . . . ouch. Well, a lot of my pride and a little of my knee."

"Maybe we should stop, rest it," she suggested.

Farnes shook his head. "The light there. It's a window. Two in fact. It's just up the bank, maybe seventy yards ahead."

"Stick with the riverbank," Lorraine insisted.

"What's the point?" Farnes barked back. "The house is up there."

"Through the woods, bimbo," Lorraine said, "You ever trekked through that shit, boy?"

Farnes admitted, even to himself, that he hadn't.

"Well in the woods hereabouts you got not only water moccasin and cottonmouth, plus a fair number of coral snakes, you got some brambles that just about skin you, not to mention little things like poison ivy and mosquitoes. And, oh, yeah, some swamps and sinkholes. No thank you. Y'all go if you want but I'm goin' *that* way." She pointed with her finger.

"What can you find," Farnes asked sarcastically, *"that* way?"

"You come along, I'll show you."

The skipper said, "Sorry, Farnes. I'm going with her."

Farnes shrugged, muttered, "What the hell."

Not two hundred yards on Lorraine stopped, stood akimbo,

and pointed. Farnes squinted into the darkness, straining till he made out a black silhouette etched against the reappearing field of stars. Behind them the storm was blowing out to sea, its distant rumblings echoes of their ordeal.

The skipper still didn't see the looming form until an errant lightning bolt lit it up with a flash. Then he said, "An overpass."

"I reckon it's Route 17," she said, screwing up her face to think. "Gotta be. Up from Brunswick, but we're north of that, so it has to be Darien. Darien it is. And just to think, Farnes, you woulda traded some dinky shack for a whole city."

As suddenly as the storm had broken and drifted off, that quickly did the riverbank fill up with the summer chorus of insects. Lorraine let out a "Shit!" as she smacked her thigh. Turning back and looking at Farnes, she said, "Mosquitoes. I'm gettin' out of here."

The skipper was close enough to Farnes to whisper, "I wouldn't mind biting that myself."

They watched as Lorraine, barefoot, in drenched bra and panties, began scaling the concrete revetment beneath the overpass. Looking back she said, "Well, you two coming or not?"

"Not quite, but almost," the skipper whispered at Farnes, who smiled back.

"What?" Lorraine demanded.

"The skipper was concerned that your arrival at a small southern town in your present attire might disturb the local Baptists," Farnes said.

Lorraine shrugged. "I been used to men lookin' at me all my life, Farnes, so I don't expect much different now. The only reason they won't look at me up there is that they're dead. If they are, you can be sure they won't mind neither."

"But we can't bring the skipper along," Farnes reminded her.

"Isn't *he* immune?"

"He was out in a boat for hours. He probably never contacted anyone with this thing. As soon as he does, it's probably just like the rest."

"You mean I'm going to die, too?" The skipper's question was another kind of whisper, not of embarrassment but of fear.

Farnes told him, "Not unless you're infected."

"How can I prevent that?"

"Stay away from people, all people."

"Jesus, you mean—"

"I mean you stay away from everybody until it's run its course."

"How long?"

"A week, ten days to be safe."

"How do I eat? Where do I sleep?"

"Eat canned foods only, ones with near current expiration dates. Those were packed months ago, sometimes years. They should be safe. Drink beers, wines, hard liquor. Sterilize everything you eat from. Boil it for ten minutes, longer if you can. Wash everything if you can, especially your hands. Use harsh soaps, even dilute Drano in boiled water, then rinse in boiled water. Microwave after. Cook everything until it's charred. If you last the week, you'll survive."

"But where do I stay? If everybody has died in their beds, wouldn't . . . ?"

Farnes had an idea. "Summer in Georgia. It's hot. And people go to the beach when it's cold up north. Find yourself a good cabana, something locked up, a rental property. Break in, sleep there. Don't move."

"Anything else?"

"Find a doctor's office, take all the antibiotics you can find. Penicillin. Streptomycin. Aureomycin. Anything and everything."

The skipper looked bewildered. "I thought this thing didn't respond to—"

"Maybe not," Farnes told him, slapping a mosquito, "but a lot of corpses are piling up with no one to bury them, which means more disease layered on this. Your only protection against that is antibiotics."

He whistled. "Jesus, I didn't even start to think—"

"Not many have." Farnes gave him a sad smile. "That's why it's likely to succeed. And pick yourself up a gun if you can, maybe a Remington pump and a couple of boxes of double-ought buck."

"What for, Farnes? Everybody is dead!"

"Not everybody. What about us?"

"Then there're others, like us. We could band together and—"

"Band together and this sickness will kill you all. And if it doesn't," Farnes sighed, "the ones left are going to be scared and suspicious and distrustful and greedy. They'll be looking after number one with a vengeance that has nothing to do with wives, children, or lovers. They're going to kill for what you have that they don't.''

Lorraine had backpedaled down the revetment and overheard. "I don't believe this shit, Farnes. People hereabouts wouldn't do nothing like that! I know—"

Farnes interrupted abruptly. "What you know is a bunch of people who used to have everything they wanted. Food, water, electricity, medical attention, protection by law, the convenience of a car, credit cards, television, booze, drugs, anything. Now they've got nothing but terror. You just watch them.''

"Anything else?" The skipper's voice croaked.

"Watch for dogs.''

"Dogs?"

"They'll start running in packs, eating the corpses.''

"Jesus!"

"Don't go far from cover. Don't kid yourself. They'll attack in packs and you won't have a chance.''

"*They* won't get sick?"

Farnes shrugged. "Maybe. But the most virulent bugs are species specific. Usually if it kills quick and fast, its range is narrow. That's a pretty good rule.''

"Anything else?" The question was barely audible.

"Just good luck.''

"Luck?"

"Some of it is always luck," Farnes told him, shaking his hand. "Like your being out on that boat when the epidemic hit. You were just lucky.''

"I don't feel very lucky, to be honest.''

"Life is good," Farnes said. "It's all you can be sure of.''

The skipper managed to raise a faint smile, barely visible in the reflected cast of the hooded bridge lights. "I'll remember that.''

"Good luck," Farnes repeated, taking Lorraine by her arm and drifting up the revetment toward Route 17.

"A week," the skipper's shadow echoed, "or ten days.''

Farnes said, "That should do it.''

"And what then?"

"Invasion.''

"Invasion?"

"The Cubans and Russians, probably in that order.''

"Why?"

"Because it beats the chance of getting blown away by an arsenal of nuclear weapons," Farnes said. "This was a prophylactic attack."

"Should I fight?"

"Why?"

"On principle."

"That's up to you."

"Are you going to fight?"

"I hadn't thought about it."

"Why not?"

"I'm too busy worrying about surviving the next ten days."

Farnes led Lorraine up the steep concrete incline beneath the bridge, turning near the top to signal silence. Looking back he could no longer see the skipper and felt strange that he never knew him by name. Steadily his bare feet measured the last few yards. When they reached the concrete rail near the bridgehead, he told Lorraine, "Stay down, out of sight."

"Why?" she whispered back.

"If anyone's alive out there, they're not exactly looking for company. And the boys at the local knife and gun club have their own idea of a reception committee," he said, raising his head just enough to view the town of Darien.

"Farnes, you got an attitude problem. Why don't you give folks a chance?"

"Because giving them a chance means taking a risk of my own and I just can't afford it. Neither can you," he told her.

"You let me worry about that."

"I would, except you don't seem to be."

"I say we just walk in, see what's happening. Maybe we can help."

Farnes shook his head, kept his voice down. "Look at yourself. You go strolling into a cracker . . ."

"Hey!"

". . . into a cracker Georgia town after social order has collapsed looking like a fold-out from Frederick's of Hollywood and people aren't going to want to help. They're going to help themselves—to you."

"You've got a real shitty attitude, Farnes, I swear."

"You keep your eyes open the next few days and tell me how shitty it is compared to what you see."

"What makes you think I want to stick with you?"

Farnes shrugged.

"Maybe you've got your own ideas of what you want with this Frederick's of Hollywood bod, bud."

"You think what you like. I'm not going to sit here and feed mosquitoes all night."

"I'm going in," she said.

"Just think, will you? Just take a quick look, tell me what you see."

Lorraine brought her eyes up, let them drift down Route 17 and play over Darien, said, "Looks calm."

"Looks dead," Farnes corrected. "If you look carefully you can see at least four bodies. One slumped by the pumps at the Texaco station. Another one under a shopping cart outside the Win Dixie. One pressed against the window inside the Chevy dealership. Another keeled over on the sidewalk, feet pointing this way, just before the second intersection. Four dead, no pickups. God knows how many inside."

"Look, Farnes. All the lights came on. Somebody's workin' 'em."

Farnes shook his head, no. "Streetlights, even a lot of commercial lights, are ignited by photocells when it gets dark. It's done automatically. All they need is electricity."

"Well, there you go, Farnes." She let her voice rise in disgust. " 'Lectricity don't grow on trees, am I right? Somebody's gotta run the damn power stations, don't ya think?"

Farnes shook his head again. "Duke Power and Florida Power and Light feed this grid. Both have nukes. A nuke with automated controls and artificial intelligence programs can deliver continuous power for a year before it needs refueling. So even the power plants can run themselves."

"Sweet Jesus," Lorraine whispered. "You mean all this—"

"Not with a bang, but with a whimper."

"Farnes?"

His mind came back. "A line from a poem."

"You picked a great time for poetry, but it won't fill my stomach. I'm hungry as a hog on a fat farm. And if you don't give me another idea, I'm gonna march straight up 17 and get some dinner."

Farnes shook his head.

"Hell I won't!"

"Hell you will. You're one of maybe five percent of folks

immune from this horror and you want to commit suicide by prancing into town damn near nude. Survivors who've escaped infection will think you're crazy. Thinking you're crazy makes them think you're dangerous, so they drop you with a thirty-ought six at a hundred yards, maybe sooner.''

Lorraine's eyes burned with anger. "Farnes, I hope y'all don't turn out to be the last man in the world, 'cause I just can't imagine doin' what we'd have to do to get the world goin' again, not with *you*. But I suppose you got a point. Do you got a plan?''

Farnes again shook his head. "I have a tactic."

"A *tactic*?"

"It's a maneuver consistent with a larger—"

"Farnes, this ain't helpin' my appetite."

"Follow me."

"You sound just like my big brother at Fort Benning. Follow me, follow me, follow me."

Farnes knew it was wrong to bring Lorraine's world-view up to date, to put her face-to-face with the reality that the life she knew had been snapped away, that her brother at Fort Benning and her contractor father and mother were probably all dead, now and forever. Instead he slapped away another mosquito and pointed to their left. "See that berm?"

"Berm?"

"Raised mound of earth . . ."

"The sort-of ridge?"

"That's it."

"Yeah." Lorraine smacked a mosquito.

"We get behind it, stay out of the light. It runs around to the back of town. We follow it."

"Farnes, if everyone's dead, and we ain't seen no one, baby—no traffic, no people, not even a goddamn dog—then who're we hidin' from?"

"The ones who leashed up the dogs."

They inched toward the berm, duckwalking and crawling, staying low in the shadows of crabgrass and kudzu. Hands and knees, close enough to whisper, Lorraine said, "You mean there *is* somebody in there and they *are* workin' together?"

Farnes nodded.

"Great!"

"Stay low," Farnes said, pointing the way. "Let's move."

They broke from the cover of the bridge and made a quick,

low scrabble. Ten seconds later, they fell panting against the shadowy back of the berm. Farnes turned to her. "Don't expect the reception to be all that great. If they have any sense to add to their fear, they've probably set up a quarantine. If they're determined to ride this thing out, to stay free of infection, they're going to shoot anyone who tries to enter town."

"You know a word for that kinda thinking, Farnes?" Lorraine skewered him with a stare, "Paranoid. You need serious help, boy. I don't know why—"

"Look." Farnes pointed.

"What?"

"You see it?"

" 'It' what?"

"The flatbed pickup over there, tipped over. The old Ford. We couldn't see it before we moved." Farnes kept pointing until Lorraine said, "Okay. Yeah, the one with its headlights on?"

"They've been on a while, running the battery down."

"They are kinda dim, yeah. So what?"

"Look at the windshield."

Lorraine lifted her head, squinted. "What?"

"I want you to see it yourself. I'm not going to tell you. Try to find an angle where you can see the glare of the streetlights on the windshield."

"Jesus!" she gasped, ducking into the curl of Farnes' body. It was, he suspected, an instinctive move, seeking refuge. He assigned nothing more to it. Still he found himself stirred by her touch.

"You saw?"

She nodded, panting with fear, her light eyes wide with terror. "It was a spiderweb crack, right over the driver's side."

"Bullet hole."

"Jesusfuckingchrist," she gasped.

"Welcome to Darien."

"Let's go all the way around, Farnes. Let's just skip Darien, right?"

Farnes shook his head.

"Are you *crazy*?"

"No," he told her, sighing. "I'm hungry and I'm wet. And I don't have much more on than you do. You're almost naked. And Darien isn't going to be any different than the next town, each one a little fortress of terror. You said it, Lorraine. They've got the food and the clothes. We don't.''

She sank down next to him. ''Why did this have to happen, Farnes?''

''It didn't. That's the worst thing of all.''

She looked up at him. ''So we go in?''

''Let's work around. Then I'll scout it out. You can wait—''

''Don't go macho on me now, Farnes. So far you're not too big a pain in the ass, but this ingenue shit—''

Farnes shrugged. ''Okay.''

In fifteen minutes they had worked their way around behind a service alley backing on what looked like a bar or liquor store. There was no store sign out back, only a delivery dock crowded with cases of Johnny Walker, Old Grandad, Southern Comfort, Budweiser, Miller, Strohs. As they got up, cautiously, and slinked forward, a stray cat leapt into the the the alley, making Lorraine shriek.

''So much for surprise,'' Farnes said.

''Well . . .''

He signaled with his hand to move ahead, to the right behind the rear door, a steel-cased model on heavy hinges that reminded him too much of Prison Perfect.

It was served by a single curved handle, no latch tab. Farnes was thinking fast now, wondering who—if anyone— would respond. Through the wooden wall where he leaned his head he heard voices, put his hands to his lips for Lorraine, behind him, to keep silent.

A minute passed, then two.

If they were going to come, they would have . . . or would they? Why wouldn't they just wait for the door to open, then cut them down as they passed through?

Possible.

Only one way to find out.

He looked down at the door, wondering how he would beat it. Or if he should simply find another way in, even another store. He didn't want to invest too much time or effort. All he wanted was a way into town where they weren't seen. Or heard. Maybe they had already lost that. All they really needed now was to get food, a change of clothes, maybe guns and a vehicle, and get the hell out. Inside was booze, nothing they needed.

And the voices, still humming throught the low walls.

Steady conversation, some urgency.

Company, the kind they didn't, or at least he didn't, need.

Intelligence.

And economy.

If they could get in here, they could learn something, waste less time. But what of the danger? What of it? Was it lowered by going somewhere else? Or were there more of them, more guns, more danger elsewhere? Not having a good answer, he decided that the bar, or liquor store, couldn't hold that many people. There was nothing of survival value to them either.

He reached down and tried the handle.

It pulled back.

He gave it a sharp jerk.

It squealed as the metal casing tore against the oak frame.

He slid in front of the door, knowing no standard rifle round would pierce it, and pulled it open with a grunt, following the swinging door away from the opening, standing clear opposite Lorraine, locking eyes with her.

From his protected position, he could see only a thin wedge of space taken by small square tables, their red-and-white-checkered tablecloths pinned down by thick chrome-orange glass ashtrays, next to a lit-up Wurlitzer jukebox.

Bar, he decided.

Crouching, he moved his head low, grabbed a quick glimpse, fell back.

No fire, no shots, no bullets.

His mind recorded more detail in the snapshot his eyes took. A neon sign over the heavy wood bar: McGinty's. Line of freestanding barstools, maybe ten. More tables. Man slumped over one, not drunk.

But it wasn't the sights that hit Farnes, it was the stench. The open door disgorged the rot of decaying bodies. Across from him it sent Lorraine reeling away, buckled her on her bare knees as she puked.

She was just stopping, her noises changing from gagging to sobbing, when the other sounds crowded in. The buzz. At first he thought it was the neon lights or the overhead fluorescents buzzing. And it might have been, at some level. But as he stood up and filled the door, he saw them swirling and pinned down what he heard.

Flies. Big, loud, buzzing. Not many. Dozens, not hundreds. Give them a few days on decomposing corpses. Then there'd be millions.

Lorraine's voice was weak behind him. "Farnes, wait."

"You don't want to see this."

She stood behind him. "That's what Daddy always said 'bout porno movies. Anyway, I don't see how I'm goin' to keep from seein' it sometime, do you?"

"Suit yourself," he said, turning back to watch her slink into the bar, one slender hand braced on the doorjamb, a glorious naked leg poking from the dark, the slender sexy body, panties and bra only, following. Still too alive amidst all the death to let that pass, he said, "If there were any men alive in here, they'd all be standing up by now, you can bet on that."

Lorraine looked shaken. Still she came back with, "I guess that makes you a real gentleman, Farnes, since you always stood up for me." Her eyes caught his. He imagined there might be something from the way she said, "Didn't you?"

Turning without response, he scanned the scene, saw the lights flashing off the walls of the alcove just beyond them to the left, and guessed about the voices he was hearing.

"TV," he said.

"You want to watch *TV*? Are you *crazy*?"

"No, no, no. The voices in there. It's just TV."

Lorraine shouldered by him. "Well TV means somebody's alive, now don't it? Somebody's broadcastin'!"

He followed her svelte body as it swiveled into the alcove, where another body had collapsed against the tucked green vinyl upholstery of a cramped inglenook. He saw her freeze, stiffen.

"What is it?"

"Looks a hell of a lot like Jimmy Horton."

Farnes pushed through, moved around, and saw a fly appear from the corpse's nose, buzz crazily at them. He waved it off, stepped forward, closed the eyelids. "We were never properly introduced." Farnes turned back, caught her face. More of her color gone, verging on shock. He finished, "Jimmy and I."

"Well," she whispered. "Ole Jimmy was All County at Jeb Stuart. Tailback. Nine years back. I s'pose it don't matter to anybody that he was the first boy inside my bra."

"Not to me," Farnes said. "Sure as hell not to him."

"He had good hands."

"No doubt," Farnes said. "All County."

Her eyes had gone back in time, thinking. She bit her trembling lip, her voice knotted, broken as she said, "Everybody wanted Jimmy Horton. Alabama. Georgia. Hell, Yankee schools like Michigan, Penn State, even Notre Dame. Why Notre Dame, I always used to wonder then. Jimmy had no God but football. Problem was, Jimmy was dumber than driftwood, Farnes. And like driftwood, he just got pushed along by the tide. Crimson Tide pushed him through freshman year, but by sophomore he found the bottle. Always thought he'd die in a bar. Guess it makes sense, in a way."

Farnes moved over, took her by the shoulder. "Let's go," he said.

The fly returned, perched on Jimmy Horton's purpled lip, rubbed its front legs together, cleaned its wings.

When Farnes' eyes returned to Lorraine, her glance had lifted, her face become cast in the harsh slapping glow of a television raised on a high bracket, where all the patrons could see it.

"There, you see," she said, almost inaudibly. "Everything's goin' to be okay, Farnes."

Her hand came up, a limp finger pointing at the screen. A headshot of an announcer, his own voice trembling, filled it up. Reading from copy on his desk, he said, "For those of you who haven't already discovered it, and we believe there are few, the country has been seized and is now paralyzed by a terrible sickness. No one seems to know where it comes from, but some California experts believe it came in by jetliner from the Far East, the starting point for most flu epidemics. Still we have no reports from Japan or the Phillipines, or Hong Kong, of any such sickness." The man, his hair parted in a razor split, his face agleam with sweat, coughed several times and struggled on, swallowing painfully and dredging up a hoarse voice that tumbled thickly on. "And while . . ." More coughing, stop, then, ". . . it is too early to speculate, the Centers for Disease Control in Atlanta calls it a major, unexpected, and devastating epidemic. Early losses of life are in the tens of thousands in Georgia alone. Hospitals in Atlanta, and statewide, were caught completely unprepared to cope with the influx of patients. Scattered reports of violence, and looting of doctor's offices, continue to roll in.

"We . . ." Another spasm of coughing, ". . . at CNN want to emphasize what we have been told by CDC, that common antibiotics are not effective against this plague. Your best chance is to avoid contact with infected people or carriers, eat only canned foods and boiled water, and wait for organized civil relief.

"A special dispatch from the American ambassador in Moscow said that Soviet men and material arriving from Cuba will be put ashore in Florida as soon . . ." A cough interrupted the speech, buckled him over. When he came back up, red-faced and panting, he continued in a hoarse voice, ". . . as soon as Hurricane Clyde subsides. These soldiers bring food, material, medicine. Godspeed to them."

The man folded his hands, let his eyes hold the camera as he said, "We have sickness here in the studio. Some of our staff never made it to work this morning. Calls to their homes go unanswered. We cannot say how much longer we will be able to maintain our reporting. But as long as we have power here we will broadcast an automatic replay of our message, updated to reflect . . ." More coughing, now blood dripping from the newscaster's mouth, ". . . additional information. God bless you and be with you. Doug Lawless, CNN News, Atlanta."

The screen broke up with snow, hissing, then recovered, cuing up the same man, the same tape, over again. "For those who haven't already discovered it . . ."

Farnes stepped over, reached up, snapped off the set. "Let's go."

"Where to? Everybody's dead."

"Not everybody. Not us. And I'm still hungry."

"How can you be hungry at a time like this?"

Farnes cut her off. "Because I'm alive. And living people need food."

Lorraine had a shallow laugh for him. "Living people, Farnes, need hope."

He turned and grabbed her with his eyes. "Maybe we're responsible for making our own when the supply runs short."

"Maybe," she sighed. "But I just can't feel it. Not right now."

Before Lorraine finished saying the word "now," the front window exploded, followed by the report of the bullet that burst through. Farnes tackled and dropped her to the hardwood floor as a rain of glass shards tinkled down around them.

# THE BATTLE OF JACKSONVILLE

Igor Yustechenko sat huddled in the iron womb of his command vehicle as it rushed north through the night, buffeted by blasts of wind and rain. Satellite downlink bursts reported winds exceeding one hundred and twenty kilometers per hour. Hindered by unexpected floods and downed power lines, they had averaged only forty kilometers an hour since landing.

Even that, if known, would make their cover story look suspicious.

If the epidemic is so dreadful, why would the Soviets rush into it so carelessly? Just one answer would make sense. Only an assault force presses on through the night, against the weather. But how could the Americans even know? Rostenkov and Saranov guessed right. Death was everywhere. And through the clouds and darkness American reconnaissance satellites could see nothing.

What advantage could he make of this disadvantage? If they were moving faster they could have disappeared as they moved north, melting in with American armored columns moving martial law from town to town. But their advance was bogged down. He struggled to rethink his tactics. Air support would not come until Clyde rained itself out. Then the wings of MiG-29 Fulcrums and Hind-D support helicopter gunships would erupt from the decks of the Soviet carriers now plowing through the heavy weather off Florida's Atlantic coast. Until then, he would have to wait and worry.

If he were religious he would pray. If he were an optimist he would hope. But since he was a realist he would have to wait, adjusting his tactics to fit the changing circumstances, keeping the objectives foremost in his thinking. Saranov had told the U.S. Ambassador in Moscow through the new Secretary General that the American President's dying wish was to send aid. Would they believe him? If so, they would accept that the easiest way to get men and material to the United States was to redeploy men and commandeer vehicles from Cuba. But what these vehicles did once they landed would determine how long the lie went undiscovered. If they stopped in every town to establish field hospitals, flying Red Cross flags, they would be believed. But if they drove north in armored columns, they would be immediately revealed.

That was why Yustechencko decided to split his forces at Tampa, to spread them out in a pattern totally unlike any Soviet battle plan ever used. Next he decided to take the separate columns *through* the towns. American military intelligence would figure that no Russian tank commander would move his tanks through towns, not after what the European resistance did to them in the Great Patriotic War. But there was another reason for his decision.

With most civilians dead and unarmed, his problems would not come from armed resistance. Against modern Soviet tank armor, civilian weapons were completely ineffective. But American interceptors like the F-16, with their Maverick air-to-ground missiles, could destroy the entire invasion force in short order, unless air support arrived in time.

Without air support and on open roads, their lethargic armor columns were sitting ducks for the armor-piercing cannons of the A-10 Warthog tank killer.

But if they passed through towns, stalled and hid between buildings, then Americans would hesitate to fire on their own civilians. He knew that he would. In a soldier's war, it is the soldiers who have chosen to fight. As many others as possible should be spared.

No, he could not reconcile that with the terrible epidemic. But that was not his choice. The politicians chose when the soldiers should fight, and often even how. He was not a politician, only a soldier.

The APC rippled slightly, jiggling the men inside. Yustechenko tapped the driver, his head embraced by infrared-sensitive goggles. The driver looked back, said in Russian, "A body, I think. I can't be sure. If so it was long dead, the same temperature as the background."

I must remember, Yustechenko thought, to tell the men not to touch the tracks. Some virus may have squirted on from the blood from the compressed corpse.

And what else?

As an officer, he got preferred medical treatment over common soldiers. Yet it bothered him that his personal "vaccination" mark never became inflamed. The shot they gave him caused little pain, no discomfort, no fever, not even a swelling where the needle went in. For so deadly a disease, how could that be? He was not a suspicious man, but it didn't seem right.

Only after Yustechenko's insistence had the Soviet High Command provided protective suits, now stashed in the APCs. They were of the British Porton Down design, bought through espionage by the GRU, modified for Soviet use. In a spasm of fear, something dark and hidden and totally unexpected, he thought of ordering them on, now. But as suddenly as the impulse had spiked, his rational mind beat it back. What is the worry? None. They had briefed him thoroughly, answered all his hard questions. You catch this sickness as with others, through contact with infected people or things, water, or food. They said to simply keep your distance, chemically disinfect and distill water, eat only invasion provisions.

How to keep your distance when the dead cover the earth?

When you run over bodies in the road?

Remember, he told himself, not to touch the tracks.

The driver awakened Yustechenko as the APC approached Jacksonville from the west, the tracks beneath them rattling steadily on the asphalt surface of Florida 278. The Field General of the Soviet North American Invasion Force felt ashamed to have slept while his men did not.

Age.

They should have picked a younger man.

No.

They wanted him.

Stretching out, he reached under his bench, withdrew a thermos of Cuban coffee. Uncapping it, he gulped down the steaming black drink. Then, moving forward, he asked the driver, "What do we see?"

"See for yourself, Comrade General, the city."

Yustechenko used the viewing port to reconnoiter. Jacksonville lay ahead, its shape dissolving and recrystalizing from the passing rain. Squinting, he struggled to recognize shapes the reconnaissance team told him would be landmarks. Those pictures showed them against clear skies.

Idiots!

Now those landmarks dissolved like impressionist images in the steady rain and light wind. If the ferocious howling that shook them last night was gone, so was their protection from American reconnaissance satellites and the fighters that would, inevitably, follow.

"Resistance?" asked the General.

His driver shuddered. "They have to live to fight. So far, many bodies. The rest, I think, are hiding."

"Drive on."

"Yes, sir."

"And stand ready to load weapons and engage the enemy. Pass the order."

Yustechenko made his command sound like a routine precautionary direction. But as it was passed back along the column, he alone knew it was time to be ready. The first active combat-trained unit was passing below them, just ten kilometers south by southwest: the United States Marine Corps detachment at the Jacksonville Naval Air Station.

As the column entered Jacksonville, skirting the right bank of the St. John River, the multiplexed downlink from Cosmos 2290 reached Yustechenko's communication center, three vehicles behind him. As quickly as messages were decoded, they were transmitted in battlefield code to the General.

Taking the paper handed him by the decoding officer, he read it quickly.

ENEMY NUCLEAR FIRING COMMAND CHAIN BROKEN.

INTERIM TACTICAL NUCLEAR STRIKES FORBIDDEN UNTIL COMMAND AUTHORITY RESTORED.

GENERAL PANIC, WIDESPREAD CIVILIAN RIOTS AND LOOTING. MARTIAL LAW EXPECTED TO DRAW LARGE PORTION OF REMAINING US GROUND FORCES.

US MEDICAL CORPS EN ROUTE TO MEET, ASSIST YOU. ADVISE PROPHYLACTIC TERMINATION. BURN AND HIDE CORPSES. MAINTAIN COVER STORY, DENY AGGRESSION UNTIL FIRST FORCED ENCOUNTER.

AIR SUPPORT DELAYED.

Not what he wanted to hear. How long?

* * *

Jacksonville's Main Street was flanked with the kinds of buildings that Yustechenko loved: variably tall, creating canyons inaccessible to helicopter gunships, difficult target areas for fighters, even if they decided to fire on their own people. Better yet, north of the city proper, Main Street became US Highway 17, leading into American Georgia. The first important target en route to joining the Soviet Army moving south from Massachusetts was designated as Target One, Invasion Force South. To hit Target One, he had to reach Atlanta. But to reach Atlanta, he had to survive Jacksonville.

War is winning survival from one moment to the next. So fight in one moment at a time, and you may get to the next.

He looked around, using the APC periscope to reconnoiter. The number of bodies stunned him. Strewn like garbage, some covered in a mist of flies, others fodder for packs of dogs that barked and snapped at the tracks of the column as it cut north along Main Street.

Yustechenko was shocked by the number of uncontrolled fires. Lightning from the storm could have done this, but no! Sitting down to absorb the blow, he realized that this was a sign of America's war against itself. The poor striking back. Like the New York blackout, but worse. Now there was, it seemed, no control.

The thought frightened and excited him. Frightened him because he knew he could expect no humanity beyond his men. And excited him because the order showed signs of breaking down, which it did only when the numbers of those in authority had become ineffectual.

What had Rostenkov said? "By the time you land, the number of active fighting men in the American defense forces will be down to fifteen percent, badly scattered and divided into three separate and uncoordinated fighting services."

Which gave him no comfort now.

And he would have none until his air support arrived.

Popping open the hatch, Yustechenko pushed himself into the moist, warm air, enjoying the cool tickle of light rain on his face. No one here. Not a person. Perhaps they are all dead, every . . .

The sound interrupted his thoughts, wrenched him around to find it. Behind him to the right, from the southwest. It grew louder by the second, the high-pitched screaming howl, fluttering occasionally and shifting, like some killer machine hovering just beyond the rooftops.

Yelling down, Yustechenko said, "Get me ten missileers. Halt the column and break out the SA-7s. If the target is enemy, take it down."

"Firing order, sir?"

Yustechenko snapped off the word like an instinct. "Yes." There it was. World War Three.

His soldiers were out in seconds, bracing their pods on the APC tracks, seeking their target.

Before the last Soviet soldier had braced in, the Marine AV-8 Harrier jump jet shifted into view. Three hundred meters in altitude, its thrust directed down so it hovered like a helicopter, but without the chopping sound.

Yustechenko locked eyes with the pilot's, exchanged a knowledge of who they were just as the first ground-to-air heat-seeking SA-7 ripped from its pod.

The Harrier never had a chance.

Hovering dead still, its pilot could not react fast enough. If the jet seemed to pitch and start to pull away, it was only a prayer.

The missile ripped into the fuselage through the hot gases of the turbine, its sudden detonation hurling a storm of flaming white metal that clattered down around the column.

Before the last chunk of wing stopped skidding on the pavement, Yustechenko screamed, "Move out! Flank speed, due north. Thirty meters separation. Rear-facing muzzles. And send for air support. Priority One!"

The radioman held up a hand, shouted back, "Incoming message. Western Armor Column under attack!"

"On the balls of Lenin!" Yustechenko shouted. "What weapons, numbers?"

"Low flying aircraft, Comrade General. Colonel Boshti reports a white mist laid down, estimates gas."

But Yustechenko knew in the instinctive way that needs no academic proof, that it was not.

Yustechenko squinted hard through his field glasses, sweeping the low horizon just above the treetops. At the same time he strained to hear the high-pitched whistle that he knew would come in behind them.

The armored column pushed ahead at its top speed, fifty-five kilometers per hours, each tank or APC separated from the others by thirty meters. That meant the Harriers would have to pick one target. The spall and debris ejected from their strikes would not damage more than one Soviet vehicle. But surely they would return, run after run, until they were all no more than smoldering heaps of iron, hot coffins with charred Soviet soldiers inside.

Idiots!

He could almost hear Rostenkov crowing, as he had at the dacha, on the endless virtues of the new FST-2 tanks. "The largest smooth-bore mobile deployed cannon in any tank in the world. One hundred and twenty-five millimeter projectiles under laser finding and target systems with rapid fire capability. Multiply laminated fused-enamel and tungsten armor effective against any Western anti-tank weapon now deployed. In exceptional circumstances, the combination of machine gun and cannon can repulse low-flying ground-support opposition . . ."

Exceptional circumstances!

Idiots!

Even above the drumroll of track plates ripping at the asphalt below him, Yustechenko tensed at the sound. Up from the south, tracing the wreckage of the downed Harrier along US Highway 17 until they would clear a stand of pines and see them all, moving at a crawl . . .

Behind his lead vehicle the tank turrets faced south, their huge guns sighted up and fanned out. One pointed forty-five degrees off axis, the next one back straight south along the road, the one behind that forty-five degrees to the opposite side. The machine gunners on the tanks and APCs all swung their barrels toward the incoming whistle, yanking back the bolts, waiting for the target to appear.

War.

It struck him like a lance in his guts, pulled back and forth. His mouth suddenly dried, his palms moistened, his heart, the heart of the Lion of Afghanistan, hammered like a frightened child. In the moment the Harrier appeared out of the southwest, its swept-back wings heavy with ground-to-air rockets, time seemed to slow, every action drifting in a surreal syrup. The pilot dipped down at six hundred kilometers per hour, fast enough to avoid fire, slow enough for a good look.

The Soviet machine gunners opened up, nesting the jump jet in tracer fire. The passing fuselage whooshed by, the pings of ricocheting rounds singing as it pulled through a hard turn and disappeared into the swirling light gray mist above them.

The next pass, thought Yustechenko.

The next pass, someone dies.

Eight thousand men.

Idiots!

The dead would have to be left behind, or they would all be buried on the same spot.

The war would go on without them.

Where were the MiGs?

The returning Marine Corps Harrier dropped out of the mist to Yustechenko's right, strafing the slow-moving column with its twin 30mm guns. The first Soviet combat victim of the Third World War dropped away from his machine gun onto American soil, falling quickly behind the moving column.

Yustechenko screamed down to his radioman, "Tell our glorious Soviet Air Force that we are under air attack. Suggest that if they can arrived in ten minutes we may not lose this war. Otherwise no promises."

"Comrade General," the radioman shouted back, "they are only minutes away now."

At that moment a second Harrier screamed out of the southwest, releasing twin rockets on a deadly parabolic track.

Seconds later the fifth FST-2 back erupted in a wall of orange flames and thick black smoke. As Soviet machine guns rattled hopelessly at the retreating Harrier, Yustechenko yelled, "Dismount for missile attach."

"Sir?"

"Pass the order. Fan and raise the cannon, three hundred sixty degrees. Fire at will."

It would cost them to stop.

He accepted that, but what could he do?

Sitting still made it almost too easy for the Harrier, but next time would be more difficult.

Each APC disgorged a team of two men. The assistant held the SA-7 ground-to-air missile launcher, fitted the missileer. Together they waited. As they must. Each team would have to track the Harrier on its pass, stand as it fired at their vehicles, wait for their moment. Only when the Harrier had passed could the heat-seeking SA-7 lock on the afterburners and chase down its prey.

But they had help.

Through the low swirling mist came the screeching howl of the Harrier. Following their ears, the machine guns and large tanks peppered the air with shrapnel. For the first time, the quick Harriers were running a deadly gauntlet.

Except the fire was undirected.

The Harrier dropped in low, beneath it, rattling off more gunfire, before pulling up and away.

At that instant twelve teams fired SA-7s.

Hissing away, they leapt into the low gray scud. Yustechenko checked his watch, counted slowly. When he reached five, the percussive wave of a huge explosion swept down over the column.

One Harrier down.

How many to go?

The next jet overhead stunned them with its speed, whooshing by fifty meters above them without firing a shot. Instead it dipped its wings back and forth and turned into the hanging mist.

Yustechenko watched it pass, its twin fins suddenly as familiar as the Red Star on its fuselage. Standing straight up, he raised a shout. "It's ours!"

A cheer rippled through the column as they re-mounted their vehicles and pressed north, leaving the sky above them to jet pilots who would dance and twist and break until a distant flash, perhaps ten thousand meters up, signaled an end.

These men were warriors, too, but not in Yustechenko's war. His war had one ultimate objective, one target that had to be destroyed, one *sine qua non*. That was in Atlanta.

But between here and Atlanta, the troops from Ft. Benning would now be shifted to defend against the Soviet advance. He was not too concerned over the 197th Infantry Brigade, feeling his elite Soviet corps would bowl them over. Rather it was the 75th Airborne Ranger Regiment that worried him. Unless they were a lot sicker than the Harrier pilots, breaking through them would require a brilliant plan, a more brilliant execution, and more than a fair measure of plain luck. How often does that happen?

# FRIENDLY FIRE

The sticky air froze in ringing silence as they huddled together on the floor, littered with shattered glass. Lorraine's eyes held him as she whispered, "You're cut, Farnes. Here, let me . . ."

Another shot tore through the window, imploding the television tube.

Although they were well hidden, the volley of rounds kept coming. The next one ripped through the back of Jimmy Horton's skull, spouting rank gore through his forehead as it exited. Lorraine screamed. Farnes shouted, "Keep low! Follow me!"

Dragging her past the shot-out window, he shouted, "Stay down!" as the next round whirred past his ear. The passing wind from the supersonic bullet brushed his hair before its impact rang from the bar.

"Why?" Lorraine sobbed, crawling after.

"Quarantine," he said. "An idea from Venice and the Black Death."

Keeping low, he checked the line of fire coming from the outside, saw nothing. Calm. He had to reach that inner pool of calm, the one he knew was always there. He had to, as his master on Okinawa said, bathe in it. When you step into the waters of the inner circle, time is left behind. It will wait for you. You reach a sanctuary of eternity. You look forward and backward in time calmly. You see, as your face in a mirror, what you must do next. And as time begins to thaw around you, you simply do it. There is no how or why. When is nonsense. It simply is. When you have reached the state once, you will know that without question.

And Farnes knew the state.

He taught it to the shotgunning guard at Prison Perfect.

Now he entered it again as he leapt the bar, landing behind it on the barkeep's bloated stomach, jetting bile from the man's dead lips. As Farnes' eyes raced along the lower shelves, where tumblers, mixers, strainers, spigots, glasses, and water-filled ice bins stared back at him, he raised his chin and watched the next incoming round float past. If he wanted, he felt he could have reached out and filliped it. So strange and yet so real.

Turning his eyes back as the bullet invaded the hardwood bar, spinning splinters out as it destroyed itself, Farnes found what he sensed would be there: a pistol-handled scattergun, pump action. Modified Holland and Holland. Beside it was a box of shells. Double-ought buck.

Bracing his back on the bar, he loaded.

Shotgun in one hand, ammo in the other, he snaked, unseen, to the end of the bar, peered around. Below the bar, tucked under a nest of red-and-white checkered tablecloths, Lorraine remained splayed out, sobbing.

He hissed, "Stay there," and sprung, spinning, dodging, zigzagging past the broken window. Two rounds blew by him before he reached the cover of the door. His mind had already pinpointed the sniper's position by tracing the trajectories of the bullets backward to their source. Second floor window across the street. Grain store.

He had seen the store and windows as he sized up the town from the berm.

Two windows.

Which one?

Didn't matter.

By now the front window of McGinty's was reduced to jagged shards in a four-by-eight frame. Wedged against the wall, he reached his gun arm out, twisted his wrist, and exposed the muzzle.

Another shot tore by.

He checked the impact on the bar, decided from the angle of penetration that the shot came from the left window. Without exposing himself, he swung the barrel out the window and tried to spray the windows across the street with buckshot. A second after his pump action Holland and Holland roared with its first volley, the incoming fire stopped. He pumped another round into the chamber and waited, counting seconds until he figured the target would rise again.

Ducking, checking quickly with a snapped glance, Farnes

found the opposing windows free and spun into position, beading on the left one.

Fifteen seconds passed before the hunting rifle's barrel flashed yellow in the sodium vapor streetlights. All instinct and reflex, Farnes didn't wait for target identification. He tore off a shot, then another.

Bingo!

The shooter crashed through the window, rifle clattering off the stubby canopied roof below. As the remaining glass and wood shattered, he watched the sniper's body fall.

A woman, maybe fifty. Gray-haired. Flabby. Print dress. Tumbling and bouncing like a huge rag doll, her right breast and shoulder torn away as she fell, the head stopping the fall on the sidewalk, the neck snapping with such force it cracked like a dry twig.

"Oh, Jesus," he muttered, squeezing his eyes shut. *"Why?"*

The time seemed to remain frozen, or just ooze into a thaw, as Lorraine put a gentle hand on his shoulder. "Guess you were right, Farnes. This is the Brave New World."

He shook his head and blew out a long sigh. "Food and clothes. Then out."

"Right," she said, grabbing him around the waist.

Together they headed out the back door, tamping barefoot, tiptoeing around the scattered glass. Behind them, just emerging from the ringing deafness of gunfire, was the steady buzzing. McGinty's sputtering neon sign. Overhead fluorescents. Flies, dozens of flies, the only pallbearers McGinty or Jimmy Horton would ever see. Above and beyond the buzz loomed the choking stench of death. Pushing it all back, Farnes went into his mind, the only refuge where he always had control.

Think.

Cadaverine. Putricine. Five- and six-carbon terminal aliphatic diamine molecules. That's what made the smell, that's what bodies quickly become after they die. He knew that from study and experience. And he wondered what possible advantage it was now.

They started down the back steps, letting the steel-cased door slam behind them.

"Farnes?"

"Yeah?"

"I think I picked up a sliver of glass back there."

"Let's see." The security floods above them threw enough light to check the wound. "Sit down," he told her. She let herself down on the steps, favoring one foot. "Left foot," Farnes guessed.

"Um-huh," she said. "I reckon I can walk on it if I have to. It's only a scratch . . ."

"Shhhh," he whispered, still looking. Catching a glint in the oozing blood, he said, "I see it." Lacking forceps or tweezers, Farnes pinched the protruding shard between his fingernails and jerked it out.

"Better already," she said.

"Let's patch it."

"It's just a little scratch, really."

"No," he said. "It's an open door to infection. And, in Georgia, infestation. Worms. Lean on me, keep the bad foot raised."

Farnes shifted the shotgun to the side away from her, slipped his arm around her waist, a nothing of a waist, felt the press of her firm breasts against his side, fought to ignore it, could not. Not just that she was a woman—and such a woman—but that he was growing to like her. The moment she threatened splitting up, he'd known he had to convince her it was better, safer, more promising to stay with him. If she had refused he wouldn't have accepted that. Never. What was it the cavemen did? Bash them over the head and drag them off?

Brave New World, Miranda said in Shakespeare's *Tempest*, that has such people in 't. But maybe that's just what we need, he imagined, to return our sense of humanity.

In the before time he wouldn't have wasted even a smile on Lorraine. In that world she would have been another pretty face and seemingly empty mind doing a routine job who didn't change the world one bit, an assembly of self-sustaining biological cells that was born, ate, maybe mated, aged, and died without fanfare, headlines, or even Andy Warhol's fifteen minutes of fame. But there was more than that to Lorraine. And he liked it.

And who was he, or any of the superior people, to judge? Farnes could argue he had a hand in shaping and changing the world, but look at what it had become!

"Farnes," she interrupted.

"Yeah?"

"You're a zillion miles away again. Sometimes I wonder if you know I'm here."

He caught her eyes. Light eyes, open, bright. "I know."

"Where now?"

"Drugstore. Gotta bandage this foot."

Two buildings down they found it, a Rexall sign hung out back, the delivery door yawning open. The inside shone in dim, eerie light. Flies and moths flickered in it, black specks.

"We goin' in?" she asked.

"Don't expect delays at the register."

"Farnes. What if they're like, guardin' it?"

Farnes snapped up the Holland and Holland. "Then I'll have to demand a little quicker service."

As they approached the open door, Farnes stationed Lorraine to one side, out of view. Stepping out, he grabbed a snapshot glance, saw nothing, spun across the open doorway to the opposite side.

Still nothing.

No guards inside.

Nothing. Nobody.

"Let's go," he whispered.

"You sure?" she whispered back.

He nodded, shrugged.

"Farnes!" she snapped. "Don't do that! I was just getting confident in you."

His arm circled her waist again, helped her along.

Inside, the scattered security lights cast hollow yellow wedges, leaving the central aisles dark. As they inched along, their footfalls echoing off the walls, they found the shelves raided. Bottles of pills, boxes of sterile gauze, even razor blades, had been swept away. Each step was hazard to a stray bottle, dropped or forgotten in the rush.

"Some sale," Farnes said.

Lorraine drifted off, limping.

Farnes said, "If you find adhesive tape, take it. Band-Aids too. Sterile gauze . . ." Not knowing where they would find another chance, or how much would be left, or what would stand between them and what they needed, he felt like taking everything, even things he now had no use for. Same as everyone else.

From behind the next counter, Lorraine gasped.

Instinctively Farnes ducked and turned, bobbed low, swung out, barrel raised, seeking whoever had caught her there.

But when he saw her, blanched and frozen, staring down, she wasn't in danger of anything but shock. And shock he could treat. Even in the Brave New World.

Shuffling her way, he dropped the muzzle of the scatter-gun, saw what she had found. First the feet, free of their shoes. Even in Georgia, people wear shoes. So they steal from the dead. What's new? Read history, he thought.

A few steps on he cleared the end of the aisle, looked down. Beyond the chest of the bibbed denims lay a pool of blood, tissue, brain and bone fragments.

"Humpty Dumpty," Farnes muttered.

Lorraine shuddered, gasped in surprise at Farnes, snapped a look at him, and blinked. "What?"

"We used to call them Humpty Dumptys in Emergency," Farnes told her. "When not even the King's Horses and Men could put them back together again. He was dead before he hit the floor."

"Somebody killed him."

"Unless he was cleaning his gun in the drugstore, and it just went off," Farnes said.

"Somebody *shot* him," she said.

"Looks that way." Farnes leaned over, looked around. "But *why*?"

Farnes shook his head. "Antibiotics," he guessed.

"But he was their *neighbor*!"

"Once upon a fiction called civilization, he probably was their neighbor. But now everybody's just looking out for himself. That won't end soon."

"It isn't right," she said. "It *isn't*. It doesn't need to *be* like this."

Farnes smiled grimly. "You've got my vote for President. Whenever the next election comes."

"Farnes?"

He leaned over, checking the shelves. Looking up he saw the decapitated corpse had something squeezed in its hand. As he pried at the fingers he responded to Lorraine. "Yeah?"

"Would you do this to me? I mean, all for a bottle of pills?"

"I don't know, Lorraine." He pried the *rigor morted* fin-gers apart enough to read the bottle's label. Propanolol. Heart medicine, a basic need. He looked up at her. "If I thought the pills would cure me, if I thought there weren't enough for both of us, if I thought you wouldn't give them to me, if

I thought you would kill me because you thought I would kill you . . . . I don't know. But I still hope not."

Lorraine gave him a trace of a smile. "I knew you were different, Farnes."

But by that time he was walking away from her.

"Hey," she said. "Where you going?"

He didn't turn back to say, "Back room."

"What's there?"

"Prescription drugs."

"What about . . ."

"The townsfolk have liberated most of the useful stuff from the shelves. I think they must have it somewhere, maybe an armory, under lock and key, controlled by a recently self-appointed little Caesar." He turned around and watched her limp up, then looked directly into her eyes. "You just saw what they did to one of their neighbors, and they *knew* him. We're strangers. If we got within a hundred yards they'd shoot us down like rabid animals, leave our bodies for the dogs and crows. And if we wanted the medicine they took, we'd have to kill them all to get it."

"Then what . . . ?"

Farnes was already past the prescription counter. Pushing back the swinging half door fronting on the desk, he saw the pharmacist pinned in the corner by a shotgun blast, his eyes wide open, vacant with astonishment at his own death, the white bib soaked in coagulating blood. "Guess they've gone self-service," he said.

Beyond the desk and the two steps down, a hallway opened. Right gave the employees' restroom, left gave another short run, offices to the rear, an unmarked locked room dead ahead. "That is it."

"How do you know all this stuff, Farnes?"

"I'm a doctor, remember?"

"You gonna jaw or . . . ?"

"If the natives haven't stolen all the hairpins, you want to find me some?"

She limped back, muttered, "Hardly time for kinky hair-dos."

"I didn't ask for mousse or Grecian Formula 16. I asked for bobby pins."

She came back, rattled a box under his nose, "Yes, sir, doctor. Your order, doctor. We deliver, doctor."

"Service is getting better around here."

"Well I ain't plannin' on makin' a career of it."

Farnes bent two pins to ninety-degree Ls, inserted one into the lock's tumbler, worked it, felt the pins lift and stop, then worked the other bent bobby pin in to jam the first. Using them together, he coaxed the tumbler to turn. When the bolt retracted, he turned the door handle and let them in.

As he hoped, the room was untouched.

Packed shelves left and center. Bank of refrigerators right, still humming, their discharged heat bringing the uncooled room into the mid-90s. His eyes traced past familiar bottled prescription pills, searching. Straight ahead, bottom shelf. Dark blue package. Sterile gauze. Next shelf up an antibiotic-antiseptic solution, for irrigating and cleaning deep wounds after changing dressings, or for soaking cuts.

"Let's get a bag for our order," he said.

"You gonna pay for this stuff, Farnes?"

He looked around in disbelief. "Who? The pharmacist?"

"Just . . . all this belongs to someone."

"Hell, Lorraine. I'm just an escaped convict on the lam, right? It's a little hard for me to get credit. So do you . . ."

She looked distressed. "Farnes, when is all this gonna . . . pass?"

"No idea. There's still a lot of dying to go, one way or another. The trick is to stay alive."

"Ow," she hissed. "Goddamn foot."

"I can't find any adhesive tape. Never mind, we'll get some electrical tape or friction tape at the hardware store down by the first corner." He looked over his shoulder, opened his mouth to speak, but Lorraine was gone. His heart jumped as he raced for the storeroom door, nearly knocking her over as she returned.

"Whoa," she said.

"You disappeared, I was—"

"Farnes, I keep tellin' you. Look after yourself. See here? I found us a bag." She held up a vinyl bag boasting "Milton Shagmyer's Drugstore," held it open as he loaded it up, running down the shelves, picking, in addition to the gauze and antiseptic, a selection of antibiotics and a bottle of hydrazone tablets for purifying water. Then, turning to the refrigerators, he opened the door of one unit, plucked out a couple of bottles, dropped them into the bag.

"Won't those spoil?" Lorraine asked.

"Not soon," he told her. "Some shelf lives are extended

by refrigeration, but the medicine decomposes only slowly at room temperature. Some of them don't change at all when they're warmed in the absence of sunlight.''

"So that's why the dark brown bottles for some stuff?''

He nodded, locked the scattergun between his knees with its muzzle pointed behind him, and knotted the bag.

Looking up he said, "It's hot in here and we have miles to go before we sleep. Let's go.''

Together they went toward the back of Shagmyer's Drugstore as they had McGinty's Bar, but more cautiously. After the gunplay, someone now knew they were here. Maybe they would send a search party. Maybe not. Keep moving. A search party would have to split up, making it one on one. If they teamed to cover the same area, they could end up shooting each other.

Or they could move slowly, store to store, as soldiers do in war, the National Guard in riots. If so, and if he and Lorraine moved more quickly, they could get what they needed before the reception committee arrived.

What they needed was basics: food, clothing, and somewhere down the road, shelter, rest. Outside the sky still grumbled. Shards of distant sparks threw off faint flashes, dimming the streetlights.

Both barefoot, Lorraine still limping from her cut, they edged through the rear door of Shagmyer's, Farnes grabbing a quick survey of the loading area. Except for a Jeep Wagon to the right—perhaps Shagmyer's, maybe the pharmacist's— he saw nothing.

To his left, just above his shoulder and outside, a bug light buzzed garish blue, hissing and spitting as it fried flying bugs. Reaching out, grasping the shotgun muzzle, he smashed the light with the scattergun's butt, plunging the area into darkness.

"Why'd ya do that?'' Lorraine asked.

He put his index finger to his lip, signaling quiet. Then he listened, closing his eyes, letting the moment slide into an eternity, taking apart every sound he heard.

The buzzing fluorescents behind them, same as at McGinty's.

In the alleyway, all the way to the woods backing on the town, a chorus of insects. Crickets, grasshoppers, cicadas.

And the grumbling of the storm beyond, not yet passed, maybe circling for another sweep. Hard to tell.

Behind them the stench of death urged their exit. Farnes kept her behind him, one hand back, so he could knock her over if danger came. He moved slowly, so she had no trouble keeping up, even with the bad foot. When they made the alley, he stopped and explained in whispers, "I don't want the light on us, or behind us, ever. Never a better target than painted or outlined by bright light. Even amateurs can hit us. But the serious hunters will have nightscopes and light-amplifying binoculars."

"*What* serious hunters?" she returned his whisper.

"The ones who said this would come and got ready. Survivalists."

"They're nuts."

"And now they make their own laws."

Farnes had not descended from heightened awareness. Less discipline than adrenalin, he felt a keen edge on his senses, as if each impression, each sight, sound, or smell, was etched with tenebrist contrast against the steady background, so sensations no longer reached and registered, they slapped and stabbed.

In this state he had an edge. The smallest disturbance in his sensory field raised his hackles, increased his pulse and breathing, tensed his muscles. A million years of instinct honed and focused for fight or flight. One hand was occupied with the supply bag. His other, the right, gripped the stubby handle of the Holland and Holland, holding it forward at forty-five degrees, ready.

Their bare feet padded silently along, heading for the corner hardware store, when he heard them. From a block away, in the shadows, he heard them. Before their shapes condensed from the dark that spawned them, he heard them coming, running. And he knew they had to move or die.

# BASICS

Farnes didn't know why he would ever want to shout a whisper, but he put urgency in his eyes and voice as he turned to Lorraine and did. "Run! Follow me!"

Nor did he know, or understand, why his will opposed his instincts, except that survival does not depend on instinct alone, but on the validity of the assumptions used in determining responses. He assumed that they both wanted to survive. His mind screamed that retreat, even in the face of the rapidly approaching danger, would be more dangerous still, understanding, as his racing heart and pumping lungs never would, that what they needed—the basics for survival, lay ahead, not behind.

Ahead not ten yards was the cut into the loading dock of the hardware store. They could make it. He looked up, heard the sound change. From the shadows ahead had come the drumbeat of their racing feet, below that, still audible, their labored panting. When they broke recklessly into the open light and began their feral growling, it was just a matter of number and size.

He had Lorraine by the arm, tucked in with their swinging bag of medicine, racing toward the pack.

He looked up and counted.

Three so far.

German shepherds. Big ones. Maybe eighty pounds each. Fast. Hostile. Not trailing leashes. No collars. Probably attack trained.

With the pack closing full tilt, Farnes yanked Lorraine, who panted, "JesusJesusJesus," into the service alley, up, sprinting, to the rear door. He reached for it and hoped.

Yes!

As Farnes suspected, the hasp had been broken free, now

dangled loose. Instantly he snatched the handle, ripped open the door and pushed Lorraine inside. A blur later he dropped the vinyl shopping bag, swung around, and leveled the muzzle at the lead dog, now a streaked shadow in the flickering security light.

The muzzle roar ripped into the silent night.

Above him an owl took flight as what little remained of the dog splattered to the ground without a whimper.

Farnes shucked another round into the chamber, pulled a bead on the second attack. Two shepherds, flank to flank, growling and yapping, felt the blast of the scattergun, one flopping dead. The farthest one, shielded by the other, winced, snarled, and rolled up, resumed the attack. The final volley destroyed him.

Smoke and ringing silence. Nothing more. Farnes felt another squirt of adrenaline. Fear. In a few minutes, his hearing would emerge from the high-pitched ringing in his ears. Until then, he was as good as deaf.

He shut the door, drew the ringing darkness around him, and looked for Lorraine.

"Here," she said, touching him. Something gentle, provocative. Or was he imagining? Not the time. Definitely not the time.

"Let me know if you hear anything. I can't hear again, yet."

She nodded, said something indistinct.

"What?" Farnes cupped his hand behind his ear. She came closer, spoke up. "The dogs, where did they come from?"

He nodded, indicating he understood. "I would have said pack, but it's too soon for that. Besides, they're all the same breed. I think they were sicked on us."

"By who?"

He shook his head, indicating he didn't know, said, "That's who you're listening for." He pumped another shell into the chamber and handed her the pistol-gripped shotgun. "You know how to use this?"

"Where's the stock?"

"Sawed off. Use both hands, this way. It kicks like a mule."

She nodded. "What are you doing?"

Farnes was already tracing shelves in the dim security-lit hardware store, searching for the rest of their needs. Turning his head to her, he said, "Bargain hunting. You want to watch for the house dick."

She seemed to smile, as if he had meant more. The words just leapt onto his lips. He wasn't used to talking to someone like Lorraine, wanted to chose words that were familiar. Farnes knew well that his words and terms tended to be narrow and special, designed to communicate with the practicing priesthood of medical science while excluding most others. Hubris of science. Now unaffordable. Now he had to communicate. More than that, he wanted to. Now that he wasn't the last prisoner, he didn't want to be the last person in the world. And being one of a few didn't bother him as long as Lorraine was another.

Farnes' eyes and hands busied themselves, snatching things he needed, reacting to other possibilities as they occurred. What struck him as strange was the variety of goods. This hardware store had, in addition to fiber tape, a farrago of sporting items. From those he pulled down a backpack, open-trail style. Two lightweight, compact sleeping bags for protection against mosquitoes and snakes, certainly not cold. A survival knife boxed beneath the picture of a Rambo-clone.

On the wall to his left stood a gun rack. The lock and casing had been shattered, most of the guns taken, the heavy artillery carried off. Only a few .22s remained. He shrugged, remembering the first rifle his dad had ever gotten him, then took the one with the best scope, pocketed a box of ammo.

"Farnes!"

His eyes found Lorraine pressed hard against a post, frozen in fear, her finger jabbing, again and again, in the direction of the window. Instinctively Farnes moved toward her, despite her protests, her finger stabbing toward the sidewalk fronting on the store.

He was nearly to her when he saw it.

No form.

Just a shadow draining across the pane of the window, as if the form casting it from the streetlights were sneaking in, trying to surprise them. Figure it out, Farnes, he told himself. The dogs. Ergo the master. Three shots, no returning dogs. Position. Hostile. Shoot to kill.

He reached Lorraine, took the scattergun. "Stay behind the pillar."

She nodded, took the .22 as he eased the other gear onto the floor.

And he breathed, in, out. Find the rhythm.

Not this time!

Before Farnes could decelerate time, gain an advantage, the front window exploded with automatic fire. Nine millimeter, he thought. Uzi clip. When the rain of glass stopped he heard the sound of a boot—or was it a gun muzzle?—knocking shards from the broken frame.

From a high shelf on his right, Farnes snatched a small can of sterno, swung his arm back, and pitched it underhand. Arcing low above neat rows of freestanding shelves, it spun and tumbled to the rear of the store, where it landed with a sharp thwap near the service door, next to the dead dogs. He held his breath, wondering whether it would work, figuring the master must have known where his dogs died, perhaps figured the gunman was still posted, waiting. Or why would he have chosen the better-lit front?

A deafening rattle of fire raked the rear of the store, confirming his suspicion.

Seconds later a boot kicked away more glass and stepped through. Macho, Farnes thought. The door was surely open. Or did he want to keep the fields of fire covered?

The silence broke with a thick Georgia accent, not speaking but laughing the words. "You dead yet, you sorry commie maggot? We know'd you's comin'."

Farnes kept hidden in the crepuscular darkness behind the pillar, until he heard the sound of a spent clip releasing. Before the replacement slipped in, he leveled the business end of the Holland and Holland around the edge of the pillar and said, "Drop it."

"Or what, maggot?" the voice laughed.

Farnes' eyes began to condense the image out of the darkness. He looked like a South African commando, crisscrossed bandoleers of cartridges and grenades surmounting a Kevlar flack vest, camouflaged fatigues, and bush hat, weapon cradled almost at the ready.

"Just drop it," Farnes repeated, authority in his tone.

"You 'sposed to say, 'drop it or you dead,' or 'drop it or I drop you' ur somethin' like that. That is, you 'spose to say that, if you's an American, boy. But if you's not an American . . ." Farnes watched in disbelief as the man began snapping the replacement clip in.

"Don't!" he shouted.

But the Uzi muzzle came up.

Lorraine screamed, "Farnes!" and began to pull him down, exposing herself.

Farnes cut loose a blast. The spreading cone of double-ought buck caught the left side of the dodging man, spun him twice through his own gore before he hit the floor, his trigger finger frozen to the wildly firing Uzi machine pistol.

"Farnes?"

"I thought I said stay down."

"You ain't my daddy and you ain't my husband, so you don't tell me what to do. Hear?"

"I guess." Farnes advanced toward the corpse, his eyes widened with absolute astonishment at his own quick finish, blood oozing thickly from the corner of his mouth, his chest vested in viscera.

"Is he dead?"

"I hope so. If he's not, I can't save him."

"You think there's more?"

"I don't know."

"I'm scared, Farnes."

"You'd have to be crazy not to be."

"You scared?"

"I suppose."

"You suppose."

"Doctors learn to hide their feelings. Hard to say what I feel."

"What now?"

"We pick out some clothes off that rack. It's not Neiman-Marcus, but it should do. We'll do better in Atlanta."

"We goin' to Atlanta?"

"As soon as we clean and bandage your foot, pack our stuff, and find a car that's easy to steal, yeah."

"You're not hungry, Farnes?"

"I haven't been thinking about it, but, yeah, now that you remind me, I'm starving."

"There's a Win Dixie 'cross the street."

He looked up from the dead man, quickly forgave himself, and managed a weak smile. "So let's rip it off."

"Now you talkin'."

It took only minutes to slip into the baggy, odd-sized sportswear left on the racks. In adjacent half-filled bins they found marked-down flip-flops, settled for covered soles rather than inadequate shoes, stopping in front of a full-length mirror to check themselves out.

"Beats prison grays," Farnes said.

"I look like shit," Lorraine pouted, pulling at her stringy hair.

"Well, you looked too good without clothes."

"You really think?"

Farnes let her eyes go, said only, "Let's have a look at that cut."

She sat down on a one-step rise between sports clothing and hunting gear, where Farnes had found the backpack, sleeping bags, and .22 rifles. Gently he lifted her foot and examined the cut.

"You have nice hands for a man. Gentle."

"Shhh. What will the neighbors say?"

"Farnes, sometimes you're a real . . . ouch, owww!"

"Shhh . . . shhh . . . shhh," he said, holding up another thin, rapacious splinter of glass. "I got the rest of it."

"Yeah, you did. How did you see in this light?"

"Night vision, a gift."

"There goes my privacy," she said.

He tried to smile, couldn't. "Privacy isn't our main worry right now. Hold still."

He pinched her wounded foot between his thighs, squeezed it in place. Leaning over, he quickly unscrewed the antiseptic-antibiotic solution, lavaged the gash and skin flap, pressed it shut. Holding the flap down he reached down, retrieved a small gauze pad, placed it over the cut. Then, using the fiber tape, he fastened the pad in place. With the open flip-flop, the dressing didn't interfere with fit. "That should do until tomorrow," he said, helping her up.

She put her full weight on it before sighing, told him, "Feels pretty good." As he turned away to pack the medicine, she surprised him with a buss on the cheek and a simple, "Thanks."

"You're welcome," he said, surprised to feel the hot flush of embarrassment. "But my patients are . . ." corrected himself, ". . . were usually not so . . ." He searched for the right word, "expressive."

"I'm not just your patient."

He had no response for that, just cleared his throat, filled the backpack, shouldered the .22 on its strap, and found her eyes. They wouldn't let him go. Gently, his only way of responding, he cupped her nearest elbow in his hand, the shotgun in the other, and eased through the rear door into the thick, wet summer night. The ringing in Farnes' ears was damping, his hearing returning, making him aware of the gnawing buzz of flies swarming on the still-warm blood of the slain dogs, the distant din of surging chirps, the trace of thunder. Above and over that, like a towering, breaking wave, was the gagging rot of death.

Farnes moved with stealth, Lorraine now beside rather than behind him.

Eighty yards down the alley that sprung the dogs of death, they found an old Mercury Cougar shadowed beneath a wild mulberry tree. Its creamy paint was ulcerated with rust, splattered in red Georgia clay. Kicking told him all tires were hard. Both headlights intact. The slit convertible top some cover if rain came. He looked up and down the alley, once, again, then again, before unshouldering his backpack and rifle, handing the short scattergun to Lorraine, and whispering, "Anything moves, just shoot. You know how to work a pump?"

She nodded, yes, whispered back, "Daddy has one."

Farnes heard it, felt anguish. She is talking in the present about a man who, events nearly guarantee, is in the past. It hasn't hit her yet. He wondered how she would react when it did. But that would wait.

"There's a shell in the chamber," he said.

She nodded, double-handed the Holland and Holland as he had shown her, one on the stumpy pistolgrip, the other on the pump. Against the shrill ebbing cry of insects came a single dog's bark, another. A few miles away, the sky rumbled. Farnes thought—or was it just deception?—he could hear distant sheets of advancing rain. Hurry.

He whipped his eyes around. No lights came on. No alarms. All still as . . . still as death, he thought.

Go.

With Lorraine above him, half-crouched, the shotgun barrel canted half vertical, she swung first one way, her eyes just ahead of her, then the opposite direction, scanning.

Go.

He fumbled in the dark beneath the dash, muttered, "Shit," then, "Oh, here," finding the hood release, pulling. The hood popped with a sharp crack, shattering the silence. Again, as the bugs screamed, the dog yapped. But still no lights, no footfalls, no signs of response. How long would it take them? The body across from McGinty's Bar.

The raided drug closet in Shagmyer's Drugstore. The fallen commando in the hardware store. Follow the clues, straight down the alley and . . .

Move, Farnes. Move your ass!

Check out the car.

Battery? In place. But charged? He hurried a look for something to . . . saw it, picked it up. Coat hanger. He worked it quickly back and forth until it snapped, brittle fracture. Now for insulation. He looked down to the same trashcan, found a cardboard milk carton, ripped it up, put the pieces between his hands and wire, the wire on the terminals of the battery, touched the two pieces.

Out leapt a hissing spark.

Good.

Fuel gauge?

As he opened the door, the rusty hinges howled and the map lights under the dash switched on, showing the old Cougar's belly nearly three quarters full, more than he hoped for, enough to get them far from Darien. His studies at Edgewood predicted that organized hoarding would quickly follow the breakdowns in law and the distribution of essential goods. That included but wasn't limited to gasoline. As time passed, the epidemic would make gas more and more scarce, more and more precious. The town vigilance committee couldn't miss that. Even if search parties didn't find them tonight, the resource committee might catch up with them tomorrow. They couldn't wait for that. Exhaustion would get them first. They had to get out tonight.

Sleep they could get elsewhere, someplace more secure. Food they couldn't, not easily. Food was a prime essential. A hunting party might be driven from a cache of fuel, because fuel wasn't essential. It might make them more powerful, more comfortable, but they could live without it. Not food. Defending food, they would fight to the last man, or, as Farnes just learned, woman. Without food, you die. As food disappears, it takes humanity with it. He thought again of peasant women killing, eating their own babies three hundred years ago in Richelieu's France. As hope vanishes, desperation grows. Once into the black tunnel of desperation, history suggested there was no bottom, no depths to which people could not sink. Malthus and Maslow. People needed basics or they ceased to be human.

Simple as that.

While his mind was busy with philosophy, his hands were flying under the dash. The map lights made hot-wiring a cinch.

The Cougar's engine tried, failed.

Again.

"Come on," Farnes muttered. He touched the wires, pedaled the gas, nursing the engine as it sputtered, tumbled, wheezed to a halt.

"Please," he said, almost believing invocation would work. On the next turn, the engine kicked into a rough idle. He looked up at Lorraine and said, "Used to have an old Biscayne that sounded like this. You could hear it three blocks off."

"What?" Lorraine shouted back, cupping her ear.

"See what I mean?" He grabbed her elbow and hauled her around to the passenger's seat, pushed her in. "Now you know why they call it riding shotgun."

"Same as the Old West stagecoaches," she said.

He pushed the shift lever into gear and the Cougar vaulted away. "Keep low," he told her, doing the same, driving with his eyes just above the dash, remembering the toppled flatbed Ford truck near the bridge.

He ripped the car up to twenty-five, squealed through the turn at the end of the alley, hammered the accelerator, and raced across Main Street, ripped the rusty flivver into the narrow street backing on the Win Dixie, felt the cold sweat of fear, the sharp edge of adrenaline, his hot breath pulsing, his mind racing.

A long minute, a seeming eternity of time, bridged their departure from the shadows of the service alley to their screeching arrival near the loading platform of the Win Dixie.

Nothing acknowledged their presence. No shots, no shouts, not even the bark of a stray mongrel. Still Farnes was tense, uneasy, his eyes blinking as he turned to Lorraine and bit off the words, "Follow me. Stay low. Zigzag. They may just be waiting for a clean shot."

She nodded.

"Two of us moving at the same time will confuse them. So on three we go. Open the door now, push and move when I say. Okay?"

"You are a bossy man," she said, clucking. "I do hope you're not like this all the time or this relationship's goin' pure nowhere."

"We'll have to settle somewhere the neighbors don't shoot at us," he said back, then told her, "On three, run like hell."

"You ever run in flip-flops, Farnes?"

"Take 'em off. One."

"My foot . . ."

"If they don't kill you I'll patch it up again. Two."

"If they don't kill you I'll let you," she snapped back.

"Three," he said.

Barefoot, they exploded from opposite sides of the car, zigged and zagged around the corner, kept as low as they could, kept moving, using the fenders of parked cars for cover, one leaping clear for a few feet then ducking down while the other burst into view, making any marksman continually shift his sights.

First Lorraine, then Farnes hopped through the buckled doors that had once flicked over pressure mats, ducking out of view behind stacked cartons of V-8 cans. Sprawled beside the stack, only his legs and feet exposed, was an aproned employee speckled with brown, coagulated blood.

"So much for customer satisfaction," Farnes panted.

"Very funny," Lorraine said. "If you weren't probably the only civilized human being I know is left, I'd probably kill you for that kind of funnin'."

Farnes shrugged. Squatting there, thinking, as he always did, it hit him. Almost like a high velocity bullet crashing through the front windows, suddenly he realized that the Darren reception committee might wait, lull them into complaisance and take them out when they returned to the car. They'd have all the time he and Lorraine were inside to tie up the car, take aim on the gas tank, burn them to cinders.

Unless they weren't really watching. If they were just encamped, sleeping . . . another part of his mind hoped.

Stop it, Farnes, he told himself. They know damn well this the place everyone is headed. In every town everywhere, everyone would want food. This was the perfect trap. The victims come in and, like the attendant, never come out.

"Let's get this body to the rear," Farnes told her.

"What the hell you talking about, Farnes? We ain't gonna . . . at least I ain't gonna . . . eat *him*!"

"Right. He's a bit beyond his date stamp, I'm afraid."

"Farnes!"

"But he's gonna help us get out of here."

"Farnes, he's deader than shit. He ain't gonna help no body, sweetie."

"Trust me."

"The first time I fell for that line I lost somethin' I neve got back."

"Take the other arm."

She did. Together they dragged the corpse to the rear c the store, holding their guns in their free hands, scannin wildly for guards, scavengers, what Darwin called competi tors for food.

They propped the corpse against the wall near the bac door. On the other side was the parked Cougar.

"Cover me," he said to Lorraine.

"Cover you from what?"

"If I knew that, I'd know where to shoot," he said, be ginning to strip the clothes from the dead man.

"Farnes!"

He kept at it, pulling the apron and hat, dropping the ma down. "I forgot to tell you I was a necrophiliac transvestite."

"If we *ever* get out of this, I swear . . ."

"How do I look?"

"You look a little like him," she pointed to the corpse "which is none too good."

"Wrong," he said. "It's just great."

"What?"

"Shop, Lorraine. Take the back, out of easy view of cros hairs. I'll take the front."

"Farnes! There's a big window up front! They can see yo up there!"

"That's the idea."

"You crazy?"

"Like a fox. Three minutes. Grab a cart and everythir you think we could need. Canned stuff, powdered milk."

"Don't forget a can opener, genius," she said.

"I'm surprised . . ." he said, snagging a cart and pushir for the front of the store, ". . . that you don't have one those in your purse, next to the Allen wrenches."

"In case you didn't notice, Johnny Weissmueller, the purs is somewhere in the middle of the Atlantic, thanks to yo little swim."

"Shop!" he shouted.

"Shop yourself, Yankee! And get me some Tic Tacs whi you're at it."

"No junk food. The stuff will kill you."

They both pushed with one hand, brandishing guns in the other. Farnes gave Lorraine the scattergun. It was more effective and she didn't need a great aim. With the .22 Farnes could dot the i's on the Declaration of Independence at a hundred yards.

"Time," he shouted.

"Wait," she shouted back. "I'm not through!"

"Women," he scoffed, just loud enough so she could hear or ignore it, or both.

The clock had run about three minutes by his reckoning, as he cruised through the front aisles, plucking cans of peas, mixed vegetables, prepared stews, hash, anything they could eat without cooking. Ranges and stoves would soon be a luxury. Fire, the other way, was more than a way of cooking. It was a signal to the opposition.

Wheaties, the Breakfast of Champions, with a picture of Dominique Wilkins on it.

Powdered milk. Carnation. From contented cows.

Coffee. NoDoz. For staying awake, alive.

Band-Aids. Neosporin.

Pepto Bismol. Kaopectate. It happens.

Aspirin, for doctors on desert islands and Brave New Worlds.

Enough.

He headed for the rear, shielding his body from a sniper's view using the shelves and display cases. All the time up front he had not detected any movement beyond the window. Nor had he seen the red lance of a laser scope running over or around him. Which only proved, if anything, they didn't want to take them in the store. In a way, that made sense. Why delay two armed people in a store with all the food? The shelves were still almost full, consistent with Farnes' suspicions that nearly everyone died within a few hours. As a result, they were awash in food, the one essential resource. Shooting would pin them down with all the food, while everyone outside starved. The outsiders would get more desperate while the insiders were forced to wait, understanding that if they made a break for it, they were dead. No, of course. The snipers would wait.

Farnes had no illusions about his mortality. Or his luck. He knew they could have hit him up front, if they wanted to. But at best they would have felled him. That left Lorraine, who could keep them from their food almost forever. And that was too dumb to imagine.

Once they were in the open, a sniper would have a better chance. A clear shot. Surprise. Panic. A second, third shot.

Take one down, hope the other would stop to help out. Then cut down the second. All over in less time than it took a second hand to lap a stopwatch.

Farnes was determined to use the plan against them. Still wearing the apron and hat, he met Lorraine, checked what she had. Canned foods, good. Other stuff. No, he thought.

"This is shampoo," he said.

"So?"

"Conditioner?"

"Of course."

"We can't take all this stuff."

"Why not?"

"Just basics," he said.

"This is *basics*," she snapped.

Holding her eyes he grabbed another box, again not food. "What's this?"

"Tampax," she said, waited enough for the silence to hone its edge and finished. "Basics. We just have different basics, Farnes."

He could feel himself warming, coloring. "Well," he fumbled, "do you need it right now?"

"Tampax?" she barked. "Soon, if you have to know."

Farnes found his stare withered by hers, his embarrassment surge like a tidal wave. Stuttering, he tried to say, "Co-co-could we just discuss this later?"

"Sure," she said, starting for the back door. "Let's go."

He grabbed her sleeve, suddenly jolted by the fear that she might just traipse out the rear door into the field of fire. Her eyes were still hot as she came back with, "What, Farnes?"

"Let's box the food," he said, nodding at the swinging metal doors to their left. "Then we can bring it all out at once, in one run. After we see what the opposition is."

"How you plan on figurin' that out?"

"Mort's gonna help us," he said, sitting down next to the slain bagger, pulling off his shoes, trying them for size. About a half size big. He decided that would do, got up.

"What's his shoes got to do with it?"

"Except for covering my feet, nothing."

"You gonna wear a dead man's shoes?"

"No good to him anymore."

"Stealin' a dead man's shoes? What's the world come to?"

"War." The response dropped like a thermonuclear warhead.

"Right," she said quietly, brushing a strand of knotted hair from her eye. "So what are my orders?"

"Help me with Mort."

"Him?" She pointed to the corpse.

Farnes nodded, slipped off his apron and hat, put them back on the man.

"How you know his name is Mort? He ain't got no name tag, Farnes."

Farnes shrugged, grabbed one arm, tugged. He felt it give a little at the shoulder joint. Although the body had the exact temperature as the night, a dead steady eighty-four, he could tell from the underdeveloped rigidity that the man had only been dead hours. Still, the ligaments around the shoulder had started to decompose, detach.

Pulling him up as she picked up the other side, he told her, "I call him Mort for mortified. It seems more personal than Hey You."

"You doctors are really gross."

"Sometimes," he said, shouldering the door open.

The paved parking lot was vacant, except for a handful of cars left by folks like Mort and others who might have parked to shop elsewhere and never returned, like Lorraine's first boyfriend Jimmy Horton at McGinty's Bar. The garish yellow streetlamps hummed, their plastic covers swatting back at moths who flew against them. Facing the lot just beyond the Cougar, its engine still coughing, chugging, running, was a brick wall bleeding chips of white paint. No windows, probably a tar roof, but no one up there revealing themselves. Along the access road they came up, junk, grass, and high weeds stretched toward a line of dark pine trees. Beyond the door to their right ran the brick wall of the Win Dixie. Twenty yards of brick ended in a sharp corner. Around that corner to the right lay Main Street, its rubble of decaying two-story clapboard businesses, like McGinty's and Shagmyer's, windowed top and bottom, each window a niche for snipers.

They had already passed that edge once, crossed what ought to have been the field of fire, entered the store unharmed. In the front of the store he had seen no red traces of laser sights, felt no instinctive fear that someone was *cer-*

*tainly* drawing a bead on him. Why then, now, did he feel the awful, crawling certainty that this was the moment?

"Let's just go," Lorraine said, nodding at one of the packed boxes. "Make a run for it. We made it in by runnin' for it. Why can't we make it out?"

"Shooters."

"We killed two. How many more can there be, Farnes? Shit, boy, there was only three of us in two thousand not killed by this thing in MPMS. How many can there be? We may've got 'em all."

Farnes shook his head, no. "Trust me," he said.

"Trust me, trust me. I trust you, okay. But I'm still not gonna be stupid. I just wanta get outta here. Get some distance. Think."

Think. Farnes could relate. Three in two thousand. Real, okay. Better, much better, than ninety-nine percent fatal. But representative? Maybe. Maybe not. She was right on one count. They had dropped two hostiles. At a level deeper than conscience, that didn't bother him. Nor did it bother him that he had killed, not saved, another two human beings. It remained incontrovertibly true that he had defended himself, and Lorraine. Hitting the woman had been a lucky shot, no test of skill, less of intent. And he had given the commando a chance to surrender. But Pollyanna magnanimity had a low survival value. And right now all he wanted was to survive.

Their outside hands gripped the stocks of their weapons, their inside arms were filled with Mort. Dragging him along on the tips of his bare feet, his toenails made a hideous scraping noise on the concrete. Lorraine heaved him along, remarking, almost incidentally, "He don't smell as bad as the others."

"Give him a while," Farnes said back.

As they approached the edge, he told her, "Stay back. Let me have Mort."

She shifted the dead man's weight to Farnes, who took the body and exposed the capped head just beyond the wall, as if the dead man were taking a peek, then drew the body back.

"What you doin'?"

Farnes hadn't time for explanations. Again he exposed the head, this time a little more, using his left hand on the back of the corpse's neck to twist against the slowly *rigor morting* muscles, exposing the capped head to full view. He knew if people had been targeting him in the store, they knew how he was dressed. And they knew, if they had figured out his actions in McGinty's and the hardware store, that Farnes was clever. So they would figure he would make the quickest, best protected approach to escape by car.

Behind them, its trunk exposed to Main Street, the Cougar stood idling, ready to bolt.

Farnes kept working the dead man's face, figuring the bill of the cap would keep the sniper, if any, from seeing that it wasn't Farnes, wasn't, in fact, even alive.

Another second passed before the incoming round tore into the dead man's head, just above the bill of the cap, exiting near the cranial suture, blowing the rotting brains out the back of the skull in a thick, viscous plume of gore.

Lorraine screamed, dropped the shotgun, began wiping wildly at herself, drifting into the line of fire. Farnes grabbed her wrist and threw her against the brick wall so hard it knocked her wind out. "Stay here! Don't move!"

Her eyes grew huge, filled with terror as she nodded.

As he grabbed the .22, the second incoming round ricocheted from the Cougar's trunk. The sniper thinks he hit the man. Now he's taking out the car, hoping the woman will run for it, get her as she pulls away, or blow the car up beneath her.

Farnes imagined if he had to protect the food source that's the way he would have done it. If he had to. His first round was in the chamber, the bolt closed, the rifle rigidly aligned with the brick corner of the wall. He checked back over his shoulder as the sniper's third round blew out the right taillight of the Cougar.

He's not that bad a shot, Farnes knew. He made the head-shot with one. Now he was pinging, trying to raise a mis-guided hope that he couldn't hit anything, that their only chance was to run for the car, pull out, race away.

But the two shots, especially the ricochet, which left a clear etch on the trunk, told Farnes where to put his return fire. He didn't need to waste time aiming. And the shooter wouldn't believe the man was still alive. For a fraction of a second he would wonder who was returning fire after he had dropped the man in the store. That break was all he needed. Just a second. No more.

Looking back over his shoulder to check the bullet scar one more time, he saw something else. On the rear fender gleamed a hard red light. Laser sight. And in the humid night the laser light flickered off each blip of aerosol water it hit and led him right back to the source.

Taking a deep breath, Farnes closed his eyes and let himself into the state. Time slowed, floated. The chirping of crickets took on the cadence of a series of high-pitched drumbeats, the tone of the overhead sodium vapor lamps lowered. Opening his eyes he turned his head to check Lorraine. Her blinking eyelids seemed to take forever just to close, were on the way to reopening when he spun into a crouch, half protected by the wall, his racing mind taking in the narrow target area.

One window, left of the hardware store across the intersection, above Shagmyer's, flickered a pinlight red.

Bingo.

He aimed, fired.

Across the hundred yard gap to the window he actually saw the .22 bullet blur toward its target. He watched it the way he used to watch his basketball shots at Andover, each with the eager anticipation that it would swish through, all net.

At the window, as Farnes worked the bolt for a second shot, the tiny red star glimmered, shifted ever so slightly as the window above the sniper shattered. Suddenly the red light vanished.

"Go!" he told Lorraine. "Get the car."

"He's shooting," she screamed back.

"Not now."

"Is he dead?"

"Just get the car!"

Lorraine ran, leapt in, threw the gear lever into first, and shot the car behind the wall, out of the line of fire. Farnes could hear her breathing behind him, heaving the two boxes of groceries into the backseat. As he brought his barrel up for the second shot he felt the incoming round tickle his ear.

That close.

He lined up his next shot, all images molasses, took his time with the red spot, scoped it dead center on the crosshairs, squeezed the trigger. A sharp rap filled his ears. From the high window across the street came a feral shriek, the noise of an animal torn with pain.

A hit.

Farnes couldn't tell how bad it was. The target was still alive enough to scream but might be badly hurt enough to be disabled. Lung shot. A .22 doesn't do the damage of a bigger bullet, but if well placed, he knew from the emergency room, could be just as deadly. But he wasn't here for a shooting war.

He didn't know the odds. And he didn't want to find out. Behind him Lorraine was screaming, "Let's go, Farnes!"

He ducked behind the wall, covered.

"Let's go!" she screamed again, hammering on the wheel.

He nodded, circled the car, jumped in beside her. Throwing the car in reverse she smoked the tires, silencing the night noises with a plaintive scream of rubber. Still clutching the .22, Farnes was whipped against the door, then flattened against the upholstery as she shifted to first and hit the accelerator.

She blew down the access road, cut hard left and back, fishtailing out of town. Farnes turned around, draped his arm over the seat, and looked back. Behind them, diminishing by the second, was the toppled flatbed Ford truck, its headlights now completely dead. As he pulled his arm back and started to speak, an incoming round shredded the convertible's plastic rear window.

# FROM THE SEA TO ATLANTA

The Cougar fishtailed wildly, skidded and pitched onto its right sidewalls, slammed down onto four, and jittered into a slow forward roll. Farnes shot left against Lorraine's shoulder, then whipped back, struck and crunched the side window. Stars filled his eyes as he felt syncope hit, fade, then blackness begin cascading down when a force deep within him screamed "NO!" as it yanked him back. At the end of a tingling left arm, his hand pulled on the dashboard. He snapped his head to restore his sense of time, place, situation. But that just made the impact blow from the window throb. After the blackness drained off, fear iced through him. "Lorraine!" he screamed.

"Keep your voice down, Farnes! JeezyPeezy! Ain't it hard enough to drive without that kinda racket?"

"Are you hit?"

"I don't know. You're the doctor. I'm the driver. Why don't you doctor while I try to drive?" After regaining control, the Cougar was now speeding north on Route 17.

He looked her over, one side only. No blood. No exit wounds. No sign of impairment in concentration, motor coordination. No outward indications of trauma, such as coughing blood. But often shock masks damage.

"Well?" she said.

"No sign of damage on the right. I can't see your other side."

"Somebody back there was shootin' at us, if I remember. Best not to stop, don't you think?"

He nodded. "Keep moving. We have the sleeping bags. If we can find a place off the road, one of us can get some sleep while the other stands guard."

"But am I hurt?" She didn't seem worried.

Farnes' head kept throbbing. "I don't think so. You seem okay."

"But you didn't look at my left side. Right, Doctor Farnes."

"I'm sure you're okay," he said, more concerned that he had concussed himself.

"But don't you think you should look at my left side, be sure I'm not just bleedin' my guts out while we chit-chat away?"

"Your left side, I'm sure, is okay. In fact, more than okay."

"What can you mean, okay? Doctor Farnes?" He could see in the dash lights that a smile creased her lips. "I think you *should* examine my left side, closely. Otherwise I might die."

Farnes felt something wet, warm, gurgling on his thigh. He touched it, brought it up. Red, thick. He tasted it. "Oh, shit!"

"Larry! Farnes, I mean. You hit? Oh, sugar, tell me you're not hit."

Farnes had to laugh. "What about that exam you needed?"

"Don't tease me. You hit? We stop?"

"Drive on, Madam. I'm not hit. But that bullet that blew out the rear curtain has also, I'm afraid, deprived you of your V-8. Went clean through."

He groped around, found the leaky can, held it up for her to see.

"Where'd the slug end up?"

"Neither one of us, thank God," he said.

"Thought you didn't believe in God, Farnes."

"Could we go back to Larry? I kinda liked the sound of it back then, when you thought I was dying."

"Okay, Larry. What about God?"

"Just an expression."

"You're alive. You should thank God for that."

"Why? If God loved me so much, why did He, or She, discriminate against me? Why didn't He sweep me away with the rest of the ones he loved to the Great Hereafter, to sing His praises in the Hallelujah Choir? What you don't seem to consider is what Nikita Khrushchev said."

"Who?"

"Nikita Khrushchev, a Russian Premier, now dead. He said it about nuclear war, but it applies to all advanced technology war, especially this one. He said that in the next war the living would envy the dead."

"I thought Tina Turner said that. In *Beyond Thunderdome.*"

"It was such a good idea that she ripped it off from Khrushchev."

"Well I sure as hell don't envy 'em."

"We're still in the first inning, Lorraine. See how you feel by the seventh inning stretch."

"I'll *never* want to be dead."

He looked over at her, watched the wind flag her hair, the clean, vigorous line of her chin, the soft, molded, sensual ripple of her lips, and understood why.

But he still said, "Doesn't sound to me as if you have much faith in God's plans for you in the hereafter. Most serious Christians I know say they would make for themselves a hell out of this life in order to stay out of hell in the next."

"So what are you, Farnes? Jewish?"

Farnes laughed. "Farnes isn't a Jewish name."

"Hard to tell. A lot of them change it so you won't know."

"Maybe that's because of what happens if you do know."

"So what are you, Farnes?"

"Agnostic."

"I mean before. People aren't just born agnostics."

"If your parents are agnostic, you could be agnostic."

Lorraine became vehement. "If you're an agnostic you shouldn't bring children into the world. I mean, how can you think of bringin' anyone into this world without givin' them something to hope for?"

"Lorraine! It's okay to keep your eyes on the road when we're discussing theology. Look, I don't disbelieve in God. Atheists do. But I agree with the atheists that if we go slamming into an abandoned car at . . ." He leaned over to check the speedometer. In her fervor the needle was flirting with seventy-five. ". . . seventy-five miles an hour, don't expect the cherubim and seraphim to descend *deus ex machina* and put us back together again."

He slumped back in his seat, gave up a huge sigh.

"Is your seat belt on, Farnes?"

"What?"

"Is your seat belt on . . . Larry?"

"Oh, no, Lorraine, it's not. You're right, a state trooper might pull us over. Let me buckle up." He pulled the belt across his lap, snapped the buckle hard.

"You wouldn't a got your head slapped back there if you'd had seat belts on."

"Oh, oh, you're right, Lorraine." He threw his arms out expansively. "It just kind of slipped my mind while I was remembering to stay behind the wall and bring both guns back to the car, keeping my head down and my ass moving, getting whipped across the seats by your imitation of Shirley Muldowney, that I just, somehow, forgot. I'm sorry. I won't let it happen again."

He blew out a hard sigh, crossed his arms, looked over at her. Lorraine's hands shook on the steering wheel, her eyelids squeezed together, narrowed to slits. Lashing her head to his side, she skewered him with a hot glance. "We're never getting married, Farnes!"

He started to laugh, choked it back, felt the sadness sweep over him. "No," he whispered. "I suppose we won't."

They sat in silence after that, the air pushing through the open windows, the split convertible roof flapping, the scrub pines lining the road flashing by in the cachectic flicker of headlights, sat silently for what seemed a long time, the thunder still growling somewhere ahead. Lorraine finally said, "I think we're catching the storm."

Farnes growled, "Yeah, I guess so. If we didn't, it would catch us."

"You always talk in riddles?"

"Only when I'm sad."

Another silence swallowed them as the old Cougar sped north. Only a few minutes passed until the first drops of rain smacked flat on the windshield. Lorraine reached down, fumbled, clicked on the wipers. On the driver's side only, the blade began sweeping across the glass. "The other one's broke," she said.

"Shall we go back and complain?"

She started to giggle, couldn't help herself, roared in laughter, laughed until the tears welled up, screamed at Farnes to "Stop it! I'm driving, goddamnit!"

"Who's stopping you from driving?"

The rain thickened, speckling the windshield. It came through the slit in the roof, cascading into the backseat.

"Should have gotten a poncho," he said, "when I had a chance."

"If you'da stole a better car, you wouldn't need no poncho, Larry."

"If I'd stolen a better car, we both could have been shot dead."

"Well, it runs," she said. Beneath the hood, even over the sound of the hammering rain, the engine coughed back, as if dissenting.

"Uh-oh," Farnes said.

"Just shush. And tell me where we're goin'."

He cocked his head up, gave her a puzzled look. "Atlanta. I thought you knew."

"I ain't clairvoyant, Farnes. Larry, rather, but I ain't dumb neither. And the gauge says we definitely ain't gonna make Atlanta without hittin' a gas station. And I'm not real sure this thing's gonna make Atlanta even if we do find some gas."

She finished her assessment with a yawn.

"Tired?" he asked.

"I guess."

"Find a place and pull over. We'll catch some sleep."

"I pull over now and we'll get stuck in the mud."

Farnes' quick eyes spotted a gravel driveway a hundred yards ahead, raised his finger. "There," he said.

She began to decelerate, pull the wheel right. The Cougar responded sluggishly, but finally obeyed. "It's a private driveway. Surprise folks in their homes, Farnes, and a lot of 'em start shootin'."

"I'll keep my eyes open."

She yawned. "I thought we was gonna sleep."

"You're gonna sleep. I'll sleep while you're driving, to-morrow."

"How can you sleep while I'm drivin', boy?"

Farnes smiled, mostly for himself. "Lorraine. After internship, you learn to sleep anywhere, anytime you get a chance."

The wheels crunched and hissed through the wet gravel as the thundering rain battered away at the hood. She halted the Cougar, let the engine idle. "Okay?" she asked.

"Pull in beyond the trees, out of sight of the road."

"Why? Somebody might see us, help."

He sighed and shook his head. "Lorraine," he said, pulling shotgun cartridges from the glove compartment, clicking them one by one in the Holland and Holland, "if anyone sees the car, they see at least three things. A car. They can use that. If the car doesn't work, there may be gas, and gas is in short supply. If the people in the car survived, they may have stolen some food for themselves, and food is in short supply. Now the people in the car are going to want the car, the gas, and the food, too. So already we have at least a disagreement. And you saw in Darien how some people handle disagreements.''

Lorraine began pulling a sleeping bag out of the back, her eyes on the line of drops leaking through the slit in the convertible top, draining water onto the rear floor. "Larry, it's wet back there. I can't sleep in the back.''

He turned, checked. "Right. Sleep up front.''

"Where you gonna be?''

"Up front.''

"I wanta stretch out some.''

"Then stretch out some.''

"I . . .''

"Put your head in my lap. We'll spread out the other sleeping bag for a pillow.''

She yawned again, deeply, covering her mouth with the back of her hand. "Okay,'' she said, "but just because we . . . I mean, this doesn't mean . . . you know . . .''

"Just sleep. I promise not to shoot you. If you're that concerned about your virtue, feel free to go up and knock on the door of those nice people. But I don't see any lights back there, so they're either all dead or they're all waiting. Now you can go up there and sleep with all those dead people, or go up there and find out what kind of reception they've got for strangers. Me, I'm staying here.''

Slowly he rolled the side window up halfway. It instantly misted up, leaving only a slot to survey for trouble.

"I usually shower before I go down, Larry.''

"Sorry. This isn't usual.''

"I don't like sleeping in clothes. It makes me feel shitty in the morning.''

"Take them off if you want.''

"You'd like that, wouldn't you?''

He drew a deep breath, let out a slow sigh. "Lorraine. I've seen lots of women's bodies. You forget that I'm a doctor.''

She shook her head, no, unrolled the sleeping bag, began to stretch out. Slipping in, leaning her head in his lap, she looked up and said, "I didn't forget you're a doctor, Larry. I just kinda remembered you're a man.'' She turned halfway toward him, her hand on his side, her breathing gently suspiring in, pulsing against his groin. As she drifted into sleep, she muttered, "How could I forget that?"

Only seconds later she was asleep.

Around them came sheets of rain splintered by varicose lightning, the rumblings of thunder diluted by the steady torrent hissing through the pine needles, a dangerously seductive, evenly steady noise that lulled at him, played with his mind, left him, after a few minutes, playing with fluttering eyelids. For the first time since he had seen the dying visitor to Prison Perfect, Farnes felt relaxed.

Wrong, a voice inside him screamed.

Stay with it.

As carefully as possible, trying not to disturb Lorraine's repose, he twisted and stretched, slipped his hand into the backseat, fumbled into the grocery box from Win Dixie, pulled out the cellophane-wrapped box of NoDoz. Settling back in, he stripped off the celophane wrapping, tossed it out the window, slid open the box, picked out two white tablets, and popped them into his mouth. He chewed them dry, enduring the bitter taste, the smoky, biting sensation in the roof of his nose. "Yuck," he whispered, reaching a cupped hand through the half open window, waiting for rainwater to fill it, then retracting and sipping.

Lorraine turned in his lap, one hand snagging on his pants, holding. A smile crossed her half-sleeping face as she nuzzled in. What to do?

Farnes shrugged. Nothing. Do nothing. Let her sleep.

Just outside, about forty-five degrees to his right, on his side of the Cougar, he heard the sound. Steady, rhythmic. Slosh, two seconds silence. Slosh, another two seconds. Slosh, continuing. He cranked the window down, brought the shotgun muzzle to ready.

Sitting ducks, he thought. They can wait us out or shoot us through the door. Nothing we can do.

Reduce your profile.

Little light. Near dark among the pines, especially under the dark slabs of nimbus clouds, the heavy rain.

He waited on the next flash of lightning to reveal something, straining to catch a shifting silhouette, a form, a motion. Anything.

When lightning popped, it threw a shadowy cast across the pine forest just before another of the sloshing sounds. And something did move! Just beyond the rising ridge, a ducking movement preceded the slosh.

What?

He couldn't wait. Sentries don't do that. Seek it out. More than ever he wished for the poncho. If he moved, he would get wet. Wet or dead? Take your choice.

He eased Lorraine's head down and slipped out the door, holding down the light button in the frame so the dash lights didn't go on, revealing their position. Then he closed the door, wincing as the rusty hinge creaked, rushing to scamper off, aiming to outflank, encircle, surprise.

Dashing down a shallow wash, he followed the defile, pinning his eyes on the spot, the very spot where he saw the movement. Around him the rain slashed down, hammering a thin mist from the needled forest floor, obscuring his view.

He could still hear it.

Slosh. Silence. Slosh. Silence.

What?

He couldn't figure it.

He wondered at his own movements, how much the intruder could hear, how much of the sloshing of his feet, the slapping of the flip-flops protecting him from the needles, the pulses of mist from his breathing, his silhouette against the syncopated lightning. And he had to wonder, for all that, who would be revealed first.

Another slosh.

This one closer.

Not closer by its movement.

Closer because Farnes, hunkered down and slinking, covered by a pine bole or rise, was approaching.

The heavy rain had drenched him through his clothes, right down to his skin. Over his forehead and into his eyes, so he had to blink it away to see. Through the mist, through the arboreal darkness, something was still making footfalls.

What?

Farnes slipped quietly around, was standing nearly behind the sounds, still exactly rhythmic and stationary. If someone was watching the car but had not seen him leave or circle, then they would now have their back to him. Slowly and quietly he brought the shotgun barrel up in one hand, used the other to steady his approach over the slippery, needle-laden clay.

Again it came.

Ten feet, no more.

In the black downpour, dead ahead. Dead ahead a swirling mist rose like a specter, completely masking whatever lay beyond. Holding his hand out at arm's length, even his fingers started to dissolve in it.

Slosh.

Half steps, edging. Now he could tell there was more to it.

He shut out every fear and instinct to listen, to study the sound.

Slosh, hiss, silence.

Too close.

Stop. Be sure.

Slosh, hiss, silence.

What or who could it be, six feet away, that he couldn't see even a trace?

He didn't believe in ghosts, laughed at the *Halloween* movies, thought Freddy Kreuger from *Nightmare on Elm Street* was a real howl. But suddenly he was drowning in fear. Something primal that comes with danger and confusion, something his powerful reasoning mind could not quite shake.

So very close.

He had to be on top of it, he was so close.

But still nothing.

He held the barrel out, swung it in a quick arc, felt it swish.

Nothing.

Another slosh, hiss, as if he were inside of it, when the splatter of water following the hiss hit the naked tops of his feet.

"Huh?" he said, sucking in the word with a breath.

He stepped forward, looked down to where the hissing splash came.

Nothing.

Turning full circle, the pulse of water struck him from above. Instinctively he flattened, went to his back, brought the muzzle of the scattergun straight up, and saw nothing. The syncope passed and another burst of water hit him, right on his chest.

He rolled, took aim, held his fire.

Tingling with fear, he pulled himself up through the pouring rain, first to his knees, then into a crouch, finally, to full height. Close by, not a half mile west, a quiver of sparks

ignited the scene and he saw it all happen, the water-laden
pine bough dip with its burden and sluice the water in a quick
cascade before recovering.

He was too angry to laugh in relief.

And too tired.

He stood underneath, reached up with the gun barrel, and
poked. Something caught on it. He swirled, snagged it,
yanked it down, showering himself with the water it had
caught. In his hands it was simple. A windblown sheet of
vinyl plastic, maybe the tatter of a mattress cover, had become tangled in the pine bough, stuck on the needles. In the
rain it filled with water, made the branch sag and, when it
had sagged low enough, spilled enough of the water to allow
the branch to recover. And it happened over and over again,
steady, regular, unchanging, unmoving, until the plastic
ripped or the rain stopped.

Suddenly he felt stupid.

He had left Lorraine alone for this. Alone and vulnerable.

His mind told him not to get paranoid. Be cool. He was
already turning to rejoin her when Lorraine's Georgia twang
shouted through the pine trunks, "Farnes?"

"Stay put!" he shouted back.

"Where . . . ?"

"I'm coming."

Wetter than a storm sewer in a flood, Farnes pulled himself over the ridge, made his own slosh, slosh, sloshing
sounds as he tramped back to the Cougar, tried to tell himself, based on those sounds, that what he had done was
perfectly reasonable, but feeling damned foolish just the
same.

Reaching the car, he peered through the half-open window
at Lorraine, who blinked back, yawned. "I thought you ran
off on me."

"I just like to get drenched. Have since I was a kid."

"Are you crazy, Larry?"

"Maybe, maybe not. Better safe than—"

"You gonna spend the night like that, all wet?"

He shook his head. "We've got to make the house."

"But—"

"Look. I heard something, went to check it out. Turned
out to be nothing. But it made me understand. The car's a
trap. They just pick the right angle, or take us from two
flanks. We're sitting ducks."

"You're wet as a duck," she clucked. "Best get you inside, those clothes off."

"Leave the car. We'll go in on foot."

"Surprise 'em?"

"Something like that."

She stared at him, her look undefinable. "You gonna kill 'em, Larry?"

He stared back. "Not if I can help it. You're always forgetting I'm a doctor."

"Yeah? Well maybe that's 'cause I don't want you to be my doctor."

"Why not? I'm a very good doctor in a rapidly shrinking field, so you aren't going to have a large choice."

She pulled herself out of the sleeping bag, kicked it away, and stepped out into the rain. "Shut up, Larry. Do you mind if we just get some sleep?"

He couldn't feel wounded too long when he saw the exhaustion in her face. Stress does that. "Okay," he said. "Let's go."

When they reached the clapboard house raised on stacked cinderblocks in a clearing in the forest, it was unlit. Farnes ran through possibilities in his head. Power out, lights out, asleep. Not home, waiting, sleeping. His eyes ran back along the power lines serving the place, little more than an overblown shack, maybe five rooms on one floor.

"Once around," he said.

"I'm wet," Lorraine sulked. "I'm tired. Let's just go in."

Farnes shook his head. "You're alive, you're well. Let's keep it that way."

She responded with a sigh, silence, as they traced the house. On the right side, where the service lines met the house, was a glass-bubbled electrical meter. In the dark, Farnes found it with his hand as it traced around. Touching it, he felt it hum. Service. Electricity. Probably a refrigerator, freezer, something that draws a lot of juice.

So far, so good.

They turned the corner to the rear, stopped, listened.

Thunder grumbled. Rain hissed. A sheet of lightning flashed, revealing a snapshot. Doghouse. Chicken coop. Small porch. Pickup truck parked to the rear.

"Maybe home," he whispered.

Lorraine said, "Uh-uh. No dog. Where's the barkin'?"

Farnes shook his head, signaled confusion, moved closer. In the coop the chickens clucked, flapped ruffled feathers. If they're in, dog or no, that should wake them up. If they heard it through the storm.

He kept his scattergun ready, level so the rain wouldn't flood the barrel, soak through the cardboard jacket on the shells. Like a magic wand, a symbol of authority, he let the deadly muzzle lead him.

"Are you going to kill them?" Lorraine's voice rang in his head, the question on him.

He still didn't know. Not if he could help it. Still, between their confusion and his quickness he could not afford to hesitate. It was a killing time, for those who wouldn't kill under any circumstances, a dying time. And Farnes did not want to die.

Up on the small back porch, the screen door was playing in the wind, slamming, opening, slamming again. Now if anyone was home, wouldn't they latch it, quell the racket, give themselves some peace? Or did the wind play through the forest every night, making the same slapping sound with the door, so they'd gotten used to it? Or were they so drunk they could sleep through a supernova?

Good questions. But Farnes had no answers.

He felt Lorraine's hands, close on his back, gentle, almost epiphanic, move up. As he took the first step of three leading to the porch, she said, "What you gonna do?"

"Going in."

"Careful," she told him.

"Real," he said back.

The step creaked, a noise he felt more than heard. Around him the pine boughs whipped in the wind. The storm was building. Behind him, step by step, was Lorraine. He motioned her back.

She shook her head, no.

The unlatched screen door swept open, slammed closed now, a toy in the fierce, gusting wind. Farnes grabbed it, held, reached the inner door, was surprised to find it open. He made the word, expressing wonder with his lips, punctuated with his face. Lorraine whispered, "Folks hereabouts trust, still."

Farnes shook his head, let them in.

They stepped out of the storm into a quiet darkness, the water dripping off their soaked bodies onto a flat sheet of linoleum, as Farnes waited, listened. The ticking of a clock, a sudden chiming, otherwise quiet.

"They're gone," she whispered.

"Or dead," he whispered back.

"If they're here, least they don't *smell* dead."

He shrugged. He wasn't worried about gone or dead. He was worried about concealed and armed.

He stepped forward, his flip-flops slapping, squishing, sloshing. Damn. He stepped out of them, went barefoot, two-handing the shotgun.

"No flies," Lorraine said. "Not dead."

"Screens keep out flies."

"Not Georgia flies. Somehow they always get through."

"Shhhush," he tried to tell her.

Again the storm sparked, its distant light throwing a faint glow through the windows. Order. Sofa. Chairs. Coffee table. Buffet. China plates on the walls. Home.

Once, anyway.

Farnes turned up his ears, crowded out the images, strained to hear everything. Below the raindrops riveting the windows, the screen door slamming, the ticking of the clock, nothing.

No snores, no sleeping sounds.

So, awake or not here.

"They're not here, Larry," she said aloud, no attempt to conceal her disgust. Before the adrenaline iced his guts, she had flicked the wall switch and popped on the overhead lights, kitchen and living room.

He rushed back as she stomped out like a drowned rat, blowing tendrils of twisted hair from her mouth before advancing in giant heavy strides to the oval throw rug centered in the living room, spinning to face him with her hands on her hips, her eyes narrowed, flashing. "The dog's gone, Larry. Sleepin' without your dog out back is crazy. They don't need to lock their doors 'cause they have a dog to warn 'em. If they leave their dog, it's because they ain't home."

"Are you crazy . . . ?"

Before he could finish, she cupped both hands to her mouth, whooped and shouted, "Anybody home? Yooohoo! Anybody asleep in there? Wake up! Anybody lurkin' back there with guns? Start shootin'!!" She clapped her hands six or seven times, raised one of them to her mouth, and split the silence with a shrill whistle.

Farnes let the shotgun's barrel descend, whispered, "You *are* crazy."

She tossed her head back, flashed her blue eyes at him, stuck out her tongue. "I'm *not* crazy. And I'm not stupid. I just know an empty house when I see it."

She peeled off her shirt and stood in her bra and wet pants, her voice trembling. "I'm wet, and I'm scared, and I'm tired. And I feel a little PMS comin' on. Altogether I feel shitty. So if you don't mind, I'm just going to take a shower, clean up, and relax."

Her voice was still echoing down the hall as she headed back.

He followed her, terrified that she might be wrong, that holed up back there was a gunman. But as he stepped into the narrow hallway he saw her fallen pants, looked up in time to see her bra and panties fly through the open bathroom door. "Could you be a sweetie and hang them up to dry?" she said, shutting it behind her.

Farnes shook his head in disbelief, leading himself through each room with the shotgun muzzle, as the sound of the shower leaked through the closed bathroom door. Along with it came her singing, smooth, soft, nicely keyed, half a step below soprano, resonant. Pleasing and more. The word sexy tried to suggest itself, but Farnes thought it more than that. Expressive, surely. And yes, sexy. Why not?

She was right. Nobody home.

He picked up her lingerie with the muzzle of the scatter-gun, took it to the kitchen, hung it on the cup hooks beneath the cabinets, went back, picked up her pants, shirt, wrung them out in the sink, stretched them over the vinyl upholstery in the kitchenette.

That done, he trekked back to the bathroom and rapped on the door.

"Who is it?" she said, mischief in her voice.

"Meter man."

"Come back later."

"I'm going down to bring the car up."

"Larry?"

"No, this is the meter man."

"Bring in the shampoo and conditioner, will you?"

"Sure," he said.

He crunched back along the slick gravel driveway, rewired the ignition, coaxed the neglected engine to start. After three failures it burst to life with an explosion of white smoke from the exhaust pipe. Oil, he thought, wondering where he could get some.

Rest, his body told him.

Soon enough morning.

Parking lights only, Farnes pushed the Cougar ahead, parked it beside the cottage, rummaged through the toppled boxes until he found the Clairol shampoo and Balsam creme rinse. Slamming the door behind him, he mounted the rear stairs, went in.

At the bathroom door he knocked.

The water kept running as she must have stepped out, opened the door, stuck her open hand out. Into it he placed her request, watching it disappear with a "Thanks."

Leaving her, he returned to check the house. Lights. Electricity. With a sudden crack of lightning they flickered, quickly resumed their former level.

How long? If the lines go down, no crews for repair.

He thought of a line from Yeats, where the center is lost.

Still dripping, he peeled off his shirt, took it to the kitchen sink, wrung it dry. On the wall to his left, next to a small window overlooking the backyard, was a picture. Mother and two kids.

"Where are you now?" he said to no one but himself.

In a kind of trance, a mix of shock, fatigue, fear, Farnes' body demanded rest. It was not a suggestion, not a request, it was an ultimatum. His concentration was shot. Lorraine's shower had stopped and he hadn't noticed. Behind him her voice said, "You wanta shower? There's still water."

"I guess," he said, turning to face her.

She stood in a white terry cloth robe, cinched at the waist with a black belt. His admiration must have shown, made her blush, stammer, "There's only one of these, but there's towels. I'm goin' in the bedroom, dry my hair."

"No lights," he told her.

"What?"

"If I'm putting down the gun, taking a shower, I do it in the dark."

"You're the shiest man I ever—"

"Not modesty," he said. "Common sense. No need to advertise we're here."

"I'm still dryin' my hair—"

"In the dark, or no deal."

"Who you 'fraid of, Larry? All those dead people?"

He shook his head, no. "The dead are well behaved. The living are less predictable."

"Whatever." She dipped her chin and pouted, showed him a great lower lip. "But I still think you just don't want me to see you naked."

He flicked out the lights all around, returned, and stepped into the shower. It still smelled of creme rinse. Beyond the door the hair drier whirred to life. He leaned down, turned the taps, drowned out that sound with falling water.

The storm was tracking off when he stepped from the shower into the dark bathroom, groped for a towel, found it, began toweling the water from his skin, rubbing his hair.

It felt great.

The darkness across the hall had fallen silent, the hair drier no longer needed, Lorraine, presumably, asleep.

Farnes wrapped the towel around him and slipped into the hall. His earlier room check revealed a child's room, two twin beds squeezed in with a clutter of dressers. It would do.

As he took his first tiptoeing step that way, he heard Lorraine clear her throat, stuck his head in to ask, "You okay?"

"As can be, considering." Her words filled the silence.

"Okay," he whispered. "I'll see you in the morning."

"Where you goin'?"

"Down the hall. A couple of beds. One is all I need."

Silence. It was an eloquent silence, one that begged for explanation. Farnes ignored the ambiguity, said, "Well, you'll be all right, then."

"I don't think so," she said.

He could only listen, stand there in the door and hear her voice break. "This morning I took the launch to MPMS, just another ole day. I's three weeks out of a boyfriend. Which was okay, because I didn't like him. But, ya know, a woman needs a man and all that, but it was still okay because I had the rest of my life to find somebody. For sure I wasn't goin' to be at MPMS forever. One day soon I would move out of Daddy's place, maybe get an apartment in Darien, start scoutin' want ads in the *Constitution,* move along to Atlanta." Her voice was far off now, even dreamy. "Find my job, my man, my life, have kids. The whole nine yards. That was this morning. By night everyone is dead 'cept the people who are goin' crazy tryin' to kill to stay alive. And it's just,'' she sobbed, ''it's just so evil.''

He said nothing, held his place leaning against the door frame, listening. Doctors were trained for this, and he did it well.

''So there goes the dream,'' she cried.

''This will pass,'' he said. ''We just have to get through it.''

''Farnes . . . Larry . . .'' she sobbed, ''I just want to . . . I don't know . . . I don't know what I want to do . . . I just don't know how much time I have . . . or you have . . . or any of us have . . . so I just want to live for life itself, because I'm sure, right now, that's what I have. And I don't know what you will think of it, and I really don't care, really don't, because I know you must have plenty of women throw themselves at you, because you're a doctor and all . . .''

''Not many,'' Farnes tried soothing her.

''And you're good looking—''

''My mother used to say that a lot,'' he kidded her.

She cried a laugh and went on. ''And you're sexy.''

''I can't say that.'' He felt the heat of color rise in his cheeks.

''And I don't want to be alone tonight.''

''Lorraine, I think—''

''You think too damn much, Dr. Farnes. Try feelin'.''

He felt himself drawn to her, came through the door. The room was dark, a kind of uniform border of gray. His eyes, night eyes, extraordinary night eyes, almost like a lemur's, found the full, voluptuous curves of her body as she pulled herself up in bed. Her arms were outstretched, her fingers beckoning, her voice a soft, persistent melody. ''Here,'' she whispered, ''I want you here, I want . . .''

He was closer now, close enough for her to reach. His voice said, ''You're tired. You've been through a shock, need your sleep. I'm a doctor and . . .'' She had one hand, then the other, and pulled.

Caught off balance, he fell.

The towel unknotted at his waist. He crossed his legs trying to save it but it dropped to the floor with a whooshing sound as he tumbled in. ''You're a man,'' she said, taking his face in her hands. ''I want you as a man.''

Farnes fell beside her and didn't want to move.

She was too . . . too everything. Her mouth was unlike

any mouth he had tasted before, firm, pliant, insistent. And her hands were urgent, demanding, irresistible. In spite of himself, in spite of the horror and exhaustion of the day—or perhaps because of it—he couldn't be sure, not sure of anything right now except for her, the fresh, clean, fragrant hair crashing over his face and chest, and her hands, her relentless, insistent hands.

When they broke from the first kiss, an eternity of everything a kiss can be, she had coaxed him to be what she wanted him to be, smiled, and whispered, "You're magnificent down there. Tell me how you like it. Just tell me." She rolled him on his back and deftly pressed herself down, taking him inside with a new sound, as if a cry, a laugh, and a moan had been fused at high heat and extracted under torture.

Her hands gripped his wrists and led his hands to her swollen breasts, where they involuntarily closed and drew his mouth up.

"That's it," she whispered, pumping on him, drawing him into her motion. "That's it . . . uh . . . that's it . . . oh, sweet Jesus . . . that's it, that's so perfectly it."

Beyond wind-tossed curtains, the storm clouds split, revealing the stars beyond.

The first dawn of the new age burst in hard wedges of dusty light through fluttering lace curtains, slanting across the bedroom until they pinked Farnes' eyelids, forcing him awake. Instinctively he turned and groped the sheets beside him, but Lorraine was gone.

A shock ripped through him, sat him upright in a bolt, had his head snapping side to side as he vaulted nude onto the hardwood floor.

"Lorraine!" he screamed.

"Out here!" she screamed back.

Only when he heard her voice did he relax enough to smell the bacon, hear its faint sizzling in the kitchen. Picking the towel off the floor, he wrapped it again, tucked it securely at the waist, and stepped out to join her.

The Formica table was set with mats, utensils, melamine plates, the skillets brimming with bacon, scrambled eggs, hash brown potatoes.

Lorraine moved about in bra and panties, making him stir beneath the towel. But all he could mutter was, "Range still works."

She turned around, nodded, licked her fingers. "Propane," she said. "Big tank out back, behind the henhouse."

"We still have electricity?"

She nodded. "*I* still figure that means somebody's out there runnin' things, somebody in charge."

"I wouldn't bet on it," Farnes said, slipping up beside her, reaching for a strip of bacon, feeling the slap of her hand.

"You wanta sit down, I'll serve us."

He pulled up a chair, explained, "Many systems nowadays are automated. Not just electrical power, but water treatment plants. The pumps will work as long as there's electricity, keeping the pressure. And the chlorinators will keep running until they're empty of disinfectant, then the water will still get pumped, but be bad. After that, anything that would have died in treated water will grow like crazy. Typhoid, cholera, maybe even the epidemic. That's why I took the hydrazone."

"You like scrambled eggs?"

He nodded.

"Fresh. We got hens out back." She shoveled onto his plate until he said, "Whoa!"

"Bacon?"

"Sure."

"Coffee's makin'."

"It's all great. You should have gotten me up."

"I did get you up, if I remember right," she said. "Or maybe that was a dream."

"About last night . . ." he started.

Her eyes drifted up, her face looked puzzled. She put down her fork, folded her hands together. "But I reckon it had to be a dream, Larry. I figure nothin' real can be *that* good."

Farnes choked up his eggs, blushed.

"Something wrong with the food?" she asked, touching his hand.

He shook his head, moved a forkful of eggs to his mouth.

"Because we was both so tired, like you said," she went on, "that I figure we both just drifted off to sleep. Don't you?"

"Lorraine . . ."

She smiled, winked. "It's okay, Larry. It wasn't your fault. You were raped."

Again he gagged.

She got up and swiveled to the counter, poured him some

coffee. "Here," she said. "You seem to have some trouble swallowin' this."

"Look, I . . ."

"Besides, sugar, what am I gonna do? Turn you in to the AMA Board of Ethics?" She looked up. "Is there such a thing?"

"Yes, there is. Or was."

"Anyway, we don't have to talk about it."

"I think we do," Farnes said, "because . . ."

"You're not gonna tell me it was all a big mistake and you don't want to ever do it again. Because, let me guess." She bit her lip, rolled a glance at the ceiling. "You have a wife already . . ."

Farnes felt sad, must have shown it for Lorraine to say, "Or used to have. What happened?"

"She died."

"I'm sorry. Me, it was just boyfriends and ex-husbands, never more than one at a time. I hate fights."

Farnes spooned a heap of hash browns into his mouth.

"So are you free tonight? Or do I have to rape you goodbye before you walk through that door and out of my life?"

Farnes sputtered coffee. "Lorraine! Jesus!"

She laughed, a deep, throaty, sensual laugh, threw her head back, shook her hair out in the scattered sunlight, started stirring her coffee with her index finger as Farnes watched in astonishment.

"How do you do that?" he said.

"What?"

"The finger in the coffee trick."

She shrugged. "Doesn't hurt is all, or I wouldn't do it."

He looked at her, amazed, shook his head.

"So what about tonight?"

"Tonight," he sighed, "we should be in Atlanta, or close. I hope."

"What's so important about Atlanta?"

"That's where CDC is."

Her face blanked.

"CDC, Centers for Disease Control. That's the only chance we have of turning this thing around. They have a high level security lab for isolation, identification, and treatment of disease vectors that—"

"So you're gonna save the world," she said, distant.

"I can help."

"I should have supposed you'd want to," she said, drew a big breath, puffed her cheeks, blew a stream of air up.

"Tell me what else you think we should do."

Her eyes opened wide. "Find a nice deep hole until this thing blows over."

"Can't," he said.

"That's just what you told the skipper was best!" she lashed out.

"For the skipper, sure."

"And what about me?"

He shrugged. "Maybe for you, too. I shouldn't drag you into—"

She held up her hand, closed her eyes. "No macho. I'm a big girl. I do what I want. Folks been callin' me a slut since junior high school, but I still dressed the way I wanted because I have a nice body, don't you think?"

"Yeah, I do."

"And there's no reason to hide it just because the rest of them are flat-chested zit-traps."

Farnes laughed, admitted, "I knew some like that."

"So I don't need your protection."

"Okay."

"But if you want to go, because you want to go . . ."

"Not without you," he said.

"If you want to go, I just want to know what kind of names you want me to consider . . ."

"Names?"

"For the baby."

"What baby?"

She held his eyes, bit her pouting lip, sighed. "Larry. That damn rubber toy boat we was in is either sunk in the ocean or floating around right dead in the middle of it. Either way my diaphragm is in my purse along with it. Now if you're a doctor, you understand what we did last night."

"You said you were near your period!"

She shrugged. "Sometime soon. Couple of weeks. I just don't like to pass up a chance to get Tampax when I'm low. The period thing seemed a good excuse in case you . . . in case I needed an excuse, if you know . . ."

"Jesus. If that's it—"

"My body's like a clock, always has been."

"Then it's possible—"

"Very possible."

"This isn't fair, Lorraine!"

"Everything's fair in love and war, Larry. You said it yourself. And this is love and war."

"How could you? I mean, look around you!"

Lorraine flashed the palms of both hands. "I'm only asking you for a name, sugar. I take responsibility."

"Bullshit!"

It was clear from the hidden turn at the corners of her mouth that this was exactly what she wanted him to say.

"On the other hand, in my delicate condition, I might be needin' a doctor now and again. You maybe can make a recommendation?"

"I'm going to Atlanta."

"Then so am I."

He sighed, considered what he had to say, then just said it. "What we're about to walk into is going to be no picnic."

"No doubt."

"Dangerous, deadly, and sickening."

"Sounds like my ex-husband, Larry. So maybe I have some well-needed experience."

"There's no stopping you, is there?"

"Not hardly."

"Maybe you're just what I need."

She leaned across the table, bussed him with a kiss. "I knew you were a smart man the second I laid eyes on you."

He shook his head, disbelieving.

She got up, clattered the dishes into the sink, squelched a burp. Turning, she said, "You don't think these folks would mind much if I didn't clean up?"

Farnes told her, "I don't think they'd mind much of anything."

"Because housework is not my favorite thing, and the kitchen," she laced her arms around his neck, "is not my favorite room."

She kissed him, long and deep. He came away breathless, but for the word, "Atlanta."

She just shrugged. "I bet they got bargains on nice clothes there."

"Let's go."

Ten minutes and they were ready. The early sun had reached half its zenith, heating up the fragrant forest air. A light breeze played through the needles, hissing and tossing the boughs. Last night's storm had raged through without relief, leaving the air still wet, sticky. Although the work was light, the humidity bore down on him, left him trickling with sweat.

The floors of the unairconditioned Cougar rippled with last night's rain. The Win Dixie boxes were splattered and soaked, the products heavy with water. "Shit," he said aloud, bailing with his hand. An image flashed in his mind, showed the skipper at work in the Zodiac. He wondered where the man was now, if he had made it. Pausing to ponder amidst the cheery chirping of morning's birds, he soon shook off the thought and got on with preparing the car.

In the cottage Lorraine was singing again. "As Tears Go By," an old Rolling Stones song. He stopped and listened, let himself smile. "Life," he whispered to himself, suddenly understanding why it was so precious.

By the time he reached the back door she was standing inside in a frilly white dress, half a size big. "You like it?"

He fumbled, was surprised how stirring she looked, felt the flashes of last night, stammered, "Yeah, yes I like it, sure. It's just, where did you get it?"

"Closet," she said, picking up the picture Farnes had seen last night, turning, asking, "Who do you think they were?"

"Someone," he said.

"Maybe they're just away at the beach," she said, putting the picture down.

"Maybe."

"But you like the dress?"

"Yeah," he said.

She gathered her hair into a ponytail, knotted it up in a dark blue ribbon. "There. Lot cooler this way."

"Nice neck," he heard himself say.

She touched him, bussed him on the cheek, held his arm. "Look at you, Larry! You got into that wet stuff again. Why don't you rummage through the closet, see what you can find."

"We better get going," he said, checking the wall clock.

"You're goin' to be miserable." She stood akimbo, her look firm.

Shrugging, he gave in, handed her the scatter gun.

She screwed up her face as she took it. "That outfit ain't that great, Farnes. Nobody's gonna fight you for it."

"I just don't want to relax too much. There are a lot of

jittery people out there. And thanks to the NRA, a lot of guns, too.''

She leaned back on the bed behind him, propped herself on both hands, tossed her head, watched him peel off his shirt.

"Nice back," she purred.

"Do you mind?" He felt himself blush.

"No. No, I don't mind at all. You want me to leave?"

Farnes whipped on a short-sleeved cotton shirt, a nightmare of splashed color drowning in disorder, then turned for approval. She drew herself forward, eyes sparkling, one hand covering her laughing mouth. "I don't think so."

"Well, you'd never lose me in a crowd," he muttered.

"If we ever find a crowd."

He tried another, a kind of beige canvas design with flattened pleated piping and cartridge pockets.

She laughed. "You look like Indiana Jones."

"See if you can find me a bullwhip and we'll be on our way."

"Get your ass out of those wet pants," she said.

"Oh, no," he chuckled. "My mother told me about girls like you."

She got up and locked lips with him, sucked urgently. "Was she right? Am I that terrible?"

"No," he said, responding, "but we have to go."

"Why?" She played her finger gently, tracing the shape of his lips.

"Because it's light," he said. "And the name of the game is hide, move, or die."

She sat back down as he slipped into dry denim pants, rolled up the cuffs, searched for a belt. "This guy had a big ass."

She shook her head, no. "You just have a cute little ass, Farnes. I find that very endearin', even in a Yankee."

He lashed the jeans on with a belt, stalked out the door. "You happy now?" Leaving her, he took a final look around the house, found a box of twelve gauge shotgun shells on the shelf of the bedroom closet, took them. A quick search for the gun itself left him empty-handed. Nothing. Maybe it had been in a gun rack across the back window of a pickup the last time they left home.

He picked up the family picture again, examined the faces. Knowing he would never know, he put it down. Around the turn of a wall, Lorraine was clattering around the kitchen. He walked to her, leaned against the door frame, said, "What now?"

She looked up, licking mayonnaise off her finger, mumbled the word, "Lunch," continued to assemble sandwiches, ham and cheese, celery, snack-sized bags of potato chips. Scavenging a brown paper bag from under the sink to hold it all, she said, "Ready?"

"As I'll ever be," he said, picking up the Holland and Holland, holding the door open.

At the Cougar Farnes told her, "Keep an eye out," handing her the scattergun, propping the .22 against the rear door, driver's side.

"What are you doin'?"

He leaned in the front, careful not to touch the inside. "I'm trying to avoid electrocuting myself when I jump start this thing. The inside's soaked."

She nodded, brushed her soft hair back with a flicking hand, watched.

The Cougar's starter motor hacked like a lung cancer patient as it struggled, failed. Once. Again. And again. Puffs of acrid white smoke shot from the exhaust pipe with each try. Farnes disengaged the ignition wires, released the hood latch, went to look at the engine. He checked the oil, found it low.

Looking up and around, he saw a small shack, walked to it, went inside. A power lawn mower sat against the rear wall. The walls were lined with shelves. On the one to his left was an open can of motor oil. One only. "Have to do," he said to himself.

He took it back to the car, poured it in, tried and failed again to start the engine.

"What's the matter?" Lorraine asked.

"Ornery," he said.

She laughed.

"What's so funny?"

"Nothin'. Just that ornery's not a word I'd expect from a blueblood Yankee, that's all."

Farnes was already under the hood again, lifting the cowl from the air filter compartment, then removing the air filter itself, throwing it away.

"Don't we need that?" she asked.

He smiled back. "If we're concerned about the warranty, sure. And there's some chance of engine fire. But we've only got enough gas for another hundred miles and we want power, not economy, so we don't need it."

"What about back there?" Lorraine was pointing to the shack where he got the oil.

"What about it?"

"You found oil. What about gas?"

Farnes brightened. Lawn mower. Of course it would need gas. Together they went back. In a red safety can with yellow stripes, wedged behind the lawn mower, was gasoline. When he picked it up, it sloshed. About half full. Maybe a gallon. But a gallon was another fifteen miles, even in the dilapidated Cougar.

"Is it gas?" she asked.

He unscrewed the cap on the pour spout, smelled it. "Or the rankest corn mash I ever smelled."

She slapped his shoulder. "Whadda you know 'bout corn mash?"

They walked the can back to the Cougar, began emptying it into the car's tank. "A friend in med school was from the Kentucky hills. He introduced me to it."

"My, my. You're just full of surprises."

He shook out the last drop, even the last vapor, threw the can away. Then he returned to the engine, worked the butterfly on the carburetor, tried again to start the engine.

When he crossed the wires, a huge convulsion shook the engine as it sputtered to life, settled into a fickle idle, running hard, slowing, hacking, running hard again.

"We'll have to trade this in soon," he said.

"Whatever you say, sugar."

They both laughed, slipped into the car. Gently Lorraine slid the sawed-off shotgun across to Farnes, stock-first. After passing it across the dash and out his open window, he rested the barrels on the bracket of the side-view mirror. One-handing the short grip with his left, Farnes wheeled the old car around, crunched slowly down the gravel driveway, ready for trouble.

Just before the gravel bed broke from the cover of the pine forest, Lorraine was chattering, "Turn right, in a coupla miles we tie into I-95 North to Savannah . . ." when Farnes held up his hand, threw the Cougar into neutral, whispered, "Shhhh!"

"Huh?"

"Listen," he whispered.

She turned her head, cocked it like a dog. "Cain't hear a damn thing, Larry."

He reached beneath the dash, stripped the connection, killed the engine. "Hear it now?"

She strained, shook her head, first no, then, "Yeah."

Farnes should have expected it. Anyone who believed an invasion would start from Cuba would move quickly north. And when they figured out the cities were just big storehouses, they would head for the cities. Just like these people.

Lorraine hissed, "Someone's singin'!"

He nodded, got out, knew there was nothing left that a sane person would sing about. "Hand me the rifle," he said, putting the shotgun atop the car.

She did, got out to join him. Together they moved behind the line of pines concealing the driveway and started south, toward the source of the noise. As it got nearer, it got clearer. Finally he could hear the words, "I wish I was in Dixie . . ." followed by a pause, when another voice cut in, demanding, "LOUDER!"

The first voice sang, "I WISH I was in DIXIE, HOORAH, HOORAH . . ."

"LOUDER!"

"I WISH I WAS in Dixie . . ."

Farnes peered out from the sparse cover of a struggling scrub pine, down the buckled and bleached gray asphalt of Georgia 17, toward a tight switchback bend where the pavement turned toward them. Tense seconds ticked as the hoarse singing spilt the growing heat and the chugging sound of a motor broke from behind the distant curtain of pines, before the image rippled out of the roadbed convection. In that instant a flash of adrenaline detonated within him.

"It's the skipper!" Lorraine gasped.

"Not the driver," Farnes clarified, as if he couldn't believe what he saw.

Lorraine shook her head, whispered, "No."

"On the hood, chained down by the neck," he said aloud, as if checking with her to assure reality.

As it wobbled into view, the sunbaked powder-blue pickup slowly revealed its long bed, coasting toward them at a lazy ten miles an hour, fluttering a Confederate flag from a pole posted atop the rear of the cab. On both side windows and the front grill had been weld-armored thick iron plates. The job was amateur, twisted bubbling welds scarring the stripped paint. Caged between the armor plates on the burning hot hood, the skipper was manacled, his wrists handcuffed, chains festooned around his neck, laced through an eyehole in the grill armor. Squinting into the sun, his neck turned at a terrible angle, the sweat matting his hair and glistening from his sunburned face, struggling for balance on the curved hood, he half sang, half cried, ". . . In Dixie LAND to take my STAND . . ."

"LOUDER, you wormy PUKE!"

Farnes felt the rush of revulsion, said a simple, quiet, "No."

Lorraine took his arm, asked, "What're you gonna do?"

"Get to cover behind the ridge up there."

"But—"

"Do it!"

She scampered away through rustling pine needles.

Farnes took his time lining up the shot as the armored truck crawled by like a float in a parade. He eased the stock of the .22 against his shoulder, lined up the sights, and tracked the target smoothly. At this speed he would not have to lead it at all, just wait for the best shot. Nor was Farnes concerned about detection. Locked into tunnel vision by armor plates, the driver was almost blind to either side. Farnes let his finger find the trigger and waited.

In a few agonizing seconds, he understood that the skipper was more than a slave: he had become a living telltale, an invitation for assailants to reveal their position by picking off the captive, thinking that they were reducing the opposition to one.

So Farnes was absolutely precise with his aim, dead steady and on target, drawing a breath slowly and holding it. It had to be perfect. He might get a good second shot in the confusion, but a third shot was out of the question. By that time the truck would be ripping away.

He shifted from a squat, let himself down prone, using the three points for stability. Steady, steady, he had it. Exhale slowly, squeeze.

The shot cracked out.

At the truck there was a dull thwack.

"Damn," he said, working the bolt, disbelieving he could have missed. But then the right front tire began to wheeze, hiss, and soften. Sensing the deflation, the driver screamed, "Who shot my truck? Who fucking shot my fuckin' truck? I'll kill you, you mealy puke!"

Driver's side open now.

"Come on," Farnes coaxed. "Let's see your eyes, dog-shit."

Behind him Lorraine screamed, "Don't shoot him, Larry!"

He turned, screamed back, "Stay down!"

As he turned back to the truck, he saw the driver had already revealed himself, armed with a Soviet rocket-propelled grenade launcher. The redneck, draped in camouflage fatigues, raised the launcher, squealed, "Eat this, Larry, baby!" and fired a screaming volley that split the air as it passed between him and Lorraine, over the ridge, before exploding.

"Lorraine!" Larry screamed.

"Lorraine!" the redneck squealed, mocking, reloading.

Whirling, aiming as the rocket launcher leveled again, Farnes squeezed off a shot that struck the redneck in the left shoulder, turned him back, sent the second rocket screaming skyward, seconds later exploding in useless fireworks.

When the man came down again he dabbed at his shoulder with the opposite hand, barked a laugh, "Hey, Larry. What you got, boy? A pea-shooter? I think you's outgunned! You wanta come out now, I kill you quick. What I do to your little woman I'm gonna do whether I kill you first or not. You hear me?"

As he passed the grill armor, the redneck reached a thickly muscled arm up and grabbed the skipper's head, bashing it hard against the hood, invoking a piercing scream as his face hit the sizzling metal, then yelling, "Didn't I tell you to sing, maggot?"

The skipper whimpered, throbbed syncopated words, ". . . to live and DIE IN DIXIE."

"Keep singin' while I take care of this."

Farnes worked the bolt, advanced another .22 long round into the chamber, and waited as the driver disappeared behind the cover of the truck's hood, himself singing, "TO LIVE AND DIE in DIXIE!" No pitch, all volume. Never make it at the Met, he thought.

Before he could react, Lorraine had scampered back, breathless, grabbing at words. "Larry! Whatcha gonna do?"

"Get down! What are you doing here? Didn't I tell you—?"

"You don't tell me nothin', boy. I thought I told you, you wasn't my daddy or my husband."

Across the road, the redneck reappeared with his weapon. Farnes had seen it in macho fantasy movies, the kind starring

Chuck Norris or Charles Bronson. Before he saw a real one on TV coverage of the Gulf War, he didn't know if they were real or made by Mattel. Since then, he knew they were deadly real.

The M-203 packed an M-16 rifle atop a grenade launcher, creating a weapon of withering firepower. His .22 was no match for it. The contest was hopeless. It was like, he whispered his thought aloud, "David and Goliath."

One shot.

The redneck dropped to one knee, let out a rebel yell as he prepared to spray the treeline with high-caliber rounds.

Farnes took his bead.

"Larry!" Lorraine tore at his shoulder.

"Down!" he yelled back, shucking her hand.

The deadly barrels came down, gaped at him like the jaws of death. In that icy second he felt his guts clutch, preparing for the shock of the fatal round that would tear through him in the next second. And in that eternal instant of time, as he caught his breath and slowly let it out, it didn't seem to matter. Not if he died, not when so many others had gone so horribly. This would be quick and easy. All that he had to do in that final instant was to fight for his own future, to assure that he didn't just acquiesce to death, that he made a savage effort to survive. Because this life was all, and everything, he believed in.

Farnes did not even feel the shot.

Something higher, or lower, in his brain had taken over before then. Everything had tripped, almost automatically, into slow motion. He had to make no effort this time, needed no preparation. He had reached the state, as the masters in Okinawa called it, where the body and mind are infused by the aura around them, where peace brings steadiness and threat brings readiness.

So Farnes was astonished to realize that the first thing he felt was the tingling vibration from the stock of the small-caliber rifle in his hands. By that time the slug had already left the muzzle, was on its way. On its way? How long does it take a bullet traveling over two thousand feet per second to cover two hundred feet?

Before he could calculate the answer, the enemy's muzzle belched fire, exploded in a thunderous shudder as the first volley burst from the barrel. But already the weapon had dropped, lost its deadly focus, fallen to one side. The round screamed horribly as it gouged out a wedge of asphalt from the road. Shifting his attention, Farnes saw the man's face. Above and between the astonished eyes, just visible as a tiny red dot, was the entry hole of Farnes' shot.

"Larry!" Lorraine screamed.

Farnes lifted himself to his elbows, rose to his feet as the redneck wobbled, seemed to consciously struggle to hold his position, then crumpled back, catching one leg beneath him at an angle too grotesque for any living man to endure the pain.

A moment of disbelieving silence throbbed by before they stepped out of the dank forest shadows and edged toward the corpse. Not quite believing his aim, Farnes kept the rifle barrel trained on the man, in case . . . well, just in case.

As they approached the fallen warrior, Farnes was astonished at how alive he felt. Every footfall reverberated through him. Against his sweating palms he felt every grain in the polished rifle stock. The scents of Lorraine's creme rinse, the moldering decay of pine needles after last night's rain, the sharp tang of blistering asphalt filled his nose. And the sounds, the wondrous chorus of noises. Lorraine's racing breaths, the skipper's cadenced sobbing, the hissing tire as it lost its last trace of air, the distant chirping of excited birds, the steady hum, almost purr, of the breeze pulsing on his sweaty face. Most obvious and immediate were the images around him. He put his foot down and kicked the awkward angle of the man's leg out. It snapped flat with a thud. Nothing else. Not even a shudder. Death below him. To his side, a slave. Behind him, in Lorraine and himself, life.

Lorraine's voice was distant. "He's dead."

"And we're alive," he said back, turning over his shoulder to find her eyes. "How long is up to us."

But Lorraine's eyes were fixed on the dead man as she stood as motionless and perfect as a caryatid, the gusts playing with her clean hair, only her eyes moving, their lids blinking and blinking, as if each flutter might erase what she didn't want to see.

"We're killing each other," she said.

Farnes wondered if this were accusatory, was suddenly angry, then, just as suddenly, calm. Then, almost as one, their heads turned, eyes fell on the skipper, sobbing on the hood of the crippled pickup, "Help me . . ."

# DAY TWO

From the tool chests flanking the bed of the dead man's pickup, Farnes took a bolt cutter and hacksaw. But by the time he returned, Lorraine was unshackling the Master padlock that held the skipper, helping him down. Farnes joined her, eased him off the burning hood.

"I thought I told you to avoid people," Farnes tried to scold.

The skipper's parched throat swallowed hard as he winced, coughed up a response. "I *did*," he rasped. "Till I got to the cabin."

"Let's get out of the sun, get some water, cool you down," Farnes said. He and Lorraine draped the skipper's arms over their shoulders and helped him across the road, up the gravel driveway, into the shade, toward the Cougar.

"We have some O.J. in the thermos," she said. "From the lunch I made for us, Larry."

The skipper lolled his head. "Got enough for me? Geez, I'm starved."

"Hell, if we don't, there's more inside," Lorraine said.

"I'm Burt," he rasped. "Burt Abelson." He took the thermos, gulped at the orange juice.

"We just got to callin' you Skipper, for skipper of that little rubber boat, you know?"

"I guess," he panted.

"Can we keep callin' you Skipper?" she asked.

"Why not?"

Once the skipper crowded into the backseat, Farnes had a chance to examine him. His face was beet red and badly peeling. Second-degree sunburns, approaching third. Signs of dehydration, but they were fixing that. His cheek was confused and bleeding where the redneck had banged it on the

hood. Around his wrists, where handcuffs had anchored him
to the hood chains, the skin was badly abraded, worn raw,
bleeding. But even with their improvised first aid kit, Farnes
could deal with it. The skipper was lucky. A few more hours
in the sun would have been more serious.

"How you feeling?" Farnes asked.

"Still light-headed."

"That's expected."

He told Lorraine what he wanted done for the skipper and
she nodded. But he delayed asking what, eventually, needed
to be asked. Instead, he just said, "We've got to move."

"Why not wait it out here," he said, jerking his head
toward the cottage, "like you told me?"

"Larry's got to play hero," Lorraine said, her anger evi-
dent. "Or he likes gettin' shot at."

Farnes tucked himself in behind the wheel, nursed the
growling Cougar back to life, began to pull out.

"You might be better with that truck," the skipper said.
"If we change the tire."

Farnes shook his head. "Too vulnerable. We can't move
it off the road, not over gravel. If we change the tire out here
we'd be sitting ducks."

"You goin' paranoid on me, Larry?" Lorraine said.

Farnes pointed to the road. "Take a good look at Mr.
Bravado, lying there. He was so damn sure of himself that
he's dead. Normally people use the roads at different times
of the day, and going in different directions. But this isn't
normal. A lot of survivors are going north, away from the
heaviest infection. If they don't kill you out of anger, they'll
kill you out of fear, fear you'll make them sick or fear you'll
kill them. Makes little difference. Either way you get in their
crosshairs, you're just as dead."

Lorraine blinked, looked away as Farnes eased the Cougar
through the shadows. Gravel crunched beneath the old tire
as the car lumbered past the line of pines and edged into
sunlight. The skipper said, "He won't be needing all those
weapons anymore."

Farnes hit the brake, crossed his arms on the steering
wheel, placed his head in it, closed his eyes. He's right. "I'll
get them," he said.

"Careful, Larry," Lorraine yelled.

Farnes quickly collected the Soviet rocket-propelled grenade launcher with two hands, passed it through the backseat

to Lorraine, who tucked it upright beside her before returning to the skipper. Next Farnes picked up the rocket launcher, spare rounds from the flatbed, a crossbow and quiver of arrows, coaxing himself on. He hated the idea, had found himself caught in denial, even pausing a beat at the moment he pulled the trigger to kill the redneck. He was a doctor. Every instinct and belief was to save people. That was why he was going to Atlanta, everything hinged on that one hope. So why was he provisioning an assault force?

Arriving at the backseat, he saw Lorraine shake her head. "No room," she said.

"The trunk," suggested the skipper.

"No keys," said Farnes.

"Truck," the skipper said, stabbing a finger. "Tool chest."

Farnes found it, and the crowbar, popped the trunk, loaded it up. Guns and tools.

Coming back to the driver's seat he said, "This extra weight is going to kill our gas mileage. We're getting maybe fourteen to a gallon and have a little over half a tank."

"Siphon from the truck," the skipper suggested.

Farnes nodded. Why hadn't he thought of it? Normally he would have. Or was there something else working here? The tool chest contained a foot-actuated siphon pump, hose, and filter. He backed the Cougar up, rigged the siphon, filled up to overflowing, capped off, and chucked the siphon hose in the trunk with the rest. Having snapped the lock, the trunk wouldn't fasten. By now he was beginning to think again. Killing a man, that was it. Unsettling, jarring, disorienting. Was he in shock and didn't know it?

Doubtful.

But now he was functioning again, rummaging through the truck's hardware lockers. Near the bottom he found a ball of thin nylon cord, took it, lashed down the trunk. Then he hopped in the driver's seat, dropped the car in gear, and eased onto Georgia 17.

"You're not going to bury him?" the skipper asked.

"*Him?*" The sound Farnes made of the word came across as disgust. In the rearview mirror he saw the skipper nod his head, take another sip of juice. Beyond him, shrinking inside the flapping gap last night's bullet made in the convertible's rear window, was the listing truck and the body of the fallen man. "The guy who tried to kill us?"

"Since last night, before I fell asleep in the cabin, I buried five. Family of three, two others. Shallow graves," the skipper said blankly. "But it seemed the thing to do." Then he shrugged, said again, "It seemed the thing to do."

Farnes squeezed his hands on the wheel and muttered, "If we stop to bury everyone who needs it, we'll be the world's busiest undertakers."

"Still," the skipper said.

"I'd rather get somewhere that might be able to save the living."

"Because you feel guilty?" The skipper's words hit him like a blow.

Farnes stammered, "Wh-wh-what difference does it make? The plain fact is that I'm one of a handful of people who has a chance to stop it."

"So if you weren't responsible before, now you're going to become responsible."

Farnes wasn't about to suffer cross-examination. He was already burdened with enough guilt. He had already suffered both Karen's death and the social consequences for his action, provided a rallying point to bring that research to an end. Why should he be responsible for the Soviet assault?

Before he could speculate more, the skipper said, "This may explain the big flap over that defection."

"Yeah," Lorraine said. "I hadn't thought of it, but, yeah."

"What defection?" Farnes said, his adrenaline lancing through him again.

The skipper said, "Two days ago a Soviet KGB colonel—Garnolov or Garnoloski, something like that—defected under an assumed name on a Pan Am flight out of Moscow. When the plane landed in London, the Soviets demanded his return. The colonel claimed political asylum. Britain granted it. The Soviets reacted by forbidding all travel into Russia until the colonel was returned."

"It all makes sense," Farnes muttered.

"How?" The skipper again.

They were breezing north on a full tank of gas, the speedometer pinned to sixty, the engine whirring along so noisily he had to turn his head to the rear to shout his answers back. "If the Russians were going to hit us with this bug, they had to make sure it didn't hit them back. There were two ways. Either they could fake a Moscow flu and undertake a massive inoculation program, which wouldn't have been credible—"

"Why not?" Lorraine this time.

"Because flus never *start* in Russia. They always radiate from the Orient. Everyone elsewhere always has a jump on a vaccine. Plus it's the wrong season. Flu hits late fall to winter. It's the end of the summer. So they stop the bug from coming back by shutting off all their airports before they release it."

"That means there had to be people, Soviet agents, already in this country ready to act soon after the defection," concluded the skipper.

"Right," Farnes said. "And they had to move fast."

The skipper figured it out. "Because the President had gone on TV, expressing shock—what else could he do to seem like a nice guy—soon after a certain Larry Farnes was indicted for treason. And the President promised that America would immediately close and seal its secret biological labs, that the people responsible for violating the ban would be brought to justice, and that the United States would *under no circumstances* initiate or retaliate with biological weapons."

"His words exactly," Farnes said. "What else could he do after the horror Americans expressed over Saddam Hussein's biowar threat in the Gulf War? If the National Convention had been farther off, he might have reacted more cautiously. But with the economy in a pre-recessional dip, his popularity was at an all-time low, the ranks breaking within his own party. Senator Mastenborg from Minnesota was being feted in the press as a rising dark horse with a groundswell of grass-roots support. At the moment he made the statement he wasn't worried about November, he was worried about August. What's the date?" Farnes said, merely wanting to check what he already knew.

"The seventeenth," the skipper said.

"Then the convention's already started," Farnes whispered.

The skipper sat up, his eyes full of awareness. "Five days ago, in Miami."

"What are you boys talkin' about?" Lorraine snapped.

Farnes and the skipper turned to her at the same time, Farnes finding the words first. "The Soviets timed the epidemic to coincide with the President's absence from Washington and access to command. They probably got him and the Vice President at a catered dinner."

"You mean shot 'em?" Lorraine said.

"Infected them," said the skipper.

"One way or another—if they were as thorough as the Soviets can be—they infected the whole civilian leadership from the top down."

"Paralyzed everything."

"Nobody left to authorize a missile launch," Farnes said.

They drove on in silence. Minutes drifted by. Every few miles a car lay toppled on the shoulder or across the center line. As if there was nothing left to say, they shot north at a flat sixty, seeing no survivors.

More than once they saw a body fallen, a sudden feast for carrion crows. A little over seventeen miles into their journey they saw a mongrel dog look up, its jaws dripping gore. Beneath its eager, lapping tongue sprawled the body of a schoolgirl in a pinafore, her belly ripped open, a coil of intestines, like link sausage, torn away. As they flashed by, the dog growled, barked, wagged its tail.

"I think I'll be sick," Lorraine said, leaning her head toward the open window.

The skipper's eyes glazed, his words washed with wind. "It's the end of everything."

"Not yet," Farnes said. "Hand me that map back there."

Lorraine struggled for dignity as she puked out the window. It was the skipper who scrabbled through the litter, found the map, passed it forward. "I'd stick to rural roads," he said.

"We'll make better time on the Interstate. We should be just about there." The road signs told Farnes he was right.

"But what about snipers?" the skipper objected. "Everyone will be waiting."

"Like the redneck?"

The skipper seemed unusually reticent, stammered to say, "He caught me while I was sleeping. He had a gun, so—"

"You don't have to explain. Count yourself lucky."

"Am I?"

"You're alive," Farnes said.

"Yeah. I guess I am."

Time dilated in silence as Farnes pushed the Cougar up the on-ramp to I-95. Half a mile down on, the white-lettered green sign said "Savannah, 25 miles." Again the skipper urged, "I'd avoid the cities," before sinking back into silence.

Farnes felt annoyed. "You know something I don't?"

The skipper shifted and cleared his throat. Farnes watched him shrug in the rearview mirror before prompting him. "Well?"

"My major at Swarthmore was sociology, not a real marketable degree," he explained. "But I did a paper for the National Meeting of JASA on social organizations in time of upheaval."

The skipper let his stare drift out the window, stopped talking as he absorbed the carnage.

"And?" Farnes prompted him.

"And history, you know, from the plague and from places destroyed by Genghis Khan, Tamerlane, tells us that when social order is broken, it reforms in tight tribal knots in small, permanent communities with traditional values and, by contrast, in roving, looting hordes in the cities."

"Why are cities so bad?" Lorraine wanted to know.

"Because," the skipper said, "there it's always been every man—"

"Or woman," Lorraine jumped in.

"—or woman, for himself or herself. They take it for granted that you'll stab your mother in the back to get rich. So when things break down, the rules haven't changed. But instead of stabbing people in the back with words in a boardroom, they stab them in the back with a knife in the street. New mergers happen, new power is established, but this time it's physical and violent—"

"Nice theory," Farnes said, "but the towns haven't exactly greeted us with firehouse cooking."

"Terror does that," said the skipper. "But you *can* approach them, because they feel strong together. In the cities, they feel weak together. Not as weak as they do alone, but still weak. They know they can't turn their backs."

"I'd just like to stay out of everybody's way until we get to CDC," Farnes said.

"Nice theory," the skipper said. Then he coughed.

Farnes felt a chill go through him. But maybe he was overreacting. People cough for different reasons, not just from . . . this. And the skipper seemed, except for the sun, dehydration, and superficial abrasions, fine. Maybe it was nothing.

But he couldn't keep himself from leaning back and asking, "How you doing, Skipper?"

The man's eyes came up alertly, smiled with the rest of his face and said, "It's good to be out of the heat."

Farnes turned back and continued north, wondering where the next reception committee was forming and how they would deal with it.

Farnes was only half convinced by the skipper's reasoning. Not that it wasn't right, simply that it wasn't enough. The interstates ran through and between the major cities in wide, well-paved swaths, broad avenues uninterrupted by access roads and intersections. In normal times that meant fast, facile travel over long distances, unless you hit rush hour. Then you were better off on the rural roads, dodging the tie-ups and blasting horns. And as Farnes had already noted, these were anything but normal times.

What did that mean? Would it be better or worse?

He didn't know.

At worst it meant that everyone could have died behind their steering wheels *en masse,* slumped over on their horns as the batteries bleated themselves into death. But at best, the commuters could all have died behind their desks, like the workers at Prison Perfect. If so, the roads would be nearly clear. The truth was probably somewhere in between. But it only took one major snarl, one crackup or overturned semi-trailer to close an interstate down. Then there was no way off except backtracking to the preceding exit and working around.

But the main reason Farnes considered the switch to rural roads was to minimize the number of encounters. He didn't believe the skipper's theory, felt there was no class or regional restriction on wholesale barbarism. Right now the dogs were eating people. Later the people would eat the dogs. Next they'd eat their own dead. Finally they'd kill the living and eat them, as they needed. And the skipper would have to admit that history, even recent history, had seen all this.

Rural places had fewer people and more roads. Minimize difficulty, maximize options. Based on numbers and opportunity, the city would be a hotbed of atrocity and horror. Human behavior doesn't change by situation. But situations can magnify or diminish it.

On the other hand, I-95 didn't lead through Savannah. They could jog west on I-16, missing the city entirely. As long as the road stayed clear, they could make good time. And time was precious.

Lorraine's voice brought him back. "Look up there," she said, coming forward to look over the front seat.

"What?" said the skipper, who had been daydreaming out the window.

"A wreck," she said.

Three cars and a van were stacked, mashed and toppled about a mile away. Together they blocked the road, leaving only the median strip open. Farnes began to accelerate.

"What are you doin'?" she asked.

"Going around," Farnes said. "If we could go over or through, I would, but—"

"Larry, look!"

Ahead someone dragged themselves from one of the cars, was crawling along. A woman in a tattered dress was all he could make out at this distance. Slowly the woman brought herself up, waved to them.

"They need help, Larry!"

"We're going around," he said.

"Larry! You're a doctor. She's hurt. If she's hurt and needs help—"

For the first time, he exploded. "Lorraine, I can't stop every time we see a person hurt! You've got to look at the bigger picture, you've got to—"

"Then let me out," she said.

"What?"

"You heard me, Farnes. Let me out. Somebody's got to show there's something in us worth saving or else—"

"Load the scattergun," Farnes told her.

"What?" Lorraine's face crystallized in the rearview mirror, a picture of disbelief.

"Load it and pass it here."

"You're not gonna shoot her?"

"Not if I can help it. Skipper, you take the .22."

The skipper shook his head. "It's one person. There are three of us. What is she going to do? Jump us?"

"Lorraine, you take it."

"No."

"Two choices," he yelled, as the tangle of vehicles approached. "Take the rifle and I stop. Leave it and I drive on."

"Damn you, Farnes!"

"Agreed?"

She held her silence until Farnes began to swerve the Cougar around the heap of wreckage before saying, "All right!"

Farnes continued around, the tires thumping on the median strip until he cleared the pile-up, had clear road ahead.

"What are you doin'?" Lorraine screamed.

Then he hit the brake, leaned over the backseat, and said, "In case we have to take off in a hurry, I'd rather have this behind us." Leaving the engine idling, one by one they got out.

Farnes kept the scattergun raised, turreted his head around, his eyes scanning the raised berms bracketing the interstate. Several steps behind, Lorraine advanced, the .22 clutched across her chest like a doll. The skipper advanced toward the woman, her face down in the middle of the median strip, with no other concern than to help her. Suddenly he pulled up with a spasm of coughing that wrenched Farnes' head his way.

But the skipper held up a hand. "Don't worry," he sniffled. "I have allergies. Since I met that survivalist I haven't had an antihistamine. I'll be okay."

Farnes sauntered over, turned his attention to the woman again.

He was only ten feet away when the strange feeling swept over him. Not fear, exactly. Just a wisp of warning. Something not quite right, something he could feel but not quite identify, something deep, primal, that raised his hackles. He was about to dismiss it as jitters, tuck the shotgun under an arm, barrel backward to give assistance, when it all began to come together.

The dress, a red print with hideous black flowers on it, didn't quite fit the body it was on. Pulled tightly across too broad shoulders, it split at the waist as if she had outgrown it, outgrown it very quickly. And the legs, well, not every woman has great legs, not like Lorraine, but this was ludicrous. The calves were taut and bunchy, and the last shave had left a hatching of stray nicks as if only an old razor were available. The hair on her head was dull and lifeless.

Not knowing why, he brought the scattergun forward again just as the woman rolled his way. Her arm whipped from under her body so quickly he almost couldn't react. But he managed to pivot half a turn, just as the polished .357 magnum barrel flashed in the sun. Half a heartbeat later it roared, spat one round thundering by Farnes before he could swing the shotgun barrel into the woman's firing arm, knocking the pistol aside.

"Drop it!" he yelled.

But the woman jerked the deflected gun back, double-handed grip, taking aim at Lorraine. Farnes didn't hesitate, not one millionth of the frozen time he had just conjured. Without hesitation he squeezed the trigger and shredded the woman's arm, crunched his foot on her hand, kicked the huge pistol twenty feet away, ignoring her howling agony as he pumped the action, shucking another cartridge into the chamber as its smoking predecessor flew out.

"Ambush!" he screamed. "Hit the dirt."

Automatic fire from his left peppered the wreck with holes. He spun and returned fire, knowing that all he could do was pin down the assailant, trade shots.

"Lorraine!"

"Here," she yelled back, already prone.

"Shoot over there!" He pointed to the other side, away from the incoming rounds.

"Huh?"

"Just do it!"

Farnes was sure they would try to outflank them, soon pour in a withering crossfire. Trusting but not understanding, Lorraine scoped in the opposite berm, fired, worked the bolt cleanly as she had seen Farnes do it, fired again, knocking up small tufts of sod where the bullets struck.

Again, automatic fire roared beyond the berm.

Had to make it to the trunk.

The skipper was down, his hands over the back of his head, flat. When the incoming fire lulled, Farnes sprinted past him, pointing the way, passing off the sawed-off and screaming, "Pump and fire, cover me," as he raced for the Cougar.

The skipper froze a second, then grabbed the scattergun with an unexpected feral yell, propped himself up on one knee, pumping off shots as fast as he could shuck cartridges.

Farnes reached the trunk and ripped away the twine, yanked out the M-203. Spanking the clip tight, he spun to return fire. But the skipper beat him to it. Screaming, yelling, he advanced as boldly as Pickett against the protected position of the ambusher. What had gotten into him?

"Skipper! Down!"

Instead of dropping, the skipper began running, pumping until all the cartridges were gone. Then he stood there, confused, panting, upright, a perfect target. By that time Farnes was already scoped in, his aim sitting nearly on top of the sniper's position, waiting.

He didn't want to spoil his aim by warning the skipper. He'd warned him already, without effect. And, as if it was all over, the skipper had started to amble back, the empty scattergun dangling at his side, clearly unaware that the attack wasn't over.

Like a jack-in-the-box, the hidden sniper came up fast, filled Farnes' sights with his fat face, his pendulous belly, his chubby arms embracing the M-16. "Good night, Irene," Farnes whispered as he squeezed off the first round from the M-203, absorbing the punishing kick on his shoulder.

The man in the scope buckled like a folding chair, knocked through the air, exploding a spout of blood and viscera through his back before he tumbled from view. Unlike the movies, there was no scream. The breath he needed for screaming was blown out with the ejecta.

As Farnes was arcing the deadly weapon to the opposite side, someone opened up on Lorraine. Automatic fire again. Different cadence and pitch. Not M-16. Maybe an Uzi.

Farnes couldn't make the position.

By the time he had squared off, the ambusher had dropped below the edge of the berm. But from the angle of the shots tearing through the crashed auto's windows, he didn't need to see. Wasting no time, he sighted in the target in the M-203 rangefinder and launched a grenade.

Seconds later an explosion beyond the ridge shook the ground, shot shrapnel and debris into smoky white tracers, followed only seconds later by a hideous scream.

The skipper was standing beside Farnes, a grotesque snarl on his lips as he hissed, "Let's finish 'em."

Farnes shook his head, no. "Don't know how many there are, what the weapons. No good."

Except for the lingering moans of the wounded, his ringing ears heard a chilling silence settle on the muggy Georgia air. Except for the soggy crunch of his own footsteps, Farnes heard nothing. In a half crouch, spinning in tight turns, raking the horizon with his sharp eyes, Farnes assessed, reassessed.

No more incoming fire.

The skipper marched to the Cougar, scooped a handful of cartridges from the backseat, and reloaded the Holland and

Holland before joining Farnes. They passed Lorraine, still lying prone. Farnes dipped down, asked, "Okay?"

She looked up, squinted in the noon sun, nodded. "I guess."

In that little time, the skipper marched ahead, was already clearing the ridge, disappearing on the other side. Before Farnes could catch him, the skipper's voice leapt back, "You've gotta see this, Farnes."

When he did, he didn't know what he was supposed to see. Was he supposed to notice that the man from Amnesty International was holding the muzzle of a shotgun under a disabled man's chin? Or was he supposed to be noticing that the sniper was dressed in regular U.S. Army issue fatigues?

Lorraine's voice came over his shoulder. "He's from Fort Benning."

"You know him?"

She shook her head. "The shoulder patch, see?"

Farnes nodded. Black horse silhouette and diagonal slash on a gold shield.

"When my brother was there I used to date somebody at Fort Benning. That's how I know."

Farnes nodded, approached the man. The skipper kept the shotgun muzzle under the man's chin. The soldier's color was nearly gone, his fatigues seeping blood, his breathing shallow, irregular, broken by bloody coughs. Internal injuries. Viscera and lungs. If Farnes could have medivaced, if he had extraordinary support, if civilization hadn't collapsed, that and a big maybe, he could save this man. The doctor in him said that. Another voice was silent, urging nothing other than to let him die as he had lived. That was the emerging rule, growing in force by general observation.

"Where's your CO?" Farnes asked.

The man's eyes rolled up, blinked once in the glaring sun before the pupils floated lifelessly up. Farnes bent down, reflexively shut the lids. The skipper was already stomping off, his words draining behind him. "Let's check the other one."

Farnes simply wanted to make sure they were safe, that all the guns were silent, that there wasn't more of the same southern hospitality a spell down the road. That done, he wanted to press on. At CDC they had everything they needed to beat it except him. But how long the staff lasted depended on the epidemic itself. And how long CDC remained operating depended on a rapidly disintegrating social order.

He had to move.

Getting up from a crouch, he joined Lorraine and climbed the grassy hillside toward the interstate.

"What's got into the skipper?" she said.

Farnes shook his head. He had no idea.

By the time they cleared the ridge and heard the shotgun blast, the skipper had disappeared behind the heap of crashed cars. Double-handing his weapon, Farnes chopped to the scene, crouching, dipping, spinning into view as he discovered the skipper standing over the woman, the shotgun barrel still leveled at what remained of her head.

"You killed her," Farnes whispered.

The skipper nodded, pumped another cartridge into the chamber. "Him, you mean," he replied.

Farnes' shocked silence became an eloquent demand for explanation.

"He was going for his gun again."

Farnes eyes found the .357 magnum ten feet from the corpse.

"Crawling for it . . . crawling fast . . . I was a long way off, warned him to stop but . . ."

The skipper's eyes met Farnes', fell down. Then he propped a heel on the dead man's hip, pushed, rolled the corpse onto its back. The head, nearly severed by the recent blast, flopped away and nearly fell off. But the skipper had something else to show, something he felt would explain everything. He smiled as he hiked the print dress with the muzzle, revealed the jockey shorts, pointed to the bulge of the penis.

"You see?" He smiled. "It was a man."

Then he pulled the trigger. A volcano of gore erupted, splattering him red. He kept smiling, repeated, "You see?"

Farnes came over, relieved him of the weapon.

"You want to go on with us?" Farnes asked.

"Yeah. Yeah, sure. Of course. We're a team, you know, like family, we . . ."

"Rule number one: shoot only when shot at or aimed at."

The skipper froze in the midday heat.

"Rule number two: kill only in self-defense."

He nodded.

"That's all," Farnes said. But that was enough, and more rules than the rest of the world seemed to be observing. As he walked away, he heard the skipper ask, "Shouldn't we bury them?"

Farnes turned slowly, blinked. "Huh?"

"Bury them."

Farnes said, "No time."

"I'd like to bury them."

"Then stay and bury them. Lorraine and I are going."

"Why don't you let Lorraine speak for herself?" the skipper hissed.

"Skipper," Lorraine whispered. "Get in the car. Now."

As if the spirit left him, the skipper's shoulders slumped. A force lower than will, perhaps despair, perhaps resignation, perhaps even loneliness, seemed to drag him to the Cougar. Lorraine opened the creaking door and let him in, slammed it, and circled to the opposite side. Before getting in, she whispered to Farnes, "Something happened to him between the night on the boat and now."

Farnes nodded.

But what happened? And even if they found out, would the skipper be stable? Predictable? Dependable? Suddenly Atlanta seemed much farther away.

The Cougar was clattering eastbound on I-16 at almost seventy when the engine began missing. The fuel gauge told Farnes it had nearly half a tank left. The temperature and coolant gauges, nothing more than red-eye idiot lights, remained dark.

"What's the trouble?" Lorraine asked.

Farnes shook his head. "Sounds like a valve-lifter broke, maybe wedged between the exhaust manifold and engine block."

"What do we do?"

The engine still spun, if only on seven cylinders. The speedometer showed sixty-eight. From the start he knew the car would be a throwaway. All they needed now was another one that worked. But when and where to stop and look? Darien had been a nightmare. Even the fake accident turned into a trip. It hardly seemed the right time to look for a new car. But the coughing, sputtering engine wouldn't hold out forever.

They cleared a low rise and approached the Swainsboro-Oak Park exists on Route One. "How far to Macon?" Farnes asked, half turning. The skipper had dropped into sleep, sucked at air with short, rattling snores.

Lorraine snapped out a map, said, "Near 'nough eighty miles, I reckon."

"We'll get another car there."

"Whose?"

"Somebody who won't object."

"Seems like nearly everybody's gonna object, Larry."

"Seems more like nearly everybody's dead," he said.

"Then put it this way," she said. "Nearly everybody who's left thinks every *thing* that's left belongs to them. Now that seems to make it harder to steal somethin' than if a lot of people know that everythin' don't belong to them. Then you only gotta watch out for the police."

"If you see police, think about letting them take care of the skipper."

"You think the police gonna behave better than anybody else, better than that soldier back there?"

"No," he said, sighing. "I don't. I think they'll behave worse. Lord Acton."

"What?"

"Lord Acton. A British political philosopher. He said that power corrupts, absolute power corrupts absolutely. And whoever has the most guns in the hands of the most people has absolute power."

"I guess that's the cops," she said.

Farnes shook his head again. "The army, or what's left of it. At least until another army arrives with more guns, more bodies, better organization."

"That's gonna happen, you reckon?"

Farnes nodded. "As soon as death walks back and forth across the land, as soon as the stores empty and the people left begin to starve, as soon as starvation drives them to steal food, as soon as barbarism spreads rape, arson, chaos through the land. That soon will anyone who's left beg for order, any order. You see, people who have nothing will always be ahead as soon as they get something. That kind of people, the kind of people who are shaping up out there," he nodded in the direction they were heading, "will embrace anyone who promises to stop the violence, put bread in their stomachs, give them a good night's sleep. They'll gladly broker their freedom for security."

"Seems you did a lot of thinkin' about it," she said.

"Where I worked they studied it up and down, back and forth, until the studies themselves were studied. No one seemed to disagree that between the world according to Marx and the world according to Genghis Khan, the nod would go to Marx.''

"What about democracy?"

Farnes found himself smiling. "Two other political philosophers, Machiavelli and Richelieu, understood the limits of democracy. I think we've rediscovered them."

And so, Farnes reflected silently, had the Soviet High Command. It was brilliant, like their chess. He looked around him as the scenery flashed by and revealed itself. Hardly a car on the road. Nearly everyone had died so quickly that all the major obstacles to invasion and occupation were gone, all the assets of conquest intact. The roads were clear, leaving them open for the cheapest, most abundant Soviet vehicle, the T-72 tank. House-to-house fighting, or foxhole-to-foxhole combat, the slow, costly business of war, the kind that stretched campaigns out into years, that turned back the most determined armies, that broke sieges, had been swept away with the people who could have provided it. Since there had been no shelling, no long hammering of rockets, bombs, and artillery, all the machinery of industry was immediately available for resettling. For the first time in history they had enlisted a harrowing, ubiquitous weapon to suppress resistance. The weapon wasn't, Farnes realized, the germs. They were just the device. The weapon was fear. Epidemic disease, disease without cure, relief, or even hope, destroyed the human bonds of social cohesiveness. It made people, normally cooperative, psychotically solitary. It made contact equivalent to death.

Worse, it made them killers. Since infection meant death, everyone infected had to be avoided. Death is the best avoidance, easy and thorough. And since no one knew the latency period, everyone was suspect. Anyone, infected or not, would lie to get food, shelter, protection. It came down to Maslow and it came down to Nietzsche before it got around to Marx.

"Peaceful," Lorraine said.

"What?" Farnes caught his mind drifting, was brought back.

"It just looks so peaceful out there, like a painting. You see the willows and hickories, hear the mockingbirds and grackles, smell the magnolia, honeysuckle. Big old houses with white columns settin' on huge lawns go by, just like nothin' happened. And I still don't know why it did."

"When clever and powerful people get scared and decide to act on their fears, terrible things can happen."

"You mean Russians?"

"Not necessarily. I mean any clever and powerful people, anywhere."

The Cougar had slipped into a troublesome noise, a scraping hum layered over the occasional cough. If a machine could have caught this thing, it would exhibit these symptoms. But that was crazy. The car was ancient, the odometer posting a hundred and thirty thousands miles, the oil burning off, the piston rings worn. Of a hundred ailments from water pump to alternator that could disable a geriatric vehicle, Farnes didn't want to imagine. Enough that it moved.

But for how long?

The Cougar broke into banshee wails and consumptive coughs just past Warner Robbins, fifteen miles shy of Macon. The skipper had been jarred awake back near Dudley and was chattering advice. "We should stay low, keep out of trouble, avoid everybody. It's just not safe. Bad enough to have the plague out, but the snipers, the bandits, even the dogs."

"Wait until order is restored?" Farnes probed.

"Exactly."

"Who's going to restore order?"

"That's not our problem. Our problem is to survive." Less than twenty-four hours had passed since the skipper asked Farnes whether he should resist invasion.

"Are chances of survival better if order is restored?" asked Farnes.

"Of course," he said.

"Then the more active role we take in restoring order, the sooner we have better chances of survival, QED."

"We'd be better to wait for the National Guard."

"I haven't seen them much in evidence."

"They'd shoot looters," the skipper said.

"What if the looters shoot back?" Farnes asked.

"So what chance do we have?"

"Whatever chance we make."

"It's okay in small towns. There's going to be some community coherence." The sociologist's refrain. Farnes remembered too clearly the welcome wagon at Darien, grew impatient, hoped the skipper would shut up.

He didn't. "In a small town we could negotiate for a car.

There'd be no stealing, no shooting. Just come to terms with—''

"—the local vigilance committee?" Farnes suggested.

"Whoever's in charge. We could trade them for a new car."

"With what?"

"We have guns."

"So will they."

"We have food."

Lorraine unwrapped sandwiches, passed them around.

Farnes took one, sunk his teeth into it. Tuna and cheese on toasted white. Good. As he chewed he spat out a response. "They have food, too. Probably more than we do."

"Information then. Stories. How it is in the outside world."

"They have TVs, radios, and imaginations. You don't think they have a pretty good idea already?"

"You're a doctor, Farnes. You could parley your skills."

"I'm not licensed in Georgia."

"Damn, don't you see? You talk about order and you're completely unwilling to start the process."

"All I know, Skipper," Farnes said, speaking around the sandwich, "is that when they see someone coming into town, they're going to think he's coming for their food, their gas, or their women, and that the intruders won't stop at killing them to get any of those things. Their remedy is to kill the intruders before they can kill them back. Simple as that."

"What if they saw someone they recognized, Farnes? Someone who'd been on the news, someone like you?"

"Someone like me?" Farnes laughed. "Who was convicted and sentenced for treason? Someone like that free and loose in God's own Georgia? I might as well ride into town with a target on my chest."

"But a friend?"

"Friend, relative," Farnes scoffed. "Makes no difference. They've seen the dead. They know what killed them. Anyone coming into town can carry that to them, kill them all. If they do see someone, they don't just shoot at you, they empty their clips."

"Never," the skipper scoffed back. "These are decent people, at heart. They're starving for information, for news. We could warn them that the Soviets aren't coming to help, they're coming to invade."

"How long until they guess that by themselves?"

"We could tell them when."

"How do they know we're not part of it?" Farnes wanted to know.

"I'm just sick of sneaking and stealing, of shooting and—"

"Murder?"

"And what else?" Lorraine asked.

The skipper turned his head away. "Just all of it," he muttered.

Lorraine's quick eyes saw it first. "There," she said.

Just ahead and off the road, the rear doors were flung open on a van, giving a clear view to the forward seats, which appeared empty. Farnes understood that if the Cougar stopped it may be it forever. But then, going on in a dying vehicle left them unsure when or where it would quit.

"It could be out of gas," Lorraine guessed.

"We have a quarter tank to siphon," Farnes said.

"Or water," the skipper said. "Maybe the radiator boiled over."

"We have water, could just siphon it in."

"If the water pump's broken or the thermostat's down, it just boils over again," the skipper said. Minutes ago he demanded new transportation. Suddenly he was checking every tooth in the gift horse's mouth.

Farnes said, "If it works at all, it should get us to Macon. In Macon we can pluck new cars from the curbs. Right now we just need to keep moving. If you like the Cougar better, Skipper, it's yours."

"What gives you the right to decide, Farnes?" the skipper said. "You haven't asked me or Lorraine!"

"I'm with Larry," she said quietly.

"Shouldn't we talk this over? I mean . . ."

"You can stay and talk all you want," Farnes said, decoupling the jump wires from the ignition as the Cougar shuddered into what was almost certain death. "We're going on."

Farnes got out, advanced through the scorching afternoon sun to the abandoned van. Up front, its hood was raised, the battery missing.

The skipper condensed beside him. "You see, Farnes, the battery's missing!"

"I see that."

"It won't run without a battery and here we are, stuck, because you—"

"Shut up, Skipper," Lorraine said. "We've got a battery in the Cougar if you stop jawin' long enough to let us switch it."

The skipper fell into a gloomy silence.

Farnes went to work, emplaced the Cougar's battery in the Dodge van, checked the rest of the engine, found nothing obviously wrong. Only the battery was missing. But if someone in need had just stopped and taken it, why had it been abandoned in the first place? The driver was gone, disappeared without trace. Maybe someone had pulled up alongside, brandished a gun, told him to pull over. Maybe. Or maybe, as Lorraine had suggested, they had just run out of gas and been forced to walk.

He leaned into the cab and began to work open the dash panel to hotwire it when his head struck and jingled the keys, still dangling in the tumbler. He climbed into the driver's seat and rotated the ignition key counterclockwise. Lights. Buzzing from 103 on the FM dial. Power. Idiot lights showed no circuit problems. But the fuel gauge pegged at empty.

"We have to siphon over," he said. "Let's push the Cougar forward. Skipper?"

"Yeah, okay."

"Lorraine, stand watch."

"Larry, there's nobody—"

"Lorraine?"

"All right," she said.

As soon as the last precious fumes from the Cougar were aspirated into the van, they transferred all the weapons and supplies to the back, secured the rear doors, and pulled away. Leaning against the side in the aft compartment, the skipper only said, "Great! Bigger target."

In the front seat beside Farnes, Lorraine said, "Great! Air conditioning!"

Farnes smiled as she let the jets of air blow over her soaked and stretched ringlets, suggested, "Maybe we can get room service in Atlanta."

"Not if the Russians get there first," said the skipper.

Or if someone along the way gets trigger-happy with a rocket launcher. Or if they ran into a vigilante roadblock, or an armored column of tanks, or ran out of fuel. But as clusters of still neat residences began to spring up on the outskirts of Macon, he pushed those fears into the deepest locker of his mind and his foot down on the accelerator. If they could avoid trouble, they could be in Atlanta in less than three hours. If . . .

# BAIT AND SWITCH

Unable to draw heat and water from the land, Hurricane Clyde stalled and weakened. Since landing and moving north, Clyde had softened to a tropical storm that cast weak, scattered gray clouds in low slabs over the Georgia landscape. Like so many others, it was dying. But the death of a single enemy, Yustechenko knew, never decides a battle. Certainly not when a new, more powerful one rises up to replace it.

He learned enough from Colonel Boshti's communication to guess that the war had entered a new, deadlier phase. A low-flying plane had dusted the Soviet Western Armor Column with something, no one knew what. If it were chemical, it would go to work immediately, its effects diminishing with time. But if biological, it would show no immediate effects, instead incubating over time, only to strike hard later. And so far, Colonel Boshti's soldiers reported no symptoms from the strike.

So it had come to that.

So desperate were the Americans in defense of their homeland that they were willing to unleash a new germ against the invaders. He smiled. It reminded him of the sacrifices his father had made in thwarting the Nazis in the Great Patriotic War. But with a difference.

If the scenario ran its course, each side striking the other with an unknown infection, each side short of resources and organization, support and intelligence, each side pinned down in battle, then both sides would die. When they engaged a few miles ahead, someone would win the battle. But it was coming to look as if no one would win the war.

All dead.

What difference from nuclear war?

Only that the land could be re-occupied, with none of the

chronic problems of radioactivity, no damage to buildings, industries, crops, or technologies.

He stood upright in the turret of the bouncing APC, northbound on the open ribbon of pavement the Americans called Interstate 75. One hundred miles due south of the American Georgia city of Macon, Yustechenko ordered his column to pull onto the shoulder of the road. Before dismounting, he muttered, "Get the doctor up here," to his communication's specialist.

From a protected position in the middle of the column, a single figure double-timed forward. When he reached Yustechenko he snapped off a sharp salute, swallowed hard, and kept panting.

"It is hot, Comrade Doctor, is it not?"

"Humid and hot, yes."

"You are not running a fever, are you?"

"No, sir."

"Any of the men?"

"No, sir. Not that I can tell. I have no complaints."

"What are you carrying to defend against biological attack?"

"Sir?"

"Something wrong with your ears, Comrade Doctor?"

"We were told to . . ."

"I know, I know! Keep our distance. But the Western Armor Column has been sprayed."

"The medic reports no . . ."

"Give it time, Comrade Doctor. I think the Americans have returned the favor."

"Certainly not . . . their stocks were . . ."

"Destroyed? You believe that?"

"But—"

"The question, Comrade Doctor."

"If attacked, we were to use standard antibiotic and antivirals."

"Then you were provisioned?"

The doctor just shook his head. "It was figured the American die-off would be so fast that we could simply provision as we went along."

"While fighting for our lives with eight thousand men? Simply, as you put it, drop by the local American pharmacy?"

Idiots!

The doctor blinked, shook his head, said again, "We have no specific treatment for . . . we could not guess what they might choose . . . carrying a whole inventory of drugs would . . . and even if we did, they could go up in a single explosion."

Just then the communications specialist ran up to Yustechenko. Gasping in the hot August air, he said, "Colonel Boshti reports one man ill. High fever, bloody cough, incoherence . . ."

Yustechenko said, "Tell Boshti to leave him behind."

"Sir?"

"I didn't say shoot him."

"Yes, sir."

"And pass the order to don protective gear."

"Yes, sir."

As the communication's specialist raced forward to relay Yustechenko's orders to all units, the doctor slid in beside him and whispered, "The men will be hot as hell in that gear!"

Yustechenko's eyes bored through him as he replied, "Perhaps. But I promise you one thing, Comrade Doctor. On the eyes of my mother, a hotter hell awaits them outside it."

Yustechenko's spearhead armor column whirred at sixty-five kph, apparently headed directly north on I-75. Their movement would read to the opposition as vectoring Atlanta through Macon.

Close.

But not close enough.

His plan was already deploying in a way the enemy could not guess. As he sat inside the protective shell of the APC he rolled up the surveillance map and almost smiled. Nothing he did conformed to traditional Soviet battle tactics. Moscow would never approve.

But Moscow was not fighting the war.

Yustechenko was.

And if he had to succeed with eight thousand men plus reinforcements, he would have to play his way.

The problem with traditional Soviet army battle plans is that they depended on overwhelming the enemy with numbers, accepting large losses, forcing comparable losses to the other side, then winning on numbers, courage, stubbornness.

Typical Slav thinking. If you can't find the latch, batter down the door with your head.

Not Yustechenko.

Before leaving Florida he had stopped the column and briefed the Iron Hammer Brigade on his plan for them. They were to commandeer idle American automobiles, load them with weaponry, drive them north to the battle area. There they were to disperse and deploy as counterinsurgents, searching for, engaging, and destroying Special Forces Rangers from Fort Benning wherever they found them.

No, he told them, he did not expect a large, well-coordinated counterattack. The infection had destroyed men, maintenance, initiative, and communication. Some organized resistance would remain. He was ready for that. But the most significant enemy would be trained guerrillas, picking off vehicles one by one. No one knew this better than the Lion of Afghanistan.

He checked his watch.

The white dials showed sixteen hundred hours and forty-five minutes. He sat crouched down in his low seat, the sweat pooling inside his protective suit, only his hands and head free.

Soon.

Overhead, above the hissing clatter of the treads on pavement, he heard, or thought he heard, the IL-76 transports passing. From their modified cargo bays, three thousand Soviet elite paratroopers would drop just north of the battle zone.

Their canopies would bubble the hazy sky, just about now. It was light and they would drift down, some picked off by enemy fire. But numbers would triumph. Besides, to drop them later, into the gathering thunderstorms, would be murder.

He checked his watch, nervous and tense.

In minutes they would be drifting into fields, some snagged in trees, others bogged down in ponds, each doing his best to drop his chute, haul his gear, and find his unit. Then they would sweep south on foot, joining up with the Iron Hammer Brigades counterinsurgency unit.

Together they would funnel the enemy forces southeast, cutting off retreat.

The Americans would not resist.

The wedge of Soviet paratroopers was not pushing them

exactly where they wanted to go—to meet the main Soviet armor column, Yustechenko's spearhead group, and destroy it with antitank weapons.

They were the bait.

And Yustechenko would keep them on the hook just long enough.

The radioman turned back and told his general, "Colonel Boshti reports his unit is between Plains and Americus, taking up positions."

"Tell them to hold, await my order," Yustechenko said.

At the right moment, Boshti's FST-1 tanks would spring from the cover of trees, barns, and kudzu, and charge northeast, closing off any retreat to the south, trapping any attacking American tanks in a withering cross-fire.

One way out for them now.

The Americans would be forced due east.

Toward Yustechenko's spearhead group.

Where they wanted to be, the battle the Americans figured they needed to win. If they did, they would stop the invasion in its tracks. So on they would come.

Outside and above him, flanking their advance, the huge, heavily armed Hind-24D helicopter gunships swept by. In constant motion to avoid American Stinger ground-to-air missiles, they closed, crossed over, and switched back, close cover against columns of American armor.

Farther above, thousands of meters over their heads, the shrieking rattle of interceptors told him that the last of the U.S. Navy F-14 Tomcats, each one bristling deadly Maverick air-to-ground missiles, were tightly engaged by MiG-29 Fulcrums launched from the Soviet carrier *Petrov,* now cruising one hundred kilometers off Florida's Gulf coast.

Only Yustechenko and twelve tank commanders he had briefed last night knew that they would not engage the opposition.

They were the bait.

They would close and turn, battle formation.

Then they would disengage and run hard east on Georgia state road 18. Left without retreat, the Americans would follow, pursue.

Then Yustechenko would spring the trap.

The Soviet Eastern Armor column, the third tine of the spearhead, had switched behind and east of them en route north. Now it parked, silent and hidden, off the north shoulder of Georgia state road 27, waiting. On the order, they would charge straight north overland and cut off the pursuing American column while Yustechenko raced northeast on 26 to Interstate 16.

At that point he would thrust north with all possible speed, toward Atlanta. He had his target and his orders. He was a soldier, would obey. Even if he understood that the Centers for Disease control was perhaps the only place that could stop the death, he had his orders. But none of his orders said his men would be without medical support. If Moscow, for whatever reason, had not provided, Yustechenko would have to do what every good soldier does in a pinch: improvise.

Before he headed north, he would dispatch sappers of the Iron Hammer Brigade in a Hind-24 helicopter gunship to the one place he knew a good doctor to be. It was a little barrier island on the Georgia seacoast, now converted to a prison. Yustechenko decided to commute the sentence of one of those men, a certain Dr. Larry Farnes.

Yes, Moscow wanted Farnes dead.

But Yustechenko himself would determine the timing of execution. For the moment, if Farnes was alive, he wanted to keep him that way.

Interrupting Yustechenko's contemplation, the driver snapped a glance back and shouted, "American tanks! M-1A1s and Bradleys! North by northwest, turning to engage!"

# THE NEW SOUTH

Just outside Macon they pulled the van over long enough to siphon fifteen gallons of premium from a locked Cadillac Eldorado with tinted glass before flashing through town, weaving around and past the stalled, crashed, or derelict cars littering the streets, straight out the other side without any intention of stopping again. At least twice Farnes thought he heard the crack of a rifle shot, but they were not hit. In the deadly still midday heat, smoke and flames leapt from two buildings destined to join a graveyard of others they had passed, already scorched and gutted by runaway blazes, now silent, charred, smoke-streaked brick and steel frames still baking in the infernal sun. Outside the speeding van the sun was bright and searing. What exactly was the temperature? They had no way to tell. The remaining bank signs were running dots of random numbers, still displaying, but in a mindless, automatic, uncommunicative way. And from the broad range of the radio frequencies only one program broke the funereal static, and that was prerecorded, on the civil defense emergency network.

They listened in silence to the baritone announcer.

"This is the Emergency Broadcast Network. This is not a test. Yesterday, a new, lethal sickness spread to every region of the United States. Federal authorities are unsure of its nature or origin. Private and government research centers are working around the clock to identify the responsible germ and devise a cure. At this hour they have not been successful.

"Until researchers are able to produce a cure, or provide a vaccine, civil authorities are recommending that individuals who have not contracted the disease avoid contact with infectious individuals. Further, they recommend consuming only canned goods, drinking only bottled water, traveling as little as possible. Emergency response centers are being set up at local hospitals to care for infected individuals.

"Cooperation with authorized civilian authorities is necessary for recovery. In several cities, looting has jeopardized travelers and endangered residents. The National Guard has been authorized to shoot to kill if necessary to retain control. Some experts expect that the infection will run its course in a week. Until then individuals are strongly advised to stay indoors.

"Domestic protection against looters, intruders, and thieves was approved last night by a telephone conference of the Council of Governors.

"From the Republican convention in Miami, the President issued this message:

'Fellow Americans. We are in the midst of one of the most serious health epidemics in all history. Not since the Black Death in Europe has there been a disease of this deadliness, speed, or extent. Our best people are at work around the clock, looking for cure. I have full confidence that they will succeed. In the meantime, each of us must conjure the goodness and decency that I trust in God all Americans have, and continue to preserve order, property, and life. When this terrible crisis is over, I hope we can look back with pride at how we shouldered the awful burden of this tragedy, and carried on with hope. Good luck and God bless.' "

The message started to recycle:

"This is the Emergency Broadcast Network . . ."

Farnes reached up and shut it off. They rode along, their silence broken only by the whistling hum of the air conditioner that kept them, for the first time since leaving the prison, cool, comfortable, even, if only through exhaustion, relaxed. Only the skipper had a complaint. "The AC is chewing up a hell of a lot of fuel, you know?"

"I think we can afford it," Farnes said. "We only have

eighty miles to go to Atlanta, maybe another twenty after that to CDC. If we can make twelve miles a gallon, there's enough gas for that, even with the AC. There's no need to be miserable.''

The skipper made a growling sound, thunked his head against the hollow steel van wall.

As the silence began to enclose them, Lorraine cut in. ''I wonder if the tape deck works.''

Farnes suggested, ''Try it,'' figuring that if discomfort was unnecessary, depression was every bit as undesirable.

''Okay,'' Lorraine responded, pulling a tape from the glove compartment.

''What is it?''

''Bob Marley. Reggae.''

Farnes snapped his fingers, winced. ''Here I was sure there'd be a little Chopin.''

Ignoring him, Lorraine was bouncing in her seat as the first bars burst from the wraparound speakers. ''We gotta loosen you up, boy. Ain't got no room for tightass egghead Yankees in the New South.''

Along I-75 northbound to Atlanta Lorraine kept bouncing in the front seat, twisting back and forth to the reggae beat while Farnes held the van at a steady seventy-five, cutting through the sizzling heat. In the back, the skipper's coughing resumed, now intensified. Uncertain at first, Farnes became less confident in the man's self-diagnosis. It didn't sound like an allergic cough. In fact, it sounded like something quite different. If so, there was nothing he could do for the man except to hope they would get him to CDC on time. If they could, he could buy time while they fumbled at a cure.

Yet time was becoming a problem. Not on the road. In fact they were chewing up the seamed white concrete blocks of interstate, flashing by abandoned or stalled cars, cars out of fuel, or, as the van had been, out of batteries and parts. Some cars were out of drivers, the bodies hanging through the windows, bloodstained vomit streaked on their doors, some others dangling from open doors, snagged by seat belts, still others dragged away and half-gnawed to blood and bones, probably by packs of dogs. Farnes could tell one of them a mile away from the circle of carrion crows overhead. Still, as ghastly and numbing as the dead were, his concerns were not with them.

He was more worried about the living. Since the epidemic struck he had seen enough of what they became to convince him that no miracle this side of Judgment Day would save them. But so far they had been lucky. No organized resistance, no more ambushes, nor cross fire.

And except for the heavy stuff—armor-piercing bullets, rockets, anti-tank missiles and rifle-grenades—Farnes wasn't concerned. A high-speed target was hard to hit, its tires harder to puncture than a motionless one.

"I wonder what it feels like to die," the skipper asked. His voice, echoing off the naked walls in the back, seemed almost disembodied. Farnes shot a glance back at him. Clammy with sweat, despite the AC. Not good. For the first time he wondered if Lorraine was really immune, or if she had just been lucky enough to . . . Stop it, his discipline demanded.

"Everyone dies," Farnes said. "It's just a matter of when."

"And how," the skipper's voice echoed, remained distant. "I was just wondering how it felt when they . . ."

"They?"

"The people I buried . . ."

That was it, Farnes suddenly realized. In a spasm of decency the skipper had ignored Farnes' advice and decided to bury some people. But unless he made other contact, the corpses still harbored the germs. Brilliant! Diabolical, but brilliant. If the infectious organism remains virulent a few hours beyond death, its spread would be accelerated by the civilized act of burial. And for both religious and health reasons, burial will continue until they learn of the risk. As Farnes both expected and feared, the Soviets had explored every way to spread the epidemic.

". . . they looked so terrible, so shocked, as if they were fighting for air and couldn't get it and so, just suffocated." Another cough.

"We don't know enough about this thing to say," Farnes told him.

The skipper gave up a single dry cough and went on. "What was it Coleridge said in the 'Ancient Mariner'? 'Water, water everywhere, nor any drop to drink.' Well here it seemed like, air, air everywhere, but not a breath to pull."

"That's one mechanism," Farnes said.

"What?"

"Respiratory paralysis. It's well known to workers in the field, ours and the Soviets. Hell, even the Chinese. It's no big secret. A lot of these bugs are designed to anesthetize the autonomic nerves controlling breathing. I've seen effects on mice, dogs, even chimps. But like any other weapons system, the designers were never confident with the latest trick, so they threw in backups to ensure overkill. If respiratory paralysis doesn't kill fast enough, the fancier bugs do other nasty things, like inducing disorientation, madness. That part they took from nature. Hydrophobia, rabies."

"I just hope I don't have to go through that," he wheezed.

"So do I," Farnes said.

Lorraine had dialed the reggae down, was listening to the conversation, reading Farnes' expression like a book.

The skipper coughed. "I've been through enough already."

"You wanta talk about it?" Lorraine said, unbuckling, climbing into the back.

In the rearview mirror Farnes watched the skipper bury his face in his hands, begin to sob. "I didn't want to hurt him, I didn't want to steal. I just wanted a place to hide until all this . . . all this just passed. But when he caught me he just wasn't going to listen. He hit me in the stomach, hard, and laughed. I was lying on the floor, gasping for air, and he was . . . was just laughing. Then he kicked me with those boots and I really thought I was going to pass out. And I couldn't move, couldn't struggle, couldn't fight, and that's when he did it . . ."

"Did it?" Lorraine's voice had dropped to a whisper, drained up from the back. "Did what?"

Farnes snapped off the tape.

The skipper said, "I couldn't help it!"

"It's okay, Skipper," she said. Farnes watched her run her hand soothingly through his hair, pull his head against her shoulder. "Just say it. Get rid of it."

"It was horrible!"

Lorraine said nothing.

"It hurt . . . he hurt me . . . and I couldn't breathe. I thought I would die. After I wished I had . . . even wished, hoped, he was going to kill me. But he didn't. He said he needed me," he sobbed, "to ride point for him."

"Shhhhh," she cooed. "He's not gonna hurt you. He can't hurt you. He's dead."

"I'm glad. I'm actually *glad*. I'm only sorry, sorry, sorry . . ."

"What?" she asked.

"That I couldn't have killed him myself."

And suddenly Farnes understood what had happened at the ambush, and could again.

"Fifty miles to Atlanta," Farnes said.

"How long is that?" Lorraine said.

"Another hour, if all goes well."

As soon as he said it, he wished he hadn't. How much had gone well the last two days? And how much more could go wrong?

Atlanta was only twenty miles away, its skyline not quite visible on the horizon, when the red idiot light indicated that the engine was overheating. Without hesitating, he eased the van over to check it out.

Still in the back, holding the sleeping skipper's head, Lorraine said, "What's wrong, Larry?"

Before he could respond she asked, "We out of gas?"

He shook his head no. "The engine may be overheated."

"Maybe the skipper was right. Maybe we shouldn't have used the AC."

Farnes popped the hood release, pushed open the door, and circled to the front of the van. Grabbing the hood burned enough to make him hiss, "Shit!" and yank his hands back.

Reflexively he peeled off his shirt, wrapped his hands, opened the hood. No smoke. Smelled all right. He uncapped the radiator slowly, applying pressure, felt the rush of expanding vapor. The green coolant was full enough to top the pan. Not likely with an overheating problem. Not enough boiled off. No sign it had siphoned over from expansion.

He tried the oil dipstick, found it showed the level of soiled oil high.

Could be a failed send switch.

That was the problem with idiot lights, the lazy man's guide to problems. Full-range gauges show the temperature creeping up, confirm the problem, allow you to anticipate and respond before it disables. With idiot lights you never knew if the problem was real or electrical failure.

If he drove on and it was a problem, the van would die, seize up from internal friction or burn up from an oil fire, leaving them stranded. If it wasn't a problem, they were just wasting time for no reason.

What to do?

Lorraine was quickly beside him, brushing her hand through her sparkling hair, asking, "What's up?"

"The light shows the engine's overheated, but I don't think so," he said, wiping his hands on his shirt.

"Coolant?" she asked.

"Full."

"Oil?"

"Okay, more or less."

"Engine block?"

"No hotter than you'd expect."

"Well, the skipper is."

Farnes turned her way. "Say again?"

"He's hot, Larry. Burning up. I think he's got it." Her throat bobbed as she broke. "And I'm scared I might, too. I'm sorry. I should be thinking about him but . . . I'm just so afraid. I don't know I'm immune. I mean I might have just been lucky . . . or it was really in the water and you . . . we don't know . . . I . . ."

"Shhhh," Farnes cradled her in his arms, rocked her. "I think you're okay. You're an anomaly."

"I am? What's an anomaly?"

"Right now it's a very healthy thing to be."

"For real?"

He nodded.

"What if I was sick, Larry!"

"You're not."

"But what if I was? Could you cure me, make me well?"

Farnes took the question the way he had every medical problem, aggressively, confidently, some would say—had said—arrogantly, but tough problems don't succumb to humility. At another level he felt an absolute rage to believe—if only for Lorraine's sake—that the answer had to be the one he gave her. "Yes, of course I could."

She blinked, smiled, wiped the tears from her eyes. "Then you can cure the skipper, too."

Farnes winced. "I . . . uh . . . don't know. I just . . ."

"Why? I don't understand. If you could cure me, then why can't you . . . I don't understand."

"Because diseases have their own clock, Lorraine. In rabies and bubonic plague it doesn't matter if you saturate a patient with the most powerful antibiotics in the world after a certain time. You have to treat early or the patient will die.''

''How early?''

''That depends on the disease.''

''You're playing doctor's games with me. I *hate* that.''

''I'm telling you the truth,'' he snapped back, watched her head recoil with his unintended force. ''If you ask me about bubonic plague or rabies I can tell you exactly how long, and what medicines you should get. But I don't even know what this is, let alone anything about it except how fast people die. And we've both already seen that.''

''You mean how fast *most* people die, am I right?''

He nodded his head, grudgingly conceding her point. It mattered. There was no standard human body. No standard immune system. That's why some people survived the most virulent diseases and some perished from negligible ones. But on average most people are in the middle. When it comes to dread diseases, the uninoculated will die. At different rates, some sooner, some later on. But eventually they all die. That was the first and great fact of medical school, the one that let you off the hook of agonizing guilt, the one that led into what seemed like detached callousness, the one that confronted you day and night with your own pathetic limitations, but the one that, after all the wailing and gnashing of teeth, remained incontrovertibly true. Epidemics kill in great numbers. They litter the earth with dead and send survivors running for cover. Except for nuclear war, no single force can so devastate mankind as a new, virulent, and drug-resistant microorganism. It just goes on killing and killing and killing until it can't find another victim. Then it, too, dies.

Normally there were ways to play for time, to use good guesses to spell the patient while you groped for a cure, to treat the symptoms, inhabit the mechanism of infection or rate of spread and pray the immune system could show up for the fourth quarter and put enough points on the scoreboard to win the game. They had done that with a Lassa fever victim at Yale whose temperature reached a hundred and eight. They packed her in ice, infused her with interferon and gamma globulin, and prayed. It worked. Her recovery took six months, was not complete even then. But they saved her.

But they had three things Farnes didn't: time, technology, and staff support. Still, he was a doctor. And there were lots of stories of doctors who worked miracles with pluck, com-

mon sense, and inspiration. It was easy to find a legitimate
reason to quit on a patient, a disease, or an epidemic, letting
nature and time determine the outcome, trusting in the numbers and isolation to win a battle that couldn't be won in the
lab. But that approach wasn't going to work here. The evidence was pretty clear on that. It lay around them decaying,
the numbers growing hourly.

And he dreaded it would not stop, even if everybody hid.

He sensed that the Soviets, confident enough to start this
thing, would never have considered it without a multivector
strategy. The multivector strategy wasn't new. It was a pop-
ular conversational game as far back as Herman Kahn. And
it required that biowar epidemics not depend on one link that
could easily be broken by organized cooperation inside the
nation under attack. Doing that meant that the disease in-
fecting people be transmissible by other vectors: dogs, bats,
mosquitoes, anything that could spread and attack survivors.
The dying who lay helpless and the dead who followed would
feed the chain of propagation.

Lorraine snapped him back. "Larry?"

"I'll look at him now."

When Farnes pulled himself into the cab and stared into
the aft compartment, he saw the skipper maniacally grinning,
the single barrel of the sawed-off shotgun staring back.

"Easy, Skipper," he said, backing away.

"I know you want to kill me," he said, drooling a frothy
spittle from the corner of his mouth.

"No one wants to hurt you."

Lorraine's voice, flooded with concern, entered the van.
"Skipper?"

Farnes held up his hand, signaled her to stay back. Here
was another aspect of the disease he feared would strike. As
in many diseases, those who resisted quick death ran into
complications: temporary madness and hysteria with high fe-
vers, neurological assault, and permanent madness from infections themselves. And nothing destroys stability like a
single madman with an automatic weapon, loosed on an unprotected crowd. What would happen in a country filled with
them?

He didn't want to think about it, held the skipper's eyes
steadily, said, "We want to help you."

"You want to KILL ME!" he screamed.

Farnes switched quickly, forced time to slow down, felt

himself slip quickly between the bucket seats as the skipper's hand seemed to take forever sliding the pump action of the scattergun, allowing Farnes' right foot to kick up, knock the muzzle up before the cartridge exploded, blowing out the roof directly above.

The shock of the kick knocked the skipper off balance, leaving him tumbling back, his hands frozen to the handle and pump, rolling over like a wasp in early spring as Farnes vaulted through the ringing silence and seized the barrel.

Outside the word, "Larry!" cut through the ringing as the second blast perforated the van's side.

By that time he had locked the trigger with one finger, the pump action with the other hand, and was wrestling the skipper, who fought demonically, elbowing, kicking, biting, screaming, "MURDERER!"

Farnes managed to knock him out the rear doors of the van, onto the gravel shoulder, ripping the shotgun from his grip. But the skipper, frenzied with madness, scrabbled away, pounced to his feet, charged back. He reached Farnes in the middle of a maniacal scream, was met with a deftly aimed rabbit punch, crumpled unconscious into a heap of pallid, panting flesh.

Lorraine's hands were over her mouth, her eyes wide with terror.

"You're not going to kill him?"

The question stung. "No. But I don't know if I can do anything for him. And I can't let him endanger what we have to do."

"You're not going to just leave him here?"

"No," Farnes sighed, not knowing why. "Let's get him in."

Together they slid the skipper into the flat rear, laid him down. Lorraine said, "He's still burning up."

"Use the water in the canteen, try to keep him cool," Farnes said.

"What else?"

"That's all," he said, "unless we can get something in him."

"What?"

"I don't know. I have some guesses. Something from Shagmyer's in Darien, maybe. A long shot, not likely. Nothing else we have now. Maybe in a drugstore along the way, if we can safely stop. But I think the shelves will already be empty.''

"Until then, what?''

Farnes had a deeper sigh, felt the helplessness sweep over him like a huge wave. "Until then, tie his hands together.''

"What?''

"Use anything, just make sure they're secure.''

"Why?''

"Because if he revives—''

"If?''

"If he revives, he'll be even crazier than before. He'll try to kill you.''

"Larry, I don't think so.''

Farnes moved forward, dropped into the driver's seat, looked back. "And keep your face away from his.''

"What do you think? I'm going to French-kiss him?''

Farnes tried to smile but couldn't. "No. But he's going to wake up biting. He'll try for your nose, your ears, even your throat.''

He watched her blanch. "You *are* shitting me. Right, Farnes?''

"I wish I were,'' he said, starting the engine.

"So what do we do?''

"For the skipper?''

"Yeah. And the rest,'' she whispered.

He pointed out the window, to the north. "Any hope is there.'' Yet he knew as he said it how little hope there was for the skipper. And he knew, too, that the minute they got to Atlanta they could be walking right into a feudal nightmare unequaled in history. It was heaven and it was hell. But it was the only chance they had.

As he pulled away, the red TEMP light kept glowing. Ignoring it, he put his foot down and pushed the van to seventy, eighty as the hot, wet air howled in the new gaps of the van. As they cleared the next ridge he saw, in the distance, the jagged rubble of skyscrapers that was, once upon a past, the great city of Atlanta.

And now?

# HEAVEN AND HELL

Ignoring the steady glow of the idiot light, the van sliced through the midsummer swelter, its speedometer hitting seventy, eighty, and climbing before the van began to shudder. Before Farnes could even think "Shit!" Lorraine was screaming behind him. Turreting his head he saw her kicking, slapping, pushing at the skipper's snarling, twisting, clawing body. All humanity vanished, leaving a feral animal thrashing so violently the whole chassis shook.

Farnes hit the brake, jerking Lorraine free, throwing the skipper forward. The tires screamed, their smoking skid filling the cabin with acrid fumes. As soon as the speedometer dropped to forty, he yanked the van off the road, throwing the madman against the open hole in the van.

As the van crunched to a halt in the roadside gravel, Lorraine was still screaming, whatever the skipper had become still snarling, clawing, snorting. Exploding between the bucket seats, Farnes thought only of Lorraine. All instinct and no plan, he had no advantage, no leverage, no striking power. He cursed himself for making such an uncalculated move. Yet he had moved reflexively, without hesitation or doubt, now shifting to regain his balance.

With one foot he bashed open the rear doors and pushed Lorraine out, keeping the other foot and both hands busy deflecting the skipper's snapping jaws and clicking teeth.

Not a second after Lorraine was clear, Farnes spun, rolled, and coiled into attack position just outside. Like a ravenous tiger, the skipper leapt in pursuit. Farnes' hands responded. The heel of one palm struck hard beneath the skipper's chin, producing a sickening snap that meant just one thing. Broken neck. Fractured at the more levered cervical vertebrae, just below the *foramen magnum*.

The skipper's body hit the gravel with a lifeless crunch. It didn't move, didn't twitch, except the fingers, all coiling slowly, as if life was just within their grasp.

Farnes felt sick.

He had never killed a man before yesterday. Before this moment he never killed anyone he knew, or with his hands. Now it seemed it would just go on like this, kill or be killed, until it was over.

He was still panting when he turned his rage on Lorraine. "I thought I told you to tie his goddamn hands!"

"Don't scream at me!" she yelled back, her body racked with sobs, her dress torn, scratch marks across her tender flesh.

"Sorry," he said, bending down to feel for a pulse.

"He's dead," she said.

"Yes."

"You didn't need to *kill* him."

"I wasn't *trying* to kill him."

"Liar!"

He spun, looked. "You were jealous, just like all men. You didn't need to be, but you were. You're all the same when it comes to jealousy. You just want to kill the other guy."

Farnes softened his tone, pleading, "I was just trying to knock him out. Come on—" He held out his hand, but she backed away, dropped to her knees, let in the grief. It wasn't just the skipper. Maybe it wasn't even the skipper. It was all of it. Suddenly it had hit.

"When will it end?" she screamed.

"I don't know," he said back, sorry for his honesty. For her sake he should have said "Soon," even if he didn't believe it. At this point he felt he would say anything for her sake. Instead he said only, "Come on, let's go."

"Bury him," she said.

"What?"

"This isn't anyone. We knew him."

Farnes wondered what possible difference it could make. Certainly none to the skipper. He was beyond caring. None to him, because there had been so many deaths all he could think about was preventing more. Certainly none to the abstract concept of decency, which seemed to have fled in wholesale retreat in the first hour of the epidemic. But from her eyes he could see it would make a difference to Lorraine.

She'd been through enough. It was time to slow down. So he said, "Okay."

He dragged the body to the woods bordering the interstate, found a spot beneath a banner of Spanish moss, tore away the kudzu, and etched a shallow trough using the stock of the .22 rifle. Even though the sun was sinking and the shade forgiving, the air was dense and wet, making his task an ordeal. Driven by some inner demon, Lorraine joined him, puffing, pulling the orange clay with her bare hands until they had created, by twilight, a narrow slot, uneven, crude, two and a bit feet shallow, into which they lowered the skipper's body, crossed his hands, covered it with clay.

Knocking the dirt off his hands, Farnes stood up, sighed, whispered, "Let's go."

"Some words," she said.

He just blinked back.

"To remember him by. He had a life. We need to say something."

"Go ahead," Farnes said.

She drew herself up, back straight, chest out, the dress the dead man had just torn hanging in tatters from her left shoulder. "We remember you, Skipper. You didn't do no harm, not till the end. Then it wasn't your fault. You tried for a better world. Maybe that will come. Amen."

She looked expectantly at Farnes. "Now you."

"Me?"

"You knew him, too."

Farnes found a thought, brought it into words, "Thanks for the boat ride, Skipper—Burt. We wouldn't be here without you. That's worth a lot."

"Amen," Lorraine said.

He looked in her face, recognized the clinical signs of exhaustion, stress, or disorientation. That would have been enough. But the van was low on gas, the next supply uncertain. Overhead the eastern sky was inky with the coming evening, the clouds gathering in long, curdled lines that promised rain. What sun remained was tentative and diffuse, spawning long tendriled shadows. In Atlanta they would *need* light. By this time streetlights, the sentinels of security, would be broken or dark. Civilization was breaking up before their eyes. Taking his own fatigue into account, he took a deep breath, puffed up his cheeks, and let it out. "We stop here. Get some sleep. Tomorrow we move."

"Sure," she said weakly. "I guess that means I have to whip something up by campfire."

"No," Farnes said. He took a deep breath and explained, "Fire tells someone else where we are and it tells them we have food. If they don't have any, they kill us to get it. Even if they do, they could kill us for other reasons."

"Such as?" Lorraine stood akimbo, evidently sure that Farnes just wanted to keep her away from other men. He surprised her by saying, "Like you."

"What? Larry, I swear—"

The heat in his eyes was enough to stop her tirade. "Oh, I'm not jealous, Lorraine. I haven't the energy or opportunity for jealousy. It's fear—terror, actually—that just puts everything else in perspective."

She blinked, her eyes fluttered, an eloquent enough response. Then she turned, pulled the torn flap of dress over her shoulder, and cantered off toward the van, her hips shifting provocatively. Looking back over her shoulder she said, "Well, you gonna just stay there, or can I tempt you with a can of cold ham and beans?"

Leaving the skipper to the earth, Farnes followed her, knowing that Lorraine needed nothing other than herself to tempt any man. He wondered about that, whether under normal conditions he would have given her more than an appreciative glance, wondered what it was that was happening and where, finally, it was leading. But it didn't hold his attention. Tomorrow seemed far away. Tonight was much closer. And nothing was certain, nothing at all.

"Looks like cold beans and pineapple slices," she said, "and you know what that can do inside you."

They sat together in the back of the van, nested under a fall of Spanish moss in the shade of a dying oak tree, well back from the shoulder of the road, out of view. Farnes considered tearing up kudzu and camouflaging it, but the maroon and white panels resisted the idea of disguise, so he gave it up.

Through the hole the shotgun blew in the roof, the first faint stars began to speckle the indigo sky. Far to the west, visible through the other blown-out hole, the last searing orange band had begun to cool and die, surrendering to night. With the fading pastel sky, the condensing shadows deepened and darkened into a creaking, chirping, hissing wilderness.

Out of the cacophonous darkness seeping along the eastern horizon, the muted rumbling of thunder washed over them.

After leaning back, Farnes reached up and slapped the evening's first mosquito.

Lorraine heard it and laughed. "Pesky little buggers, ain't they?"

"I can maybe plug these holes."

She grabbed his arm. "I don't expect the Hilton, Larry. Enough to be alive."

Then she passed him an open can of beans and, except for her quiet chewing, went silent. After she swallowed half a mouthful, she said, "You believe in *any* kind of life after death, Larry?"

He shook his head.

"I don't know whether I believe it or not. I used to for sure, used to think that's the one place Momma deserved for sure."

"Your mother died?"

"When I was twelve, yeah."

"Sorry."

"You didn't have nothing to do with it."

"I can still be sorry."

"Somebody should. She was a good person."

"How did she die?"

"She died with an infection. Doctors never found out what exactly it was. Guess we didn't have very smart doctors back then, Larry."

"Even the best doctors can't—"

"Took a long time. She fought it, mostly by herself. Doctors gave her medicine, okay, but we never did decide if the medicine was worse than the disease."

"Was it cancer?"

"Nope. Just a long wasting illness. Never figured out what. Death certificate gave cause of death that way, said just, 'After a long illness,' you believe that? People just die and they don't know what killed 'em?"

"Sometimes."

"Bet the really *good* doctors would know."

Farnes laughed.

"Whatsamatter?"

"The really good doctors would make you believe they knew what killed her, give a cause of death, but if they couldn't cure her of an infection, why does that make them any better than the country doctor?''

"I don't know." Another silence, then, "But you know what?''

"What?'' Farnes spooned the beans in, tasted the salt, gobbled at tough strands of pork, soft globs of fat.

"I don't remember her as dead. No sir. I remember her the way she was when we went to Six Flags Over Georgia.''

"The amusement park?''

"Right. Best damn time. Jesus! Momma used to fix lunch, pile us into the pickup, my brother and me, Daddy, and we'd take off for the day, take off early, sometimes before the sun was up, so as we could have a whole day there. We'd take our bathing suits, too.''

"They had a swimming pool?''

She laughed, an infectious laugh with a little shriek in it. He loved the sound. Then she said, "No swimming pool. You don't drive over a hundred miles for a swimmin' pool when you're ten miles from the beach at home. No sir. At Six Flags Over Georgia they got White Water Park. People over five states come just for that. They got cascades and slides and raft rides down these gorges, all sorts of stuff. A course we'd never actually get wet until we did all the rides.''

"Roller coasters?'' Farnes asked, spooning out the last of his beans.

"The Great American Scream Machine!''

"The what?''

"Just about the hairiest roller coaster ride you ever had.''

"I don't know . . .''

"It is! I swear it! We should go there someday and . . .''

Farnes put his can down. "Where are those pineapple slices?''

"Here.'' She handed the can over in the darkness.

He slurped one down.

Lorraine sighed, went on. "So every once in a blue moon we'd go there. That's what I remember most about Momma. She'd do all the rides, just like a kid. Shoulda heard her scream on the damn roller coaster. Her scream scared me more than the damn ride, Larry. You believe that?''

"Sure,'' he said.

"Anyway, it was Momma convinced me there had to be a heaven, just for her, 'cause she was always there. Three squares on the table, everything clean and washed and ironed, all orderly like. And I never heard complaints from Daddy, so you know what that means.''

Farnes kept his silence.

"You listenin'?''

"Yeah," he said. "And thinking.''

"Can you listen and think at the same time? Don't know many people who can do that. It's like, if you're listenin' you listen, but if you think you stop listenin'. You listenin'?''

Farnes said, "Sorry . . . please. Go on."

"So I used to think there was surely a heaven for Momma because Earth weren't no heaven and she's an angel, a saint. I loved her. But I don't know how she coulda loved me. I was a brat!''

Farnes smiled. "You grew out of it.''

"Come here.''

He moved over next to her, felt her mouth take his earlobe, her lips whisper, "I need your sweetness tonight, Larry. I want it.''

Her mouth on his, supple and moist, firm and prying, her tongue inside his mouth, her breath pulsing hot, wet on the summer night. With a shimmy of both shoulders she shed the tattered dress.

Farnes fumbled at her bra as she unzipped his pants. "Front," she whispered. "Up front.''

He found the clasp between her breasts, released it, let them fill his hands, found his mouth eagerly kneading, heard her whisper, "Yes, yes, yes . . .''

Minutes after they crested, Lorraine drifted off, swept as much by exhaustion as rapture into a sleep that embraced her as urgently as Farnes had, carried her away from the horror around them. Letting her gently down, he slid her into an unzipped sleeping bag, covered her with the flap, tucked her rolled dress under her head, watched carefully in the near darkness as a smile crept over her lips, the warm air rushed in and out of her fluttering nostrils.

He sat up and pulled his trousers back on, raked in the scattergun, pushed three more cartridges in, set it down beside him. Then he leaned against the side of the cargo compartment and drew a deep breath. Except for the holes in the van it was secure. For as long as possible, he had to stay awake. Sleeping now risked a slit carotid artery.

Damn!

He should have picked up amphetamines at Shagmyer's in Darien. Wasn't thinking. Should have prepared . . . Farnes felt wasted, useless. Stubbornly, he propped himself up, played consciousness games, struggled to remain awake. He thought of the NoDoz, fished around in the jumble left when he swerved the van, found some, swallowed three down. Enough?

The buzz surged through him.

Outside, as the moon rose, lancing broken wedges of light through the windshield, the insect chorus gnawed at the silence, the percussive booms of advancing thunderheads bore down, washing the wafts of soggy air that flooded the breached van with the sweet tang of ozone.

What seemed about thirty minutes passed.

Far away, its molten image dodging heavy clouds, the moon had scarcely moved against the steady field of stars. A long yawn pushed his eyelids shut as Farnes felt his will begin to dissolve, release overtake him. Laying the shotgun across his lap, its muzzle aimed dead aft, he settled in, leaned his body back, closed his eyes. Rest, just a little rest, Eyes are burning, tired. Again he yawned. Five minutes, then awake. Just five minutes.

The first one was half through the hole in the side of the van before Farnes could react. As he shifted out of sleep the word leapt at him. Cerberus. Three-headed dog of hell. One head completely inside, to his right, struggling its snarling, snapping jaws, another head clearly visible, snarling and barking on the roof, still another leaping again and again onto the steep hood, grabbing at the windshield wipers with its teeth for purchase.

Farnes lashed the barrel of the shotgun like a whip, cracking on the snout of the intruder. Yelping and whining, it feinted, turned, and snarled.

Suddenly awake, Lorraine filled the cabin with her scream.

Farnes lashed out, struck the invader again with such savage force that he knocked its head outside. When the dog's muzzle reappeared, Farnes had already pivoted the barrel. Leveling the scattergun at the hole, he pulled the trigger. The drooling snarl exploded in a mist of gore.

Above him on the roof, the second dog poised to drop.

Farnes spun and shucked in another round, snapped the

barrel up, fired. Instants after the dog's body shattered, a warm, sticky mist descended from the roof.

Up front, the third dog was still attacking the laminated glass, its claws busy scratching, its jaws tearing at the windshield wipers.

Just below the ringing in his ears, Lorraine continued to scream, clutching the sleeping bag, saying, "No, no, no, not again, not again, not again . . ." then just screaming.

Farnes hunkered over to the rear doors, lowered a shoulder, and crashed out, pivoting just as the third dog was turning his way. A single shot decapitated the dog, ending it.

Inside, Lorraine was still whimpering, "No, no, no, please don't, no . . ."

"It's okay," he said.

But he could see her head, silhouetted in the golden moonlight, still shaking as she murmured, "No, no, no . . ."

He climbed inside, pulled the doors shut. "Just dogs, a pack of wild dogs. They're all dead."

"Good," she trembled. "Good. They're dead. Good. They'll never do it again."

He slipped back in through the rear doors, closed and latched them behind, clambered forward, patted her gently, slipped into the driver's seat. Above him and east, low in the sky, the moon was setting. Sleep. He had slept, what? Five hours? He didn't know. Darkness had no clocks, and the clouds had settled in, masking the moon, flaring sheet lightning. Whatever time, time to move. He turned the key in the ignition, watched the dashlights ignite. Quarter tank of gas. Should do. In the back Lorraine asked, "Where we goin'?"

"Atlanta," he said.

"Do we have to?" she sobbed.

He didn't know what was going on, didn't have time to figure it out, not now. Now he had to move. The shots had revealed his position. Maybe nobody was out there. But maybe someone was. They couldn't afford to wait and find out. Throwing the transmission in drive, he pressed on the accelerator. Re-entering the road, he passed a green and white interstate sign that read:

Atlanta, Host of the XXIII Olympic Games, 15

Fifteen miles. For Farnes, it could have been a thousand.

# DARKNESS AT DAWN

Fifteen miles.

Not much. The van should stand up. As soon as he thought that, the TEMP indicator lit up again.

He just shook his head.

Hell, if they had to they could *walk* fifteen miles. Besides, the van showed no signs of quitting, kept purring along. Lorraine moved forward, slipped into the passenger seat.

"What led the dogs to us?" she said.

He kept his eyes ahead as the road unraveled in the long throw of the high beams. "What?" he said, biting off another yawn.

"Why'd them dogs 'tack us? Dogs don't 'tack people."

"What dogs are we talking about here? Pit bulls? Dobermans? Shephards? Those kinds of dogs attack people for a living. As for the rest, if you look at their genes, they're just wolves pretending to be man's best friend. Maybe they're trying to get even. Asians, even American Indians, eat dog. Turnabout, as they say, is fair play."

"Can't you depend on nothin'?"

Farnes shook his head. "Everything has changed. And nothing has. Civilization was always just a veneer. We're getting a look at ourselves up close and personal, the way we really are. When the going gets tough, the tough get vicious, even murderous, anything to keep food in their guts, a roof over their heads, and a woman to use."

Lorraine caught her breath as if he had hit her, then she let it go, lapsing into silence.

"What?" he asked.

"Nothin'. Just drive, Farnes."

"Farnes? Not Larry? What's wrong?"

"Nothin'," she snapped. "I just woke up, if you recall."

"Where were we?" He cleared his throat, struggling to break the silence. "Dogs?"

"I've got a dog. Beethoven."

"Beethoven? What instruments does he play?"

In the dash lights he could see a faint smile, sadness beneath it. "Hope someone's feedin' him."

Farnes knew the timing stunk to tell her it was more probable that someone was eating him, or would be soon. Or to suggest that the Beethoven she knew could get hungry enough to eat her. They had already seen enough strays, singles and packs, feeding on the dead. Once they got a taste of something, including man, it became food. After that, only Darwin was rule maker. But Farnes only whispered, "Maybe."

"He's a good dog."

"No doubt."

"Maybe some day you'll meet him, Larry."

"Maybe."

"I'd like that. Then you could meet Daddy, too."

"Maybe."

"You don't think we'll ever get back, do you?"

He knew she didn't mean back to a place, the geographical location she had come to know as home, but back to a condition, a way of life. Still, he sensed she didn't wanted candor, only that he not completely lie to her. So he said only, "I don't know."

Her tension seemed to break with a heavy sigh. Maybe she settled for his answer. Maybe that was the straw she needed to grasp right now. Almost immediately her voice became stronger. "I thought we's gonna wait till dawn. So why're we movin' now?"

Farnes decided to give her a little harder honesty. "The dogs could have been hunters."

"You mean like 'coon dogs? Retrievers?"

"No. Man hunters."

"Pack dogs, like you said."

"That wouldn't have bothered me."

"Larry, talk to me."

"I was afraid someone was using them to sniff us out. If so, the dogs would have outrun their master, tried to pin us down until he arrived. That's why we had to move."

"What would anyone want with us?"

"Either nothing, in which case he would have killed me; or you, in which case he still would have killed me."

Her silence went up again, like a wall of ice.

After a minute it shattered in confusion, "You mean . . . to . . . for . . ."

"Yes," he said, sensing something here. In the dash lights he could see her eyelids flutter, her throat surge with a hard swallow. "Or," he went on, "according to a study we did on recovering societies, they could have wanted me, as a slave."

"A slave?" She laughed. "Now I've seen some rednecks . . . I mean people even I call rednecks, but just because you're a Yankee, Larry, the south rising again won't make a slave of a white man."

"I'm sure the same thing is happening up North."

"What?"

"Strong men with guns and no hesitation, taking charge. They conscript who they can, starting with family, friends, and shoot anyone who resists . . ."

"Even family?"

"Especially family," Farnes said, "Look at the Mafia. Killing your own brother shows you'll kill anyone, anytime, in any number, to stay in charge."

The van slowed as it approached a twisted, blackened heap of wreckage, pulled slowly around it, and slowed more to read a green interstate sign, leaning at an angle, that promised only ten miles of darkened highway stood between them and Atlanta.

"In this kind of chaos, everybody's looking for a leader, someone to take charge, protect them, show them the way. Compared to anarchy, they'll take a dictator. Dictators start at the smallest social unit, the family."

"Families with slaves?"

"More like clans, groups with social connections, similar interests, common experience."

"But the skipper said—"

"The skipper was wrong," Farnes almost snapped. "The leaders of these clans will appear to be the only ones to trust. For a time they'll be able to act more like gods, have the power of life and death, of food or starvation, of sex or castration, and use all these powers to graduate slaves into soldiers, then as far as their abilities and loyalty can take them."

"I don't like the picture you're paintin'."

"Why do you think I exposed the Edgewood Bunker?"

"But see what happened?"

"It could have happened anyway, maybe worse than this. Every day we got something a little more lethal, with more mechanisms for shutting down the body's systems—respiration, circulation, cognition, neural synapses—everything, even intracellular osmosis, hematolysis . . ."

"I don't understand those words," she said.

"We were developing bugs that would leave a country the size of the Soviet Union without a single, living human being in it—not one."

"Jesus," she whispered.

"And when we were pretty sure they could do that, the brass wanted us to see how fast they could spread it, to be sure that people or other vectors could get it to the next settlement, however remote, before the initially infected population simply keeled over in place."

"This is making me sick, Larry."

"Lucky you're not sick."

"Am I?"

"Goddamn right you're lucky, Lorraine, because—"

"Better Red than dead, huh?"

"I didn't say that."

"How soon?"

"How soon what?"

"Till the Russians come ashore."

"I don't know."

"But soon?"

"Yeah," he said weakly. "I suppose it's getting close."

"Will we be able to win?"

"You mean beat the plague?"

Lorraine laughed. "No," she said, her turn to speak in whispers. "I don't think anything can stop *that*. I mean the Russians. Is there gonna be enough folks left willin' to fight so's we can stop 'em?"

Farnes shrugged. "I don't know."

"You mean we're goin' to be like East Germany was?"

"No. I think we'll probably turn out a little more like Finland."

"You think?"

"Maybe," he said.

"Why maybe?"

"I think we'll have to wait to see how many of these clans kill one another off first."

She was silent for more than a minute before she said, "Will it really come to that, here?"

He waited nearly as long before protecting her confidence in his honesty by saying. "The Russians have learned the lessons of history better than we have. During the Thirty Years War in Europe, the invading soldiers that crisscrossed Germany left so little food that people tore down the bodies of executed criminals from the gallows to eat them, exhumed corpses of the recently buried for food. And these were devout Christians, mind. Will it come to that? The Russians are counting on it."

Ahead, against the pinking dawn, the silhouetted jumble of Atlanta's skyline staggered out of the dark like a specter, hard and black and silent. In the pit of his stomach Farnes felt the ice of terror condensing as he pushed his foot down, knowing that whatever happened, he had to try. At some level he still believed that this was his own, very personal nightmare and that he, and only he, could stop it. Russians or not, invasion or not, murder, arson, theft, and rape or not, he had to try. Odds be damned, he had to try.

As they got closer, individual buildings loomed up and stood out, like old friends in a crowd. He comforted himself with the thought that he knew Atlanta fairly well. He had spent four months here on loan to CDC after they established the link between AIDS and HIV, as part of a research team shuttling between NIH in Bethesda and here, charged with devising strategies for thwarting the virus. It seemed a reasonable assignment, as part of his work at The Bunker had involved developing vaccines to protect against backlash infections in the United States after a clandestine pre-emptive attack by the United States on the Soviet Union.

It was too clear now that the Soviets had similar thoughts, comparable resolve, had waited only for the opportunity and authorization. Make the leaders believe that if we don't do it to them, they'll do it to us and anything could happen. And since Hiroshima anything was everything.

His foot jammed down the accelerator. The wind howled through the shotgun holes. Just beyond the Farmers Market south of the city he slowed for the ramp to I-285, planning to avoid the city, head east, cut back on North Decatur Road toward Emory University, then CDC. As he approached the exit he felt his heart sink. It was blocked by smoldering wreckage, no way down. Before he could think to switch lanes, hop down the opposite way, jump the median strip, he was swept toward the city. Daylight was breaking. He was shattered. He had to find a place to rest. A few hours only, then on. But he had to stop, just for that long. Suddenly it hit him and he couldn't help but smile.

Lorraine must have noticed, because she said, "What's so funny?"

"Nothing," he said. "Just a thought."

"What? Some dirty thought?"

"No, just strange. We're going someplace there," he jabbed his finger, "that everybody used to go, but now will be empty."

"Where?"

He turned his head, said, "Load the scattergun. First we've got to get there."

She jacked a cartridge into the chamber.

"You're riding shotgun," he said. "Watch out for bandits."

"Bandits?"

"Shoot anyone who gets in our way."

*"Shoot* 'em? *Why?"*

"Impure thoughts?"

"Can't we warn 'em off, tell 'em we're serious?"

"A barrelful of double-ought buck'll get the message through real quick, Lorraine."

The city folded around them at better than seventy miles an hour, its outline slowly ignited by stubby wedges of pink dawn that groped to discover the new Atlanta, not of peach trees, magnolia, booming business, and Olympic pageantry, but of shattered windows, smoke-streaked buildings, and now, forcing them to slow down, tangles of wrecks, abandoned cars and overturned semitrailers, their rear doors ripped open, loads disgorged onto the road.

"Heads up," Farnes said.

"Don't make me nervous, Larry. I'll blow another goddamn hole through the roof."

He wished he could be more alert, but the nearly sleepless night had left him slow, tense, edgy. He wished he could feel more horror at the corpses littering the land, not all dead of plague, many simply shot down, women's bodies with their clothes ripped away, throats slashed, reminding him again of the comedy of law and the tragedy of impulse. The fires had come. Around them, every other building showed smoke puking from windows.

"Why fire?" Lorraine whispered.

"Huh?"

"Why is there so much fire? The sickness kills, it don't burn."

"There's a tertiary infection."

"A what?"

"A third and final form of these sicknesses designed after known diseases like syphilis that acts more quickly, inducing—"

"Doctor Farnes, please."

"—bringing on a psychosis, madness, disorientation, where the patient doesn't relate cause and effect, perceives that the world is out to get him."

"Paranoid? Like with the skipper?"

"More or less. And believing he is trapped by pursuers, is willing that they *all* die rather than let himself be captured. That explains part of it. The rest is, well, bitter people run amok. Society was the only lid on their anger. Now there's nothing to hold it down."

"Like a volcano?"

"Exactly . . . *watch out!*"

Farnes swerved the van, felt it wobble, heard the tires whine painfully as they deformed and skidded, finally righted before the first pipe bashed the side.

"White muthafuck!" came the shout.

He counted twelve. Over the retaining wall they came as he crept up on a snarl of cars that narrowed I-75 to a single lane just past the Omni. They closed on the van like a knot, shouting, screaming, battering the side.

A shot rang out. Large-caliber pistol, Farnes made it. The pavement sang with the ricochet. "They're shooting at the tires!" he screamed. "Return fire!"

Lorraine swung the muzzle of the sawed-off around and caught a black bandit on the chin as he yelled, "White pooooosy," made a sucking noise, and began to laugh as she squeezed the trigger. A nova of blood bathed the cab.

Farnes aimed the van at the obstructed passage. Now closer, he could tell it wasn't just a wreck. The cars had been pushed and dragged together to form a partial roadblock, designed to do just what it had: slow drivers down in confusion. Once they were slowed and confused, and unexpectant, they could be taken. And it was working.

As they pulled away, a short metallic sound left a gleaming hubcab dancing away from the right front tire. He watched it bounce in the rearview mirror, caught a glimpse of the bandit who clung to the rear bumper, and tried to duck out of view.

"Coming in the rear!" he shouted to Lorraine.

She spun around and leveled the shotgun barrel, bracing it on her seat as Farnes crashed the van straight through the hole in the roadblock, tearing away the fenders of both sides.

"Did we lose 'im?" Lorraine screamed.

Farnes shook his head in confusion. He didn't know. The jarring impact should have, could have thrown the bandit off but . . .

To end the confusion, the rear doors popped open, revealing the muscular torso of a huge black man. In the rearview mirror Farnes could see his left arm was welded to a white steel, long barreled .44 magnum.

He was lowering the barrel inside, pulling it toward the back of Farnes' head when Lorraine unleashed her volley. The cab exploded with noise and the tang of burnt gunpowder. In the rearview mirror Farnes watched the intruder's chest open, its contents blow out in back, his eyes roll back as his hands lost purchase, the body fall away and bounce in the retreating roadbed. Farther behind, the gang was still running, waving pipes, shouting, chanting, "Honky! Honky! Honky!"

"Jesus!" Lorraine screamed. "What's *their* problem?"

"Power," Farnes said. "And fear."

"Fear makes them crazy?"

"Oh, yes," Farnes said. "Especially fear. They know they're going to die soon. But they want to live first. And to live they've got to get rid of all their anger."

"Jesus!"

"Mary and Joseph," Farnes repeated her own words from Prison Perfect.

Farnes pushed the van through the sticky morning air as the sun climbed in the eastern sky. Dodging obstructions, they passed the Capitol Building, left the gleaming jumble of downtown skyscrapers to their left, swung north and hit the steep off-ramp to Spring Street.

"You know where you're goin'?"

Farnes nodded. At Fourteenth he darted right, scattered a

knot of punked-up teenagers, headed the damaged van east three blocks past the pyramid-topped IBM Tower, then north on Peachtree to Inman. On Peachtree a Shell station was charred, gutted, twisted and sagging metal and streaked concrete.

"So much for filling up," he said.

"They burned down the gas station? How can they be *that* crazy?"

"They're not," he sighed. "They're that smart."

"Huh?"

"It's not the crazies. It's the Army, our Army."

"But why?"

"The Russian tanks need fuel. No fuel, no movement."

"Then they'll go back?"

"Never," he said. "If we burned gas like Saddam Hussein in Kuwait it might slow them down, but our trip up didn't look like a replay of Sherman's march to the sea."

"But the people need gas, damn it!"

"Why?"

"Why, Farnes? So we can get the hell away from the Ruskies!"

"Oh, so we can move."

"Natch, what else?"

"Figure it out, Lorraine. The more people move, the more people get infected, the more people die. Torch the gas stations and you slow the epidemic, too."

She shook her head, tossed a hand up as Larry pulled the van into its final turn. "Here we are," he said.

"What is it?"

"High Museum of Art."

The clean, curvilinear white tiles of Richard Meier's modern design coruscated pink in the fading dawn. Farnes pulled the van into the parking lot. The TEMP light was still glowing as he turned off the engine, packed and gathered their weapons, food, and sleeping bags, and headed inside.

"Why?" she said.

"Why, what?"

"Why here?"

"Because the age of culture is over for a while. There's nothing worth killing for here. All the bargain hunters have come and gone. It's too public for a great hiding place, so who would look? There's nothing else anyone would want. Not food, maybe not water. Plenty of other places have shelter, so there's no premium. And, if we don't run out of gas, we're only ten minutes from CDC. It's perfect.''

They strolled up the long, railed ramp and through the open door, Lorraine sporting the shotgun like a scepter.

The lobby embraced them in silence. Behind the desk, his eyes frozen straight ahead at the last moment of his life, the receptionist was braced on folded hands, a small-caliber bullet hole between his eyes.

"Wonder why they killed him," whispered Lorraine.

Farnes shook his head. "Studies call it the second epidemic. The first is the disease. The second is disorder. No one ever decided which was worse."

"But why?"

"Because, like Everest for the climbing, the man was here for the killing."

"Has it come to that?"

"For a while."

"And after that?"

Farnes tried to fight off a yawn, couldn't. "I'm too tired to think about after that. I need to sleep."

"And what about me?"

"Stand guard. Shoot anything before it has a chance to shoot you."

Farnes moved through the toppled bronze and chrome statues, past the empty pedestals, toward the stairs. The echos of his footfalls rippled through the silence.

"Where you goin'?" Lorraine said.

"Upstairs, to a back gallery, some place more defensible."

"Mind if I join you?"

"Kind of hoping you would."

She fell in behind him. "Sometimes you drift, Farnes. Sometimes I'm not sure 'bout you at all."

He turned around and held her eyes. "Sometimes I'm not sure of myself. Now I am. Now I know exactly what I have to do. But it's not your problem. And if you want to take off, I'll understand."

She tried to smile. "A girl alone, in the middle of Atlanta. That's never been safe. I know better than . . ." She stopped, stumbled, blinked crazily before shifting. "But now, now it's crazy. Now you need a man more than ever."

"Then pick a good one."

She gave him everything in a glance, said only, "I have," and followed him up.

Farnes climbed to the top floor toward the rear, spun around, and examined the walls before dropping into a shaded corner, curling up in the fetal position, enclosed by sprawling canvases splashed with iridescent pastels, a chromatic asymmetric madness that seemed suddenly, poignantly resonant with the world around it. Formerly rebellious, brash, daring, the acrylics had overnight become the epitome and standard of the New Disorder. Abstract art became representation, expression became depiction, exorcism had become invocation. The scale reminded him of Soviet public art, and he began to wonder how those who created these paintings—at least those who survived—would serve a Marxist-Leninist regime. Struggling with that, he was carried slowly down the currents of exhaustion into a deep yet restless sleep.

When he woke, the late afternoon sun was hammering through the window. Lorraine leaned over him, combing her thin fingers through his hair. Softly, almost cooing, she said, "You snore, did you know that?"

He shook off the slumber with a quick snap of his head, turned up blinking into the hard light. "When I'm tired I do, yeah." Or so Karen had said, in the before time. Forcing himself to forget, he gave her a puzzled look and said, "It's cool."

She laughed. "AC still works. Ain't that a bitch?"

"Must be ninety outside."

"More like a hundred."

"How do you know?"

"I snuck down to the front door, had a look around."

He shook his head. "Not good. Stay out of sight."

"I didn't see nobody."

"Still . . ."

"I think they're all dead. Or holed up somewhere with food, too scared to show."

"Except for the sociopaths," he yawned, getting up to stretch, "you may be right. Still, it only takes one well-aimed bullet."

"Your optimism is depressin'," she snapped.

"Or my realism is essential." Before he finished talking, the ground outside the museum began to shake, the mechanized noises rattled through the window, and both of their heads turreted toward the front door.

"What's that?" Lorraine said.

"Too early for the curators from the Hermitage."

"From *where*?"

"Famous Russian art museum."

Lorraine began to raise her eyes over the windowsill for a look when Farnes pulled her back, snapped a finger to his lips, whispered almost inaudibly, "Stay down!"

"Who is it?"

Farnes shushed her again. "Maybe they'll snoop, find nothing, leave."

Lorraine looked frightened, confused, must have felt trapped. But there was something more than natural fear that Farnes saw, something evoked from the past, something that the moment couldn't suppress.

"Gotta get out of here," she said, breathing hard.

He grabbed her. She shot him a look of hate, defiance, gulped the words, "You don't understand . . ."

"Trust me."

Something in his eyes, maybe a bedside manner, maybe something more, made her settle, stay down. But she was still agitated. "Who are they?"

Farnes snatched a quick glimpse through the window.

"Tanks. Soldiers."

"Ours or theirs?"

"I don't know. Our markings. But one way for an invading force to overrun an uncoordinated defense is to disguise themselves as defenders."

"So they could be Ruskies?"

Farnes nodded. "They're in CBW gear, biological protection. Must be hotter than hell in that stuff. Maybe they want to stop, bivouac, get out of the sun."

"You mean they're gonna camp out in the lobby?"

The front door swung open three floors below as the beat of combat boots echoed through the building. A loud, deep voice commanded, "Secure the area. Check it out."

"Ours?" Lorraine said.

"Maybe," Farnes said, then decided, "probably." The Soviets would never risk a forward unit so isolated, unsupported, vulnerable. And there had been no sign of the air support that generally precedes an invasion by ground forces.

"What do we do?"

"They're going to go through this place, room by room."

"Then they'll find us."

Farnes nodded.

"Then what?"

"One possibility? They shoot us."

"*Shoot* us?"

Farnes nodded.

"Why?"

"Because they think we're infected and they don't want to die."

"Just for that, they shoot us?"

"The rage to live? To live, people will do anything."

"But we're Americans."

"They don't know that either, do they?"

Farnes' sharp retort left her blinking. The Soviets had agents in every region of the United States, agents who injected the virus into food supplies. Probably immune, these agents would hide until invasion forces could liberate them. Knowing that, defenders would suspect anyone who was uninfected, hiding, or on the run, anyone without credentials or a credible story. Where did that put them? The truth Farnes needed to convince them of was crazier than the suspicion they would be likely to embrace.

Two immune people together? What were the chances of that?

Statistically, pretty low. But *situationally,* in a crisis where some small number of people are driven to band together to survive, inevitably high. Still, the soldiers' perceptions would narrow to a choice between two deadly conclusions. Either they were infected too recently to show symptoms, requiring summary execution and burial before dogs could get to them and spread the disease through their saliva. Or they were Soviet agents waiting for the invasion forces to pacify the area. An ununiformed agent of a foreign power in a theater of war is a spy, subject to summary field court martial and execution.

Neither case was true. Yet if Farnes himself were told that truth, that the one person most capable of organizing and conducting a biological defense of the United States had escaped unaided from a maximum security facility and crossed three miles of storm-raked ocean, survived a rash of ambushes, and acquired a small arsenal en route to the CDC, not to destroy the facility, but to help save the country that rewarded his courage by prosecution and imprisonment, he wouldn't believe it for an instant. No way.

"What do we do?"

"We don't wait," he said.

"What?"

"We don't get caught looking like we're hiding."

Farnes got up and stormed to the door, making no attempt to be quiet. From the passageway leading from the gallery to the walkway, he shouted, "Hey, we're up here. Don't shoot!"

A panicked voice shouted, "Major, someone's up there!"

"They alive?" Soldier's voice.

"Ain't heard a corpse yet talk that good."

The ratcheting action of automatic weapons advancing rounds, locking in clips.

"Don't shoot!" Farnes said. "We're Americans."

"We're scared!" screamed Lorraine.

Soldier's voice again, "Hey, a broad!"

Another. "Shut up, Sinclair. Could be a trick."

"No tricks," Farnes shouted back. "We're coming down unarmed."

Voice of authority saying, "You folks feel all right?"

"I'm a doctor," Farnes said. "Neither one of us is infected. I can show you that."

"You're a doctor?"

"I'm a research doctor, yes."

"You know what the hell's goin' on, doc?"

"Yes."

"Come on out. Let us have a look. Just come down to the lobby. We'll wait."

When Farnes and Lorraine cleared the last turn, they saw the company of soldiers below assembled in loose formation, their faces enclosed in the hooded gas masks, M-16s raised. Lifting their hands to show they were unarmed, Farnes said, "No guns, no infection. We can't hurt you. And we can help."

"Anyone else up there?" Major speaking? Voice of authority anyway.

"Just us."

"Come down." The muzzles trained on them, the masks stayed on.

"Sinclair. Barkley. Check out the upper floors."

A moment's hesitation before the answer, "Yes, sir."

Two soldiers shouldered by, backs to the wall, and clat-

tered off to sweep the deserted museum while Farnes and
Lorraine descended to the lobby. By the time they reached
it, arms still raised, the soldiers reappeared, saying, ''All
clear, Major.''

''Then fall in,'' said the major, turning his goggled eyes
to Farnes. ''Now *who* do you say you are?''

''I'm an immunologist. I've worked at CDC. You can call
and check with the director.''

''The director at CDC is dead. Maybe you knew that.''

''No way,'' said Farnes, shaking his head, swallowing
hard, and going on. ''And I worked for DOD at Edgewood,
in The Bunker.''

''How do I know that?''

''Reach out and touch someone. Call,'' Farnes said.

''Facility is sealed. Fifty-five percent fatalities. Only NO-
RAD can call in. Seems the Russians took the federal prison
at Morriset Island. Word is they got the one guy that Edgewood feels can turn this thing around, a guy named Farnes.''

Farnes blinked, swallowed hard again, said evenly, ''That's
me.''

''Say what?'' said the major, dropping the muzzle of his
M-16.

''I'm Larry Farnes.''

''How the fuck . . . sorry, ma'am . . . but . . .''

''It's a long story.''

''How do I know you're Farnes, not a saboteur or nut-
case?''

''Get in touch with someone who's worked with Larry
Farnes before.''

''Where?''

''CDC,'' Farnes said.

''CDC has been declared part of the Emergency National
Defense Plan by the President.''

''He survived?'' Farnes gasped.

''Declaration before he died.''

''Who's is charge?''

''NORAD. Everyone in the silos and Cheyenne Mountains
made it.''

''Then see if CDC would want Larry Farnes, if he's available.''

''Who's she?'' The major pointed the muzzle of his automatic rifle at Lorraine. Farnes batted it away. Before he could

say, "Don't point guns unless you mean to use them," the ten closest weapons were at his head and neck.

"Relax," the major said to his troops, then to Farnes, "We're a little nervous."

"Are we under attack?"

"The way I figure, we've been under attack since before the first case of this sickness. It's too big an enemy for any army. Hell, we can't shoot it or bomb it. We can't see it or hear it or smell it until it's too late. Nobody knows how long you look well till you get sick, so we can't coordinate counterattacks."

"So the Russians are ashore?"

"Florida's already fallen; the Soviets are using Pensacola for close air support. Not that they need it. We've got practically nothing up to oppose them. They're moving fast. Maybe to join another landing force up north. We don't know. Communications for shit . . . sorry, ma'am, but either nobody knows, or nobody's getting the poop out. All we know for sure is that their tanks just engaged ours near Macon."

"How bad?"

"Heavy combat losses on both sides, especially the Soviets. But the numbers did it. They took everything from Miami to Pensacola Naval Air Station in thirty hours. Every time they secure an area they start running MiG sorties ahead, softening up defense for the armored columns to follow."

"And our forces?"

The major heaved a great sigh behind his mask. "Some units, like us, hold together. But there's a lot of desertion, even in uninfected units. They seem to know we can't lick this bug. They know the enemy can hit us with canisters of it in the field. A lot of National Guard units have no protection, no masks, nothing. And the people, the folks like the NRA who say the Russians will never take us . . ." another sigh, deeper than the first, ". . . well they were wrong. They're so busy shooting looters, rapists, and tresspassers that nobody's gonna be left after the plague. That's where we stand."

"But if the forces did know we had a cure?"

Behind the mask, the major's laugh sounded coarse and hollow. "If they heard it and believed it, then sure, everybody'd fight like hell. They're madder'n shit about what Ivan did."

"Then, Major, I suggest that you get Larry Farnes to CDC as soon as possible."

The major entitled himself to one more sigh, both a catharsis and exorcism, then said, "Shit, yeah. What do we have to lose that we aren't going to lose if we don't take a chance? You ever ride a tank, Dr. Farnes?"

"Can't say I have."

The major turned his head and summoned with a wave of his arm. "Martinez. Show Dr. Farnes to the M1A1."

"Yes, sir."

"Can this lady come with me, Major?"

"Martinez?" asked the Major.

Martinez was all eyes and testosterone. "Sí . . . I mean yes, sir."

"Then let's roll."

"Sullivan," barked the major into the mobile command radio, "coming in from the High Museum of Art with Dr. Larry Farnes."

"Say again," barked a voice through the static.

"Dr. Larry Farnes, the Messiah."

"Where'd you find him?"

"He managed to get this far himself."

"Can you verify the real Farnes?"

"No," Sullivan said.

"We'll have to hold him at a checkpoint for security."

"Do whatever you have to. We're rolling. Look for our column eastbound via Ponce de Leon and Briarcliff. ETA 1800 hours, out."

Farnes let Lorraine through the turret hatch and hopped down behind her, Martinez squinting up at the orange-tinted sky and shutting them in. His eyes came up from behind the goggle lenses. "Hope we can run into some bandit roadblocks so you can see what this baby can do."

Farnes just nodded and hoped they didn't. CDC was too close. Any delays could be catastrophic.

The tank whined, jerked backward, and swung around like a sports car. Martinez turned. His eyes were smiling as he patted the controls. "Lee Iacocca built this baby," he said.

Outside the military cordon that isolated CDC from the outside world, Major Sullivan went facemask to facemask with a sentry, pleading for Farnes' admission, getting only a swing of the man's head side to side. Orders were orders.

Sullivan returned, said, "I have to go through and argue with Colonel Henderson, the CO. But I'll be back."

Farnes and Lorraine had exited the tank, were standing amidst the soldiers in protective clothing, the two of them being guarded like a national asset by a company of heavily armed men.

A pair of adjutants broke off to accompany Sullivan to the facade of the yellow brick complex. Minutes later they had passed two more checkpoints and were swallowed by a sand-bagged door.

Farnes stepped forward to catch a glimpse of where, exactly, Sullivan was heading when the sentry stepped between him and the complex, placing a firm hand squarely in the center of his chest. "I'm afraid you'll have to wait here, sir," he said.

Lorraine led Farnes away by the arm, asked, "What happens when you go in there?"

Farnes began to open his mouth when the distant southern skies whined with a low, eerie rumble, like captured thunder. That brought all eyes, large and full and insect-like behind their goggled facemasks, up and south. At first they saw nothing. But the roar was real. Its awful gutwrenching screech grew second by second until Martinez lifted a finger and shouted, "MiGs inbound!"

The sentry had time for "Shit!" before racing for his command phone. In the same moment Martinez was atop the tank turret, spinning the machine gun around as the other soldiers fell to one knee. Five sentries shouldered their Stinger missiles, tracking the incoming blurs. Others began peppering the air with M-16 rounds. Two seconds later Martinez opened up the brutal hammering of the fifty-caliber machine gun. Beyond the gunfire the sentry huddled with his phone, shouting, "Enemy aircraft inbound from the south, ETA . . ." He looked up. "NOW!"

A wedge of five needle-nosed MiG-29s roared in, bearing down just subsonic at five hundred feet, just above the tree-tops. As Farnes watched, paralyzed, he had no doubt about their mission. Stunned, he muttered to himself, as if he were watching it from a million miles away, "Makes sense, makes perfect sense."

The words were scarcely out of his mouth when the pilots

began releasing the smart bombs, television-guided high explosives with penetrating armor tips.

Martinez swung the machine gun up and around as the MiGs swept overhead, their deadly cargo already descending in a spooky whistling chorus. In Farnes' mind, where time had again been forced to relax, he saw the bombs drift in, like barrels sinking in the sea, until they had almost penetrated the CDC roof.

Lorraine and one of the soldiers pulled Farnes down as the explosions thundered through the complex, erupting pulverized yellow brick in lethal projectiles that whistled and tumbled, pattering down, annihilating the sentry post. Only the nearby sandbags, themselves now disemboweled, saved Farnes and Lorraine.

When the choking smoke and debris cleared, Martinez's decapitated body lay twisted and slumped over his machine gun. Other soldiers were dead, some dying. The fire spawned by the explosion was spilling their way.

Instinctively Farnes dragged himself to his feet and began the numbing process of triage. Spreading flames thwarted him. The less seriously wounded men he pulled away, laying them in rows beyond the range of the fire. Lorraine stumbled along, helping, crying, stopping, then crying some more.

The soldier who had pulled Farnes down survived uninjured. He followed Farnes' directions, stammering, "Jesus," then biting his lip, lifting men under the arms, pulling them like rag dolls to where Farnes could minister to them. Together they got fourteen out before the target area was overtaken by the growing conflagration.

"Why?" Lorraine finally screamed. "Why, why, why, why?"

"Because they're playing for keeps. It's a real war and they're taking away our only real defense."

But reasons meant nothing to her. The words, however true, had no comfort. Breaking down, she just cried.

"What do I do, sir?" asked the soldier.

"Whatever we can, with what we have," Farnes said numbly.

"Is it over?"

Farnes gave him a look without meaning, as if he didn't understand what the real question was. Then he looked back to the wounded and began looking after them. Suddenly, over his shoulder, a mobile command receiver barked, "Come in, all US Forces. Come in."

The lone soldier picked up and shouldered his M-16, stumbled over, and snatched the handset up, said a simple unmilitary, "Hello."

"Soldier?"

"Darnelles, Corporal. USA."

"Where's your unit?"

"Dead and wounded, sir."

"*All* of them?"

"Except me," he said, silent for only a second before adding, almost perfunctorily, "sir."

"We're mustering at the intersection of I-85 and I-75. You know the place?"

"Yes, sir."

"This is Colonel Jerome Sharp, USA. Spread the word. Then mobilize. See you there."

"No, sir."

"*What?*"

"Beg your holy pardon . . . sir, but I got charge of the most important weapon in America. It's not a tank and it's not a missile, it's a doctor . . . sir, a doctor who can beat the real enemy, the one that's not leaving even if we beat Ivan."

"You've received a direct order and—"

"Roger and out." Darnelles snapped the transmission off. "Well, doc, looks like you picked yourself up an armed bodyguard, at government expense. So what's next?"

That was the question all right. And Farnes had no idea what the answer would be.

# REVERSALS

Two hours later the last fires in the rubble of CDC flickered low as the skies roared and flashed with dogfighting jets. As night inked the sky, the MiG-29s and F-16s banked, spun, fired, exploded, and dropped in flames. Two survivors of the earlier bombing died, one hovered near death. The others, unless they were shot or starved, should make it, even with the crude medical attention available. Lorraine sat braced against a sturdy oak, her eyes vacant and fixed, unblinking. Farnes busied himself with the wounded, fighting a numbness that seeped into him.

Intellectually he wanted to play out the options in his head, to see what the chances were for turning the situation around, to think his way out, as he always had. But spiritually he was as dead and thoughtless as the decapitated Martinez, whose dismembered body he had removed from the tank and set aside for burial.

The Russians were coming.

Soon.

But what did it mean?

Stumbling toward Lorraine, he reached her, leaned over, put a gentle hand on her shoulder. "We can't stay here."

"Why?" she asked, eyes still hollow.

"They could strafe or bomb again."

"What about them?" She pointed to the wounded.

"They'll make it," he said, not entirely confident. Instinctively he stooped over and pulled an M-16 from one of the dead.

"Sure?"

"Let's get to cover. It's too open." He pulled her up and they began moving.

He cinched her waist with his powerful arm and half carried her away, pressing her body against his. And that was a reason for concern, too. Not just feelings, real as they were. The reputation of the Red Army for casual rape was as robust as any conquering army. And Lorraine made any man think sex.

Nearby, in the fading twilight, the silhouetted buildings of Emory University etched the sky.

"There," Farnes pointed.

She nodded.

"For the night."

"Then what?"

"Let's just get through the night."

As they trekked across the neatly trimmed grass, he thought how lucky they had been to find the one place that wouldn't be littered with corpses. A school out for the summer, operated only by a skeleton crew. Skeleton crew? Strange expression. Ahead and to the right, through a idyllic quadrangle, he guided them.

Behind them the dying heat of the conflagration ebbed against their backs, crackling like maniacal laughter.

"Through the night," Farnes mumbled again, not knowing why.

They woke to a howling, screeching hammering at their second story window, a sound that made them clinch one another tighter than did last night's passions. Farnes lifted his head and squinted past the chintz curtains into the hard morning light. Suddenly he relaxed, laughed.

But Lorraine was still confused. "Farnes."

"It's a chimp," he said, getting up. "They have the Yerkes Primate Center here. I guess all their handlers died and this guy escaped."

Lorraine got up behind him, her eyes soft with the wonder of survival. "Poor baby," she said, drawing close.

Before she could reach the window to unlatch it, a single round of automatic fire tore through the chimp, sharded the glass, and echoed through the small dormitory room. The chimp blinked once, made no sound, then slipped away and fell into the courtyard below.

"Down." Farnes said, his heart racing, his breathing short, shallow. Who and where were they? How many? As he turned to retrieve the M-16 the door swung open and smashed against the wall.

Lorraine screamed.

Farnes looked up.

Behind a quiver of AK-47 muzzles stood a two-star general in the Red Army. Farnes tried to get behind his eyes, into the man's brain. No sadism, not that. Control, yes, but harsh. Discipline. That, yes, but more. It was a somber Slavic face, touched with Tatar lines, especially in the hint of epicanthic folds around the eyes, but framed in a strong Teutonic jaw beneath tight lips, a large, almost Roman nose. Hair grayed around the temple, but on a hairline that held on, not receding. The whole face glistened with sweat, yet the general held a full military brace as his eyes swept the room, switching from Farnes to Lorraine, lingering, then going back to Farnes.

What was he thinking?

"Who are you?" the general asked in accented English.

"Who are *you*?" Farnes asked back.

"I ask the questions," he said, then, softening a bit, ran his hands over his uniform. "This can be difficult or quite easy. You believe that?"

Farnes nodded.

"Good. We have trust. Something, I fear, politicians miss."

Farnes could only blink. How to read the man?

"Now, who are you?"

"I'm a doctor," Farnes said.

"That is good. We need doctors. And American doctors are, despite their vulgar greed, good. Are you a very good doctor?" The general stepped into the room, turned back to his men, said something in Russian, and closed the door behind him.

"And who is the woman?"

"The woman is my wife," Farnes said, too vehemently.

The general went to the windows, pulled back the torn curtain, and squinted into the hard light. At his own convenience he turned and sighed. "That, too, is good, because we will need wives. And mothers, of course. A wife is good," he murmured. "In Soviet Union we have much divorce. Not a good thing. You agree?"

Farnes refused to follow idle banter, especially if he didn't know where it was going.

"I am Igor Yustechenko, Field General of the Red Army, Commander of the North American Invasionary Force. I have learned that this Georgia is as unsufferably hot as ours, although I am not Georgian. Myself am Belorussian, White Russian, though not the drink, the ethnic group.''

"You seem to think this is pretty funny," Farnes said.

Yustechenko's expression hardened suddenly as he shot back, "No, I do not. But I sometimes laugh to keep from crying and drink to keep from feeling. You have never done this?''

"It's happened," Farnes said.

"Then you understand something of life.''

Farnes nodded.

"And as a doctor, something of death.''

Again Farnes nodded.

"We have much death," said the general.

"There's a lot more where that came from.''

The general slowly unbuttoned the flap on his uniform pocket and retrieved a small photograph. Holding it up in the space between them, he looked at it, back to Farnes, again at the picture. "You are Farnes, no?''

"Who?" It was a feeble bluff. He knew instantly that they had targeted him as one of the few who could thwart the epidemic in time. His picture was as common as a week-old copy of *Newsweek*. If the major's story was right, they must have tried to scoop him up at Prison Perfect and missed. Then it got urgent. By now his name was at the top of a list for summary post-invasion executions.

"Your Corporal Darnelles said our picture was very good—''

"Before you shot him?''

Yustechenko snapped Farnes a look of pure contempt. "For soldiers, the fear of bullets is real. But for American soldiers, he might have been more persuaded by money, no? And for American doctors, perhaps we would get to the truth more quickly—or at least to co-operation—by starting with money. Isn't that the thing, Dr. Farnes, about American doctors? They would do anything for money, even use their profession to plan a sickness to end the world?''

Farnes sensed that Yustechenko didn't want answers, was more interested in staking out his position.

The Field General proved him right. "And if money is it, how much did the KGB pay you to expose your work? Americans say everyone has his price. So what is yours, Dr. Farnes? What is the price on your life and freedom? And how will you be paid? Gold, diamonds? What?''

"You ain't got that kinda money, even if he was this guy you're lookin' for," Lorraine snapped.

"Lady, I believe that Dr. Farnes is calculating a figure. Whatever he believes, we are not murderers. Darnelles surrendered, is now prisoner of war. Geneva Conventions rule."

"If you have so much intelligence, you must not be regular Army. What is it Yustechenko. GRU?"

Yustechenko exploded the silence with a thunderous huff, stared back. "No, not GRU. And KGB wears the proud blue uniform. Our political officer came ashore with us, of course. Unfortunately he took a bullet in the throat from paying too little attention to a tense tactical development. A combat officer would have seen this coming, of course."

"I thought you weren't a murderer."

"Politicians make me more barbarous than greedy capitalists. Can you understand that?"

Farnes half nodded, remembering the trial, the press, the freak show.

"So you are Farnes, no?"

Lorraine sensed something. "No. That's not his name."

Yustechenko's bushy eyebrows lifted and dropped. "No? Then who?"

To take the Red general's hard stare off Lorraine, Farnes broke in. "If I say no, what happens then? You torture me until I say yes, even if I'm not. Hell, I've got more time left if I tell you I'm Farnes, even if I'm not, rather than deny it if I am."

Yustechenko took his time reforming the English thought into its Russian counterpart, translating the conceit from the American value system into the Russian understanding of it, before simply asking, "You play chess, Dr. Farnes?"

"Middling well," said Farnes.

"At least that, I would bet."

"You think?"

"Not as you do. I am simple soldier."

"Not so simple, I would bet."

"Then troubled soldier."

"Why troubled? You're winning."

Yustechenko heeled and gave Farnes the saddest eyes he had ever seen, understanding better from them than anything in Pasternak what the Russian soul was. "No, Dr. Farnes. We are losing. Soldiers cannot win this war. The weapons we have . . . fail. Whereas all soldiers take duty to country deeply enough to give our lives, we need men of, perhaps, a higher sense of duty to save us from an enemy greater than any weapons ever made.''

Farnes was so stunned he couldn't speak. No words came. No glib repartee, no defensive banter, no defiance or contempt, only disbelief. The one word he got out before the general resumed was, ''But . . .''

''We are army, Dr. Farnes. You understand?''

Farnes nodded.

''We have only combat doctors with Invasion Force. Sawbones, I believe you call them. You understand?''

Farnes gave him another nod.

''Army is not civilization, you understand?''

Farnes looked over at Lorraine, saw the fear in her eyes, and turned back to Yustechenko, nodding again.

''No industry, no university, no scholars, no researchers, no—how do I say this?—intellectuals.''

''Yustechenko. What's this all about? If you were that sure it was me, you could have shot me when you came through that door.''

''Shoot you?'' Yustechenko's face reddened, his fist tightened into hard knots. ''I can tell you if I knew the one man who started this . . . this, what is the English word?''

''Horror?'' Farnes suggested.

''Yes, horror. If I could find the one man, I would stand him up against a wall and shoot him all right. If I could go back in time and find any men, anywhere, who made this sickness, I would shoot them all, without delay. And if I ran out of bullets, I would have killed them one by one, with my own hands if necessary. And may still. That is why, Farnes, you should not push me too hard. Time is shorter than patience, and that is short enough. It is not time to choose sides, or there may, in the end, be no sides. So quickly is death upon us.''

''Yustechenko, if I could turn this around, how can I be sure you won't use it against Americans, or shoot me as soon as you learn what to do?''

Yustechenko's face split in a cruel smile. Arching his full eyebrows he said, ''Better, no, than dying now. At least you have followed your Hippocratic oath, rather than your greed. But if you were to decide to help, even to help us, *Dr.* Farnes, what share of the new Soviet order in America would you require as reward? State Head of Medicine? *What*?'' The Russian shouted the last question.

''I've done enough damage working as a government doctor, for any side.''

''Your mind can be changed.''

''Don't bet on it,'' Farnes shot back.

''Betting, Farnes is for men who are excited by luck. I prefer something both more predictable and methodical.'' Raising his voice, Yustechenko bellowed to the soldiers outside, ''Take Dr. Farnes to isolation.''

''Wait! What about my . . . my wife!''

''She will be treated with Soviet courtesy.''

''Yustechenko, this gets you nowhere!''

The general had turned his back, was already leaving, but suddenly stopped, pivoted in a quick about-face, and smiled. ''Don't bet on it.''

The wood-slatted crate was just a few inches more than five feet long. By coiling up, Farnes fit, but couldn't hold one position long. The short sides of the box were so tight they jammed his shoulders. Whenever he moved to relieve the aching in his crooked back, splinters gouged his shoulder.

They put the crate on the floor of a basement, wet it down with a hose, turned off the lights. The Georgia summer heat began its slow persuasion, surging in palpable waves that mirrored his thudding heart. In minutes he began panting, as if he were running hard. Not long after—he had no sense of time—the thirst began to work.

In time, that might have been enough. But after what seemed like an hour came the first sounds of frantic scurrying. Maybe large bugs—roaches?—but no, too big. Cats? Feral cats. But no, there was more than one. More than two. Three and more. What? Rats!

When the first brush of whiskers intruded through the wooden slats, Farnes screamed and rolled, cursing and screaming. Immediately the scampering lulled. Gone? No, just waiting. Jesus, they could wait . . . how long? Until he passed out or fell asleep? Then what?

He didn't know.

They kept coming, each time bolder, less tentative, learning the folly of his shouting and pitching. And each time he threw himself, rolling the crate, splinters dug into his flesh, raising the scent of blood in the darkness.

* * *

No sense of time, only the crushing weight of fatigue. Hours? Of course, but how many? Was it day or night? If night, which night? Had he been in two hours or twenty-two? Where was Lorraine? Would Yustechenko be back, ever? Or would battle draw him away?

All good questions. He wished he knew. The only question he refused to ask was the most obvious. Was it going to end here, slowly devoured by a pack of ravenous rats?

Farnes felt something sag inside him, like rotten roofing timbers in an old mine, fought off a secret sobbing, wondered if they were listening, waiting, calculating the moment he broke.

In a flash, before he could wonder more, a blinding light burst from the stairwell they'd brought him down. Silhouetted against it was the huge outline of Igor Yustechenko. Into the echoing darkness, he said, "We need to resume our discussions, Dr. Farnes. The luxury of delay has vanished even in your short confinement."

For reasons clear only to Yustechenko, Farnes was brought to the same room where he last saw Lorraine. Before he could ask after her, the Soviet General said, "Dr. Farnes. The epidemic has," he stammered here as if unsure, searching, perhaps for the proper English word before going on, "taken new turn."

"New turn?"

"Or is perhaps another sickness. It is sweeping north with our advance, killing our troops."

"But what of protective clothing?"

Yustechenko shrugged his massive shoulders. "No good."

"But . . ."

"Don't ask for understanding or explanation," Yustechenko said. "I am not scientist. That is why I need you, Farnes, as you must understand, by now, that you need me. You understand?"

"Not completely," he said.

"By time Moscow figures this out, all my men are dead."

"What do you want me to do?"

"Save us."

Farnes' heart thudded in his chest.

Yustechenko's eyes were humble, desperate. "Save us all, Farnes. Soviets and, yes, Americans alike. I don't know who else there is.'' He went to the window and pointed to the ruins of CDC. ''I can't think who is left. And if they are out there, we would never get to them in time.''

Bleeding, bruised, sweaty, and exhausted, Farnes convulsed. He didn't know whether he was laughing or crying. The distinction was gone between the two. He couldn't figure out whether it was too absurd or too tragic to consider. When the seizure lifted, he said ''You *bloody* idiots! You blew up your best hope!''

''Moscow orders, put in place before this . . . surprise.'' Yustechenko didn't even blink as he said, ''So we need the second best hope, because without hope is no point to go on.''

Farnes blinked, said only, ''What?''

''The Bunker.''

''Edgewood?''

The general nodded.

''Intact?''

''Unless *your* people have destroyed it.''

Farnes muttered, ''Mothballed, not destroyed, I think,'' hedging slightly on what he suspected.

''We must go,'' said Yustechenko.

''You've already taken Maryland?''

''No. You'll go with us.''

''I'm not a soldier.''

''We do not invade Maryland. We take The Bunker. Soviet Special Assault Force. And you.''

''And more MiGs? This is crazy.''

''No MiGs. But you have to be little crazy to survive war, Dr. Farnes. But we use U.S. Son Tay mission as model. And I will be Bull Simons.''

''I'm a doctor,'' Farnes said. ''My job is not killing.''

''Is like operation, Doctor. You want to save a lot of lives, Dr. Farnes, you have to spill a little blood first. I do not create this horror. You and men like you in my country, playing little bloodless games on big bloodless boards in big comfortable rooms, far away from twisted bodies that will come from twisted thinking, you and they made this. Now only question is, do you want to stop it?''

''Yes,'' Farnes said, getting up.

''So do I,'' Yustechenko said.

''Let's go.''

''She stays,'' the general said.

"She comes."

The general shook his head, no. "This is no, what you call, Sunday school picnic, no Hollywood movie. You want her safety, leave her here."

"But she's naturally immune. How do you think she survived this long without protective clothing? Her antibodies are the quickest way to create a vaccine against the Soviet virus. She's *vital.*" In scientific fact, Farnes knew that even an immune person was at risk from a rapidly mutating virus, and what Yustechenko described could be just that. Scientists aren't gods, creating life and knowing exactly how it will play out in the grand evolutionary theater. They are more like meddlers and children, excited about learning as they go. The naked truth was that Farnes *wanted* Lorraine along. And the general, as he admitted, was no scientist.

Yustechenko regarded him silently. A trace of a smile creased his lips as he said, "Maybe she's not quite as vital as you argue, Farnes, but you are the doctor and I, but a simple soldier."

"Then let's get going."

They raised their eyes and blinked, shading them from the noon sun, as the sprawling Soviet Mi-6 Hook helicopter settled into a slow, controlled descent onto the grassy quadrangle. The prop wash hit them like a firehose, tearing at lose clothing, forcing them to backpedal until they wanted to be knocked over. When it settled in and down-throttled its engines, Yustechenko shouted, "Soviet land speed record over a one hundred kilometer course for a horizontal rotor aircraft. It will take us."

Farnes took the three steps up, pulling Lorraine behind. Once Yustechenko boarded, the ladder was withdrawn and door secured as the chopper powered into the hot Georgia sky.

"Do we have the range?" Farnes asked.

"Oh, yes." Yustechenko nodded.

"Where are the assault troops?" Farnes asked, scanning the empty fuselage.

"At rendezvous point."

"In Maryland?"

Yustechenko frowned, as if Farnes had just said something stupid, sighed, and explained, "No. Off your Cape Hatteras."

"Off?" Lorraine repeated, not sure the Soviet had chosen the right English word.

"Yes, Madam. Off. On Soviet submarine."

For an hour the Hook helicopter played tag with the tree-tops along the Georgia coastal plain, edging dead east south of Augusta to avoid the Savannah River Weapons Plant, then skimming north by northeast over water toward the southern Carolina coast. Farnes had few concerns about interception by United States aircraft, fewer about the possibilities of scattered ground fire bringing down the huge chopper. Inside, the vibration of overhead props was so deafening that Yustechenko yelled himself hoarse extolling the virtues of the Soviet Quebec class submarines, an old model from the Sudomekh naval yard at Leningrad, recently refurbished and returned to service for the invasion. Only a hundred and eighty-five feet long, it drew only thirteen feet at the folsom line, making it nearly as invisible as a submarine could be. More important, at this size it could infiltrate submerged right up estuaries without running aground. The main problem, the general noted, was the diesel propulsion and old design. They were slow and they were noisy. And yes, if detected, they were too slow to escape. Otherwise, they were quite fine.

"Dandy," Farnes muttered.

Yustechenko clapped him on the back. "Not to worry. Our submarine is the *Rodina*. I know skipper. He will get us there."

"Us?"

"Yes," Yustechenko shouted. "Twenty of elite Soviet Assault Force and us. That should prove enough to overrun a handful of scientists and janitors."

"Time will tell," Farnes said.

A Russian word barked from a mounted speaker.

"Aha," Yustechenko yelled. "Our transportation."

Lorraine joined Farnes and Yustechenko at a Plexiglas observation bubble blistering the left side of the fuselage. Beneath them, lolling placidly on the twinkling Atlantic waves, was the low black shape of the *Rodina*, its narrow deck crammed with waiting sailors.

"They are wondering," Yustechenko said, "if we are sick. So they are nervous."

"They ought to be," Farnes said.

''But they know that if we do not succeed, we must retreat. If we retreat, they fear that may make us seem weak. Seeming weak, everyone may attack us.''

''Everyone?'' Farnes wondered.

''Look at history. Everyone always has.''

''Now is different,'' Farnes said.

''Is it?''

The Hook settled deftly abaft of the submarine, hovered neatly above the bobbing deck as they slipped into winched harnesses for lowering to the waiting crew.

''Yes,'' Farnes yelled to be heard above the roaring turbine, ''now winning is losing. Now total war means both sides launching all the nukes. When that starts, it's the end of everything, everyone.''

They were already strapped in and dangling, the electric motors of the winches playing out corded cable as the Russian general shouted, ''One danger at a time, Dr. Farnes.''

''This place makes me claustrophobic,'' Lorraine groused.

Yustechenko turned a hard eye on her, said, ''Not compared to the crew. They sleep on top of one another in berths, nose to the next man's backside, night after night, and cannot even turn in their sleep. So this is flattery, here.''

''Flattery is a Russian euphemism for fear,'' Farnes said to Lorraine.

The general shrugged. ''Yes they are afraid, but you are not?''

''Yes. But not for myself.''

''Hippocrates, is it?''

''No, immune is it. I'm just another primate, like the chimps we tested for years with experimental vaccines. And their immunity lasted an average of seven years, much longer for their life spans than seven of ours. And if the antibodies are close enough to fight a new virus, you've got a damn good chance of survival. With luck and hustle and one good antiviral research lab, we can beat this epidemic. But can we stop the madness it's unleashed?''

''In Soviet Union, restoring order only a matter of giving masses more to fear than fear driving them to riot.''

''The world according to Papa Joe?''

''The world we see could use a Stalin.''

''Yeah? I bet you'll find a lot of applicants out there.''

''Maybe not so many, if we don't hurry. No?''

\* \* \*

"The oil smell is makin' me sick," said Lorraine.

Sliding through the Chesapeake shallows, only ten feet submerged, wrapped in hard, tight turns of dense steel, the compact diesel sub drowned them in the stench of heavy machine oil. Newer designs, especially the nukes, had eliminated it. Older models, like the *Rodina,* carried it like an indelible birthmark. Seasoned crews adjusted, Farnes knew, through olfactory fatigue, the way scent glands at the top of the nose, just beneath the brain, ignore a constant smell to detect new ones. But as an experienced doctor, he also knew that some people, like Lorraine, can't help reacting. For them it's almost reflexive.

"She must not appear sick," warned Yustechenko, the urgency in his voice almost palpable.

Farnes nodded. If Lorraine came down sick, even with motion sickness or nausea, the crew and attack force would assume the worst, that the plague had been taken on board. Then they would panic. Worse, they might be driven to something desperate, like sealing off part of the sub and flooding it, hoping the sea would cleanse the germs. Enough fear and reason flees. Then anything can happen.

"Can you get me any Dramamine?" Farnes asked.

Yustechenko said, "We have only military doctors, essentials, I would think. But I ask. Discreetly, of course."

"How many more hours?" Farnes asked.

In the dim yellow cabin light Yustechenko checked his watch and sighed heavily. "One, if all goes well."

"That close?"

The general nodded.

"Troops ready?"

Another nod.

"They won't kill needlessly?"

"Any good soldier hates killing. But I make no promises. The objective, is take facility with minimum damage. And if we slip detection, get inside defensive perimeter fast, a lot of ifs . . . but there will be death. In war, always is there death."

"But no explosives?"

"Silent but quick, knife to throat, hand to hand," Yustechenko said. "So you see your enemy, feel his breath, hold him as he dies."

"Great," Farnes muttered.

"No, not great. Worst nightmare. Red Army would be

happy for illusion of 'strength in numbers.' But even in Afghanistan we had overwhelming advantage on rebels, yet did not win. Then came the Gulf War, where Iraq exposed our jugu'ar. Four thousand tanks! And what effect? Everything picked apart by weapons so far away the crews never knew they were under attack until the second they died. Then come the Huns rattling their high tech on Polish borders. Leave us defenseless, you invite a counterstrike. Now only way to peace is knowing that alternative is more horrible by far.''

"Let's not talk about it, okay?" Lorraine pleaded.

"Of course," Yustechenko said, almost gently, leaving them alone.

Farnes turned her way. She looked pale. "Less than an hour. Can you hold out?"

"I'll try," she said weakly, but could not manage a smile.

"Soon," he said, stuffing his hands deep in his pockets. At the bottom he felt a small bottle, his one memento from Prison Perfect, the same bottle he used to quell the fear in the dying rapist in the cell beside him. Simple aspirin, and a promise. Turning to Lorraine, he snapped his fingers and shook his head hard.

"What?" she asked.

"Almost forgot. Picked these up at Shagmyer's, with the other stuff."

"What?"

"Dramamine."

"Really?"

"I just forgot, what with so much going on. Here."

"Two?"

"Two is fine. The general will get us some water."

"Thanks," she said. "I feel better already."

Sixty minutes later the deck hatch popped, opening the tight compartments to the lapidary blaze of summer stars. The cool air over the Chesapeake Bay filled the sub like a balm as the elite Soviet Assault Force scrambled silently onto the deck beneath the moonless sky, dragging their limp rubber boats behind, yanking the levers on the $CO_2$ cartridges, hissing gas into the pods, lashing bandoliers, knives and Kalashnikov AK-47 rifles firmly on their bodies they dipped the swelling boats into the black waters. Slipping quickly into their shoulder harnesses, each man snatched an oar from a tending yeoman before lowering himself in.

Farnes followed Yustechenko in the lead boat. Should he stay behind? Was he the indispensible man they should return for when they had secured the Bunker? Or would they all be driven away by withering fusilades from the defending forces? Surely they must have heard about CDC by now. Or had they? How good, or bad, was communication? Who was passing messages? And who at NORAD was in charge? And when, as they eventually must, would they give the order for nuclear retaliation? Or was the chain of command broken? Maybe. So many unknowns, including the ultimate one. Could he do it? Answer. Easy. If The Bunker's facilities were intact, he had nearly as good a chance as at CDC. And that's why he had to be here now. To say no. Soldiers would use all deliberate force to take the objectives without understanding why. He had to be on Yustechenko's shoulder to tell him no, not to blow up a door, not to take out an emergency power source. It was a deadly race against time and they could afford no errors. Just one could kill them, kill millions more, maybe, in time, kill everybody.

To either side, paddles dipped and stroked through the glassy water as they left the submerging form of the *Rodina* behind. A hundred yards of shallow water lay between them and the shore. Two hundred yards inland and as many feet underground lay The Bunker.

"Some homecoming," Farnes muttered, just before Yustechenko slapped a huge hand over his mouth.

"You," Yustechenko whispered, surveying the shore with infrared binoculars, "are the ace in this hole. You stay behind the troops. To get you shot proves nothing but stupidity. Already there is enough stupidity."

The boat slipped quietly shoreward as Yustechenko said something in Russian. The men responded by dropping one hand from their oars, crooking the other over their shoulders, and retrieving compact wire cutters. "Spools of concertina," Yustechenko said, "from reception committee." As the lead boat's bloated bow snubbed the sandy shore, Yustechenko circled his arm.

The commandos exploded off the bow, dragging the boat ashore behind them. Turning quickly, one reached back and slashed the pontoons with his combat knife. Farnes froze as the air hissed out. He could almost see the commander's smile in the faint starlight. "You will see."

A pair of commandos rushed ahead and snaked forward,

low, hands and knees pumping, clutching the wire cutters, reaching the first tangle of concertina wire and razor ribbon, shearing it, pulling with heavy leather gloves, cutting more. Others flanking them pulled away, opening a wedge to give access to more wire.

Yustechenko joined the last one in dragging the deflated boat toward the wedge. When the men finished cutting, they leapt over and waited on the other side. The general crouched down and entered the breach, passing the leading edge of the flattened boat across. The pair on the other side grabbed it, waited for Yustechenko to clear, then stretched it tightly through the path.

"Boat is armored. Use it to protect us," he said.

"What about getting back?"

Yustechenko whispered, "We lose one boat, same amount of men. We know that. This is no video game, Farnes."

They moved like ground fog, seeping silently, almost invisibly, condensing here and there in pockets. No rattles, no taps, no coughing or panting, just blackfaced phantoms eating up ground.

Steadily, invisibly, closer.

Since the concertina wire, nothing.

No machine gun nests, no mines, not even searchlights sweeping the grounds. Why?

"Where are they?" Yustechenko hissed.

Farnes shook his head, not knowing, still thinking.

"Is trap?"

Farnes shook his head.

"Are they all dead?"

"There!" Farnes whispered.

Surrounding The Bunker's concealed entrance a small wall of sandbags had been set up. On its edges, spotlights swept the night, all skyward.

"They're waiting for planes, like at CDC," Farnes said.

"No," Yustechenko whispered back. "Planes cannot hit two hundred feet underground, yes?"

"Burrowing bombs," Farnes shot back. "You have them?"

"Not invasionary force. What is need? Our scientists tell us everyone will be dead."

"Surprise, surprise."

"But why are they not ready for surprise attack?"

"Because," Farnes whispered back, "it's so much easier to send in MiGs or assault helicopters or Scud missiles. Why would you waste the men when you can just wait until everyone dies or starves?"

"Because our men are dying, too."

"They don't know that. They think there's only one thing you want to do to The Bunker, to take it out. They can't imagine you'd want to capture it. So they'll do anything to keep you from destroying it. Up there they've got the best ground-to-air missiles in the world."

"You too much believe your defense contractors, I'm afraid," Yustechenko said, unsnapping a canister, punching it onto the muzzle of his AK-47.

"What's that?"

"I ask questions. That is only way in?"

Farnes nodded. "Yes."

Yustechenko shouldered the rifle butt and aimed. The soldiers at The Bunker stood maskless, their bare faces suctioned to nightscopes. To the north above Philadelphia, the sky began igniting with tracer fire and air-to-air missiles. Just sparks. Far away as they were, it was an eerie display, so silent, so deadly. The soldier's nightscopes turned that way just as Yustechenko pulled the trigger.

"What is it?" Farnes said.

"Tear gas. Trichloroamine, Dr. Farnes."

The canister whistled as it arced and dropped behind the sandbags, exploding in a dull poof like a dropped bag of flour. A panicked spray of machine-gun fire scythed into the night before the defenders came stumbling out, coughing, rubbing their eyes, holding their throats, one grabbing at his pistol scabbard as the gas-masked invaders surged forward in a wide arcing wave, ready to cut down the opposition.

There was none.

The American soldiers were knocked flat, disarmed, shackled, left coughing as the Soviets raced through the clearing smoke of tear gas and began to descend the stairwell to the elevator platform down. As quickly as he could, Farnes raced along, donning a gas mask Yustechenko shoved at him.

Farnes was shoulder to shoulder with Yustechenko when the Soviet commander faced the elevator door and said, "Locked!"

Farnes held up a hand as the eddies of tear gas swirled around them and said, "Wait. It's my system."

Not entirely true. Again it was Gerhardt Siemens' program, modified by Larry Farnes to give The Bunker security and safety. It was his choice to leave in the bypass and access commands Siemens had built into the program logic, the same ones that remained in the system at Prison Perfect, the same ones that would work on the modified Rabson Cyberus-Sentinel Prototype lock on the elevator.

Pressing his hand against the panel to the right of the door frame activated the red light system. "Come on, come on."

Synthavoice came back smoothly, an anodyne lobotomized calm forming the words, **"Enter access code, please."**

"JABBERWOCK," Farnes said, ignoring Yustechenko's puzzled expression.

Nothing.

Had they debugged after he left?

Why?

It was Siemens' system as far as they knew. Farnes should have been seen only as an installer, a user, not a programmer.

Capacitance delay?

Situation override for DEFCON 1?

What?

As Farnes' mind raced, attempting to discover what was thwarting his override command, the pincered doors slid open. Still masked, he led Yustechenko and four elite commandos into the cab. Pushing a button for Level Seven, he felt his stomach fall behind as they dropped to the restricted research area, where Karen Karlsen had died what seemed a lifetime ago. The back of his mind rang with the jarring sound of the alarm that day as he tried to forget. When the cab hit Level Seven, he shook the budding tears away and pushed through the opening door.

Ten feet away stood Bill Wentworth, a diamond-hard glare in his squinting eyes, his right hand clawed around a modular detonator, its red light pulsing. He swallowed hard as he chirped the threat, "One more step, comrades, and we all find out if there is a heaven after this hell."

# TIME BOMB

"Easy, Bill, very easy," said Farnes, his hands up.

Wentworth let out a maniacal laugh, less human than a hyena, his eyes welling up with tears, his hand clutched firmly on the detonator.

"We don't want to kill anyone," Farnes said.

"Then why are so many dead?" Wentworth screamed.

"We can end it."

"Do you have any idea how long we've been locked up down here *trying* to end it?"

"Then you're too close to give up now."

Wentworth's hand quivered on the detonator, his red eyes blinking, his breath spasms of sobs and anger. "Mary's dead," he told Farnes. "I listened to her die on the phone, while I was trying to turn around this mess you and your comrades caused."

"*I* caused?"

"The FBI said you were probably a Soviet agent. No, they couldn't prove anything, as always with clever people. They couldn't prove a thing, but they *knew* anyway. They said you had damaged national security irreparably and they were *right,* weren't they?"

Wentworth's finger shifted toward the button.

"Easy, Bill. Where's the crew? Is Andy Cross around?"

"Dead."

"Sorry . . ."

Yustechenko's men stood motionless behind him, as Farnes took one cautious step forward.

"Don't," Wentworth said, stepping back.

Just behind Wentworth came Cindy Chin, who gasped before stammering, "Dr. Wentworth. We have telemetric satellite reports from Florida that the Red Army is dying in droves.''

Wentworth's eyes clicked onto Yustechenko. ''Pravda, Comrade?''

Yustechenko's head nodded.

''Tit for tat.'' Wentworth laughed. ''You really didn't think you could beat American science at its best game, did you?''

''Jesus,'' Farnes whispered. ''You mean you counterattacked? After seeing what theirs was doing to us?''

Wentworth made a chirping noise, squeaked, ''What did we have to lose? Running eighty-seven percent mortality in heavily infected areas, Comrade Farnes. It is Comrade Farnes, isn't it? You were part of this all along. That's how you got out of that hole you should have died in, am I right?''

''No,'' Farnes said, understanding that Wentworth was beyond logic.

Yustechenko stepped forward, shouldered Farnes aside. Wentworth took another step back and said, ''Don't or I'll—''

''Dr. Farnes is not ours,'' Yustechenko said, ''but we wish he was, because he can stop this.''

''Can't take a dose of your own medicine, eh?''

''It was not my choice,'' Yustechenko said directly, holding Wentworth's eyes.

''But you'll settle for it, eh?''

''I am soldier. If needed I die for my country. I know that. Thirty-five million Soviets died in Great Patriotic War. Is not first time I have seen this. When I was seven, I promised myself that if a soldier I would keep civilians from dying. But,'' he shrugged, ''I am soldier and my country sent me to die. I am long way from home. No one comes for my body, or what's left if you push button. For me does not matter. If I don't die here, I die somewhere else, maybe from knife or bullet or missile, maybe from these killing germs, maybe, if madness goes on, from nuclear detonation. If we don't stop it, it comes to that.''

Wentworth blinked.

Farnes said, ''He's right. We've got to stop it or the hand is played out to the last card.''

''Why should I believe you?'' Wentworth hissed the word, retreated another step, brandished the detonator.

''What's holding the launch command back, Bill? You've

had continuous contact with the SAC Omaha and Cheyenne Mountain since the epidemic began, right?''

Wentworth's head dipped slightly. A nod.

"Did you ever tell them the plague was incurable?"

"Of course not!" Wentworth snarled. "We know anything is curable, if . . .'' His wild eyes seemed to drift.

"Then we better hurry up with that cure, Bill. Otherwise there's no telling how much time we have left before they give the launch order.''

"SAC won't launch," Wentworth muttered, "unless we get incomings.''

"Maybe. Maybe not. But what about the last card in the nuclear game, the one that was designed to guarantee the Soviets would never survive a pre-emptive strike? What about the boomers, Bill?'' Farnes pleaded.

Wentworth's eyes went to Yustechenko's, who blinked slowly as he nodded, sighed hard.

"Moscow did not balance equation," the Soviet said. "That means even if everyone in United States dies, thirty missile submarines destroy Soviet Union. One Trident submarine can destroy thirty major Soviet cities. If only one survives and launches, the motherland is crippled for thirty years, at least. Maybe forever. And it will happen.''

"Good, you heathen bastard!" snarled Wentworth.

"Then *our* submarines do same.''

Wentworth buckled as if hit.

"Until is nothing left but vast, burned wasteland of blackened bodies and melted buildings. I want no part in final madness. So if you must, Dr. Wentworth, spare me, a poor soldier, the pain of going on. Push your little button.''

Farnes tensed, unsure that Yustechenko knew his game.

"Bill . . .'' he started.

"Back, you bastard!" Wentworth's hand tightened on the detonator, smiled as he said, "It doesn't matter.'' He threw down the box. It clattered on the floor, the red light still pulsing.

Yustechenko picked it up, signaled his men forward. "Show them what you need.''

"I need you," he said, grabbing Wentworth by the lab coat collar.

"Too late," he said laughing. "I infected myself this morning.''

"What?''

He shuddered through a chill and buckled over, his eyes rolling, fighting for the words. "I knew you'd come back . . . so damn smart . . . just had to show every . . . everybody . . . but it's set to blow. Hah! Find *that* . . . genius."

Wentworth twisted backward and surged in convulsive tentanic spasms, his body arching, his limbs stretching spastically out, unable to control his sphincters, becoming a writhing vessel of death, grabbing for air in huge, hideous gulps, gurgling and frothing, showing nothing but the sclera of his eyes, then, in one quivering convulsion, pouncing into death.

Cindy Chin screamed, then began sobbing.

Farnes grabbed her. "Files. Computer, hard copy. Wentworth's notes. Everything. Let's go."

"Okay," she whimpered, her eyes locked on what had been Wentworth.

"General?" Farnes said.

Yustechenko nodded.

"Signal the sub. We need Lorraine."

"Why?"

"Vaccines. She's immune."

"But I thought . . ."

"General, we've got a lot to do and next to no time."

"Certainly." He nodded.

"And that's not all."

"What more can I do?"

"We've got to transmit a priority message to SAC at Cheyenne Mountain. Next we've somehow got to open communications to the Submarine Base at New London, Connecticut."

"Yes?"

"Very much yes. Unless we want World War III."

"I see. And what is it we have been fighting here?"

"I'm not a soldier, General. I'm a doctor. My fight is against disease and this fight is to the death. Some will die, some will linger, some will live. If we succeed, some will never get sick. If you succeed, General, there will be a future worth saving them for."

"But I am a soldier, Farnes, not a diplomat!"

"You're the best diplomat the Soviets have in America, General, so I guess you'll have to do."

"But I don't know what to say."

"My guess is they won't care what you say, but what you offer."

Cindy Chin returned, her hands stuffed with folders. "We have a terminal up in Dr. Wentworth's office, and—"

"You know what they released, the counteragent?"

Chin nodded. "Of course. It's well characterized."

"Labs working?"

"Yes."

"And Wentworth's bomb?"

Chin shook her head, confused. "I don't know. I think he was into the psychotic phase of the disease. Confused. He could have deluded himself to think he had a way of protecting the vaccine from capture—"

"Or he could have actually planted a bomb."

Yustechenko turned the detonator in his hand. "It would need receiver, of course. We can find receivers, little bugs and listening devices, all the same. We have thirty men. I will find it."

"But in time?"

Yustechenko tried to smile as he shrugged. "You run your race. I run mine. We must both win."

Farnes nodded. "I developed the vaccine against our illness. Emergency treatment, too. Lorraine has antibodies against the Soviet virus. With both we have a real chance, if we run full speed, nonstop, and without delay."


Only twenty minutes later Farnes pressed the jet inoculator against Yustechenko's powerful bicep and injected him with the vaccine. He looked up from his intense search and winced. "Don't like injections," he said.

"Progress?" Farnes said.

"We know very much where it *isn't*."

"Hurry."

"Yes, but we cannot miss something," Yustechenko said. "You deal with your problem. I with mine. What do you have?"

"All your soldiers are protected, and we have lots of vaccine in stock."

"What if we are already sick?"

Farnes shook his head. "Not likely. Incubation period is twelve hours, plus or minus two. You'd be sick by now."

"And for those who are?"

"Treatment. We have that, too. But to save a nation, we need to stop a war and start a system of distribution."

"I can offer peace, plus use Soviet invasionary machinery."

"Without trouble from Moscow?"

"Who, Dr. Farnes, will walk into a lethal epidemic and tell me no? Before we meet I learn that sickness spreads to Cuba with wounded invasion troops. From there, how far? So you see, now the sickness is second in danger to only one thing."

Farnes nodded. "So what about New London?"

"First the bomb. Next a telephone."

"You're going to call them?"

"America has best telephone system of all. We have orders to spare it, so could study. Orders stand."

"But—Jesus! A phone call . . ."

"As you said, Dr. Farnes, reach out and touch someone."

Repressing a silly urge to laugh, Farnes said. "All right, call. But do you have any idea what your scientists threw at us?"

"I am only soldier."

Farnes struggled to get a handle on what he was up against. "Can I borrow your protective gear?"

"Of course."

"What else did they tell you?"

"Who?"

"The people who briefed you for invasion."

Yustechenko looked up, furrowed his brow, said, "Avoid water and people who are sick, coughing."

Farnes lit up. "So after the primary distribution through infected food, secondary is waterborne, like cholera. Tertiary vector is airborne aerosol droplets from the lungs, like pneumatic plague."

"And this is help?"

"Isolate, then cure. Quarantine," said Farnes. "If you know where it's coming from, it's easier to keep people away from the disease than to keep the disease away from the people who don't know where they're catching it."

"I give you radio stations."

"Soon," Farnes said.

"What to say?"

"The truth."

''That means I must say Soviet High Command is a bunch of assholes. Not great for career, *da*?''

''Say they were all, Soviet and American, a bunch of assholes. Lay it on the line. But say that no one should fight in a burning house. The fighting has to stop. Armistice. Cease-fire.''

''This will stop it?''

''Maybe.''

''Maybe, Farnes?''

''We have to beat your bug, Yustechenko.''

The general shrugged. ''We have your dossier. You are genius.''

''I can't change the speed of chemical reactions or alter the laws of nature. Even geniuses need time.''

A shout rang out down the hall. Yustechenko struggled to his feet and joined Farnes rushing from the computer room, down the central corridor, and into a small, unoccupied lab. One of the commandos stood pointing to a small refrigerator, its door open, the light-switch button depressed by tape. Inside, unlighted but visible, sitting on a shelf as innocently as a carton of milk, was a cubical package of plastic explosives wired into the power cord.

A burst of Russian. Yustechenko translated, ''Double detonator. One on opening is deactivated. Other, they say, connects to main power. If move outside, blows when break connection.''

''How much time?''

''Dial says five minutes.''

''Can you find the switch?''

After Yustechenko's quick translation, one soldier shook his head, no. Turning back to Farnes, the general said, ''No promises. Another way. We take suggestions.''

''Don't unplug it,'' he said.

''What?''

''Run an extension cord, a long one joining every cord in the complex, hurry . . .'' He moved off at a run, ''. . . from another outlet then bridge across to the refrigerator plug as you remove it. Don't interrupt the power, JUST GET IT THE FUCK OUT OF HERE!''

Taking a deep breath and closing his eyes, Farnes dropped himself deep into meditation. Time became thick; the seconds flicking digitally on the detonator's timer seemed more like hours. Around him, what was seconds ago chaos seemed now casual, the spinning motions of soldiers responding to commands now slowed to lazy turns, ghosts of motion, as Farnes pulled himself up and out, running out the door and down the main corridor to the supply closet, reaching the handle, feeling it pull back. He stepped away, whirled in a roundhouse kick and sheared off the locked handle as the door pulled away from its frame. A quick snap later it was open, his hands feverishly yanking spool after axled spool of electrical cord from the floor, stacking it beside him as the Soviets drifted in, picked them up in slow motion, began their strange, jerky run back to the bomb.

Farnes spun and sprinted, racing past them, snatching one roll of cord away, turning and sliding across the polished floor to the closest free outlet, plugging in extension after extension until they were all connected together in a run of seven hundred feet. Then, leaping up, he reached one of the soldier's belts, snatched the combat knife from its scabbard, and slit the terminal cord's receptacle, baring sparking wires. Stooping down, he touched them to the half-pulled refrigerator plug before pulling it slowly out. Having found a conducting circuit, the electricity ran into the refrigerator, so Farnes could wrap his hands around it without danger. Holding the leads firmly in place, he motioned the nearest commandos to pick up the refrigerator, head for the elevator.

Instantly understanding what needed to be done, others picked up the connected spools, last one first, and began to play out the cord.

The detonator passed three minutes and kept ticking down.

Together they raced down three intersecting corridors, playing out three hundred feet of spooled cord.

Two minutes, ten seconds.

Farnes hammered on the elevator call button.

"Access code . . ."

"JABBERWOCK!"

It snapped open.

Two minutes.

One of the Soviets simply pointed to the cord.

No way.

The elevator door could not close unless they disconnected the cord. Without the door closed, the elevator would not ascend. Without ascent, the bomb would go off right here, sealing them in with all the deadly germs blown up as the labs buckled.

In one minute and forty-five seconds.

Farnes pointed up, signaled for the soldiers to open the maintenance access port to the overhead motor.

They started levering the panel off, stripping the threaded screws away.

Ninety seconds.

As two soldiers let down the refrigerator to assist, the bare wires pulled from his hands with a snapping spark.

Farnes felt it coming in slow motion, but couldn't stop it. He grabbed a breath and prepared to die. But when the wires had broken completely free, lay sparking and smoldering beside him, nothing happened.

"Decoy!" he shouted.

Although the Soviets could never know the word, they followed Farnes' pointing finger, winced, froze, then understood. There *were* no booby-trapping connections.

The detonator was entirely internal.

Seizing the package and pulling it away from the housing, he felt the fear all over him, pure, primal, powerful.

Seventy-five seconds.

Maybe this was it.

He kicked the cord out the door and let it shut, hit the panel marked SURFACE.

The elevator lurched up.

Sixty.

Level Three blurred by.

Fifty.

Level One passed.

Forty.

Slowing for arrival.

Thirty.

The doors started back, remained closed.

Farnes hit the OPEN button. Nothing.

Twenty.

The doors yawned open.

Fifteen.

Farnes shot through, surprising the Soviets posted above with, "Down!" Motioning with his free hand, running for the sandbag wall.

Ten.

Holding the bomb in both hands he spun once, read

Eight.

Twice, saw

Six.

Released it into the night, remembering four.

A Russian hand reached up and pulled him down just before the bomb exploded, tracing the night sky with hot trails of burning white phosphorus.

He stumbled back to the elevator, descended numbly to the Level Seven, where Yustechenko greeted him with, "You should have let my men . . ."

Farnes shook his head. "No. Bravery is fine. I draw the line at stupidity."

"Stupidity," Yustechenko said, "sometimes seems stubborness. No?"

"New London," Farnes said.

"Radios," Yustechenko said back. "I have seventeen stations controlled. So far we have made no occupation messages. What do you propose?"

"What is the objective?"

"To avoid the abyss."

"Then you'll have to leave our country."

Yustechenko shrugged. "Occupations are often difficult. History tells us that. It would have happened anyway. We could not have survived the epidemic you threw at us."

Farnes smiled back. "You could not have survived the epidemic your own people threw at you," he said.

"Protective clothing," he said.

"I've had a close look. Any respectable virus will have no trouble defeating your respirators."

Yustechenko's head dropped, his eyes closed. After a few seconds he opened them, looked right at Farnes. "You are saying . . . what?"

"You figure it out. Why didn't they send doctors who could care for your sick?"

"We are a long way from home. Supplies are difficult."

"But vaccination travels with the soldier."

"We received some shots. I do not know why . . . perhaps they could not . . ."

"They could. That's the game, Yustechenko. You don't make a killer bug unless you've got a cure. If you don't have a cure, it always turns on you."

"Like a mad dog."

"Very."

"I do not make policy. Perhaps if one of us were captured, they felt he could provide immunity, as Lorraine is doing now."

"Perhaps, but were you led to expect that much resistance?"

"No. That is why they send only thousands."

"And?"

"Little resistance, Farnes, but men who fought well."

"But not enough to resist you."

"No."

"So how does all this make any sense—vaccinations that don't work, protective suits that don't protect, an invasion that's not followed by massive reinforcements?"

"I am simple soldier."

"But not a stupid man."

"You have answer."

Farnes took the general's eyes, hard. "As I have it figured, you were sent to preoccupy us with a fight and spread the infection by panic. If you could win and occupy while avoiding disease, that was fine. But that wasn't the plan. The plan was to break down the last pockets of resistance, destroy the command centers for nuclear retaliation, and wait to be relieved. Then while you were waiting, you were expected to die out as the infection caught up with you."

"You say I am not stupid, but makes me seem . . . the word is naive?"

"You said to look at history. In history, plague turned back more invading armies than it ever helped. Name me one army that won during a full-blown epidemic."

Yustechenko closed his eyes, went into his studies, sighed, and shook his head. "My memory is not clear now, but there must be cases where disease helped. Sieges, for example."

"The diseases were inside the walls, and always after the population had been weakened by hunger and exhaustion."

"And if you are right, Farnes? What are you saying?"

"They sent you unprotected against a weapon you couldn't beat. When did the plan call for you to be relieved?"

"When we had won."

"Won? Against who? Us or them?" He waved his hands across the lab windows where the germs had been bred. "Because you had to beat us both."

"Perhaps this takes some thought."

"Perhaps you should remember that strong conquering generals, in history, could set up their own nations, become strong political figures that Moscow couldn't control. Either that or you become a returning hero, maybe even take over at home. Nobody in the Politburo wanted that. So how do you eliminate that possibility?''

"A diabolical thought," Yustechenko said.

"But a possibility you admit."

"We have other concerns, no?"

Farnes let it go, accepted the suggestion. "So let's work on the broadcast. When we return we can get some vaccine back to the sub for distribution to your troops in the rear and,'' Farnes drew a breath, "to our civilians, if that's not too much to ask."

"Your soldiers will not trust us, not after our trick."

"Then we have to convince them. No one survives if the war goes on. Before you landed, Yustechenko; all our National Guard and many in our army were already deployed for epidemic relief. All we have to do is resume that same system to distribute the vaccine!''

"If we can, yes. And we will broadcast a plea for your forces to join us, for all your people to come, for water and food, as well as medicine. You will help us to make this announcement?"

"I will."

"And if they do not respond?"

"Then I won't risk your men to hunt them down. It's trust or die. If they'd rather be dead than see Red, they'll die. Some will. If they'd rather live, they'll soon understand that they have to take a chance."

"Thanks to you, Dr. Farnes."

"If the missiles don't fly."

"New London."

Farnes nodded.

"What will they want?"

"A plan for cooperative relief of the epidemic, plus a timetable for eventual Soviet withdrawal, with the first deployments confirmed by reconnaissance satellite tomorrow."

"Tomorrow?"

"They're soldiers, general. For the first time in history a foreign army is overrunning the country they love. And they've got their finger on the trigger of the gun that was supposed to keep that from happening. Since deterrence has failed, how long will they wait for retaliation?"

"Long enough for a telephone call?"

# ON THE BRINK

"I am General Igor Yustechenko, Supreme Commander of the Soviet North American Invasionary Forces."

"Yes, sir," came the response over the staticky telephone connection.

"I must speak to your ranking officer."

"One moment." The line went silent for a minute before a clear voice, showing a single quaver, took up the conversation. "Chaney speaking."

Yustechenko asked, "Who am I speaking to?"

"Lieutenant Commander Richard G. Chaney."

"You are ranking officer?"

"I'm what's left at the top, yes, sir."

"I have important message."

"I am listening, sir."

"Soviet Invasionary Force begins withdrawal tomorrow morning."

"Say again, sir."

"Repeat what you thought I said," Yustechenko told him.

"Soviet forces begin withdrawal . . . tomorrow?"

"Correct."

"I don't understand."

"We are leaving United States."

A long silence ended in a sigh and, "Sir, we are not in the mood for jokes here."

"I do not joke."

"And *I* do not understand."

"We have lost."

"Our reports—"

"We request immediate cease-fire and armistice."

"Sir . . . ?"

"Fighting ends tomorrow morning. Our healthy troops

disengage now to redeploy for civilian relief. Look to your satellites to confirm this.''

"Jesus," the voice said.

"I do not understand, Lieutenant Commander, why you say Jesus.''

"General, we are three hours into countdown for an all-out nuclear attack against the Soviet Union.''

"You must stop this!''

"I . . . I don't know if I can . . .''

"You must try! Do you understand?''

"General, they're never going to believe me. I'm just a Naval reserve officer who hit rotation at the wrong time. You'll have to talk to our command structure, the real brass . . . at NORAD . . .''

"You are ranking officer and must take responsibility. Tell your brass, as you call them, to monitor commercial emergency broadcast stations for important message. One hour from now, to repeat every hour, so everyone with radio can hear. We must end this now, or it will end everything forever. Cancel the launch. Abort it. You *must*.''

"I will try," he said, his voice breaking, "but we must see the disengagement and demobilization, plus evidence of withdrawal, very soon.''

"Watch from the sky. Now we stop attack. Now we start pulling back our forward lines. Soon we start to help your people with water, food, medicine.''

"Say again?''

Farnes took the handset. "Commander Chaney, my name is Larry Farnes. I'm a civilian doctor who worked for DOD.''

"*The* Larry Farnes?''

"The same.''

Another silence, broken suddenly by, "Is this for real? Do *you* know how to stop this, how to stop the dying or at least slow it down?''

"Yes," Farnes said.

"What can we do to help?''

"First, stop the launch, get the message to our submarines, or it doesn't matter. Second, listen to the broadcast and arrange for our armed forces—''

"What's left of them . . .''

"To do exactly as we say.''

Another silence. "I'll see what I can do. But whatever you do, hurry.''

* * *

Without allowing its five-bladed rotor to stop, the huge Soviet Mi-24 Hind-D helicopter gunship plucked them off the field above The Bunker and banked into the moonlit night, heading due north at two hundred miles an hour. Looking down, Farnes saw—perhaps imagined—starlight twinkling off the quiet Chesapeake. Beside that, only the nearly tactile whooshing of the treetops below disturbed the darkened silence. Ahead, skies that earlier roared and exploded with dogfights now settled into a tense calm that drew them on. Drawing a long breath, Farnes snapped out a ballpoint pen and began to draft his speech.

An hour later the pilot spotted the circle of barium green flares marking the landing area as the gunship banked sharply before leveling off and floating down, hovering tentatively only feet above the ground as its clattering props engulfed them in a thick swirling cloud of dust. Only when the pilot felt the wheels touch evenly did he cut the powerful turbocharged engines and settle into the smoldering wreckage of south Philadelphia. Only two hours had passed since it fell to Soviet assault after intense door-to-door fighting and heavy losses on both sides. Descending the ladder, Yustechenko snapped off a salute to waiting staff officers and shepherded Farnes to a waiting jeep. Racing along dodging rubble and fire, the driver covered only three blocks before dropping them at the blackened walls and shattered windows of the WCBL studio on Franklin Street.

Crunching through the fallen glass, they were swept off by Red Army majors to the broadcast booth. Inside, exhausted Soviet technicians had labored through smoke, fire, and explosions to link the signals from this station into local affiliates in Richmond, Durham, Atlanta, Nashville, Mobile, and Orlando and were just finishing up their checklist. Jumping to attention as Yustechenko entered, they assured him that the boosted signal would reach as far west as the Rockies.

When they sat down, Yustechenko nodded to Farnes. The technician swung the boom mike his way as Farnes set the yellow legal pad in front of him, cleared his throat, and began reading slowly.

"Fellow Americans, civilian and military. My name is Larry Farnes. I am an American speaking to you from a half-burned radio station in Philadelphia, the city that gave birth to American freedom over two hundred years ago. If, God willing, all goes well, following this message from the birthplace of our freedom, we will once again be free.

"These words may seem incredible. Even as I hear myself speak them, they seem incredible to me. Many have died in the most terrible war we have ever fought, more terrible by far than the trench warfare of World War I. Our enemies were two. The first was disease, which I am ashamed to admit, as many of you will recognize, that I, as well as my Soviet counterparts, designed and created to ravage the human body. Over eighty percent of the millions dead have fallen to disease. More will fall if we don't act now to stop it. This very evening the Soviet forces have begun assisting in distributing vaccine and treatments to centers we have established to minister to the sick and inoculate the well. Relief centers are being established in every American city with a pre-invasion population of two hundred thousand or more people. The sick are directed to the large Red Cross disaster tents which are going up even as we speak. The well are directed to large olive-colored military command tents with markings. Both sick and well will receive assistance.

"People who are not sick should be advised not to eat uncanned foods or drink unboiled or chemically untreated water. The disease is able to travel in water, as well as through the coughing of those infected. So avoid drinking suspect water or contacting infected individuals. Of the two diseases out there, both will make you sick in twelve hours. If you have been well that long and drunk bottled water and avoided contact, go immediately for vaccination.

"Despite the deception used in the Soviet invasion, this offer is no trick, and may be your only chance to avoid death. Without doubt, these germs are the most lethal in human experience, more than three times as deadly as bubonic plague.

"The Soviet Army was badly hit by a biological counterattack of our own. In Florida and Georgia it has already experienced staggering losses. Nonetheless we have found a vaccine and are now administering it to the invading forces, as well as our own civilians who otherwise may become infected.

"Except for Soviet personnel remaining behind to inoculate and treat our own people, the invading Soviet forces have agreed to complete a speedy withdrawal. The timetable of their withdrawal depends on voluntary replacement at plague relief tents by our own American military personnel. As that happens, they will be on their way home. Their commander, General Igor Yustechenko, is right beside me . . ."

Farnes passed the boom mike to Yustechenko.

"Dr. Farnes speaks truth. Even tomorrow some Soviets leave.

This war is not won by any man. Not Soviet, not American. Winning means after waves of death, nothing keeps life from returning, as flowers in spring. If we cannot stop this, Farnes, next spring is only death. So stop it we must, and now, before no one is left. And we must now hope your countrymen who control missiles will find mercy and wisdom to see that they, too, must permit life. We have all great sadness. Perhaps we have now learned to know how to live. And with this, we have perhaps learned that we all live in a time where no war can be won, where we must all live together or we must all die together. And so we will leave, return to life we believe in, leave you with life you believe in. I cannot say I am sorry because the sorrow I feel is unspeakable, seems, even to me, unknowable, but I hope that we learn from this horror to destroy all things that can destroy us.''

Farnes took back the microphone, said only, ''If, as I believe, the Soviets in Russia are monitoring our broadcast, we ask that you send your best doctors and researchers to help us stop this thing, stop it here, before it circles the globe.''

Yustechenko reached over and snapped off the broadcast toggle.

''Well?'' Farnes said.

The general shrugged. ''We will see.''

Inside Cheyenne Mountain, NORAD's Commanding Officer, General Brent Sanderson, asked his Executive Officer, ''Estimated forty million dead and the thing hasn't even hit stride. How are the Soviets going to pay for it?''

''Surviving targeteers at Omaha are expanding our inventory to include Soviet population centers, sir.''

''Are we rigged to re-program trajectories of our land-based launches based on secure link-up, Doug?''

''Roger that, General.''

''The real mystery is . . .'' He stopped to rub the throbbing ache at his temples before drawing a hard breath, blinking his eyes open and staring at the huge backlit maps on the high walls. ''Where the hell is the incoming Soviet volley? Why haven't they emptied their silos?''

''Because they want everything intact. Our technology, our resources, even as many of our people as—''

''Damn it, Doug! If this is a goddam commie trick, they'll just walk in and take over!''

"Like the broadcast said, satellites show the battle lines breaking, redeployment to vulnerable civilian relief posts, company strength max, unsupported, all over the place in a lot of little cities. Scattered around like that they're either suicidal—which I don't believe—or they're for real. Now if you're them and you don't mean what you say, why leave your men behind to get slaughtered?"

"Who's left to slaughter them?"

"Come on, Brent. We still got a couple hundred thousand fighting mad dogfaces in uniform out there. And there's always someone who wants to hit back. You can always fire, if it's a trick."

"Unless they hit the mountain."

"This guy Farnes says he can beat the sickness, if we can support him and get the stuff distributed."

"And stand down the missiles? Not on your life! Reprogram for new targets, using coordinates from Omaha. Do we have contact with our boomers?"

"Through New London, yes, sir."

"We launch in eighteen hours, or when their first silo lights up on our recon birds."

Aboard SSBN *Nathaniel Green,* four hundred feet beneath the choppy waves of the Bay of Bengal and fifty miles off the city of Madras on the eastern coast of India, Captain Allan Perry had already ordered General Alarm sounded as he began to run the launch control sequence with his Executive Officer, Charley Genovese.

Turning to Genovese, he whispered the command he had prayed his lips would never form. "Sound battle stations missile."

"Aye, aye, Captain."

"Advise when the launch control center is ready."

Genovese left Perry alone at the con and stepped away. Ordinarily everything in a drill was done by voice communication, for maximum efficiency, minimum time. But they both knew this was no drill, so he made no objection to the departure from procedure. It would take a few extra minutes, only that. As far as they knew, they weren't being pinged, had no evidence of hunters, below or above, were in no apparent danger. In his judgment they could afford the time, ought to take it if there was any chance, any chance at all, that someone back home had worked out a way to avoid it.

He pictured Genovese ambling down the ladder, his ungainly six feet six inch Texan frame descending to the deck below and ducking along aft, until he reached the Missile Control Center. He knew it well. Stepping through the hatchway into the busy MCC, he was always struck by its similarity to a video arcade. Bright lights, patterns, and intersecting cartographic grids, but no bells, no jingling tunes goading players to the next level. As the red panel glowing DEFCON 1 reminded everyone, the game they were playing was already at the highest level, and for the highest stakes of all. As he bent down to hear Genovese's voice twang up, ''Battle stations missile,'' he tried not to think of his grandson Jamie popping up and down as Mario stomped along in the Nintendo game at home. He tried not to think of Jamie, or of Jamie's mother and his oldest daughter Dawn, tried not to think of his wife and Dawn's mother Sonja, tried, hardest of all, to avoid thinking about the inevitable, that they were all gone.

Without being told, Perry knew where the birds were headed. They were targeted across industrial and agricultural sites in the south and manufacturing and military targets in Siberia, plus main centers of population and command. Minsk. Leningrad. Kiev. Moscow. But shit, he realized, everyone has at least one for Moscow.

After launch, Moscow would be a big black hole.

Finally responding to Genovese in the MCC he said, ''Are you ready to launch?''

''Yes, sir, Captain.''

''Spin up the missiles. Stand by for launch sequence orders.''

''Pressure tubes go.''

Surrounded by a forest of missile tubes, Lieutenant Arne Skoldebrand lifted his key, one of the three required for launch, into the tumbler facing him on the panel and inserted it.

Where from here? This was what he had been trained for all his life. He still had two things to confirm.

First, that no one took them out by surprise.

Slowly he rose from his chair in the con and padded across to the sonar room. Inside that room, Sonarman first class Carl Yarboro kept his eyes on the electronic displays, alert for the slightest sign that they were being shadowed. Although they had lain silent, drifting at neutral buoyancy, their antiecho coating concealing them from even active pinging, they had to be dead sure to avoid being dead.

''Anything?'' said the captain.

''No, sir,'' whispered Yarboro.

"Confidence?"

"High. Only contact a tramp steamer, noisier than a fish-wife, making for port. Otherwise, nothing."

Perry walked back to the con. "Make your depth sixty feet. Ahead one third."

"Aye, aye, sir."

The sub nosed up and began sliding toward the surface. Perry had to do it. He had to be sure, for two reasons. Number one, the command reason, was that the satellite passing overhead would downlink the coordinates that linked the missiles to their targets inside Russia. Second, a distant second, but one Perry needed to live with, and one all the sub commanders shared, was the need to authenticate the firing order. Although they were always in contact by trailing wire, he had received no message since the strange one that told him to prepare to attack. Once he authenticated the launch order, any hope the Soviets put on compassion vanished. Enough that it was necessary. Enough that he obeyed orders. And if he had any thought beyond that, if he needed any more reason than what he had accepted years ago, he only had to think of Jamie, or Dawn, or Sonja.

From the con the skipper could reach anywhere in the boat. Pressing one button he said, "Sonar report."

"Negative, sir."

"Depth?"

"Passing one hundred feet, sir."

Perry waited.

"Passing sixty, sir."

"Up periscope." Beside him the tube moved and stopped when the lenses reached eye level. Stepping in to embrace it, he swung the scope around, had a good look. Nothing.

"Passing fifty feet, sir."

"Level off. Up radio mast."

"Aye, aye, sir."

Missile Control reported, "Second key inserted and turned, sir."

"Give me final position from navigator, as soon as you get it," Perry said, his mouth dry, his heart racing, his hands wet. He went to his control panel, inserted his own key, ready to turn. So this was it. A gently whirring noise filled the con as the radio mast went up.

"Radio?"

"Preparing for burst transmission on downlink, sir. Countdown to transmission, sir. Five, four, three, two, one, now. Channel open.''

Seconds yawned like hours.

The radioman's voice came to him suddenly, "We have a message, sir.''

"Decode and bring it up.''

Perry waited only two minutes before the footfalls came hammering into the con. The radioman stood breathless, said only, "Here.''

Perry feared the worst, was afraid his eyes would refuse to focus. So he said, simply, "Read it.''

The radioman stuttered twice before he got the decoding out. "Sir,'' he shouted, unable to restrain himself, "it says 'ABORT LAUNCH. STAND DOWN FROM READY STATUS. GO TO DEFCON 2. RETURN TO PATROL AND STAND BY. NEXT CONTACT OH-SIX HUNDRED. SO-VIET INVASION TERMINATED. OVER.' ''

Then nothing but silence.

"Make your depth three hundred feet,'' he sighed, his whole body shaking, the sweat soaking his khaki uniform.

His exec slipped in the door as Perry withdrew his key. Puzzled, Genovese said, "Ain't it time we hit back?''

Perry rubbed his key between his index finger and turned to Genovese. "Charlie? We can kill them just as dead at oh-six hundred. Am I right?''

"Yes, sir.''

"Then let's see what happens.''

"But Al . . . they could open up on us . . . and . . .''

The skipper spoke in a dull, flat, almost emotionless voice, keeping his passion in his eyes, which he gave, full, wide, and direct, to his exec. "Charlie. Ivan hasn't a clue where we are. Shit, we can kill him anytime. But if he's pulling back, if they've found something to stop this, if there really is a cease-fire, I can tell you that I don't want to go down in what little is left of history as the man who ended life on Earth as we know it.''

Other than a quick blink, Genovese had no response. The silence flooding in around them was quickly filled with the dull, muted humming of the greatest killing machine ever to swim beneath the great oceans of the Earth, cruising ahead and biding time, still waiting, like a hungry shark—a little nervous, a little eager, and even, at depths greater than it had ever plumbed, more than a little scared.

# WITHDRAWAL SYMPTOMS

Just behind the three of them, a US Air Force C-5A was loading the last detachment of Soviet troops into its mammoth hold, waiting only for Yustechenko to join them before taxiing down the hardstands of the Pensacola Naval Air Station for the flight to Havana.

General Igor Yustechenko stood in a rigid military brace and sniffed the hot Florida breeze a final time before extending a hand to Farnes. "I salute you, Dr. Farnes. If you have not saved a world, you have at least kept it from committing suicide."

Farnes shook his head. "But it took a man of vision and courage to understand what was at stake, and to act."

The general shrugged his massive shoulders. "All Slavs are stubborn but not all are stupid."

"You will not receive a hero's welcome," Farnes guessed.

"At home the order has changed, so I may not be shot."

"You could stay here," Lorraine said.

Yustechenko laughed. "I have more chance of shooting here than at home. And if I have to die, let it be in Russia."

"We didn't win," said Farnes, joining Yustechenko's stroll toward the gaping tailgate of the C-5A.

"Neither did we."

"No." Farnes shook his head. "I mean we, humankind, all of us. We didn't win. We haven't beaten this thing. It's showing up beyond Cuba. It rode along with infected American tourists during their incubation periods and has exploded in Britain, Germany, France, Spain, Greece, Egypt, India, Thailand, Korea, Japan, Australia, Mexico, especially Canada. Everywhere cases are being quarantined while we push production of the vaccine and experimental antiviral drugs."

Yustechenko shook his head. "We have opened Pandora's chest."

Farnes laughed. "You mean Pandora's box."

"Sorry," he said, very seriously. "We learn in language school at Kiev never to use the word 'box' after possessive form of proper woman's name."

Farnes surrendered to a sad smile at the irony of such trifling diplomacy in the face of such terrible slaughter. "What I meant to say is that once you let something like this out, it becomes the world's problem. First world travelers spread it to places without the resources or organization to stop it. Then, like all viruses, it mutates, and mutates fast. Then whatever genetic resistance and virulence we scientists added from antibiotic-resistant microbes, whatever neurotoxins or immunosuppressant properties we gave it to start with just get stronger. For the near future we can ignore the chance of nuclear war. Right now we have a new threat to deal with. And we have to work like demons just to stay ahead of this thing. Like flu, but worse, it will circle the earth, season after season, for years, until we find a way to stop it."

"What will it take?" Yustechenko asked.

"All the resources we're putting into killing each other."

"And if not?"

"Then it's medieval, like the plague, but worse. Again and again, until we're whittled down to a few, too few and too poor to fight."

Yustechenko nodded, took Farnes' eyes and smiled. "So this is your new quest?"

Farnes' turn to shrug. "Who knows?"

"You will become one of these hardworking American doctor heros?"

Farnes stuffed his hands nonchalantly in his pockets, shrugged again.

"And what of Lorraine here?"

Farnes gave her his eyes, then turned them to Yustechenko. "She's well, she's alive, and she's free. What she does is up to her. That's America."

Yustechenko waggled a thick finger at him. "In Soviet Union many men would fight for woman like this!"

"Well, I've seen enough fighting for a while," Farnes told him.

Yustechenko sighed, shrugged. "In my country is a saying. Tomorrow finds yesterday's mistakes as today's despair. *Do svidanya.*''

In quick, strong steps, Yustechenko strode up into the cargo bay. As the tailgate began to groan shut, he waved a final time.

Farnes lifted a hand, waved back.

In retrospect it seemed miraculous that for over a month uniformed Soviets and Americas, who for so long seemed so ready to kill each other, could work shoulder to shoulder, hand to hand, often without translators, battling a common enemy that threatened the only bond that no one would deny, their humanity. As the C-5A moved off, he stood beside Lorraine in the prop wash and let the early October sun bake his skin.

It felt good.

Gentle breezes wafting off the Gulf filled his nostrils with the tang of salt.

And it felt good.

Beside him Lorraine laced her slender fingers through his.

And it felt good.

She drew in the air, threw her head in the breeze, her blonde hair flying, snapping banners that sparkled in the summer sun. "So what now?" she asked.

He looked back, shrugged, kept his pace toward the control tower.

"You're not going to tell me this thing has left me sterile, are you?"

He smiled, shook his head.

"Or that it's left you sterile?"

Again he shook his head.

"And for sure you're not impotent."

He laughed.

"So what are we going to do about it?"

"Is this a nag?"

"Look, Larry. In case you didn't notice it, we're down by about fifty million or so in this country. Why don't you think about some patriotic service here?"

"Lorraine . . ."

"He speaks!"

He laughed.

"You don't think I'm going to let some other woman snap you up, do you?"

Another shrug.

" 'Cause if there were damn few good men to begin with, it's surer than hell that there are damn few good men left.''

He managed a smile, turned his eyes to watch the plane carrying one of them storm through the shimmering convection currents and lift into the blue-white sky.

"And it's not just because you're a doctor, Farnes.''

Above him the C-5A lurched into a hard bank and headed south.

"What if I told you I was pregnant?''

He kept his eyes on the plane as it receded to a point.

Then he brought them back to her, circled his arm around her waist, and said, "Then we better start talking about names.''